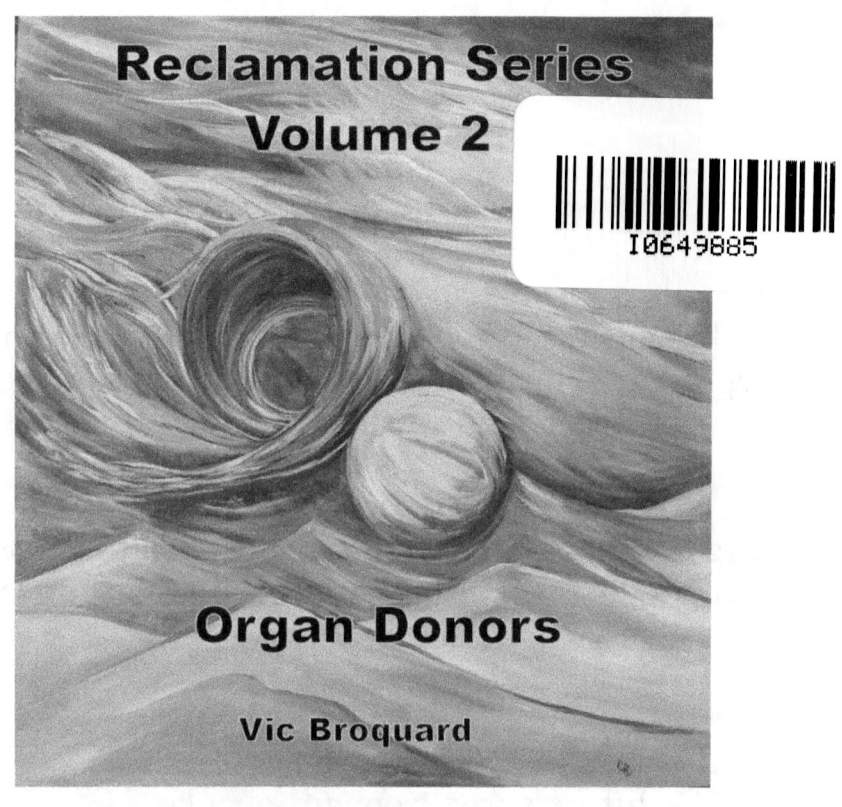

Reclamation Series
Volume 2
Organ Donors

Vic Broquard

Published by Broquard eBooks, East Peoria, IL
61611

Reclamation Series Volume 2 Organ Donors
First Edition
Copyrighted © 2010, 2013, 2014, 2015 by Vic
Broquard
ISBN: 978-1-941415-77-1

This is a work of fiction. All characters,
organizations, and events portrayed in this novel
are products of the author's imagination and are
used fictiously.

Published by:
http://www.Broquard-ebooks.com
Broquard eBooks
103 Timberlane
East Peoria, IL 61611
author@Broquard-eBooks.com

Artwork by Crooked Willow Studios.

For Morgan and L. Ron Hubbard

Table of Contents

Chapter 1—Discovery

September 1, 2272, Franco Helu sat in his private office located in a secure wing of his heavily guarded and remote compound just outside Mexico City. He had no choice but to place this videophone conference call to the other eight members of the Camarilla, the leading circle of nine top members of the secretive and illusive Cabal, which consisted of the ninety-nine wealthiest men in the world. Entrance to the Cabal had always been a net worth of at least ten billion gold-backed dollars, not the universal credits in use throughout the world in 2272, but rather a scaled and fictitious dollar that was backed by gold, a financial system devised by the original members of the Cabal back in 1990, nearly three centuries ago when many disparate currencies were in use among the countries of the world.

The nine richest men of the Cabal formed the inner circle called the Camarilla, headed or chaired by the wealthiest of these nine men. For many years, that honor fell upon Franco Helu. Unless circumstances took a very wild swing, his position was secure, because James Buffett's standardized wealth was a good ten billion less than Franco's.

One by one, the other eight members of the Camarilla joined the video conference, one that was guaranteed to be totally secure from any potential hackers. James Buffett's connection popped up first. Soon, the others appeared: Jacques Arnault in Paris, Francisco Ortega in Madrid, Ben Michaelson-Waberly in London, Delius Pogs in Hong Kong, Al Rumani in Mumbai, Henry Koch in New York City, and Tom Walton in St. Louis. Franco's fortune came from the telecommunications industry. James made his in finance. Jacques headed up the world's largest arms manufacturing operations. Francesco controlled the worldwide production of Pytalon, the awful drug which turned people into easily controlled "zombies." Ben had cleverly usurped the fortunes of the women engineers who had pioneered the EMAC and Air Liners. Delius had invented the original concept of the PDH implant machine, but worked closely with the illusive Lin brothers to get it developed and was their "front man." With an implant, a person could be made to slavishly follow orders, particularly when combined with Pytalon. Al made his fortune in the medical arena. Henry's fortune came from controlling the Total Care Program worldwide, and Tom's fortune still came from the sales of commercial goods, now worldwide in scope.

Franco stared at the eight other images on his large monitor. One couldn't tell much about the age of these nine men for various reasons. Some had made use of the Lin brother's Transference Machine, which allowed them to "swap" bodies with a young person, but all had made use of Total Care's Organ Donor program, often many times. Nearly every organ or limb could be replaced. Thus, these men had controlled the world for nearly two centuries. Franco himself was well over two hundred years old, but his current body certainly looked as if it was fifty. His father had been Carlos, now dead for centuries.

"Gentlemen, we have three serious anomalies that simply must be handled before the next Cabal meeting. If we don't, they're certain to bring these up, and I, for one, do not want to be embarrassed by these. I'm sending you the summaries I've received. First, there has been some kind of internal shakeup within the Feds organization. Apparently, one Peter Delius has taken over the position of Supreme Commander of the Feds. None of us has made that appointment. This rogue must be brought under our control as soon as possible or else appropriately replaced. James, this falls under your jurisdiction, so handle it. Second, an alarming number of high school graduates are not being implanted, put on Pytalon, and given permanent job assignments. Somehow Chicago is leading the way. This must be investigated and ended immediately. Henry, this one belongs to you; it's a Total Care problem in spades, so handle it. Third, Delius has discovered a most alarming situation. The Lin brothers have been abducted, and all three of their secret and secure installations have been raided. Their extremely vital Transference Machines have been stolen by parties unknown."

Delius Pogs spoke up, "Aye. Both brothers have been abducted, twice if my sources are correct. I have it on good authority the Feds were behind their abductions and raids. It's my belief the Feds have their hands on our precious Transference Machines. The machines are vitally important to us. I don't have to elaborate that point, but we should retrieve at least one of the Lin brothers, unless you know someone else who knows how to run their machines."

Eight faces grimaced. Al Rumani spoke up, "I can make the case that the Transference Machines belong to the Medical Arm. Once we know who has them, perhaps I can acquire them for our facilities in India. I've argued this point with you for years, Delius. Now the worst has happened, and we are so screwed if we don't get them back. Maybe now you'll listen to me." He was extremely annoyed with this sudden news. The loss of these machines was of gargantuan proportions.

"Indeed, Al," James Buffett spoke up. "Look, I'll see what I can get out of this Peter Delius fellow. I'm sure we can get our hands on our Transference Machines again." Al seemed somewhat relieved, as did Delius Pogs.

"As long as I have you on conference call, James, are there going to be any surprises at the next full Cabal meeting on January 1?" Franco asked what was also gnawing in the back of his mind.

"No. The bottom rung members aren't in danger of being bumped from the list, and there are no up and coming new billionaires," James replied formally. "While there may be some slight jockeying among the bottom tier of members, I anticipate nothing of any real importance at this time." He added jocularly, "Your positions are still secure." Several grinned.

"Okay, then. That's all I have. Just get these three situations terminally handled before full Cabal meets," Franco ordered.

One by one, the men signed off, all except Ben. When only he and Franco remained, Ben spoke up, "Might I have a private word with you?" Franco nodded. "With the Transference Machines temporarily out of service, might this be a convenient time for some consolidations within our Cabal?" His tone was extremely covert, but Franco knew what he was alluding to.

"It would seem now is a particularly judicious time for consolidations," Franco replied, just as covertly. "Besides, such will give James something to do."

Both men laughed and Ben signed off as well. He had plans to make. The loss of the Transference Machines was ideal for his big move.
***

Three of these ninety-nine Cabal members lived in the greater Chicago area, but on the outskirts, and in very secure compounds that were both well-guarded and had top of the line security measures in place. Yes, these three billionaires could afford only the very best of everything, and they most certainly did just that.

While these three men were considered lesser Cabal members, that was only due to a coup pulled off around a hundred-fifty years ago. First, Randal Raven controlled the fortune made by the MTE system, that's the Mass Transit Escalators system based on EM technology and which is in widespread use throughout the civilized world, replacing all manner of older systems for moving many people from one place to another. His was a minor fortune. The other two men felt cheated. How did that come about?

Years ago with the incredible invention of the EM engines, two female engineers applied the technology to build the EMACs, that is, the ElectroMagentic Air Cars

(Joanne Waberly) and Air Liners (Jena Michaelson). Between the two, they amassed close to fifty billion each, later dividing their estate among their children. Back in 2122, Ben Michaelson cleverly managed to merge eighty percent of the Michaelson fortune with a similar amount of the Waberly fortune by marrying Jana Waberly, forcing her to become an EE woman and making her sign over her fortune to him, thus merging the greater share of their wealth into his sole hands. That coup also bumped his total fortune up sufficiently to enable him to knock one of the Camarilla members out, taking his place as one of the nine wealthiest billionaires in the world.

Hence, Ace Waberly and Alan Michaelson felt cheated of their inheritance, and rightly so, for they were stuck at being lesser Cabal members because of the coup brilliantly pulled off by Ben Michaelson-Waberly back in 2122. Alan and Ace were quite furious but could do nothing about it, except fume and plot. Here in 2272, they hatched a new scheme to attempt to drastically increase their total wealth, since all their previous schemes had failed. It should be noted here that both men were quite old, but had once made use of the Lin brothers' Transference Machine and had numerous organs replaced before that, extending their longevity considerably.

Randal Raven's wife was Regina; Ace Waberly's wife was Marcy; Alan Michaelson's wife was Christa, and yes, their wives were recent additions. In fact, these were the men's third wives, since neither chose to "extend" the lives of their former wives. What of their children? Simple. When their children came of age, eighteen, they were implanted, put on Pytalon, and sent off to run some of their companies. With their third wives, they had more children, destined to play a vital role in their latest schemes.

Randal and Regina had two sons, Roy, twenty, and Rob, seventeen, and one daughter, Rachel Roxanne, eighteen. Ace and Marcy had a son, Scott, twenty, and a daughter, Mary Jane, eighteen. Alan and Christa had two sons, Steve, twenty, and Felix, eighteen. Their new plan called for having Scott marry Rachel and Steve marry Mary Jane. Once done, their sons would have legal rights to the other fortunes. What Ace left unsaid was if Randal, Roy, and Rob should meet with an untimely accident, then Scott would inherit the entire Raven fortune, more than doubling his net worth. Likewise unsaid, Alan anticipated that once Ace pulled off his big power play, gaining the Raven fortune for the Waberly's, then he would arrange an untimely accident to Ace and Scott, allowing Steve to inherit that combined fortune. Alan estimated with the merging of all three's fortunes, Steve would have enough to push himself into the Camarilla, displacing Tom Walton at least. However, Alan had to be extra careful, because Ace could well do the same thing to his own family!

What of the women in the lives of these Cabal families? Every woman was made into an EE woman, just as soon as she reached eighteen. Women certainly didn't count or matter, beyond being sex dolls and occasionally giving them children at opportune times. Such had been the attitudes of the Cabal men for many centuries, during which time, they managed to implant their viewpoint on the world. Normal women were implanted and put on Pytalon, just as most men were, turned into unthinking, unemotional zombies or morons, who went about their assigned lifetime jobs unquestioningly. Only a few of the prettier young women were physically altered into the sex dolls for the wealthy corporate executives and of course the Cabal men.

Alan also planned to have his younger son, Felix, implanted, dosed on Pytalon, and sent off to run one of his Air Liner companies down in Memphis. At this time, September 2272, none of these children knew of their father's plans. By tacit agreement between the three men, they would "initiate" their children just after supper on the same day, September 1.

After dinner on that day, Ace summoned Scott and Mary Jane to his private office. He'd already opened his secure safe, retrieving the Waberly Family Journal, his most prized possession. It outlined precisely what the role of the Waberly family had been since around the year 1990! In fact, each of the Cabal family heads had similar journals. It might be interesting to compare the entries between them, but of course, such isn't possible.

"Ah, Scott, Mary Jane. Please have a seat. It's time you're inducted into our family's long and illustrative history," he began.

Scott sat up straight, knowing this was vitally important. At last he would become privy to everything. No more secrets! Likewise, Mary Jane was intrigued, but knew whatever role her father was planning for her would be a minor one at best. Still, she was excited to finally hear such things. Before, all she heard were rumors, though some were very wild.

"Our family is a member of the Cabal, the most wealthy and powerful families in the entire world. We control the world and everything in it, well very nearly," Ace began. "It's all documented here in this journal. It's time to share our family's history with the both of you."

"Back in 1990, the world was on a self-destruction course. Overpopulation, food shortages, starving people, ruthless dictators, and worse, the slow destruction of the earth's atmosphere from greenhouse gases from extensive use of fossil fuels were combining to wipe out our world. Governments of the many countries were unable or unwilling to do anything about it. That's when the ninety-nine wealthiest families in the world formed up the Cabal, fully intent upon doing what the pathetic populations were unable to do for themselves."

Ace went on, "The first steps happened before the Waberly dynasty began. The Cabal took two actions. First, they induced all major US companies to ship their factories and highly skilled workers overseas to China and India. Why? Back then, US workers were unionized and demanded huge salaries, making it very difficult if not impossible for these corporations to make a profit on the world markets or to compete. A US worker got $40 per hour, while the same worker in China or India got maybe $2 per hour."

"During the next score of years, huge numbers of jobs were sent overseas. The result was two-fold. The corporations, their executives, and the shareholders—Cabal members—became extremely wealthy, while the huge middle class literally evaporated.
Baby Boomers, named for the exponential increase in birth rate just after World War II, grew to retirement age, at which point their healthcare costs ballooned!"

"Enter Phase II as Cabal calls it. The Cabal pumped huge amounts of funds into the US elections. The result was they got Obama elected as president—twice. He was then obligated to pass a Health Care Reform, often called Obama-care in those days. Supposedly, every person had to have health care. It was promised as a way to ensure every person got the care they needed. That's how it was sold. If you were poor, you couldn't afford any health care. Heck, I'm told a simple emergency room visit cost over three thousand dollars, drastically more if the doctors had to do much of anything for the patient. However, under this new Health Care law, insurance companies covered the costs for everyone."

"Of course, the Cabal was well aware of the staggering costs that were going to have to be covered. That was part of their overall Phase II plan. Within a decade, the US national debt exploded. Bailout debts swelled into the tens of trillion dollars range, and by 2022, the national debt exceeded two hundred trillion dollars, thanks in part to this Affordable Care program. To keep the poorer people happy, which by then meant nearly everyone in the country, government handouts were needed, playing perfectly into our hands."

"With the total economic collapse of the US, most other countries of the world collapsed as well, and we entered Phase III of the Cabal's long-range plans. Cleverly, they had their handpicked government leaders implement their long-thought out Total Care Program, From the

Cradle to the Grave. Absolutely brilliant piece of work, if I do say so myself. Facing desperate times, starvation, runaway inflation, lack of any means to provide food on the table, the population jumped onboard the Total Care Program. As you kids know, it promises every person a job and funds for food, clothing, and a home. It was at this point the Universal Credit replaced all other forms of monetary exchange, part of the Total Care package."

"During those early years, the psychs and the drug companies were making a killing dumping their supposedly anti-psychotic drugs onto the market. The Total Care package demanded every person be taking them. That's when the Ortega clan invented the perfect drug for the masses, Pytalon. I hear a new version is now in the testing phase. Hopefully, it will help eliminate these sporadic outbreaks of insanity that we've had."

"Kids, here's where our family fits into the picture. Until about this point in time, the voluminous carbon pollution of the earth's atmosphere was skyrocketing. The polar caps were melting. In fact, the breadbasket lands moved from the corn and soybean fields of the Midwest on up to Canada! The ocean levels rose considerably. That's why we have that huge concrete barrier wall around Lake Michigan. The water levels back then nearly overflowed them! Incredible."

"At this time, the EM engine was invented. Our family enters here, with our own matriarch, Joanne Waberly. She invented the EMACs, while Jena Michaelson invented the Air Liners. Also, Raven invented the MTE system for mass transit, based in part on the EM engines. Our matriarch, Joanne, totally undid the atmospheric pollution! Within a decade, all forms of oil burning machines were obsolete and abandoned. More importantly, given time, Mother Earth healed our world, ending global warming. Today, we're pretty much back to normal. You see, our family heritage is an enormous one. We're right to have immense pride."

"Phase IV began after the Delius Pogs and the Lin

9

brothers, three brilliant Chinese men, invented the implant machines. Only then could we guarantee workers did what they were supposed to do. In today's world, a job implant combined with the proper dose of Pytalon guarantees the worker will do precisely his or her own job and cause no troubles whatsoever. In fact, during the last century and a half, crime has been almost eliminated in the civilized world. No country has any need for an army. Wars are a thing of the distant past. While we do keep a National Guard around, their job is to assist the population in times of national disasters, such as a hurricane or tornado. They're simply relief helpers."

"We have inherited a perfectly run world. Countries don't need or have any rulers—no kings, monarchs, presidents, dictators. Nor do they need anyone making the laws. The Cabal makes them for them. So yes, the Cabal now runs the entire world, except for a few isolated, uncivilized areas. The AP-cops handle the minor annoyances caused by a few insane people. The very few larger difficulties are handled by the Feds for us."

"You see just how important our family is. We're helping run the entire world. It takes a net worth of at least ten billion to become a Cabal member. That brings me to the Great Betrayal, back when Joanne Waberly and Jena Michaelson divided up their vast estates among their children. Not long after that, Ben Michaelson-Waberly cleverly managed to merge eighty percent of the Michaelson fortune with a similar amount of the Waberly fortune by marrying Jana Waberly, forcing her to become an EE woman and signing over her fortune to him, thus merging the greater share of their wealth into his sole hands. That coup also bumped his total fortune up sufficiently to enable him to knock one of the Camarilla members out, taking his place as one of the nine wealthiest billionaires in the world."

"Alan and I swore that one day we would get revenge. We owe it to you to do so."

Mary Jane protested, "But dad, you aren't that old.

10

Mom says you're fifty."

Ace smiled. "There's more to the story, Mary Jane. You see, after the mass exodus of talent to India occurred, there have been some subsequent incredible medical advances made. Dr. Rumani is incredibly brilliant. You see, organ transplants used to take a huge staff of highly trained doctors and cost a fortune. If a person's kidneys failed, the sheer cost of the operation was overwhelming, to say nothing of the huge problem of finding a compatible organ donor. In fact, on the black market, a kidney went for nearly a hundred thousand dollars!"

"Dr. Rumani approached this monumental problem from two directions, both of which benefit us all, particularly yourselves. First, he developed the Medical Machines, which are now able to replace that whole staff of highly trained personnel needed to do the complex operations. I'm told it's virtually a foolproof operation to install replacement organs. That alone saves a huge amount of otherwise wasted funds. You see, back when Obama-care was going strong, such operations nearly bankrupted the US. The trustees of the National Health Care program had to adopt strict organ donor methods. Anyone over sixty was always refused such operations. They had only a short while to live anyway, so why waste millions on them just to allow them to live another ten years? Made no sense. Eventually, the upper age for an organ donor operation was lowered to thirty. After Dr. Rumani's breakthroughs, it has been upped back to sixty for the normal population."

"How does this apply to you and me? Simple. There is a Case A category that all Cabal members and our families fall into. Mind you, this is top-secret information I'm telling you right now. We're permitted any type of organ donor transplant operation. Whenever we need a replacement organ, be it a kidney or a heart or even a hand or foot, we get it immediately—all at no cost. It's free to us, the world leaders."

"So you see, I've had many such organ transplants,

mostly before fifty years ago though. Those transplants and skin graphs kept me alive long after my body should've died of very old age and organ failures. Now listen carefully, kids. Dr. Rumani's second breakthrough affects the both of you, as well as your mother and me. Finding compatible organs used to be a monumental barrier. However, he solved that one by inventing a fool-proof cloning procedure."

He paused to let that detail sink into their minds before continuing, "When you were born, a swab was taken of your DNA. From that, the doctors created a clone of you. Yes, in a super secure, highly secret, medical facility, there is a duplicate of your bodies, mine, and your mother's as well. Thus, if you are injured, we have an immediate organ donor ready to provide you with your needed transplant! Furthermore, there are several younger clones of yourselves there as well. After all, when your body reaches sixty years, it's pointless to transplant a sixty-year-old kidney into your body. So approximately every ten years or so, another clone is created. So when you are sixty and need a new pair of kidneys, they can be harvested from your own personal organ donor whose body is say twenty years old, giving you the best chance for a much longer survival."

Mary Jane spoke up, "You mean there are more of me's out there somewhere?"

"Organ Donors, dear. That's all they are, simple ODs as we call them. There is only one you, Mary Jane. So don't worry about that. They are kept locked away in a pristine environment and are not on Pytalon. Their bodies are kept in perfect health, ready to donate an organ to you, but let's hope you don't need any anytime soon."

She seemed satisfied and he continued. "There is one final piece of the overall picture. Again, the Lin brothers are responsible for this one, another terrific invention of theirs. This is incredibly top-secret, mind you. Not even your mother knows about this one. It is a Transference Machine. With it, they can transfer you into a completely new body. So yes, this body you see here, me, is fifty years old. I was transferred into it some thirty-two years ago, around the time I met your mother, bless her heart."

"Dad, you have got to be kidding, right?" Scott broke in.

"Hardly, son. The procedure was done over in China. I was taken there to a secret location. I've no idea what city it was in. My body was in bad shape, quite old, and riddled with many transplanted organs. I laid down on a table. They attached some electrodes to my head. Beside me on another table, electrodes were attached to this body that you see here. They activated the machine. The next thing I knew, I awoke in this new eighteen-year-old body. I had all my memories; everything was perfect. I did watch as my old body quickly died. God, I felt rejuvenated, as I watched my old body being cremated before I left China."

They gasped, shocked to hear this unbelievable story. Yet, there their dad sat. Now they knew why he seemed to have some Chinese features.

"So kids, what I'm telling you is when the time comes, we should be able to get entirely new bodies for you, making us, in fact, immortal. Considering the immense power we Cabal members have, we need to be immortal to make sure the world runs right."

"All right, kids. So why am I telling you all this right now? Simple," Ace got to the real reason for this family conference and the revelations. "Alan, Randal, and I are going to try to regain some of what we lost to Ben when he stole most of our family's fortunes. Scott, soon you're going to marry Randal's Rachel Roxanne, joining our family to the Raven's fortune. Mary Jane, you'll soon be marrying Alan's Steve, joining the Michaelson's fortune with ours as well. Once you two are married, the Waberly fortune and thus power should be at least tripled, maybe even enough to get us into the elite Camarilla, but we'll have to see how that plays out."

"But I don't want to marry Steve. I don't like him,"

Mary Jane protested.

"Well, don't worry your pretty head about that, Mary Jane. I won't make you. Scott, Randal will be getting Rachel Roxanne prepared for you. We'll talk more about such things later on. As my heirs, I want you both to read over all the details here in our family journal. When you're done, I'll lock it back up in my safe. Mind you, this is the only time you're going to get to read this. I won't bring this journal out for you again," he added very seriously.
***

Around this same time, Ray and Rachel Roxanne Raven and Steve and Felix Michaelson also heard nearly the same stories from their fathers. Both Rachel Roxanne and Mary Jane had long suspected when they turned eighteen they'd become EE women, since the only adult women they'd ever seen among the Cabal families they'd met over the years were EE women. They had seen the implanted and drugged women of the world around them, who performed their lifelong jobs as unthinking, unfeeling, zombies. Of course, seeing the beautiful EE women in their lives, they had no desire to become "ordinary women." They didn't want to become zombies.

Chapter 2—Days in Life

R³ grew up in Ward 4 of the Ramani Chicago Medical Institute, well mostly on Ward 4. Rachel Roxanne Raven-A had some vague memories of a smaller, different ward, but those were when she was very little. For the last fourteen years, she lived her whole life here on Ward 4, along with eighteen others—roughly equal numbers of boys and girls. She, like all the others, knew she was an OD, an organ donor, giving the gift of life to some of the most important people of the world. That was drilled into all their heads, as far back as she could remember.

Wall placards strategically located around the huge ward displayed clever sayings. There is no higher calling than to be an Organ Donor.

Organ Donors are second in importance only to their hosts.

There is no higher purpose than to be an Organ Donor.

Organ Donors command the very highest respect from everyone in the world!

An Organ Donor gives the gift of life to those in dire need.

Near the central meeting room, one wall contained the names of previous ODs. The listing was lengthy and added to periodically, though until now, none of the eighteen recognized any of the names. Once a month, they were read a listing of the invaluable contributions being made by other ODs from other medical institutes. As each name was called off, they were required to clap and cheer, the former only if it was physically possible for them to clap.

The ward held nine bedrooms, two to a room. R³ and Mary Jane Waberly-A shared a room since they were six. During their first eight years in the ward, they received a basic education so they could read and write, handle math, and other topics. R³ picked up her nickname when she was twelve and she and her friends learned their basic math powers. She was Rachel Roxanne Raven-A, hence her nickname which stuck.

While they never left Ward 4 during these years, that isn't to say they lacked mobility. At one end of the huge ward, they had access to a full gym and were required to spend one hour each day getting their exercise in. Often the boys played basketball, but several joined the girls running laps around the gym. A placard there read:

An OD must keep totally fit at all times for the benefit of their host.

Another read:

Be prepared at all times, for who knows when your host's life will depend upon your precious gift of life.

Besides proper exercise, they all received nourishing meals with proper vitamins and received medical checkups once a month. In the doctor's office, a placard read:

An OD must maintain perfect health for the benefit of their host.

However, after the equivalent of eighth grade, none were required to study any further. At this point, six of the boys spent their time playing video games, excepting the mandatory hour in the gym. Six of the girls spent their time playing dollhouse games, card games, and browsing women's fashion pages on the web. In contrast, three boys and three girls followed another avenue entirely, calling themselves the Circle of Six.

R³ was keenly interested in learning more about the real world, the world beyond her glass windows. She had waist length black hair, thick, wavy, and shiny. Her face was somewhat angular and her eyes were bright. R³ always had a smile on her face and an encouraging word for her five friends. While romances were strictly taboo among the ODs, she had a crush on Felix Michaelson-A; and he, her. He was tall, thin, and wiry, with a keen mind. In fact, he and Rachel Roxanne had very high IQs, far above the norm. Further, Felix had an overpowering drive to learn all about computers and their systems. When he was fourteen, he discovered how to hack into the medical facility's system, gaining them access to the world at large. This then gave Rachel Roxanne access to every university course in the world, for they were all online somewhere.

During the last two years, R³ devoured every course she could find, pushing Felix hard to keep up with her by finding more sites and courses for her to explore. In contrast to these two, Mary Jane Waberly-A was more interested in all things medical, while her heart throb, Todd Kingmann-A was fascinated by the marvelous Medical Machines. Mary Jane had waist length blonde hair, wavy and curly. Her face was round with lips that always seemed to be smiling. Like R³, she always encouraged her friends, always finding a positive side to everything. Todd had bushy brown hair and an angular face, with an overly large nose.

The other two members of the Circle of Six were Rhianna Winslow-A, a fiery redhead, whose flaming, wavy locks also fell to her waist. The three young women kept their hair at equal lengths, an unspoken pact between them. To others, they claimed to be ready to provide their hosts with super hair transplants, if needed, but that wasn't their true reason behind it, rather they loved long hair. Rhianna was keenly into both geography and history, devouring all such courses she could find online, compliments of the hacking by Felix. Her boyfriend was Trevor Goode-A. A mesomorph, he was into physical forms of combat, watching and studying every martial arts video he could find, again aided by the hacking skills of Felix. "I have to be able to protect my Red Rose," he teased Rhianna, who always flashed him a big smile.

As ODs, they knew they would never be allowed to marry, much less even have any kind of close relationship. Kissing was verboten. Even holding hands was not allowed in Ward 4. Instead, the six found alternate means to express themselves, often by seemingly innocuous phrases, such as "My Red Rose," in Trevor's case.

Three times a day, the eighteen met at the opposite end of the ward from the gym. Here, they had a small dining room and were served their properly balanced meals. However, there were also healthy snack machines here as well. The growing teens often made use of them; sometimes eating more from the machines than they did from their formal meals. At least these past four years, they were allowed to drink tea, and in their eighteenth year, they were given access to coffee as well, but none really cared for it yet.

A year ago, the education of the six took a very wrong turn, considering they were ODs. R^3 asked the wrong question. "Say, I wonder if we are real people? ODs, I mean. Is an OD a real person, like we see out there in the world? Or is an OD somehow very different?" None had any answer and that began their investigations.

Before long, Mary Jane found an answer. "Look, from all I can tell, the real people are implanted and taking a drug called Pytalon. We aren't. So maybe that makes us not real people. What do you think?"

"Dunno. What's an implant? What's Pytalon do?" asked Trevor. None knew, prompting further research. Thanks to further "Felix Skills," as they now referred to his uncanny ability to "find" things on the internet, they learned that Pytalon was supposed to be an anti-insanity drug, but in the secret medical databases they discovered the drug turned people into near zombies, sapping their self-determinism, intelligence, and reasoning abilities, lowering them to nearly that of a small child. Further, one of its ingredients prevented all sexual arousals in men and infertility in women.

After studying up on the PDH implants, methods, and scripts, Todd concluded, "Gang, I think the implants help a person do their job well and nothing else, but I'm going to look into it further. Are real people so stupid that they don't know how to do their jobs? Something doesn't seem quite right with these implants."

"Well, I'm looking into this Pytalon thing," Mary Jane pronounced. "Surely, there aren't that many crazy, real people. Certainly none of us are nuts, at least I don't think so. Maybe ODs can't get insane, do you suppose?"

Not long after that, Rhianna discovered Total Care online. "Gang, I've found the basic health care real people get. Funny, we aren't listed there. So maybe R³ is right. We ODs aren't real people."

"We have to be there, because we're the second most important people in the world, second only to our hosts," Trevor protested. "Surely, we're in there somewhere. Let me have a look see." He looked over her shoulder, whispering My Red Rose in her ear, causing her to flush slightly. "Hey she's right. We aren't there. Wait. They list Case B, C, D, and E. It seems Case A is missing. See, it says, 'Case B is for the wealthy Lords and Ladies, though some have other titles, such as corporate executives, and presidents. Case C is solely for EE women. Case D is for all the professional personnel and highly skilled workers. Case E is for all the unskilled workers, the common laborers.' What is an EE woman?"

"Yes, what's an EE woman?" asked R³.

"I'm on it, R³," Felix called out from his nearby computer. "Wow. Look at these images!" All five stopped and crowded around his monitor, and Felix scrolled through a number of images and descriptions. "I think they're supposed to be sex dolls, the epitome of feminine beauty," he added. "That's what it says here."

R³ countered, "But Felix, none of the caretaker women around here have chests that big. The EE women's breasts must be positively huge. Still, I see what you mean. Marilyn has been looking at those fancy fashions. She showed me one of her fashion pages last week. I think we should see what the missing Case A is all about. Maybe we ODs are in there somehow. What do you all think?"

All agreed they should learn about this missing case. However, there wasn't anything on any Total Care page that even mentioned Case A.

Nonplused, Felix continued working his magic. A week later, he hacked into a Medical Center File and hit pay dirt. "Got it. Gang, come here! There is a Case A, and we are in it, though as Organ Donors. Come see. What's a Cabal anyway?"

R³ replied, "Some kind of secret political society."

Rhianna added, "It comes from a committee of five ministers under King Charles II back in the sixteenth century—from the first letters of the minister's names. Kind of an evil group, I think."

Felix pointed out, "Hey, there are ninety-nine families in the Case A Cabal. Oh, and the Organ Donors are providing organs for these people. Say, these are our hosts. I wonder what makes these people so special." A bit later, he had his answer. "Gosh, these are the wealthiest people on the planet! Billionaires several times over—all them."

R³ gushed, "Hey wait a minute! There's a Raven family among them. And a Waberly, too. Michaelson, Kingmann, Goode, Winslow. Hey, we're all in there! Wait, we aren't them. We don't have any families. We aren't real people. We have no father, no mother, no brothers, no sisters, but we have those last names."

"Not exactly, R³," Rhianna pointed out. "You're Raven-A and I'm Winslow-A. I wonder what the A means. Felix, can you find that out?"

It took him another day of sleuthing to uncover Dr. Rumani's cloning project. At last, Felix discovered the entire organ donor program. All six were positively stunned, as they read the lengthy description over his shoulder!

Rhianna gasped, "I've never thought about us donors this way. So we're basically nothing more than lab rats, donating our bodies to keep these few people alive, not anyone who gets badly injured. I don't think we were ever supposed to see this, Felix! I hope we don't get into big trouble over it."

Biting her lip, R³ said, "So out there somewhere is another me, another Rachel Roxanne, and my whole purpose in life is to donate my organs to her when she needs them? That doesn't seem fair to me at all. I'm a real person too. I think so anyway."

Felix whispered, "I wonder what the other Rachel Roxanne looks like?" He spent another day trying this and that before he uncovered their medical records. "Eureka! R3, come here. I found your family—er your host family anyway. Everyone, come look at the other R3."

"Weirder than weird," R3 exclaimed. "She looks just like me."

"Er, no, R3," Rhianna pointed out, "I think you look just like her. You're a clone of her. Maybe that's what the A means in Raven-A, do you suppose? Felix, can you find my doppelganger?" An hour later, Felix displayed each of their "families." The Circle of Six were extremely shocked to discover their hosts looked nearly identical to themselves. Only their clothing and hairstyles were different.

The next day, Felix uncovered more startling news. "Hey R3, there's more of you right here in the Med Lab! There's an eight-year-old version of you on the floor above us and a baby version of you on the floor above that! Oh, I see. The eight-year-old is Raven-B, while the baby version is Raven-C. Clever, but why three of you?"

Rhianna declared, "I don't like this at all. I'm going to do some serious history digging! This just doesn't seem right to me."

"Why not? Our hosts are supposed to be the most important people in the world. Our job is to provide organs when they get ill so they can stay alive," Trevor countered.

Later that day, a gong sounded. All were conditioned with weekly practice sessions to respond when they heard that signal. It meant one of them was needed to perform their duty as an OD. They all headed straight to their bedrooms as drilled into their heads. A bit later, a caretaker came by and told them, "Okay, you can leave your rooms now. You'll be most pleased to know one of you has just gotten the opportunity to fulfill his noble purpose. Able is off donating to save his vitally important host."

R³ breathed a sigh of relief, thankful it wasn't one of the Circle of Six. This was the first time the OD call came to these eighteen of Ward 4. Hence, everyone gathered around the main station, centrally located, waiting for news about Able, speculating what organs he would be donating.

Hours later, Able was wheeled back up the elevator into Ward 4. He was sitting up on a Gurney. His right shoulder was heavily bandaged as was his right pelvis, but his face displayed a proud smile. Spontaneously, the remaining seventeen began clapping for him. He smiled. "Thanks everyone. I've given up my right arm and leg. I guess my host suffered a really, really bad accident," he explained.

"Doesn't it hurt?" asked Rhianna.

Able smiled. "Only a little bit. Didn't take them long to do it, I don't think, but I was unconscious. They say I'll be fine in another week. More importantly, my host is doing very well now. I've saved him."

Able looked very proud of his accomplishment, but the nurse who came with him quickly shooed the others away, while two men pushed his Gurney on down to his room. The Circle of Six stopped by Felix's room.

"Gosh, he's got no right arm at all, and no right leg!" whispered Rhianna.

"He can't tie his own shoes anymore," Trevor added.

"Bet he can't write either. He was right handed," added the observant R³.

"How can he even walk?" asked Felix. "He has nothing left to attach a prosthetic arm or leg to."

"I don't think being an OD is right," Mary Jane whispered. "How awful for Able."

The next day when the eighteen got together for breakfast, Able was there too, sitting in a wheel chair. Their caretaker spoke up, "Before we eat, let's give Able here a loud round of applause for his selfless act of heroism, saving his valuable host's life."

"Here, here!" his roommate called out loudly, and the seventeen clapped and cheered him, bringing a smile to

Able's face. Then they chatted and had their breakfast, though everyone kept stealing glances at Able. He managed to eat fairly well with his left hand though.

A week later, Able was getting around on his own using a crutch on his left side. He still seemed pleased with his accomplishment, though he complained his video game was now suffering badly. In addition, his name now appeared on their wall of Hero Notices, kindly pointed out by their caretaker.

***

The Circle of Six continued their clandestine investigations with renewed vigor. A month later, they began to believe the entire organ donor program was somehow evil, certainly not right, especially for the ODs!

Things took a strange turn on September 2, 2272. R³, Mary Jane, and Rhianna were summoned to the central nurse's station. In her emotionless monotone, the nurse explained, "I've wonderful news for you young women. Fabulous news, in fact. Your hosts are about to become EE women, and thus you three are also going to become EE women too. Isn't that just fabulous? You three will be the epitome of feminine beauty. If you will follow me, we'll get started. I'll be bringing you back in three days, looking absolutely gorgeous. You'll be the envy of the other young women in Ward 4."

"But can you tell the others what's happening to us?" R³ hastily spoke up. "We don't want them to be worrying about us for three days."

"Of course, just as soon as I get back here. Satin dresses. My gosh. So very few women ever get to wear such fancy dresses. I'm drooling with envy over you three," she chatted away in her monotone Pytalon voice, as she led them into the elevator. They went down several floors, entering what appeared to be a medical wing. The nurse handed them off to another nurse who led them into a waiting room. She handed them each a cup of berry juice, instructing them to drink it down and she'd be back. The three nervously obliged, not daring to speak up, for fear of revealing they knew far too much! The knockout drug took nearly immediate effect. All three slumped unconscious a minute after finishing the drink.

All three woke up hours later. They were each lying on small recovery beds, but were fully dressed. R³ roused first. Her breasts ached, and she reached for them, noticing that her nails were several inches long, painted a bright red. Her lips felt thick and funny. She sat up and saw her enormous bosom partially obscuring her vision. She was wearing a bright red satin gown. Her legs felt funny, slippery sort of. She now wore black seamed nylons, but her red patent leather pumps got her attention, for they had a seemingly enormous tiny spiked heel. As she sat up, her luscious black hair seemed even longer than it had been, though she didn't yet know it now reached down to her knees. All at once, she found herself reciting words that told all.

She whispered, "My body is hypersensitive to sensual touches. My body needs sexual sensations and stimulations several times each day. I exist to provide elegant and sensual experiences to men and women of power. I am an exotic escort. I must look my very best at all times. I must be ready to flirt at any time. I must be ready to engage and satisfy the sexual fantasies and satisfactions of both men and women at any time. I am a super-sexual, hypersensitive woman. I must wear only the finest and exotic gowns. I must always wear nylons and the tallest heels. I must look perfect at all times. I will repeat to myself these words several times each day. I must not forget these words. If I fail, I will get an intense migraine headache."

Only now did she cry out, rousing Mary Jane and Rhianna, who were just as shocked as she was. Mary Jane wore a blue satin gown, greatly highlighting her wavy blonde hair that was also lengthened some, while Rhianna wore a green satin gown that contrasted with her lengthened flaming red hair. Just as R³ had done, both began reciting the same words that R³ had, and R³ found herself repeating them to herself once again, while also noticing that her head throbbed, and she felt very fuzzy somehow, groggy.

A nurse appeared speaking calmly to the three teens. "There, there, now you three are absolutely perfect EE women. You should be proud of your dresses. I'm told there is none finer anywhere in the world. Nothing is too good for you EE woman. Now then, you probably have a slight headache and feel a bit groggy. That is perfectly normal. It will pass in a day or so. I know you need pleasuring frequently. So go ahead and do it anytime you feel the need. You may pleasure each other as well. Just remember do *not* pleasure any of the boys in your ward. Your caretakers will keep an eye on you and remind you three when appropriate. Just relax. A light meal is on its way. Between you and me, I think all three of you are simply gorgeous young women now. You're emulating your hosts superbly and will be ready to provide any organs that they might need."

R3 barked, "I thought we're EE women now, not ODs."

The nurse laughed. "Of course, you're still beautiful and highly honored ODs. That's not changed at all. It is just you're also now EE women too."

Undaunted, R3 countered slightly antagonistically, "Why? So we can donate monster boobs?"

Again, the nurse chuckled. "Oh, I suppose that's true too, but no. You see, each organ donor must parallel the life of their host so that if a disaster harms their host, the organ donor's body is as close a fit as possible to their host's body. That way, there will be less trouble for the host. After all, you're the true heroes here, providing life for the most important people in the entire world." She then left the recovery room.

"My breasts hurt," R3 muttered.

"Oh, I'm rubbing mine and that's helping some," Mary Jane advised. Then, she had a strange look on her face. A big, sheepish grin followed, and she began pleasuring herself. R^3 and Rhianna soon followed suit.

After an explosive relief, R^3 commented, "Wow. That's sure different. Oh, I can think now. I'm hungry. Gee, Mary Jane, Rhianna, you both look gorgeous, just as she said."

"You too, R^3," Mary Jane replied. "Gosh, my hair is down to my butt! So is yours, R^3."

"Mine too, but I look like a Christmas tree!" Rhianna added, annoyed with the clashing of her red hair and bright green dress. All three giggled. That was true. Just then, a caretaker wheeled in a cart of food.

After eating, their minds cleared some, and their nurse got them up and walking around the recovery floor. She fully expected their wild exclamations. "Small steps. Take tiny steps. Do stand up straight. Don't be bending your knees so. It takes practice to learn to walk in such impressive heels."

"This is impossible!" grumbled Mary Jane, her arms flailing wildly.

"Too big a step. Tiny steps, Mary Jane, tiny steps. That's more like it," the nurse insisted in her unemotional monotone.

After getting the three used to walking some, she had them sit down again for two reasons. One, their knees and feet were throbbing, and two, all three began to recite their litany. After they recovered some, she left them with their orders. "I want you to practice your walking this afternoon. Tomorrow, a beautician will come by to teach you how to put on your makeup and handle your nails. The next day, a therapist will be by to help you learn to dress yourselves elegantly. After that, you will be taken to our local EE women's store and pick out seven complete outfits for yourselves, since Rhianna doesn't like her green gown." The three giggled nervously, for they began to see that their new implants wouldn't allow them to wear anything but such elegant apparel. "After that, you'll get to return to your ward and your friends there."

R^3 declared, "Well, that's not soon enough for me!"

Her two friends agreed with her.

***

"You think they'll be all right?" Todd asked Felix. They'd watched the three girls leave the ward.

"I really don't know. The implants are supposed to make a person competent at doing their job, but why would they want them to be EE women? It's not as if they're going to be kissing us or something. The caretakers don't allow even holding hands," Felix replied. "To be honest, Todd, I'm kind of worried about them."

Just after supper, Able came crutching his way into Felix and Todd's bedroom. "Hi fellows. Say, can one of you lend me a hand with my video game? Rob's been taken away and I need some help."

"Sure Able," Felix replied, jumping up. "Lead on. Say, what happened to Rob?" He followed behind the very slow moving Able, who was only barely able to walk. He looked strange to Felix. His entire right side was gone, well not really, just his right arm and leg.

After getting his fancy game console fired up for the teen, Felix asked again. "So what happened to Rob?"

"Not sure. Said he now had new hosts and that he was being transferred to another building. They said they'll be moving someone else in here tomorrow to help me out. Thanks Felix. Sure glad I can still play my games. Best part—I don't have to run in the mornings anymore." Both chuckled, and Felix headed back to his room, but stopped at his computer station.

His hands flew over the keyboard before he sat back reviewing what he'd found. Rob was transferred to Cook County Hospital and was to undergo extensive donor compatibility testing tomorrow. However, what caught his attention was Rob's host, R^3's host's brother, Rob. That Rob had been appointed the CEO of the Chicago MTE Construction Company. Further, he had been scheduled for the appropriate implant at nine this very morning, and his chart indicated his Pytalon dosage was the maximum allowed.

Felix cleared his screen and walked slowly back to his bedroom, pondering these results. "So did you get Able fixed up?" Todd asked as he entered.

"Oh sure. He's getting a new roommate tomorrow. No, I just checked on Rob. Rob's been sent to a regular hospital and is getting donor compatibility tests. Even stranger, his host, the real Rob Raven, has been implanted and heavily dosed on Pytalon and is now the CEO of the Chicago MTE Construction Company."

Trevor poked his head in and overheard Felix. "So what does all this mean?" he asked. "Kind of strange that the real Rob gets a real job and our Rob leaves here. Isn't our Rob still the OD for the real Rob?"

"Not any longer," Felix replied hesitantly. "Sure doesn't look like it. I'm going to check on what happens at Cook County tomorrow and see if others have gone there. We need more information."

"I hate being kept totally in the dark," Todd exclaimed.

"We're kept birds," Trevor declared. "We live only to donate our organs, nothing else. We don't even have a life of our own. This isn't living, not from what we've seen on Felix's monitor."

The next day, Felix whispered to Todd and Trevor, "Our girls are all right. They are on the eighth floor of this building right now. In recovery. Doing okay according to their charts. So that's something."

"How did you find—never mind," Todd whispered back. "Don't ask." Felix grinned.

That evening, Felix had a very pale face when he entered his bedroom where Todd was already getting ready for bed. "What's up? Girls still okay?" Todd asked, growing worried. Seldom had Felix looked so distressed, if that was the right observation.

"Lot of us ODs have been sent away. Lots. Whenever one of our hosts is appointed to a new job, like Rob's, the host is implanted and put on Pytalon. At the same time, their OD ends up in Cook County or similar hospitals around the world. Not long after that, their organs get donated to a whole bunch of other real people and that's the end of them."

"What? That's not right. We're supposed to be the ODs for our hosts only," Todd protested.

"I guess when our hosts get a real job, they're no longer considered valuable. Further, their Total Care situation gets lowered from Case A to Case D!" Felix added glumly.

"We're being lied to and abused," Todd declared vehemently.

"Duh!" Felix retorted.

"Well, at least the girls will be back sometime tomorrow," Felix added. "I wonder how they will look."

The next morning, their nurse commented to Felix, "Well, fellows, the three girls will be back in time for supper tonight. I'm told they look positively gorgeous, so that's something. Now they will match their hosts superbly and be far better able to provide any needed organs to their most valuable hosts. We should all be quite proud of them. Did you see Rob's name on our Hero's Plaque?"

"Yes, we did," Todd replied. The three waited anxiously all day long, wishing the hour hand of the wall clock would somehow move faster.

Around four that afternoon, a loud explosion shook the medical complex. Everyone raced to the windows, though Able couldn't move quickly at all. They saw smoke rising, black acrid smoke. Soon, they saw fire trucks arriving, but they couldn't see much else. Over the intercom, they heard a worried-sounding voice explain, "The medical center has just been bombed by some mad terrorist. Fortunately, the bomb only affected the EE Women's store down on ground level. The rest of the medical complex is undamaged. So relax. No one is in danger here."

Not long after that, a caretaker and the three girls appeared on the ward. The elevator's doors opened and there they were. All three looked shocked though; their hair, disheveled. "Okay ladies. Your things will be brought up later on."

Felix, Todd, and Trevor rushed to their three dear friends, their mouths reflecting their shock at just how incredible the three looked.

"Hi Todd! They bombed the store while we were in it!" Mary Jane gushed. "Oh, we can't walk much. Tiny steps. Remember, tiny steps," she added to Rachel Roxanne and Rhianna.

"Wow, R³! You look fantastic!" Felix exclaimed. "Are you okay now? Come on; we want to hear all about everything. You look so different now. Can you even walk in them?" Seeing that she needed a bit of support, he slipped an arm around her, "I'll help you." The three fellows helped the three into R³'s bedroom.

"Where am I?" R³ exclaimed, totally confused. "I'm not hurt, I don't think. What is this place? I want to go home. Aren't you Mr. Michaelson's youngest son? Who are these other boys? What's going on? I want to go home now. Oh no!" Suddenly, she began reciting her implanted litany. The mere mention of boys had triggered it. Worse, as soon as she began reciting it, Rhianna and Mary Jane did so as well. All three boys stood there dumbfounded, not understanding what was happening at all.

Several minutes later, the three seemed to come back to the present. Mary Jane spoke up first, "It's all right, R³. You're safe here with us. I'm your best friend Mary Jane. This is your boyfriend Felix. We're the Circle of Six. Remember now? Guys, that implant thing is just awful! We can't help ourselves any more. Oh god! Not again!" Her eyes fogged over, and she began reciting it once more. Right on cue, the other two did so as well.

By now, the three boys knew enough to be patient and didn't interfere. A bit later, they were back. "But I don't even know you!" R³ protested. "Where are we? What is this place? Who are you?"

"Has she lost her mind?" Felix whispered to Mary Jane and Rhianna.

"She wasn't like this before the bomb went off," Rhianna whispered. "Maybe the bomb did something to her. Is that possible Felix?"

"You're in the OD Ward 4," Todd answered her original question. "I'm Todd. That's Trevor. He's Felix. We're your Circle of Six. Have you forgotten everything, R3?"

"What's R3? I've never met you two or Rhianna here either. I've seen Mary Jane a few times I think. OD Ward? What's that? I'm so confused. I just want to go home!"

"Gosh, she's forgotten everything," Mary Jane whispered, though she didn't know why she was whispering.

"The organ donor ward," Todd answered her question. "You're Rachel Roxanne Raven-A, the OD for your host, Rachel Roxanne. We're all ODs here."

"What? That's impossible. I'm Rachel Roxanne. I'm not an OD. There must be some mix up here," she replied, growing quite fearful. "I'm a proper EE woman now. I'm supposed to marry Steve, soon I think. This is all so confusing. The bomb, the confusion, the rush. Oh god. Not again!" She began reciting her litany once more.

This time, Mary Jane and Rhianna had the bright idea to leave the room quietly, and the three boys followed them to Rhianna's bedroom, leaving R3, or whoever she was, to herself.

"Something's not right. R3 has lost her mind," Rhianna gushed. "This has been just awful for us, the implant thing. We can barely walk, and we have to keep saying that stuff over and over or we get these hideous headaches.

"What happened with the bomb?" Felix asked.

"We were all down in the EE Women's Store getting our new outfits when there was this loud explosion. Smoke and flying glass went everywhere. They have the EE Women's Store down on the first level of the Medical Center, you see. Then, our caretaker rounded us all up and got us out of there very fast. It was so confusing. I think one of the women workers was badly wounded—so much blood. Anyway, something's not right with R^3, that's for sure. So what's been happening while we were gone?"

Felix explained, "It's Rob! His host was implanted and put on Pytalon. At the same time, they took our Rob to the Chicago County Hospital and donated many of his organs to all sorts of people. He's dead now, but they did put his name on the Hero's Plaque. Look, this is serious. I dug deeper and found lots of us, er our hosts, have been given real jobs, implanted, and put on Pytalon. In every case, their OD was removed from their OD ward and taken to a general hospital, where their organs were donated to many others. Worse, the real Rob's Total Care case was demoted from Case A down to Case D. Some of the others were demoted to Case E, the very lowest. Things are very wrong around here."

"Wow! That is strange, Felix. Oh, crap. Here it comes again," Mary Jane said disgustedly. She began reciting her litany, and Rhianna soon followed suit. The three boys left them alone and went to check on R^3. They found her face was quite flushed, but didn't know why.

"So this is not right. I want to go home. Now. Take me home, please," R^3 said.

"We can't leave the ward, R^3," Todd explained.

"Why not? And stop calling me by that weird name! I'm Rachel Roxanne," she declared, pouting a little.

Felix decided to try a different approach. "Say did you know your younger brother, Rob, got a new job?"

"Oh," she seemed to be struggling to remember something. "Ah yes, I think dad said he was to take over running one of his companies. Oh, I'm to be an heiress. That's why I'm to marry Steve. Yes, that's it. Now can I go home?"

"Look Rachel Roxanne, you can't leave the OD Ward. They have it all locked up. You're stuck here," Trevor explained, growing annoyed with her insistence on leaving. "So you best play along with us for now."

Felix added, "Until we can figure all this out. Okay?"

He added, "If you don't, they will probably do something awful to you."

Rachel Roxanne rubbed her throbbing head. "You mean like another implant thing? God! No. Okay, okay. I'll be quiet and play along. What do I do?"

Rachel Roxanne calmed down and followed the others to the dining area for supper. All three girls were constantly stared at, though. Each did shoot flirting glances at everyone, but Rachel Roxanne was pleased with the meal. It was up to her standards. "Well, this won't be so bad after all, I expect," she whispered to Mary Jane, as they dined.

Just then, a nurse entered, "Mary Jane, we need you now. It is time for you to become our newest Hero. Your host is in desperate need. Everyone—a huge round of applause for Mary Jane, our newest Hero. We're so very proud of her!"

"But I don't want," Mary Jane started to protest, but hastily shut up, realizing she could well give everything away. Instead, she whispered to Felix, "Rescue R3!" Teetering on her six-inch heels, Mary Jane followed the kindly looking young nurse. Fear tensed her stomach. For a moment, she thought she might just lose her partially eaten supper.

"We're so proud of you, Mary Jane," the nurse chatted with her, opening the elevator doors for the pair. "Honestly, you're still recovering from your conversion to an EE woman. So very brave of you, Mary Jane. I'm sure your host will definitely be so utterly grateful for your sacrifice. She's in whole lot of pain. The bomb, you know. Such insane violence! Honestly, I do wish the Feds would get all those insane people rounded up and onto their Pytalon. You know everyone on Pytalon is totally sane, don't you? Why never have we had even the tiniest troubles from them. Oh no. The terrorists are insane and not on the sanity-causing Pytalon. Dear me, but then I'm only a nurse." For a moment, Mary Jane heard her whispering her own litany, shocking her some.

Mary Jane suddenly realized everyone here in charge of their care was implanted, just as she was! "What will happen to me?" she asked nervously.

"Oh you'll be just fine. Your beautiful host doesn't need any critical, life-threatening organs, at least that's what I was told. I expect with our modern surgery techniques, you'll be back with your friends tomorrow doing just fine. Relax, Mary Jane. Think about the very important young woman whose life you are saving. There is no more honorable purpose in life, now is there?"

While Mary Jane could think of many more purposes, right now, she dared not speak of them. Her Circle of Six had uncovered numerous other purposes. She felt more like a useless, kept animal, dreading what must surely lie ahead. Honestly, if she ended up looking as Able did, how could she possibly live like that? Worse, would Todd even be interested in her after this? She flushed and knew she had to be very silent! However, merely thinking of Todd reactivated her implant, and she softly recited it while following the nurse.

They were on an upper floor—Mary Jane was sure of that detail, just not which one. Everything smelled so sterile. She was led into a room and told to lie down. The nurse placed a cloth over her face and told her to breathe deeply. That was the last thing Mary Jane could recall. Blackness came.

She awoke some five hours later. Her face felt funny, and she reached up to rub it, being careful not to poke herself with her two inch nails. Nothing happened. Panic struck. Her stomach knotted. Her shoulders throbbed and one glance at them told all. She screamed.

A nurse entered, glassy-eyed. "Ah, you're awake, my Hero. You've saved your host, Mary Jane. Very well done indeed. Yes, your arms were needed, but that was all that was needed. See? You'll be just fine now. Here, sip this." She held up a cup and Mary Jane sipped. Whatever it was, she fell into a deep sleep again.

This time when she awoke, she didn't feel so

terrified and wondered why that was. Her arms were gone. She was just as helpless as before. Perhaps it was something they gave her, she thought rather muddled. The nurse entered, fed her some light broth, and helped her into a chair. She noticed she was wearing most of her EE woman's outfit, less her bright blue satin gown. Her strapless slip still covered her, and she could see the heavy bandages on her shoulders quite clearly.

"Don't worry, Mary Jane. There should be very little scarring. With the modern surgical procedures, we'll remove those bandages tomorrow. If so, you can rejoin your friends in Ward 4. I'm sure they want to give you a huge Hero's welcome, Mary Jane. Don't worry. Rachel Roxanne and Rhianna will be helping you with everything from now on. Already a caretaker has told them about your new needs. See, everything is taken care of for our brave, valiant heroes! Now you just sit there and recover some. If the broth stays down, the doctor says you can have solid foods soon."

***

That first evening after Mary Jane was pulled out of supper, Todd was frantic with worry. Hence, Felix took him over to his computer station. "Come on. Let's see what we can find out." After some routine hacking, they discovered the real Mary Jane had been injured in the bomb blast. Flying glass had ripped through her arms. The initial report on her stated it was unlikely that either arm could be saved, and a recommendation for her OD donation made.

Todd swallowed hard. "Both her arms? My god! How can she live?" Both boys paled.

"Let's see how they do this surgery," Felix suggested, unable to think of anything better to help calm Todd's fright. After a bit more hacking, they began reading up on the Rumani Medical Machine. Several minutes later, Felix added, "Well, that thing is so simple, a child could run it. Look, it says the healing time is now down to a week for the recipient and just a couple days for the donor. That's positive I think, Todd."

"Yes, but," Todd countered, "this is getting horrible. We could be next. How can she live with no arms? Seriously, I think we need to get us all out of here—soon, before anything bad happens to us."

"I know. Rachel Roxanne is the wrong one. She's not my R^3. Right now, our R^3 could be in bad trouble. We're going to have to rescue her, get the real Rachel Roxanne back to her home, and get ours back," Felix declared. "Come on; we need to make some plans."

Chapter 3—Implementations

Felix Michaelson wasn't a fool. He'd watched his father like a hawk, as well as his older brother, Steve. When they announced Steve would soon be marrying Mary Jane Waberly, merging those two Cabal families, Felix knew his own days were numbered. Why?

For years, he had attended the annual Cabal meetings. Always, the family heads had one son present, their heir-designate. He wasn't his dad's—that was Steve. Keeping his ears open during those years, he found out the younger sons ended up becoming CEOs of their father's companies or similar positions. They were implanted and put on Pytalon as well. In fact, quite by accident, he once met one of them. The man was glassy-eyed and a zombie, just as the billions on earth were. That woke Felix up!

Therefore, when he heard his father, Alan, making the wedding announcement, Felix knew his days were numbered. If he did nothing, he'd end up just another mindless moron, while his older brother lived the high-life. He needed to do something, anything to forestall his doom. But what?

Days later, he realized he needed to stop the marriage. If Steve couldn't marry Mary Jane, then his father would have to look elsewhere, devise a new plan, giving Felix far more time to come up with a workable plan. He knew the women were taken to the Medical Center to become implanted EE women. Thinking about them, he realized he would have just the opportunity he needed. There was a big EE Women's Store located on the ground floor of the Medical Center, where the newly created EE women would be soon shopping for their new wardrobe. Perfect.

Felix found all he needed in his father's arsenal. Here were vast quantities of guns of all kinds and a goodly supply of explosives. He set to work in the privacy of his own room, assembling what he thought was a perfect bomb. He also knew the schedule being followed. Always on the third day of recovery, the new EE women were taken shopping for their new wardrobe. Felix was prepared.

That day, he hung around the outside of the giant medical complex. He could see the relatively small shop from the street. It had numerous large windows, and he could easily see the women inside. Patience, he kept reminding himself, steeling his will for what had to be done. That afternoon, he spotted the three new EE women making their slow way into the store. For a moment, he regretted having to kill Mary Jane. She looked incredibly stunning, and he felt envious of Steve. He should have such a woman hanging on his arm, not his brother.

At last he acted. He moved over to the windows. Only glassy-eyed zombies were on the street, paying him no attention whatsoever. He planted his bomb and set the timer. Perfect. Mary Jane was moving towards this window. He hit the Activate button and made a very hasty exit, trying not to draw attention to himself. Boom!

It's done. Now I have far more time to find a way out of this mess. I sure as hell am not going to become a mindless zombie! Felix headed on home, ignoring the wailing sirens.

He was in his room when his father raised the alarm. "Steve! There's been a terrorist attack on the EE Women's Store. Women have been injured. Come on; we need to get to the hospital fast. Mary Jane is in a bad way. You too, Felix. Your brother needs us now."

Mary Jane? Excellent. I got her, Felix thought, grabbing his jacket and following the two. Steve said, "Hey, what about Rachel Roxanne, dad? Any word on her? She's supposed to marry Scott Waberly."

"Don't know. It's chaos there right now. All I know is they have my future daughter-in-law in intensive care right now. Thank god for the ODs. If we're lucky, they can fix her up from her OD," Alan replied, his voice sounding terribly worried. Plans were crumbling around him.

Chaos. They arrived at the Medical Center amid a chaos of fire trucks and AP-cop cars. A number of other EMACs were just leaving, but Alan spotted both Randal and Ace hovering around the Medical Center entrance.

"Sorry to hear about Mary Jane," Randal was saying apologetically to Ace as Alan, Steve, and Felix walked up to them. "We got Rachel Roxanne out of there. She's unharmed, just terribly shaken up. Alan, Mary Jane is in critical condition. We were just about to go up to the waiting area now. Care to join us?"

"Of course. Anyone have a clue who did this? Another insane terrorist attack?" Alan asked.

"Damned if I know," Ace barked angrily. "My own daughter. God, the city isn't safe anymore. We should bring this up at the next Cabal meeting. I won't stand for this any longer. It could easily have been Randal's Rachel Roxanne. Still, it once more proves our brilliant OD program. Always be prepared, right? Still," his voice trailed off, leaving unsaid his worry the proposed marriages wouldn't come about now.

Randal spoke up, "Yes, the OD program can fix up just about anything at all, as long as it isn't the brain. Don't worry, Steve. When the doctors are done with her, you probably won't even be able to see any scaring at all. Come on; let's get an update on her condition now."

Later, the doctor came out to meet with Ace. "We have her stabilized now. The flying glass has shredded her arms. We're going with her OD now, prepping the OD for surgery as we speak. I'm confident in a week Mary Jane will be just fine. We seldom have any problems with this new Rumani Medical Machine and procedures. I'll know more in about five hours." The men thanked him, and he ducked back into the surgery room.

Just then, a Chinese-looking man walked up to the three men. "Excuse me. I'm looking for Mr. Ace Waberly."

"Yes," Ace replied, not recognizing the man.

"I'm Peter Delius, Supreme Commander of the Feds.

I want to extend my sincere apologies for this unfortunate incident. I've instructed the Chicago Feds to leave no stone unturned. We'll find this mad, insane terrorist and bring him to justice. I wanted to relay this to you personally. I won't stand for such barbaric crimes in this city or any other one for that matter."

"Thank you, Supreme Commander. So are there any leads? Who could have done this hideous thing?" Ace asked, sizing up this leader. He suspected the Cabal would like any and all information on this man. Likewise, Alan and Randal were doing the very same thing.

"Surveillance cameras have picked him up. They're running it through facial recognition now. I'm sure in time we'll know his identity. I assure you the moment we have him apprehended, you'll be the first to know. I'll see to that. If you'll excuse me, I want to oversee the Chicago Feds on this one, personally."

Ace commented, "Thanks sir."

Felix cringed, but kept a straight face. He'd not thought of facial recognition or surveillance cameras! Once the Feds leader left, Alan and his sons did so as well, since there wasn't anything more they could do.

As he left, Alan said, "Ace, keep me posted." Ace nodded.

As they drove home, Steve asked, "So dad, will Mary Jane look the same? I mean after the organ donation. Will her arms be all scarred up? That wouldn't be a good thing. If so, I don't think I could handle being married to her."

"Oh, I'm certain you'll not be able to tell she's had her arms replaced. That's why we have the OD program. Son, I've had mountains of replacement organs. That was before the Transference Machine came along. Once, there was a trace of scaring, but usually I couldn't tell any difference. That's why we're so particular about the ODs. Her OD is a clone, a duplicate of her, probably eighteen too, if I know Ace. They'll simply remove the arms from her OD and install them on Mary Jane. Recovery is about a week these days, thanks to Dr. Rumani's incredible

Medical Machines. So put such thoughts out of your mind. Me, I'm more worried about finding the idiot who bombed the place. It's the why that eludes me. Why bomb an EE women's apparel store? Males no sense at all."

Steve spoke up. "Hey, not unless they wanted to kill the EE women, dad."

"Yes, but who would want to do that? Someone with a beef against the ultimate in feminine beauty? No sense," Alan replied.

"Unless someone wanted to stop my getting married—wanted to stop the merging of the Waberly's fortunes and ours, dad," Steve theorized.

"Say, you have a point there. I think you're on to something. We do have many enemies. But wait. Ace, Randal, and I have kept this totally secret from outsiders," Alan pointed out.

"Still, as soon as we can get a look at those images on the surveillance cameras, maybe we can recognize the bomber," Steve suggested. Felix cringed, but was fortunately in the back seat, as always.

"Good idea, son. I have a few connections in the Feds. Tomorrow, I'll see if I can get a copy of those images, and we'll see if we can recognize this beast," Alan declared with some passion. He added, "At least, Ace and Randal aren't calling off the two marriages. That's what's truly important, Steve."

Late the next day, Alan received word Mary Jane was expected to make a full recovery and was due to be released from the hospital in a week. After that, she would confined to bed rest for two more weeks. However, that wasn't what was bothering Alan. No, he'd pulled some strings and had his hands on a copy of the surveillance footage. True, it was fuzzy and ill defined, but it sure looked like Felix!

Just then, Felix knocked. "You wanted to see me, dad?" He'd sent for his younger son.

"Yes, come in. Shut the door and lock it. Come here. Look at this." He motioned him over to his monitor. Felix obeyed, still without any real plan for the future.

His face flushed when he saw himself planting the bomb on the window and then backing away hastily.

That reaction was all Alan needed. He sighed. "Damn, Felix. Why? Why? You could have wiped out our grand plans to merge the three families into one. Why?"

"I sure as hell don't want to be implanted and turned into one of those mindless zombies as all the other Cabal leaders do to their second sons!" Felix spat out with a vengeance Alan had never seen before. He ran his fingers over his chin, contemplating what Felix had said.

"You know, in a way, you've shown brilliance with this move—misguided perhaps, but with a certain flair that is totally lacking in your older brother. I believe I've totally misjudged you, son. You're right, you know. Once Steve was married, I had planned to install you as a CEO of one of the companies—yes a mindless zombie as you put it. But now—this casts a different light on things. We're going to have to have you disappear, of course. Eventually, the Feds will be on to you, son, so you're going to have to vanish without a trace and yet leave behind a believable trail. Okay. Let me do some planning, Felix. I give you my word you won't be implanted or put on Pytalon."

"What? You aren't?" Felix exclaimed, shocked. He figured he was doomed when he saw his image on the monitor.

"No. Such brilliance must be rewarded, not wasted on a mindless zombie. I need some time to work something out. Go now. Say nothing of this to anyone. Let me think about it." Felix quietly left the room, greatly relieved.

Alan knew the "system" would have to have Felix logged as either deceased or as an implanted/Pytalon drugged person. If not, the Feds would be all over him. Nowhere would be safe from their reach. That was the whole point of the Feds in the first place, but there was one remaining avenue open to him, one that could make use of his newfound talent. He fired up his email program and sent off a secure email.

Later that night, he received a reply and smiled, sending for Felix. "Well son, I have two solutions for you—you choose. Well, actually three solutions. One, you could surrender to the Feds, but let's ignore that one. Two, you could be promoted to a CEO and become implanted and on Pytalon, as are all the CEOs. I'll see you have a proper EE woman as your wife though and want for nothing." Felix grimaced and started to protest, but Alan continued. "Three, as far as the system is concerned, you could become dead, but in fact join up with the Marshals Militia and Security. I've gotten confirmation they would train you for the position of a captain. You would be a leader of soldiers. So make your choice, son. These are the best I can offer."

"How soon do I have to choose?"

"A day or so. Eventually, the Feds will uncover your identity and come knocking. When they do, I won't be able to do much for you. So make your choice soon, son."

"Okay then, the militia it is," Felix replied, thinking that at least he would be alive and trained as a fighter. Perhaps one day he could return and take over the family fortune. His dad wouldn't live forever. Steve wouldn't either for that matter.

The next day, the official orders were filed. Felix Michaelson was scheduled for CEO implanting and to be given a maximum dosage of Pytalon in two days. At that time, a second notice was filed: Felix Michaelson passed away during the implanting operation. However, Felix was aboard an Air Liner bound for the Middle East and the training camp of Marshals Militia and Security.

Later, Alan and Steve joined Ace and Scott when they picked up Mary Jane from the hospital. Steve insisted on seeing the condition of his proposed bride firsthand. "Oh Steve, it was so horrible!" Mary Jane exclaimed. "Please, a steadying hand on me. I'm not used to these heels yet, and my shoulders are a bit sore still, but look, my hands work just fine." She wiggled her fingers, flashing her long red nails for him, doing her best to flirt with him and to show him that she was just fine now.

"You look gorgeous, Mary Jane. That must have been awful for you," Steve replied.

"Oh yes, but then fortunately I don't remember much of it. I think that's a good thing—not to remember such an awful thing, don't you? I can't wait to get married, but they say I have to remain mostly in bed another two weeks, until my shoulders have fully healed. You do still want me, don't you? I'm an EE woman now."

Suddenly, she began reciting her litany once more, bringing a smile to the four men's faces. Steve felt all was well in the world now. Before today, Mary Jane hardly spoke to him, and now she was fawning all over him. Besides, he found her highly attractive and wished they didn't have to wait two weeks.

***

Boom! A massive explosion shook the EE Women's Store, knocking R^3 to the floor. A wrack of dresses fell over on her adding to the confusion. Suddenly, strange men raced into the smoke filled store, while she struggled to get out from under the pile of dresses. She got into a sitting position, but sat there dazed. She couldn't hear well at all and was just as confused as everyone else was. Two men came up to her. One yelled, "Rachel Roxanne? You hurt?" Strong arms lifted her up to her feet.

"I don't think so," she said, but was in fact yelling loudly. "What happened? What's going on?"

"Come with us. We'll get you out of here," one of the men said. Just then, R^3 wanted nothing more than to get out of the store. She was coughing from the acrid smoke, while wondering if there was a fire too. She had no idea where the men were leading her, but in her heels, she couldn't move at all fast. One of the men picked her up and carried her out of the building. She could see a fire truck arriving and vaguely heard what must be sirens, but they were so faint.

Before she knew what was happening, she was carried inside an EMAC. While one of the men fastened her seat belt, the other headed to the controls. She felt it lifting off before she realized what was happening.

"Where are we going?" she asked, still yelling, though she thought she was talking normally.

"Going to get you home, Rachel Roxanne. Randal's orders. Sit tight. Only be a few minutes. You sure you're all right?" one asked her. Mechanically, R3 began feeling herself. That triggered another bout of litany recital much to her dismay, but she couldn't do anything but recite the words.

R3 was lifted down from the EMAC and found herself in a strange location. Ahead, she saw a very ritzy home. Two older people walked towards her, as well as a younger man. Suddenly, R3 recognized them from the images Felix had discovered with his computer. The older man was Randal Raven himself, while the older EE woman was his wife, Regina. The young man was their son Roy. All three had very worried expressions on their faces.

The man who had sat beside her during the trip seemed to be whispering, "She's fine. The blast has temporarily deafened her."

"Rachel Roxanne!" her father declared. "Thank god for this miracle. Come on in. Are you sure you're okay?" He too seemed to be whispering.

R3 replied, "I think so. A bomb. I don't think I can hear well. Where am I? What's going on? Something's not quite right."

"You don't have to yell, sis," Roy whispered.

"I'm not, am I?" R3 answered, realizing she must be yelling. Everything was so strange, so confusing.

"Regina, take her to her room. Get her cleaned up. Maybe some of your gowns will fit her. I should go to the medical center and be with Ace," Randal ordered.

"I don't know where anything is," R3 declared, growing more confused. She was here in the real world, not in her Ward 4. She was totally lost. "This isn't right."

"Dear, dear. It'll be okay. You've suffered a whole lot. Come on. I'll get you fixed up. This isn't how it is supposed to go for a new EE woman," Regina explained.

That triggered her implant again. "I don't look perfect, do I?" R3 gushed and began reciting her litany once more, only adding to her confusion.

The rest of the day and the next became a stream of unending confusions for R3. Nothing was familiar, but thankfully, Randal and Regina chalked all this up to the shock and disorientation of the bombing. Adding to her misery was the frequent triggering of her implant. Fortunately, her mother was familiar with what she was going through and "educated" her daughter, particularly in the following days.

Randal returned the second day with all of her dress purchases, claiming the EE women's store was sorting out the mess. What truly bothered her was Randal's reporting on the severe injuries Mary Jane had had.

"Is she badly hurt?" R3 asked, very worried about her dearest friend, before she realized he was talking about the real Mary Jane, not the OD Mary Jane, who was her friend. That only added to her confusions. If she hadn't been implanted, R3 probably could have managed very well, but as it was, she spent several very confused days.

"Don't worry, Rachel Roxanne. Mary Jane will be just fine. Her OD will be donating her needed organs. Why, in a week, I'm told, she'll be returning home in perfect condition," Randal explained.

Unfortunately, he said the wrong word, perfect. That triggered another round of litany chanting for R3, who wished she could stop saying those words, but was helpless to cease.

At least, Randal and Regina took that embarrassing detail into account. He added, "Don't worry, dear. In a few weeks, you won't be reciting that all the time. Your mom certainly doesn't. Now why don't you go try on your new dresses? You want to look your best for Scott, don't you?"

"Who's Scott?" R3 replied without thinking, barely finished with her reciting.

"Your fiancé, dear. Remember? You're getting

married to him, but we're going to postpone the wedding until Mary Jane has recovered," Randal explained.

R³ wanted to yell out, "but I don't want to marry him. I want to marry Felix," but was able to bit her lip and say nothing at all. *I have to get back to the ward somehow.* After her mind calmed, she thought about telling them about the big mix up—that his men picked up the OD Rachel Roxanne not the real one, but that only got confused in her mind. I'm real, aren't I? Maybe they'll harm me. Maybe I'm not ever supposed to see my hosts. R³ decided to keep quiet for now.

The second day, Regina discovered Rachel Roxanne's ID card was missing. Figuring it got lost in the bombing, she brought it to Randal's attention, and he had a new ID card made for her.

"Now don't lose this one, Rachel Roxanne." He clipped it to her dress. "I've news for you. Mary Jane is in recovery. Mary Jane's arms were shredded by flying glass in the explosion, but her OD donated a new set of arms, so you can rest your pretty head. Mary Jane is going to be just fine with her new arms."

That registered in R³'s mind. Her Mary Jane, her dearest friend, had donated her arms? She'd be utterly helpless. Tears flowed down her cheeks, messing up her makeup. Randal misinterpreted that. "I know. I know. It is such a blessing we have our ODs around for emergencies like these. She'll be just fine, but I'm told they want her to spend two weeks resting up before they give her medical clearance. So the weddings will be shortly after that."

That night in her new, strange bed, R³ cried. *Mary Jane needs me now more than ever before! I just have to find a way to get back to her. I just must!* Unfortunately, she had no idea where she was, rather where this home was located, or where her Ward 4 was located, that is, the Medical Center. Worse, she had no idea how she could find it. R³ also knew her walking was now severely limited, excruciatingly slow. She experimented a little by removing her tall heels, but that only turned on a severe headache and yet another recital of her implant script. If she were to walk now, she'd have to wear these impossible heels, yet another setback.

Ten days after her arrival, she had adopted a plan. First, she had to get her legs and feet toughened up so she could walk long distances. Second, she needed to learn the layout of the mansion so she could work out a way to escape. How she could possibly find her way back to the Medical Center slipped to the back of her mind. Slowly, she wandered around the ritzy mansion, observing everything.

Regina praised her and encouraged her. "Just the proper thing to do, Rachel Roxanne, practice walking gracefully. It does take much practice as I recall, though I admit my memory is rather fuzzy too. I'm sure you'll learn quickly." That emboldened R^3, and she persisted, though she had aching feet each evening.

That tenth day, she passed by Randal's private office. The door was slightly ajar, and she overhead him talking with Roy. "So we'll wait until five days after the two weddings. Then we will strike around two in the morning. Rachel Roxanne will then inherit the Waberly fortune." R^3 moved on, her heels clicking on the tile floor.

What did they mean by that, she wondered. How can Rachel Roxanne inherit the Waberly's fortune? Suddenly, it jelled. They were planning to kill all the other Waberly family members! Now she knew she had to escape and very soon. How could she warn the Waberly's? Would Mary Jane, her Mary Jane, be hurt more? R^3 felt real fear, but had no idea how to handle the situation. She knew Felix would have a solution, a plan. He always did. Oh, how she missed Felix now. Then, she began to wonder what Felix was doing with the real Rachel Roxanne. *She must have taken my place,* she thought, and again panicked. Her Felix would get all mixed up and forsake her. R^3 felt utterly miserable that evening, crying herself to sleep.
***

James Buffett hated to be outside in the real world— hated it with a passion! Still, he'd worked for close to two centuries to make the world into what he considered a habitable, survivable world, one in which he was in total control and in no danger. That meant everyone else had to be a zombie. That was the answer, now pretty well implemented in the habitable portion of the world. That he was also the second richest person in the entire world was secondary. Still, he felt very nervous walking out in the open in Chicago of all places. He only felt safe in his secure compound in remote New York State.

Yet, things were unraveling, if only slightly. Presuming Franco's intelligence was right, then this new self-appointed Supreme Commander Peter Delius posed a major threat. Worse, he'd somehow discovered the Lin bothers and stolen their precious Transference Machines. Further, this business of no longer enforcing the Total Care program on recent high school graduates was unthinkable. *My god, we'll have thinking, acting people running around again. That's beyond scary! We simply cannot tolerate that!*

He was on his way to meet this Supreme Commander Peter Delius, which was why his mind was in such turmoil and why he had to appear out in public, the latter being most terrifying to him. He entered the Feds building in downtown Chicago and walked up to the proper moron in reception. "Here to see Peter Delius," he said without emotion. After signing in, he clipped his visitor's card to his immaculate business suit pocket, making sure the letter B of his handkerchief was not obscured in any way by the plastic card and clip. Satisfied, he headed to the elevators.

Peter Delius sat in his office pondering the email message he'd received from a James Buffett, demanding a formal meeting with him. Peter had searched the databases for any record of this person, but to his amazement, found none, except to a man who must obviously be long dead. No one lived to be two hundred plus years old. The man didn't exist and yet he was due to arrive within minutes. The front deskman notified him that a James Buffett was on his way up, and Peter sat back waiting to see what this was all about.

He saw an immaculately dressed man, perhaps fifty, entering his office. Peter rose, "I'm Supreme Commander Peter Delius. Have a seat. How can I help you today?" The man refused to shake, but took a seat opposite Peter and cleared his throat.

"We have a number of things to discuss. First of all, I'm your boss, the boss of all the Feds, worldwide."

Peter looked up and stared at this man, whom he had never heard of before now. "I beg your pardon. We have no knowledge of you in our databases."

"Well, let's approach this from a different angle. Who do you suppose pays your salaries, the wages for all the Feds, your operating funds?"

"It comes in regularly. We have a yearly budget. The funds are always there," Peter replied.

"Of course. My job is to see that occurs without any interruptions. That is, as long as you do your job and follow any orders I may give you. Mind you, I very seldom do that—give orders I mean," James explained in his quiet manner.

"Now then, Mr. Delius, it has come to my attention you've kidnaped the Lin brothers and have raided and stolen their many medical devices. The Lin brothers are highly respected members of the entire world. Thus, I must insist the Lin brothers be returned to me and their medical devices too, as soon as possible," James stated softly, having decided to minimize this meeting.

He longed to get out of this building. Peter Delius was not on Pytalon nor was he implanted, but then in the past the top Feds had not been. Still, this alone caused James considerable worry. He wasn't safe, not remotely. Like most all Cabal heads, he greatly feared people, especially those who were not now zombies. In fact, it was more like utter terror that he felt when he was around people—almost any people for that matter.

"I'm sorry, but Bo Bin Lin and Han Lin have been

found guilty of very severe crimes against numerous men and women. They were using their machines to perpetuate their many crimes. We've dutifully taken both them and their machines out of circulation, Mr. Buffett. Just doing my job," Peter replied, wondering how much detail he should divulge. He thought better of saying too much. He simply didn't trust this man in the slightest.

"If you'll consult your records, you will find the Lin brothers have been instrumental in developing many medical devices that have greatly aided our entire world. Of course, we all have committed certain, shall we say, indiscretions in our past. I'm sure you yourself have done some things that perhaps you should not have done, and yet here you are still performing your sworn duty to the world, capturing criminals and the like, and you haven't arrested yourself. Surely, we can come to some understanding in this matter. While I'm sure the Lin brothers may have committed some crimes in their past, the benefits they have made to our world surely outweigh those. Am I not correct?"

Peter found himself flinching, because he'd done numerous things in his past for which he could have been arrested, but he had changed, turned over a new leaf and was trying his best to help the whole world now. "I'm sorry, but their crimes are far too serious for any one of us to consider releasing them. On top of that, their medical machines are simply something the world should not have in its possession. They are far, far too dangerous, in the wrong hands, mind you. You'll just have to accept my word on that."

James didn't like Peter's response, but wisely changed topics. Peter had to go. "Another smaller matter. It seems a fair number of Chicago high school graduates were not implanted, put on Pytalon, and given their appropriate jobs per the Total Care program. Perhaps you know something about this?"

"Yes, our doing. We want to help get this world on the right track again. Implanted Pytalon morons have brought the world to its knees. We are allowing those bright graduates the opportunity to flourish and work at jobs of their choosing. Thus far, it's producing remarkable results. In time, we hope to implement this worldwide. Surely, you can see the tremendous benefits of having a keen mind working on any particular job, as opposed to unthinking idiots."

"I see. Well, I've taken up too much of your valuable time. I'll see myself out."

"One second. If you're my boss, how do I contact you? You see, not only didn't I know about you, I had no way to contact you about the Lin brothers mess."

"Point taken. I contact you, not the other way around. Good day, Supreme Commander Peter Delius," James said softly.

He rose, and left. Only when he was safely in his Air Liner did he finally relax. Sipping a fine wine, James fired off several emails, only one of which went to Franco Helu.

Several days later, he received another email back. It read:

Feds operative captured and questioned. Peter Delius ordered the raid, twice. Four others of Chinese descent accompanied him. Names attached. These four are often found around the Feds Chicago office, where they have offices.

Now James fired off another email and sat back smiling.

***

"Well, well, gentlemen, we have an assignment worthy of us," Al Hamadi grinned. He'd just received an email from James Buffett. "Pay is guaranteed and some of you could retire on this one. Load up the guns. We've a job to do." Five other men of Arab descent also smiled. All six were superb assassins, with over twenty kills between them.

A day later, they landed at New O'Hare and rented an EMAC, using fake ID cards. They flew over the tall Feds building and landed on a nearby skyscraper. Al Hamadi and four of his men assembled their scopes and fifty-

caliber sniper rifles, while the other companion stood guard and watched for their targets via a powerful scope. All had photographs of the five targets of Chinese descent in their hands, namely Peter, Ben, Tim, Jessi, and Mandy. Now they waited, each with their own target.
***

After James Buffett left, Peter called in his friends, Ben, Tim, Jessi, and Mandy. Carefully, he replayed back the recording he'd cleverly made of the encounter with this mysterious James Buffett. "Well, what do you make of this? I can't find him in our databases, so perhaps that is an alias name."

Tim replied, "I don't like this. He wants the Transference Machines back. That alone is highly suspicious, to say nothing of having the Lin brothers back. I think we're again facing another plot of the Lin brothers, like before. This time, we have them at a severe disadvantage, unless they have more of their machines hidden from us. I don't like this at all. I think it wise to let Lady Persephone and the professor know about this. Send them your video file. Ben, do some sleuthing on this mysterious James Buffett."

"Already on it," Ben teased.

Mandy added, "Darn. He didn't touch anything in the room, so no fingerprints. Clever man. I'll go check the visitor's badge. Maybe he left some on it." She rose and headed off to do just that. By the time she returned with a sour look on her face, Lady Persephone and the professor were on conference call with the others. "No go on fingerprints. Wiped clean," she reported.

"We should take this very seriously," Lady Persephone spoke up. "I'm going to move a number of these machines to alternate, secure locations. What about moving the Lin brothers, professor? If they should come after them, we sure as hell don't want them in Phoenix."

"Bloody right you are. Besides, they're a royal pain. Sometimes, I wish we'd just killed them. Still, we may be able to get more useful information from them. I'm always hopeful on that line. These Transference Machines of theirs are something else," the professor replied. "I'll arrange for them to stay at a small home in Flagstaff, under guard of course."

Peter took charge. "Okay. We'll all take precautions. Perhaps this will amount to nothing. Ben, keep me posted on what you find. Also, since he alluded to somehow paying our Feds, see if you and Jessi can track where we get our yearly funds. I'm curious. Thanks everyone." The professor and Lady Persephone hung up.

Peter changed the topic. "So how is everything working out with your other bodies?" He was referring to their four armless EE women's bodies, that is, Beth, Tilly, Amanda, and Jessica. He and the four had used the Transference Machine and were in fact running two bodies each—their original bodies and the young Chinese ones. They had recently arrived from London and were now staying in their fancy new penthouse suite not too far from the Feds building, along with their four Chinese bodies, that is, Ben, Tim, Jessi, and Mandy.

"So far so good," Tim replied. "By the way, tell Chan and Yan congratulations on becoming mothers. Beth, Tilly, Jessica, and Amanda are also considering becoming mothers soon too. We've been holding off a bit, hoping everything dies down."

Peter chuckled. "We're about a month along now. Over the morning sickness, we hope. Honestly, that's the weirdest thing. I mean being in this body while experiencing that in my Chan body." All five chuckled and the four returned to their own offices to get onto the trail of this new potential situation.

By the next day, Ben was quite frustrated. He'd learned nothing more than Peter had. James Buffett didn't exist, unless one counted one that was over two hundred years old. Further, the Feds operational funds came directly from the Total Care Program Worldwide. From there, Ben hit a dead end. "Looks as if we're going to have to fully investigate this Total Care network," he commented that evening to the others.

A week passed without incident, except Captain Lech had one of his Feds turn up missing for several days. Later, his body was found in Lake Michigan. He had no leads on that one, though he forwarded all the scanty details on up to Peter, along with the autopsy findings that the man had a huge dose of Truth Drug A in his system. This detail bothered Peter, who relayed this finding onto Tim to see what he made of it.

Since the man had no significant clearance codes, Captain Lech didn't change any passwords. Peter agreed with his decision. He did suggest, "If other men go missing, I would recommend using the buddy system. Always pair your men up."

"Already wrote out those orders boss," Lech smiled at Peter.

"Say, are we getting anywhere on the Medical Center bombing last week?" Peter asked.

"Strange one, boss. We believe we've finally identified the bomber, but it seems he died on the implant table a few days ago. No motive. Guess it's just another insane action. I've forwarded the information to Ace Waberly like you asked. Case is closed now. Fortunately, no one was killed. One woman was badly wounded, but has survived."

On September 15, Peter walked out of the Feds building, accompanying Ben, Tim, Jessi, and Mandy. They were chatting about the nice fall weather, while heading for the MET and the short trip to their penthouse suites. A dozen other Feds were around them, all heading home.

"Got mine," one man whispered. One by one, his accomplices acknowledged target acquisition. "On my mark. 3-2-1. Now." Five high-caliber rounds fired within split seconds of each other, their noise masked by silencers. The range: a startling six hundred feet. The men rolled back from the edge of the building and climbed into their EMAC. It quickly lifted off, joining the hundreds of others sailing the skies of downtown Chicago at rush time.

In an instant, Peter, Ben, Tim, Jessi, and Mandy were sent smashing into their other bodies' heads, complete with splitting headaches. The death of their young Chinese bodies forced each to go solely into their other body. Down on the street, the Feds swarmed around the crime scene, but the five were dead. The large caliber rounds had taken the back of their heads off. Captain Lech came rushing out of the building, taking charge, but none of his men had heard gunshots or seen anything at all! It was thus far a perfect assassination!

An hour later, still nursing headaches, the five were on a conference call with Lady Persephone, the professor, and Captain Lech. Speculation ran rampant. "Crap. Now we have another dire situation to handle, and we're barely able to function," Beth grumbled. "It takes me forever to do anything now."

"Tell me about it, love!" Jessica added. She still became frustrated at her eternal slowness using her toes to manipulate her computer systems.

At least, we have accommodations here that we can manage to handle," Tilly tried to think of something positive to say. Their other bodies had reworked much of the large suite bringing most everything lower to the ground so the four could manage with their feet, mostly.

"Okay," Lady Persephone took charge. "I want you to get some of the Trikuza together and have them be your bodyguards from now on. If anyone can stop these assassins, it'll be them."

Chan-Petra replied, "I'll see to it in the morning. I think that's a very wise idea. Crap, do you realize what would have happened if we hadn't had these extra bodies?"

The professor answered, "The freedom movement would have been set back severely. I might also suggest sending some Trikuza to protect the other Feds heads as well, Chan-Petra."

"Right, particularly those who aren't on Pytalon and haven't been implanted. I'll see to that in the morning. I bet James Buffett will make another appearance one day soon.

Should I arrest him?"

"What charges?" Tilly countered. "We know nothing about him—yet anyway."

"Be bloody vigilant," the professor added. "Bloody vigilant." At that, they ended the conference call.

Tilly commented, "I'm glad we held off on starting a family. Without the helping hands of our other bodies, a pregnancy would be challenging, to say nothing of caring for the babies."

Jessica sighed. She had so hoped they could've started a family soon, in spite of the awful society around her. Yan Delius had already given birth to a son, Dan. Chan-Petra was due any day now.

A week later, Captain Lech had few clues. Crime scene reconstruction pointed them to the location of the shooters, the top of a nearby building. A thorough search suggested six men had been there recently and that five had fired high-caliber guns. The only clues were several dried spots of spit. DNA samples were taken, but no hits were found in the US database. As a last resort, Lech sent a request for worldwide search of other countries databases. He didn't hold out much hope though.

Chapter 4—Offers

On October 1, nine-month pregnant Chan-Petra got the call she was expecting. The deskman notified her that a James Buffett was on his way up to see her. Once again, she activated her auto recording and patched in a concealed speakerphone to Beth and Jessica so they could overhear the conversation as well. Shortly, the immaculately dressed man entered her office. His appearance hadn't changed, and she wondered if he'd even changed his suit, but then perhaps he had several identical suits. Some men were like that, she thought.

"Supreme Commander Chan-Petra Delius?" he said, raising an eyebrow slightly.

"Precisely. James Buffett?"

"Indeed." He sat down precisely as he had before.

"Again, it's noted that I didn't appoint you to your post. I'm your boss, in case the late Peter Delius has not so informed you," he began.

"Yes, consider me fully informed."

"An EE woman. What are the Feds coming to anyway?"

"Women are just as capable as men, perhaps more so. The reason for your visit?" Chan replied coldly.

"Your predecessor raided the Lin brothers and took them prisoner and confiscated their invaluable medical machines. This must be rectified immediately. However, I've become aware of a rather unique situation. Apparently, you're well acquainted with four other most unfortunate EE women who have met with an accident and lost their arms. Is this not correct?"

Chan didn't want to divulge any more than she had to. "Yes, we EE women tend to stick together and help each other when the need arises. I have been helping four unfortunate young women who are having a most difficult time just surviving. Why do you ask?"

"The Lin brothers' Transference Machines are extremely important to the medical arena. I would like to make you a most generous offer. See that two complete sets of these machines, in full working order, are sent to the Rumani Medical Institute for Medical Research in India, along with the Lin brothers. In return, I'll see that Total Care finds appropriate organ donors so your four EE women can have new arms, just as good as their old ones were. Surely, you're aware of our highly advanced surgical procedures? The process takes a few hours to complete. Expect a week in recovery and then another two weeks of rest and little activity. After that, they'll never know they had even lost their arms in their unfortunate accidents. Mind you, EE women aren't allowed such organ donations, as they are Case C recipients. They could obtain new arms if they are willing to pay for them. The going rate for new arms is thirty million credits. Times four, yields a staggering one hundred twenty million credits. You see, I'm offering you a very remunerative deal. Surely, the loss of two sets of the stolen medical machines donated to medical research and the return of the two Lin brothers is worth one hundred twenty million credits to you and your organization."

Chan-Petra was a bit surprised with his offer. "I'm sorry. I didn't know arms could be regrown or re-attached."

"Miracles happen, thanks to the Rumani Medical Research Foundation in India. Once a compatible organ donor is found, the process is extremely simple. I'm told a child could operate these incredibly sophisticated medical machines," he replied.

"So you can guarantee me that these machines will be used solely for proper and ethical medical research purposes?" Chan asked.

"Absolutely. I suggest you check up on the Rumani Medical Research Foundation in India before committing to this offer of mine."

Chan knew just how helpless her four friends were.

That they could have new arms and hands would be a true miracle, and yet, he wasn't asking for all the machines back, just two, and they were going to a medical research foundation, which potentially could benefit mankind. Still the Lin brothers were a problem. "Perhaps we could agree upon everything but the Lin brothers. I don't have the authority to release tried and convicted master criminals. Believe me, the Lin brothers got off easy. They should have been executed for their crimes, which include murder as well."

"I can see how that could be a problem for you. In the name of medical research, I too must compromise. These machines offer new horizons in medical research, perhaps saving countless lives in the near future. I'll then withdraw my request for you to turn over the Lin brothers. Will that be acceptable?"

"As you suggest, I must look over this Rumani Medical Research Foundation in India before I can make any commitments. It shouldn't take too long to do that. How do I contact you if I wish to proceed in helping my four EE women friends out?"

"Write this number down." James gave her a disposable cell phone number to call. "When you hear my voice, say only yes or no, and I will get back to you. Thank you. I do hope we can proceed in this matter." He rose and left, taking care not to leave any fingerprints this time as well.

Once onboard his own Air Liner, James fired off another email, one that would handle the Lin brothers. He had many contacts and had recently learned that they had been moved to a safe house in Flagstaff. He could use other means to acquire the brothers. However, nothing could happen until he received the two machines. His extensive network of spies learned nothing about the machines, other than the Feds loaded them onto a private EMAC operated by some woman. He was definitely running out of options. The only remaining one was to kidnap this EE woman, Chan-Petra, dose her up with Truth Drug A, and hope and pray she knew something about these machines. He kept that as a last resort, because she could well not know their location. He hoped this last bit of sleuthing, the discovery of the close relationship with these helpless and unfortunate four EE women, would pan out. Women had soft spots. Perhaps this Chan-Petra would too.

James had barely left the building before Chan had everyone on a conference call. First, she replayed the video recording for everyone, though Beth and Jessica had already heard it live. Once it finished, Chan asked, "So what do you think? It seems a reasonable request—medical research. If there is a chance you four could have arms and hands, I feel obligated to make the attempt."

Beth didn't like the sound of it. What about the organ donors? Were they merely transferring their disabilities onto their organ donors? However, one look at Jessica and his heart melted. If there was any chance, she felt she owed it to Jessica and to Amanda too.

Tilly broke the ice, "Well, my and Amanda's initial calculations suggest this has a seventy percent chance of success, but much rests on just what this Rumani Medical Research Foundation in India actually did. Give us a day to investigate it. We're incredibly slow typing with our feet. God, it would be fabulous to be whole once more."

The professor added, "I agree. It would be highly advantageous to our cause if the Weasel and the Wart were at full potential, to say nothing of Jessica and Amanda. I have the Lin brothers in a secure facility, so I think we're safe on that account."

"I agree, with many reservations," Lady Persephone added her viewpoint. "I'll go ahead and get two sets ready for shipment, just in case. I would advise the operation be conducted there in Chicago if possible. You're familiar with the city. The odds are more in your favor. Tilly, I don't need your calculations to tell me that," she jested. Tilly laughed.

A day later, Chan-Petra called the number and recorded her "yes." A day after that, James Buffett visited the Feds headquarters, bringing along a nurse with him.

Chan-Petra spoke first. "We can have a deal, but I would like the surgery to be performed here in Chicago. It is terribly hard on the four women to do much traveling, as you probably can imagine."

"The Ramani Chicago Medical Institute is more than highly qualified to perform such organ transplants. They have had a good deal of experience in doing these. I'm told that recently they did just this very operation for a young EE woman who lost her arms in a terrorist bombing attack on the EE women's store, just below the medical institute. She has fully recovered now. I would like my nurse here to collect DNA samples from the four women so that compatible donors can be found. Sometimes, this takes some time, but I do hope to have them found before your delivery arrives in India. Just as soon as donors can be found, we should proceed. Sometimes, the donors have recently died and thus, I'm told, it's imperative the organs be harvested immediately. Will that be acceptable?"

Chan agreed and got the process started. James provided her with the shipping address, which she verified was actually the medical institute. The two left shortly after the glassy-eyed nurse had her swab samples and correctly labeled. James promised to call her as soon as donors were lined up. Now the five waited, though Lady Persephone went ahead and shipped the heavy containers off to India, but set it up so they would arrive around October 15. Moreover, if things didn't work out for the four by then, she could delay the arrival date as much as desired.

On October 3, Chan-Petra gave birth to a son. She named him Peter. A few days later, she was released and joined Yan. Now she was a mother, a completely new arena for her! In some ways, bringing forth this new life changed her viewpoint, particularly being so tired the first few days.

What the group found utterly amazing was the speed at which four compatible donors were found! In barely one week's time, the Ramani Chicago Medical Institute called Chan-Petra, notifying her that donors were found and that the surgery was scheduled for nine o'clock on October 10!

She and four Trikuza members accompanied Beth, Tilly, Jessica, and Amanda to the medical center. The five then nervously waited in the waiting area for news, while the four were taken to another floor. After drinking a concoction, the four were rendered unconscious. Later they awoke and found themselves in dual bedrooms with two Trikuza members sitting with them, their personal guards. Chan-Petra received notification all had gone perfectly about five hours later. Curiously, the doctor said some twenty other transplants were being handled this day as well.

***

Back in Ward 4, Felix continued to monitor the situation. He had Rachel Roxanne calmed down and playing along with them, but she just couldn't bring herself to help poor Mary Jane. Instead, Rhianna became her constant arms and hands. For those next few days, Mary Jane fought hard to keep from breaking down, though at night when she and Rhianna were finally alone in the bedroom, she did allow her tears to flow freely. "I don't want to be an organ donor, Rhianna. Look at me. I'm completely helpless now. I can't do anything for me. Oh god, no, not now," she wailed as she found herself having to recite her implant script yet again. Unfortunately, that triggered Rhianna's as well.

Then, Felix discovered the real Felix was apparently scheduled for implanting in two days' time. "Oh shit!" he exclaimed and hastily got the Circle of Six together, even though Rachel Roxanne was the wrong R³. "They're going to implant Felix Michaelson in two days!" he exclaimed.

"So what of it?" Rachel Roxanne declared. "People get implanted all the time. Still, it's unusual for him to get it. Must be part of the Cabal's plan."

"Are you an idiot?" Todd barked. "That means our Felix is going to get his body chopped up into little pieces and donated to god knows who, that's what."

"Oh. Well, you are the ODs, aren't you?" she replied

naively.

Trevor spoke up, "Rachel Roxanne, if you ever want to get out of this place and back to your home, then you have to help Felix. Without his help, you're just another one of us organ donors. Sooner or later, they'll be cutting your body parts off too."

"Oh!" She exclaimed and shut up.

"We have to get out of here soon," Todd declared.

"Best try it at night," Felix explained. "The problem, gang, is that none of us have ever been out there in the world. We have no idea where her home is at or how to get there. Okay, Rachel Roxanne, let's make a deal. I'll get us out of here, but you have to get us to your place and help us get our Rachel Roxanne out of there. Deal?"

"Deal. This is exciting. Oh shit," Rachel Roxanne gushed, as her implant began forcing her to recite the words yet again. The word "exciting" triggered it. Shortly after that, Mary Jane and Rhianna followed suit, much to the consternation and annoyance of the three boys.

The next day, Felix devoted his time to figuring a way out of the medical center. The elevator was out. That was heavily guarded at all times. A camera was also constantly focused on the main entrance; besides, it was well lighted for arriving emergency vehicles, particularly EMACs. He needed a clever way out, one that held the fewest opportunities for discovery. It wasn't until late afternoon when he finally found it. There was an emergency exit chute, a tube that circled round and round until it reached the ground. There was only one camera focused on its entrance, and its door latch was computer controlled, for ease of use in emergencies. Felix muttered, "In an emergency, this place could lose power. Then, how would it be open-able? Idiots."

By supper, he had worked out two critical programs. Timing was everything. The first program would feed a replay loop through the camera on the entrance. When he gave the unlock command, the loop would play for no longer than five minutes. Everyone would have to start sliding down it in that time. The second one was even more problematical: the exit latch and camera. He had no idea how long it would take them to descend, particularly with Mary Jane being so helpless and dependent upon their help. If he made the time too short, they would become trapped at the exit point. If he made it too long, they'd be sitting ducks if any guards walked by, and there were guards patrolling the perimeter, especially since the bombing attack. He made a wild guess and set it to activate five minutes later. Finally, he set up a computer bomb that would totally wipe his hard drive clean a half hour after that. Once he initiated the first program, the rest would follow like clockwork.

Just after supper, he whispered to everyone to be ready to go at midnight. "Girls, if you have to recite your scripts, please do it in a whisper," Felix advised.

Rhianna spoke up, "What about Mary Jane? You know she has no way to pleasure herself now and has been wearing special panties that do it for her. Should she continue to wear them? Honestly, Felix, you have no idea how awful it is for us. She'll get migraines if she can't get pleasuring when she needs it. We all do."

"Let her continue to wear them," Felix advised.

"You might have to wait a bit from time to time. When it happens, she can hardly move. This is so utterly humiliating and embarrassing to talk about to you guys," Rhianna admitted. Even saying this much reactivated her implant, and she silently repeated the words again. Felix saw her eyes sort of fog out and knew what was happening. He remained quiet until she recovered, her face as crimson as her long flaming locks.

When she was coherent again, he suggested, "Say, when it happens, why don't you alert us by saying something like 'dogs.' When we heard that word, we'll know. I'll let the other guys know. Maybe that will help all three of you." She flashed him a big smile.

Hours passed anxiously for the six. Rachel Roxanne kept asking, "Is it time yet?"

Felix continued to say, "Not yet. Not yet. Patience."

Finally the clock at the caretaker's station stoked midnight. The entire ward was asleep except for the six. "Okay, get everyone over to the emergency door. Wave your hand when everyone is set to go. I'll launch the program," Felix whispered, mostly to Todd and Trevor. "I'll come as fast as I can. Remember, five minutes and we all have to be inside the slide, and five minutes after that, we have to be outside, no matter what." Todd gave him a thumb's up sign and a big grin.

Trevor, the burly fighter type, took point, moving quickly but silently to the emergency door where he waited for the others and keeping watch. Rhianna, a steadying arm around Mary Jane, made her slow way down the hall. In their tall heels, the two moved very slowly. Rachel Roxanne walked right behind them, while Todd brought up the rear, his eyes darting side to side. After what seemed an eternity to Felix, Todd waved his hand.

Well, this is it. Either we get out of this abysmal ward or I get sliced and diced, Felix thought. His finger poised over the Enter key. It wasn't too late to abort. But why? He knew he had no future. Everything he'd uncovered suggested his body would shortly be cut up, organs going to many unknown persons. He'd be dead. His finger hit the key. He watched his carefully crafted script begin execution. Then, he made a dash down the hall to the emergency door.

As soon as it opened, Trevor saw nothing more than a black circle opening, a tunnel. He slipped inside, sitting on his butt. "Okay, it's like some kind of slide. Sit on your butt and push off." He did so. The four heard a faint sliding sound that rapidly fell silent. "I can't do this!" Mary Jane whispered, more afraid than ever. She knew she had no way to get herself inside as Trevor had.

"Got you," Todd whispered. She felt his strong arms lifting her up and sitting her into position. "Stay still a bit. Rhianna, you go next and put your arms around her. Control her descent." He then lifted her in and watched as

Rhianna did her best to get into position. Perhaps a bit too soon, Mary Jane began sliding off into the blackness of the tunnel, but at least Rhianna was right behind her. Todd helped Rachel Roxanne into position and gave her a push off. Down she went. He hopped in after her, while behind him, Felix kept saying, "Hurry up!" Felix just barely got himself into position when the automatic door shut behind him. Hastily he shoved off and felt his body sliding away, going downward rather rapidly. He could see nothing whatsoever!

Down below, Trevor came sliding to a stop before the exit gate, which was currently closed. So far so good, he presumed. He scooted as close to the door as he could and listened to the outside sounds. Mary Jane and Rhianna came sliding to a stop a few feet behind him. "Scoot on up close to me," he whispered.

"We can't. Little help," Rhianna whispered back. Trevor turned around and felt for the girls. He found Mary Jane's foot and pulled her on down close to him. Somehow, Rhianna managed to get herself scooted up behind her, just as Rachel Roxanne joined them. Before long, all six were crowded close together, waiting for the door to open.

"Now what?" whispered Rachel Roxanne, nervously?

"Patience," Felix whispered back. Click. Trevor heard a noise from the gate door and gave it a push. It opened. As fast as he could he scooted outside, before realizing the girls needed help. He leaned back in and dragged Mary Jane on out, standing her up on her feet. Then he did the same for the other two. Todd and Felix scooted out just as the door swung shut and locked. Felix had timed it almost too closely!

"Okay, I got us this far. Rachel Roxanne, you're up. What do we do now?" Felix whispered.

"We find an EMAC. Follow me," she whispered. She was so nervous that her legs were shaking. At this point, they were walking on the concrete sidewalk. The women's heels seemed to make very loud noises as they took their tiny steps. "Maybe it'll look better if you guys put an arm around us girls," she whispered back. Felix moved up, and she felt his arm sliding around her waist. Suddenly, her EE woman's implant kicked in, but she remembered to say "dog" and whispered her chant under her breath. However, the six paused for a couple of minutes, the fellows growing more and more worried.

That done, she led them on down the street. She knew the MET system didn't run all the way to her place. That would make their compound insecure. Her mind tried to figure out where she could get an EMAC at this time of night. Then it came to her: New O'Hare. "This way. We're taking the MET," she whispered.

"Thank god. I can't walk much farther. Dog. Dog. Dog," Mary Jane whispered frantically. She was very relieved finally to be standing on the moving escalator track.

Felix looked around. Hardly anyone was in sight. "So how do we get this EMAC, Rachel Roxanne?"

"We pass my ID card over the scanner. It debits my account for the EMAC fee. Once inside, I think I can program it to fly us close to my home. Of course, the problem is getting inside and getting your person out. Dad has all kinds of security devices. I think I know how we can do it," she replied. Before getting her implant, she knew she could do this, but now with her mind constantly thinking about the man's hand around her waist, she could barely focus and keep from continuously reciting her chant. *I wonder what it'll be like when I can kiss Scott. No, I can't think about that!* She fought to keep her mind focused, but was slowly losing that battle.

"Keep following the signs that say 'To New O'Hare,'" she whispered back to the others.

Trevor whispered, "Guys, this is incredibly exciting!"

Rhianna whispered back, "I know. I can hardly keep from throwing my arms around you and kissing you to death! Oh! That's not what you meant," she flushed as red as her hair, but in the near darkness, it wasn't visible.

"Sorry. Bad choice of words. I'd love to kiss you too, Rhianna. I meant this is, well exciting. We're really escaping. We're going to be free to do what we want to do, I think."

"I'm sorry, Todd. I'm a helpless cripple now. You can dump me whenever you want," Mary Jane whispered.

"Don't be silly, Mary Jane. I'm not dumping you, not ever, but we best wait to kiss, don't you think?" Todd whispered back. She sighed and said "dog" again.

"How much longer?" Felix whispered.

"Probably an hour," Rachel Roxanne answered. "I've never made this trip before. Dad's never let me out on my own much, ever, but I do know it's a long way from downtown—where we were—to New O'Hare."

"Okay. What does this ID card thing actually do?" Felix asked.

"Oh that's simple. Everyone has one, well, excepting you people. It's electronically tied to your bank account, so when you need to buy something, you pass the card over the card reader and the machine debits the cost from your account. Of course, if you don't have enough money in it, then the machine won't allow you to buy it," she explained as best she could. Such things were automatic for her. Besides, she had no real understanding of what actually went on when she swiped her card—just that it always worked.

Around an hour later, they stepped off the MET near a long line of empty EMACs. She walked up to the purchasing kiosk and swiped her card. Automatically the nearest EMAC activated its outside lights and its door opened. She didn't need to tell the others this was it. The boys helped the girls into it. While Todd and Trevor strapped Rhianna and Mary Jane in, Felix and Rachel Roxanne headed to the driver's seats up front. "Now what do we do?" he asked.

"Not sure. Never done this before. Let's see," she swiped her card over the reader and a menu of choices appeared on the dash. Admiring her long red nails in the pale blue light, she was distracted for a moment. Then she focused again and found an entry that read, "Home." She pressed it and the EMAC silently lifted off.

"How do we drive it?" Felix whispered.

"We don't need to do anything. It's on automatic. I think it detected my home address from my card and is now taking us there. Of course, when we get close, I'm going to have to do something different. If we land inside our complex, dozens of guards are going to come out with their guns blazing. Besides, we need to get your person out and me in. I would rather not have to explain all this. Too hard. Damn. Not again! Dog," she whispered.

Felix fell silent, allowing her time to recover. He was certain these implants were wicked and evil, imagining the horrors his R^3 must be going through!

Fifteen minutes later, they were out over farmlands. She spotted her complex coming up and hastily disengaged the autopilot. A message appeared on the monitor: Action required. She fumbled around and finally decided to press the option to land immediately. The EMAC responded, landing in a grove of oak trees outside her home complex. Once everyone got out and Rachel Roxanne shut the door, the EMAC silently lifted off once more.

"What?" asked Felix?

"Oh, it's probably returning to where we got it. Automatic, see?" she said, wishing her implant wasn't automatic. It triggered again, annoying her no end. While silently repeating her chant, she looked around getting her bearings. "Okay. I think it will be best if you hide out here in the trees. I'll take Felix with me and see if we can sneak inside without alerting anyone. If so, she and I will switch places, and they can join you later on."

Felix whispered, "Gang, if I'm not back by morning, you can split. I may have been caught and killed or something." None of the four liked the sound of that, but agreed to wait here. Besides, the girls found walking on the soft and uneven ground nearly impossible. As Felix and Rachel Roxanne headed off, she too nearly fell until he slipped a steadying arm around her. "Where are we going?" he whispered.

"That old shed over there," she pointed out. "There's a secret escape tunnel that opens up in there. In case of an emergency, we have a secret way out. It's got some booby traps in it, but I'll show you how to disarm them."

It was three in the morning before they entered the shed filled with rusting machinery. She pressed a concealed button on the back wall and a small keypad appeared. "912," she whispered and deftly punched in the numbers. A sliding door opened, revealing a very dimly illuminated tunnel. It was only three feet wide, but tall enough that they could stand up. It was made from concrete, Felix observed, and he felt a bit safer walking along. Twice, she stopped at a keypad along the walls and entered the same three numbers, disarming the traps and alert sirens. At last, they exited the tunnel and were in her home's basement.

She whispered, "Felix, you stay here. I'll go find my room, help her get dressed, and bring her to you. If someone sees me, they won't think anything about it, but if they see you, bad things will happen, if I know my dad." He sighed, but suspected she was right. He would have to trust her to bring his precious R^3 to him.

It seemed like an eternity that he stood there in the darkness of the basement. Just when he began to lose all hope, he heard the telltale clicking of their heels on the concrete basement floor. "R^3? Is that you?" he whispered, scarcely daring to hope.

"Felix? Is that you? I've never been so glad to see you ever! I need help. The implant is driving me nuts. Are we free now?" she whispered back, slowly closing the distance between them.

"Yes, it's me. The others are waiting for us," he whispered back, his arms outstretched waiting to hold her tightly.

"Okay, I'll open the passage. Remember the codes?" the other Rachel whispered.

"912."

"Right. Thanks and good luck," she replied, as the tunnel door opened again. Felix led his precious R3 down the dimly lit tunnel. Behind them, they heard the stone door sliding shut sealing them in.

Neither dared to talk. He needed to keep alert for the two keypads, while she had to keep her balance and fought hard to keep from reciting her implanted chant aloud. She found merely thinking them through was sufficient just now, but his warm arm around her waist continually electrified her body, causing the recitation to repeat itself. *God, I'm going crazy, but I have to hold it together. I just have to!*

Around four in the morning, the two finally joined the others, who were shivering. The late fall night was quite chilly. After a brief reunion, Felix decided their best bet was to go back into that shed and hide out. At least, they would be slightly warmer inside. With the men mostly supporting young women, Felix led them back into the shed. There, Trevor spotted a number of old blankets piled in one corner and finally the exhausted Circle of Six laid down, covered up, and fell asleep, the girls resting upon their long time boyfriends, free at last to do so.

In the morning, the six friends woke to find themselves hungry and rather dirty. While the fellows worried about the former, the three young women also found their implants kicking in heavily merely because they were disheveled and their gowns dirty. The three boys learned more about how debilitating their girlfriend's implants were.

Felix summed up their situation. "Well, gang, we're free. I got us this far, but now what do we do? I've no idea. I don't see anything but empty countryside outside this shed."

R3 shivered. "I've missed you all so badly. This is torture—trying to live with this implant thing and having to pretend I was her—Rachel Roxanne. I couldn't think properly, not really. Worse, they were going to marry me today, er Rachel that is, so I told her about it last night. She knows about it. Please, implant, not now. Let me finish this." R³ was obviously fighting reciting it again. "They're all leaving—for the wedding—place will be empty—except perimeter guards—safe for us to go inside—clean up—eat. Damn. My body is hypersensitive to sensual touches." Her eyes glazed over as she continued repeating the script words.

While R³ was lost in her recitation, Felix took charge. "Okay. She's worked out our next step. We'll go inside via that secret tunnel, get cleaned up, get something to eat, and make some more plans."

"But where will we go?" asked Rhianna.

Todd laughed. "I don't think any of us expected to get this far. Me, I'm just going to look after my Mary Jane here."

Trevor added, "Hey. Don't worry. R³ and Felix will figure something out. They always do." He shut up, thinking, *well she always did before she got implanted. Maybe she can't anymore. Shit!*

They waited until the sun was high in the sky before heading into the tunnel. Carefully, Felix pointed out the two keypad traps and made sure they all knew the number sequence to enter. When they opened the basement concealed door, he and R³ stood there silently, listening for sounds of the family. Utter silence.

R³ whispered, "I think they're gone. Come on, but be as quiet as we can." She led them up a stair and into the kitchen of this fabulous mansion. All stood gawking at the unbelievable sights. She showed them where the food was at, and the six rummaged through the refrigerator and cupboards, putting together something to eat.

While they ate at the small table, unwilling to make any mess in the spacious dining room, and while R³ and Todd helped Mary Jane eat, R³ explained the entire layout. "I've walked all over here, getting used to walking in these heels. Their security guards are always outside. They've their own bunkhouse. They took their four servants with them to the big wedding. They aren't planning to return until late tonight. She said we could have some of her dresses too, so now we need to clean up."

Felix replied, "R^3, we get it. You have to look your best. We'll scout around and keep watch while you three get cleaned up. Maybe we can snitch more food to take with us. What I wouldn't give for a computer or maybe even a smartphone. I'm lost, you know."

Trevor laughed. "Heck, you're always glued to that darn computer, Felix. Live it up a bit. We're free for the first time in our lives."

"Speak for yourself, Trevor!" Rhianna declared, quite annoyed. "We girls aren't. Not now. Probably not ever again." She fought against having to recite the damned words yet again. Trevor gave her a sympathetic look.

R^3 bit her lip and reached a decision. "Felix. Guys, I think this is important. Our minds are mostly wiped out from this damned EE women's implant. We're free, but for how long? I don't know. Can't think properly anymore, but we're supposed to please our husbands. Felix, I do love you. Before anything else bad happens, I would like to sleep with you once, if only to know what sex is like—what we're implanted to do. It might help us, guys."

That broke the ice between them. They were in love, but such feelings had to be totally suppressed all those years in Ward 4, where even holding hands was outlawed. Although unspoken, none of the six held out much hope they could remain free for very long. Here was perhaps their lone chance to show the depths of their love for each other. None of the six were fettered with societal taboos on sexual relations—such things did not even exist in Ward 4. None of the six needed any further encouragement.

Felix took his precious R^3, while Todd took his Mary Jane ignoring her protests about being helpless and not worthy of him, and Trevor took his Red Rose Rhianna. Knowing no better, the fellows led them into the living room and laid down on the soft carpet. A passionate kiss later led to passions long suppressed exploding, but for the

EE women, their first taste of real sex was more like a pleasure bomb somehow exploding.

Sometime later, R³ suddenly exclaimed, "Felix! My mind! It's finally clear! Oh god, it's clear! I can think again!"

"Mine too!" gushed Mary Jane, quite shocked that her dull headache and mental fog was gone.

"Me too," Rhianna added. "Somehow, Trevor, you did it. I can think normally again! I do so love you. It's the greatest feeling in the world to just be able to say that to you." He replied by giving her another passionate kiss.

R³ took control. "Okay. We best get cleaned up. Felix, I think there are laptops around here somewhere. I've seen several, unless they took them when they left. Fellows, see if you can pack us some food and maybe a blanket or two. I still have the ID card they made for me when they brought me here. They said I must have lost it in the bombing and made me a new one. So with it, I have access to all her credits. That should help for a while, until they catch on. Come on. We should be ready to leave in about an hour. We don't want to get caught."

The three young women bathed and then rummaged through the seeming mountain of new gowns R³ had acquired while being Rachel Roxanne and got themselves dressed appropriately. "Well, red isn't my color, but we don't have much choice," Mary Jane commented, while R³ zipped up the back of her gown.

R³ explained, "See, none of us can really zip ourselves up, so we too need help dressing, Mary Jane. Once more, she resumed hovering over her longtime roommate and best friend, hoping to make her a tad more comfortable with her unique situation. She sensed how terrible Mary Jane felt about her loss of arms and desperately wanted to lessen her burden somehow, someway.

When they joined the fellows, they found Todd and Trevor had made two large bundles of food and blankets for them. Felix had found a laptop and other computer equipment; he was more than content, having spent all this time tinkering.

He looked up, "Hi gorgeous. I'm making some discoveries. Do you know Mr. Raven has a complete ID card making machine in his office? From what I have discovered, that's illegal because the Feds and the Total Care people are the ones that are supposed to be making the ID cards. I think given enough time, I can make us some ID cards. Still working on how to get us bank accounts with credits in them so the cards would actually be useful. Can we spend the night in the tunnel? Maybe by tomorrow I can figure out how to do it. If so, then we can go anywhere we want."

R³ replied, "Good idea. Let's do that. If nothing else, we can use my Rachel Roxanne ID card for a while at least. Come on. I'm not sure when they'll be back. Make sure we leave everything as we found it. We don't want them to know we were in here. God, Felix. You can't imagine how wonderful it is to have my mind clear again, even though it's only temporary. We're going to need sex frequently if only to have periods where we can think properly. It satisfied the EE woman implant."

"I'll second that!" Mary Jane added, "even if I am helpless now. At least, I can think and that's something!"

The group darted about making sure all was acceptable and then headed into the basement. A few minutes later, they set up a "home" in the tunnel, near the basement's concealed door. Then, they settled down for the night, with Felix still tinkering with his "new" laptop.

"I found us a gun," Trevor explained. "Now I can really protect us, but I'm going to have to figure out how to use it. Maybe one of us should hide out in the basement and spy on the Ravens when they get back. You know, gather intelligence and all that."

R³ responded, "Say Trevor, that's a good idea. You can alert us if they suspect someone has been in their home today. Give us advance warning and all that. Oh, crap! The implant stuff is coming back again. I can feel it."

Mary Jane declared, "You're right. It's coming back again. Damn. Hey wait; we now know how to defuse it. Oh Todd honey, I need you again."

A half hour later, Mary Jane added, "Damn. That worked! My mind is clear again. Todd, you're going to have to do this with me lots!"

No one argued this point. Later, they decided to hold up here for a few days, while Felix tried to find out if the Feds or anyone was now after them. To the six, this seemed to be the most critical point. If they were not missed, then they could go anywhere. On the other hand— well, they didn't want to think about that just yet.

***

The morning after their escape from Ward 4, no one missed the six. However, later in the afternoon, one fellow came up to the central desk and asked about them. The glassy eyed caretaker looked at her daily printout. "Oh, they were transferred to Cook County last night. Sorry. That's all that's listed here." No one else paid any attention to their disappearance.

Chapter 5—Strikes

"Rachel Roxanne, dear, time to wake up. It's your wedding day," Regina called out, rousing the overly tired teen.

"God, mom. It's so wonderful being home!" she said, before realizing her gaff.

"What's that honey?"

"Oh, my mind is clearing up some."

"Oh goodness. That is so wonderful! You suffered a bad concussion or so dad said. Memory loss and all that. Have you forgotten it's your wedding day, dear?"

"No. I need a bath first. I must look my best. Shit," she cursed, reciting her litany once more.

Regina chuckled. "Dear, after your wedding night bed, you'll find things will change for the better. I always have. Come on. We have to make you look your very best today. Double wedding. Impressive. So we must, really look our very best today. So many men to please, you know."

Around noon, Randal put his arm around Rachel Roxanne's waist and proudly escorted his daughter in her new white satin gown into the mansion of Ace Waberly. Roy held on to his mother's waist, following behind them. Four servants brought up the rear. Ace and Marcy were there waiting for them. "Come on in. Everything is all set," Ace declared. "The Michaelson's are already here."

Within minutes, the whole group took their designated positions in the expansive living room, appropriately decorated for the occasion. Up front before the glassy-eyed pastor, Rachel Roxanne stood beside Scott Waberly. Mary Jane stood beside Steve. Three sets of parents stood behind the two young couples: Randal and Regina, Ace and Marcy, and Alan and Christa. Roy stood behind them, wondering when Randal was going to arrange his marriage. He felt a bit envious of the two younger men, for their EE women looked positively stunning. For a time, he mulled over whether or not he could seduce Mary Jane. Surely, she would now be desirous of pleasing any man. He'd seen his own mother do it often enough.

The signing of the official documents by the two couples took far longer than the wedding ceremony, a fact not lost on the two new brides, who continually begged to be kissed again. Once all the papers were signed, Ace, Randal, and Alan carefully packed them into mailers, and Ace sent them off with a courier. None of the three men were taking any chances. Once these documents were filed with the Cabal, the inheritance, the merger of these three families was sealed, though each man had their own subsequent plans for how this merger would play out.

The reception came next. Both young men played their ordered role perfectly. They held up a juice glass for their brides to drink their first toast as a married couple. Carefully, the men didn't sip the juice. Why? Their fathers had put a maximum dose of Pytalon in the juice. From now on, both Rachel Roxanne and Mary Jane would be heavily dosed on Pytalon, becoming glassy-eyed EE women, unable to think, but fully able to perform their roles as sex dolls, but little more.

Slowly the mind-altering drug took effect, but Rachel Roxanne quickly noticed what was happening to her. *Oh god! No! Not Pytalon! Oh no!* By then, she was helpless to say or do anything about it. Fear swept over her, but the drug kept all outward signs invisible. Later when Scott took her in her wedding bed, she felt the explosive result of her EE implant.

After Scott finally fell asleep, she realized her mind was finally clear of the implant torture, at least temporarily. Now she knew what her mother had meant. As long as she had sex frequently, her implant remained in the background. However, she was still terrified over what the Pytalon was doing to her ability to think, but she was unable to do anything about it. In the morning, she saw her body automatically taking another Pytalon pill; she felt as though she was some distant spectator of life, that this wasn't real or her, but it was. Taking Pytalon was now an automatic response. Try as she might, she couldn't stop herself from taking it each morning! *I don't want to be only a sex doll,* she screamed in her mind, while she heard her body saying, "Oh Scott, please let's do it again. I so need it." Thankfully, he responded to her plea.

***

General John Smith, as he often liked to call himself—that wasn't his real name and few knew it—looked over these latest secure emails. Yes, these would be particularly dangerous missions for his Marshals Militia and Security men. Cabal heads were known for their utterly ruthless actions. That he knew well. Without a doubt, these three independent missions would be most challenging and deadly. On the other hand, the pay—ten million credits—times three if he accepted each one—was simply too good to pass up. However, considering the targets, he accepted only upon full payment in advance.

While awaiting the payments, he sent for his top three platoons. They arrived two days later. The emails provided details of the three target locations, and the general doled one out to each of his platoon leaders. "Silencers mandatory. Everyone dies. Leave no trace of us behind. I must have photos of these dead men, before you handle the cleanup details. The assignment nets each of your platoons a cool million. Divide it up as you see fit, lieutenants."

"Simultaneous strikes, general?" one lieutenant asked.

"Aye. Midnight. That should give plenty of time for the cleanup work," General Smith answered. "Other questions?"

"Dangerous mission," another commented.

"Aye. That's why I picked your platoons. A Cabal strike is always dangerous. No looting though. My orders were specific on that detail. Make sure the cleanup is done properly. Oh, make sure their security systems are still operational when you depart. I know, strange orders, but the pay is far above average."

A lieutenant chuckled, "Aye, sir. That it is!"

***

At midnight, thirty extremely well-armed men dressed entirely in black and with night vision goggles, slipped over the outer walls of the Raven Compound. Alarms did go off, but that was expected. Muzzle flashes and soft popping sounds echoed from the silencer equipped, automatic rifles, dropping the few security guards patrolling the perimeter. As more staggered out of their bunkhouse responding to the security breech, one by one, they too were picked off.

The lieutenant signaled for one squad to search the bunkhouse, while another squad fanned out securing the perimeter of the large estate. He and the remaining squad entered the mansion proper, beginning with the servant's quarters. Four pops later, they moved out into the main portion, where a partially dressed Randal and Roy, guns in hand, were heading for the security center room, trying to figure out what was happening. Pop. Pop. Both men dropped. Two more pops guaranteed they were both dead, holes in their foreheads.

The lieutenant signaled one man, who stopped and photographed the two dead men, while the rest fanned out, searching the remaining rooms. Another lone pop signaled the discovery of Regina. One by one, "clear," messages came over the lieutenant's ear receiver. Satisfied the assault was complete, he gave the sign that meant, "Clean up detail." Men scurried about dragging the dead bodies outside, while others dug a hasty, but shallow pit. One by one, the deceased were dumped into the mass grave. Eventually, the dirt was pushed back over the top and mounded up.

Inside, the lieutenant went from location to location verifying the blood and bits were cleaned up. Around four in the morning, he was finally satisfied the cleanup work was done properly. Quietly, he and his platoon slipped

back over the outer wall, marched into their EMAC, and lifted silently off, heading for New O'Hare and their Air Liner, where they awaited the arrival of the other two platoons. As they waited, the lieutenant fired off the photos of the two dead men to General Smith, as ordered.
***

"What's that noise?" R³ whispered.

"Dunno. Sounded like a popping noise. I hear lots more of them," Felix whispered. Already, he had established a link between his stolen laptop and the security video feeds of the Raven Compound. Hastily, he made the connection. Five separate windows opened up. All six looked at his small monitor. There were men dressed in black and carrying strange looking rifles, whose barrels seemed overly long. In silence, the Circle of Six witnessed many of the slayings that wiped out the Raven family and security guards.

"Now what are they doing?" asked a fearful R³.

"Looks as if they're burying the dead bodies," Trevor whispered back.

"Are we safe here?" she asked what was really on her mind and most of the others for that matter.

"Sure. They probably don't know about this secret tunnel," Trevor declared. "Otherwise, it wouldn't be secret." At least he hoped so, but was very, very glad that he and Rhianna had at least shared their love.

When dawn came, the strange men left. The compound was eerily silent. However, the six slipped out of the tunnel, going back inside to check on things. To their amazement, the found no trace of the attack. They even found the spot where the two men had been slain. Small bullet chips marked where the slugs had chipped part of the tiling on the floor.

"Well, now what do we do?" asked Mary Jane.

"Looks like we have a place to stay—at least for a while," R³ declared. "Come on. If they're all dead, let's see what we can use around here." The six began a detailed search of the place. Trevor was elated when he discovered a

small room filled with guns, ammunition, and even bombs!
***

Rachel Roxanne was miserable, more miserable than she could imagine possible. True, her implant was now staying pretty much in the background, since Scott was doing her in the morning and at night. No, it was the damnable Pytalon that was ruining her life. Her body craved it. Try as she might, she couldn't keep her fingers from opening the bottle and from swallowing the pill each morning. She acted as if she were in some kind of daze, going through motions, while she sat back out of the way and unable to make her body do anything else. She couldn't even communicate what she felt, for only silly words came out, such as "Oh dearest, kiss me. I need it." That she'd said this to Mr. Waberly himself shocked her. It was as though she no longer had any control over her own body.

Desperate for sexual attention, she'd wandered towards the two men, who were in Alan's private study. Vaguely, she noted he too had a secret wall safe. The two men were looking over a small book. Did he have a journal as her father had? Someone was speaking. The words filtered into her ears, but her body took no note of them, while the helpless Rachel Roxanne did.

"Well, Scott. It's going to go down tonight. General Smith's men will strike the Ravens. By tomorrow, son, you'll be in control of the Raven fortune and eventually inherit mine too, merging these two fortunes into one. You won't have any trouble with Rachel, since she's a mindless sex doll now."

"Hey dad, a sexy sex doll at that. Excellent. But what about the Michaelson's?" Scott asked.

"The general will be taking care of them too. Once done, we'll get our Mary Jane back. She'll inherit the Michaelson's fortune as well, but she's a sex doll now too, so we won't have any trouble signing her fortune over to you. After all, you are her big brother, but you might have to sleep with her too. Sex dolls do need some upkeep." Both men laughed wickedly.

"A word of advice son, do her three times a day for a while. That will keep Rachel nicely contented. A few months from now, you can ease off and just do it twice a day. That's how it went with Marcy and me. Keep her content for a few months, then the cravings subside somewhat," Ace explained.

Inwardly, Rachel was horrified several times over. Her mind struggled with the confusing ideas she'd just heard. They were going to kill her parents? They were going to kill the Michaelson's? She was a sex doll? The last idea hit her hard and sent her mind reeling, and she ambled on down the hall reciting her implanted words, proving beyond any doubt that she was a sex doll and that was her only purpose, to give pleasure and to get it. She just knew she had to have it three times a day. The implant said so.

"Dear Rachel, stop fingering yourself. It's not lady-like. If you have to do it, go into the bathroom," Marcy chided her. She had met Rachel in the hallway, saw her trying to get relief, and had admonished her. "Goodness. Didn't they teach you anything at the implant center?"

Rachel Roxanne flushed and hurried to the bathroom. She had no choice.

That evening after Scott finished up with her and fell asleep, Rachel Roxanne had a moment of lucidness. Now the idea they were going to murder her parents came into her mind again, followed by the idea they were going to kill the Michaelson's too. In her Pytalon daze, she tried to think what she could do about it. She had no idea that three hours had passed while she was just trying to think about what she could do about it.

She heard popping sounds. Then some loud alarms went off. Scott lunged out of bed. "Hell, what's going on?" he yelled. More popping sounds echoed around the halls. For a moment, Rachel Roxanne thought perhaps someone was playing with firecrackers. Vaguely, she thought she'd once seen them when she was a little girl, but accessing memories was terribly difficult to do. Were they even real memories? Her mind spun. "Hide!" Scott barked to her and left the room.

Hide? Hide? The word bounced around her mind. Surely, that word meant something, didn't it? It wasn't sexy. Hide. Hide. What does that mean? Somehow, she forced herself to get out of bed, standing on the floor. Hide? She heard more popping sounds. Maybe he meant a hide-a-bed. They had one of those at her house. She'd slept on it once. Or maybe that wasn't real. She couldn't remember right. She bent down to look under the large bed. She spotted a magazine of some kind. In the dim light, she saw a naked woman. That alone drew her towards it. To reach it, she had to crawl under the bed. Scooting under it, her hands reached it at last. Oh, so sexy, she thought. Naked women. Oh, they don't have big boobs, do they? She didn't notice the pages were well worn. More popping sounds came and cries of pain. Rachel Roxanne didn't like those sounds, so she focused instead on the naked women, particularly on the two-page foldout. So pretty, she thought.

"Clear." She heard someone calling out. Then, more men said that word.

Why do they have to say it so many times, she wondered, but continued staring at Scott's dirty magazine.

"Drag Scott over beside Alan. Photograph them both. We need to upload proof of their deaths."

Deaths? Scott dead? Oh no. Who will pleasure me? I need it three times a day. I need it now, she thought. *Oh, I can do it here. Marcy said not to do it in public. No one can see me here.* Her finger began its work, while the black-clad men launched into their extensive cleanup work. Later, she fell asleep, somewhat contented, oblivious to the fact she was underneath Scott's bed.

***

At the Michaelson Compound, the lieutenant cursed. "Damn that woman!" Mary Jane had accidentally gotten in the way when one of his men was shooting Steve in the head. She'd taken the shot to her head. "Our orders were specific. Leave this EE woman alive and take her over to the Waberly Compound. Shit."

"So what the hell do we do now?" asked the shooter. "She's still breathing, but probably won't make it."

"Crap! Hell's to pay on this one. Okay, we follow orders. We'll take her over to the Waberly Compound, but we'll notify the rescue squad on this one," the lieutenant decided, firing off an email outlining the error made and what they were going to do about it. He received confirmation of his decision from the general.

***

Men. Rachel heard men's voices. *Coming into this very room. After me? No.* Thump. Something landed on her bed. *A moan? Voices. Leaving again? Quiet. No, a moan. Is Scott on the bed? Maybe. Maybe I can make love to him.* Slowly, she crawled out from beneath the bed and looked. Her body gasped, but she shrieked in spite of her Pytalon haze. It was Mary Jane. She had been shot in the head, but she was still alive.

Rachel Roxanne knew she needed help. Quickly, she called out for Scott and then anyone. She saw her body running barefoot around the home. Empty. Returning to her bedroom, she sat down beside Mary Jane; her eyes, foggy from the Pytalon, but her mind racing. Help. She desperately needed help, but who? Like a bolt, the memory of those five from the OD ward appeared in her mind. *Yes, they can help. They are OD people. They must know what to do. How to reach them?*

She recalled having given Felix a cell phone. She could see the number in her mind, but was unable to make her body respond. Still, she got up, found her own phone, and stared at it, her body wondering why. Only with great willpower was she finally able to dial the number.

"Rachel Roxanne. Help. Help. They are all dead. Mary Jane. Shot in head. Alive. Help me." *Is that my voice,* she wondered?

"Where are you?" Felix responded, though the other five were listening in, wondering who was calling him.

"Here. Oh. Waberly's. Help me."

"We don't know where that is. How do we find you?" he answered rapidly.

Rachel Roxanne forced herself to say, "Dad's EMAC. Menu. Waberly. Help. Hurry. All dead."

"Okay. We'll try," Felix answered. Turning to the others, he added, "We should try to help her."

R³ agreed. "Yes we must. I think I can figure out what she was trying to tell us. Come on. I know where they keep their EMAC. Her mother showed me."

The six headed into the basement, up the stairs, and out into the courtyard. Though it was quite dark and chilly, the EMAC was there. Once everyone was inside and with Felix and R³ in the control seats, he pressed the Menu button. "Cool. We don't have to swipe your ID card on this one."

"Okay, press Destinations," R³ suggested. "Ah, press Waberly. Now Go." Felix did and the autopilot took over, gently lifting them off, though the EM engines were almost completely silent. In fifteen minutes, the EMAC landed in the courtyard of another rural estate. Again, eerie silence greeted them. Following Rachel Roxanne's hints, they headed inside and called out for her.

"In here!" Rachel Roxanne answered back. "I need help."

"My god! She looks exactly like me!" Mary Jane exclaimed, when she entered the bedroom and saw herself lying on the bed, a bullet hole in her head.

Todd felt for a pulse. "She is still alive. Now what?"

"Someone else is coming!" Rhianna alerted them. She was still just outside the bedroom and spotted some men wearing uniforms and carrying some bags coming their way.

"Excuse us. Got a call that someone was shot in this residence?" one of the men called out.

"Yes, in here. We just got here. Our dear friend Rachel Roxanne called us and we came to help," Todd explained, looking over his shoulder at the emergency technicians. He recognized their uniforms from his extensive studies of medical technology. Todd was a would-be doctor, if he ever had a choice. "She has been shot, but is still alive."

"Okay kids. You back out of the room. Let us do our job. The AP-cops are also on their way," the man ordered. They did so.

Both men looked Mary Jane over and attached a diagnostic machine to her arm. Then, he shook his head sadly. "I'm afraid she's dying, miss. The best that we can do is to stabilize her. Does anyone know if she has an organ donor or is to be an organ donor?"

Poor Rachel Roxanne. The effects of the drug were lessening and finally the magnitude of what she was seeing hit her hard. She broke down and started crying.

R3 thought quickly. She glanced at Mary Jane and at the host version. "Sir, I believe she is. I believe she would want MJ Kingmann here to have her arms, if that is possible and compatible—I think that's the right word for it."

"Excellent. Let me check your ID card," he replied. She had it on a chain around her neck, just as Rachel Roxanne had. He swiped it. "Ah yes, Case A. Good. Now then, let us take sample DNA from each for testing." He took a swab out of his case and had Mary Jane open her mouth, swirling it around inside. At the same time, the other technician swabbed the wounded Mary Jane.

"We're from Cook County. That's where we'll be taking her. As you know, in cases like this, time is the worst enemy. If possible, we'd like MJ here to come along with us. If this donor is compatible with MJ, then she will be prepped for surgery at once."

"Sir, I'll come along with her. She's my wife," Todd interjected.

"Perfect sir. Okay, let's get going. Time is precious in these cases."

"Here, take my cell," R3 whispered to Todd, knowing they would have a way to reach him. Mary Jane and Todd followed the two men, as they carried the dying body out to their medical EMAC. Just as they lifted off, another arrived, bringing the AP-cops.

Two glassy-eyed men stepped out. "What happened here?" one asked.

R³ decided to speak for Rachel Roxanne. "Sir, I'm her cousin. She called us, but as you can see, she is terribly broken up by all this. Let me tell you what she told us." That satisfied the man, so she explained about the entire family having been murdered.

When she finished, he asked the sobbing Rachel Roxanne if that was correct. All she could do was nod repeatedly. After that, one of the men began searching the home and then the grounds. Later, he whispered, "Found a fresh mass grave just outside. Best call in the Feds on this one."

"Sir," R³ spoke up. "Rachel Roxanne here is so shaken up by this, would it be all right if we took her back to her home? She was only recently married to Scott who just got murdered in her bedroom."

"Yes, we've swiped her ID card, so we have her data. That would be best. Probably the Feds will want to question her tomorrow," the man replied in his monotone, unfeeling voice. R³ wondered how the man could ever be effective at his job.

A half hour later, the five were back at the Raven Compound. Rachel Roxanne also knew her family had been slain, but that was mostly unreal to her. The murder of Scott was now rather vivid in her mind. R³ wisely ordered to her take a bath and to go to bed, which Rachel Roxanne was very willing to do. However, she did take another Pytalon pill before crawling into her old bed.

The four gathered in the kitchen, too wound up to sleep. Besides, it was almost dawn. They fixed a snack and some tea. "Damned fast thinking, R³! With Mary Jane, I mean," Felix praised her.

She smiled. "I hope it works out. At least, it's at Cook County and not our medical center. Maybe no one will be the wiser. Clever of Todd to go along with her pretending to be her husband."

"Hey, you and I are married too—so is Trevor and Rhianna," Felix hinted. "Wish we had real ID cards though. Rachel—she's really drugged up on Pytalon now, isn't she?"

"Right. She could hardly function at all," R³ pointed out. "From now on, gang, we should 'speak' for her as much as we can get away with. She'll just nod yes and no, more than likely."

Felix's new cell vibrated. It was Todd. The call was short. "It was a match. Mary Jane is in surgery right now! Brilliant thinking, R³!"

The others cheered her and she broke into a big smile. "We stick together," R³ declared.

"Tomorrow, I have to see if we can somehow get proper ID cards. Todd is on his own at the hospital. Without a card, he's stuck," Felix pointed out.

R³ suddenly gasped. "Gang! Wait a minute. I just thought of something. If all the people in the Raven, Waberly, and Michaelson families have been murdered, what's going to happen to all their ODs in Ward 4?"

Felix answered her. "They'll likely be gotten rid of, since their hosts are dead. I'm looking into that right now!"

"We can't just let them cut them to pieces," Trevor exclaimed. By that, the others knew he meant having their organs removed and donated to a whole lot of other different people.

"That's inhuman," Rhianna added.

"But Red, you are forgetting one detail," R³ countered, a serious frown on her face. "They're ODs. Not everyone on our floor is like us. For some of them, like a bunch of the boys, that's all they're living for—to donate parts. Just look at Able for example. Damn, I'm getting a headache again. I think the big rush has ended. Oh Felix dearest?" she teased him, causing him to look up from his monitor and smile.

Rhianna added her "me too" to the mix, and Trevor gave her a kiss. All four had to take a lengthy timeout from all else, a very pleasant one that is.

Around seven, the two young women scrounged around the kitchen to find something for everyone to eat, while Felix and Trevor helped get Rachel Roxanne roused and collected together. They found her in quite a mess. She felt the loss of her own family rather hard, but had little feelings at all for the loss of Scott, except she craved sex from him, which she finally realized was never going to happen again. Combined with this was her steadily growing migraine dictating behavior and the fogginess of her mind from Pytalon, it was a miracle Rachel Roxanne could even function.

Neither boy wanted to satisfy her pleading needs, since they didn't love her, but Felix took the suggestion of Trevor and helped him put the dong latex panties on her. As Trevor suggested, if it helped Mary Jane, it probably would her. "Come on. R³ and Rhianna have something for us to eat," Felix then said, pushing her up to her feet.

As she walked out of her room and to the kitchen, she began moaning slightly, which Trevor took as a good sign. By the time they got her to the kitchen, Rachel Roxanne had finally gotten some relief and became more coherent, particularly after Trevor insisted she eat something. "They're dead—all of them," she said morosely.

"We know, but we need to make some more ID cards soon. The Feds are likely to come by soon to find out what happened," Felix pointed out.

"What's the use? They're all dead. Now I can't ever get satisfied anymore. I do so need it," Rachel Roxanne wailed, but immediately began reciting her litany, frustrating the four. Trevor had her get up and show him around her home. She did so, sensing an opportunity to flirt some with a boy, but the walking once more triggered her into a realm of pleasure, bringing her more into the present again.

Good timing. Just then, six Feds arrived, including a Captain Lech. First, he read back the story given to the AP-cops last night, asking for verification from her. She nodded repeatedly as he spoke, and Captain Lech realized he was unlikely to get anything more significant from her. She was newly implanted and heavily dosed on Pytalon, but her grief was overlying all that.

Her four companions were in drastically better shape, he observed. Since two were also EE women, he focused his attention onto Felix and Trevor, rightly figuring he could get "straight dope" from them.

"Yes, somehow they didn't find us. We heard popping sounds. When we investigated, it was all over. They wore black clothing and masks," Felix said.

"I think the popping sounds meant they had silencers on their guns. We believe they buried everyone outside. There's a new mound out there. Then, we got a frantic call from Mrs. Rachel Roxanne Waberly here, begging us for help," Trevor continued. "So we hopped in the EMAC and headed over to the Waberly's. She's only recently gotten married to Scott Waberly, you see. That family was murdered too, and we found her with Mrs. Mary Jane Michaelson, who had been shot in the head. What's strange is that Mrs. Michaelson was living in the Michaelson estate; she's also recently married. The murderers brought Mrs. Michaelson over to the Waberly's home, dumping her onto Mrs. Waberly's bed. Isn't that the strangest thing? The emergency fellows arrived and then the AP-cops. So why did the killers bring Mrs. Michaelson's body over to the Waberly's home?"

Captain Lech pulled his chin before answering. "Son, if we knew that, we'd probably know a whole lot more about this hideous crime. I can tell you the entire Michaelson family was murdered as well, so we have three crime scenes here—three mass murderers. This is the weirdest one I've ever seen. I don't suppose either of you know if she or her family or her husband had any enemies?" Lech fished for any remote clue. This crime was beyond baffling.

"Sorry sir. We don't. I think the families were all friends, particularly so with the two recent marriages,"

Felix answered. "Rachel Roxanne is taking this rather hard. I'm sure glad that we can be here for her."

"Indeed so, son, indeed so. Okay then. The crime lab boys will be here shortly and go over everything to see if there are any clues. They're already at the Waberly Compound. Excuse me, I have to take this call," Lech said, backing away out of hearing range. A moment later, a very relieved Captain Lech said, "Thank you ma'am!"

***

Chan-Petra was awakened by an incoming call. What startled her was the caller id indicated it was coming from the special phone number given to her, or rather the late Peter, by the mysterious James Buffett! Chan-Petra was instantly alert. "Hello. Chan-Petra here."

She wasn't surprise to hear his soft voice. "You should personally take charge of the latest case that has fallen into the lap of the Chicago Feds. Happened last night. Three mass murders of three very important families. Billionaires." Click. The line went dead.

A couple of hours later, from her office on the top floor of the Feds building, Supreme Commander Chan-Petra finished reading the initial reports submitted by the AP-cops, along with their referral of the case to the Feds. Captain Lech was already on it so she gave him a call. After telling him she would oversee this case and hearing his huge relief, she asked, "So is there anything new yet?"

"No boss. The kids' stories are matching what was reported. Three mass murders. Occurring about the same time late last night. Scenes have been wiped clean. Bodies all buried in three mass graves, one on each site. I have the CSIs on it now. Big mess. No clues. One survivor, a recently married EE woman, Mrs. Rachel Roxanne Waberly, Raven is her maiden name. Her friends brought her back to her family home last night. She's on Pytalon too. Can't get much useful information out of her."

"What about those friends of hers?" Chan-Petra asked. "I don't see their ID cards on file yet." For these first few weeks as a new mother, she appreciated being able to do some of her work at home, using her new computer system there.

"Claims they didn't think to bring them with them when they responded to Mrs. Waberly's call for help."

"Okay for now. Understandable. I'll join you on site after checking up on the pair that was taken to Cook County General," Chan-Petra replied and hung up.

Some twenty minutes later, she walked into the recovery room where the organ recipient, a MJ Kingmann, was located. He found her husband, a Todd Kingmann, sitting beside her bed. The woman was still unconscious. Her shoulders were heavily bandaged, but her arms looked otherwise okay. Todd looked up, bags under his eyes.

"Supreme Commander Chan-Petra Delius. I've taken over this mass murder case. Lucky woman. How's she doing? Transplant went well?" she began politely.

"Yes, the doctors said it went perfect. She will have to remain here for a week and then spend two more weeks at home in recovery, ma'am," Todd replied.

"Good son, very good. Amazing what modern medicine is capable of. Now then, about last night. The reports said that you got a call from a Mrs. Waberly?"

"Yes sir. She was almost incoherent. Frantic. Desperate. Out of her mind, begging us for help."

"So you six are close friends with Mrs. Waberly?" Chan-Petra asked.

"Yes sir. We rushed over there immediately. Good thing that we did. It was awful. I mean Mrs. Michaelson. There she was, lying on Rachel's bed, ghastly hole in her head and all. She shouldn't have been there. Rachel Roxanne was in bed with her new husband, Scott Waberly sir. I think Mrs. Michaelson was supposed to be with her new husband, Steve Michaelson, I think that's the name. Never met him. Why would Mrs. Michealson be there in Mrs. Waberly's bed?"

"Son, we don't know. Now then, did any of the victims that you know have any enemies? Anyone against these recent marriages? Other boyfriends in the picture?"

"No sir. None that we know about. Rachel Roxanne was happy to be married—EE implant and all. You know how that goes," he added, since Chan-Petra was obviously an EE woman herself.

"Indeed. Okay. We'll need your ID cards when you get a chance to get them."

"I don't want to leave her just yet."

"That's fine. Understandable. If you think of anything else, here's my card. I'll get back to you both later on."

Chan-Petra rose and left, thinking hard, ignoring the clicking sounds of her heels on the hard, polished floor of the hospital hallway as she headed out. None of this made the slightest sense. Obviously, the murderers had taken the time and trouble to move the nearly dead woman from one home to the other, some twenty miles away. Why? They'd murdered everyone else. Why didn't they finish the woman off? Why move her, since she wasn't going to survive anyway? Chan-Petra had more questions than answers. She had a strong hunch they wouldn't learn anything useful until the CSIs finished their work on the three crime scenes.

As she rode her EMAC over to the Raven Compound, she tried to look up Randal Raven in the Chicago database. Nothing. He didn't exist there. Strange. She tried Ace Waberly. Nothing. At last, she entered the ID code the AP-cops had swiped from Mrs. Waberly. Restricted Access flashed on her screen. Weird, she thought, and entered the second code, the one from the deceased Mrs. Michaelson. Restricted Access flashed. Now this was interesting, she thought, but put that on hold, since the EMAC was landing.

A swarm of glassy-eyed CSIs was swarming over the mass grave. Several bodies had already been uncovered and were lying in a grizzly line. All had gunshot wounds to their heads. One CSI was logging ID cards and Chan-Petra looked over the man's shoulder. Several men were identified: security guards. One woman was a maid and another, a cook. Curiously, another read only Restricted Access.

Chan-Petra went on inside and got an update from Captain Lech, who was very grateful for her stepping in on this one. She also met with the five but saw they would get very little useful information from Mrs. Rachel Roxanne Waberly. She also saw some of the technicians were cataloging the cleaned up blood trails, via their special lighting equipment. She could see where several of the Ravens had been executed, their bodies later moved. Someone had gone to a great deal of cleanup work, but why? The mass grave was obvious.

"We'll need your ID cards when you get a chance to fetch them," Chan-Petra advised the four. "Meantime, it is best if you stay here with Mrs. Waberly. Right now, she really does need your help." She then left to visit the other two sites. Hours later, she returned to her office, completely mystified by these three mass murders.

Her first action upon returning was to fire off requests to the Feds office personnel to get her access to these Restricted files. At this point, she turned her attention onto other matters, because until the CSIs finished and her technicians got her access to the files, there really wasn't any line of inquiry to follow. All three families were mystery families. She couldn't even provide next of kin notifications!

Some initial results were in by the next day. Many of the bodies had been identified. Most were security guards, but there were also housekeepers and cooks among them. Dutifully, their next of kin were notified, but as expected, those were implanted Pytalon zombies who didn't realize they had these relatives or husbands or wives. No help there.

However, what alarmed Chan-Petra the most was that the ten main family members all were unidentified— their files marked Restricted Access. Further, her technicians had yet to gain access to them or their identities, though from Mrs. Waberly and her friends, they knew their names, for the little good that did. The names didn't show up in any database.

Reluctantly, that evening she decided she needed the services of the Weasel or Shifty Eyes. However, even that had to be put off. Amazingly, compatible donors had been found, and all four were now being prepped for arm transplant surgery. Well, that was the best news Chan-Petra had in a very long time, except for her having a baby. She forgot about this case and headed to the Medical Center to wait on her dear friends, but she also brought along five Trikuza members to guarantee their security.

Many anxious hours passed, before one by one, Beth, Tilly, Amanda, and Jessica were brought into the recovery room. While their shoulders were heavily bandaged, each had new arms plainly visible, and Chan-Petra was elated. Patiently, she waited until each one roused from their anesthesia and shared their joy at discovering the operation was successful.

"Beth, after you recover, I have a really serious sleuthing task for you. We've had three mass murders, but we can't even get access to their files," she explained.

"Just enter their ID card numbers," a fuzzy headed Beth whispered.

"Done that. Restricted Access comes back. My technicians can't get into those files."

"Crap. Bad timing. Here I lay when there's a mystery to be solved," Beth lamented.

"Well, you rest up and get healed. I'm more than pleased with the results. You four are whole once more. That alone is a huge miracle," Chan-Petra declared. "I'll be leaving two Trikuza guards with you at all times. I'll drop by each day."

Beth grinned and closed her eyes. The painkillers were working well. She dozed.

Chapter 6—Are Clones People?

The CSIs hauled out Randal Raven's computer system. They'd finished their examination and photographing of the home, as well as removing the bodies. At least, they'd covered the grave site back up, leaving the planting of new grass seed until spring came.

Finally left alone, none of the five knew how to cook. The Ravens always depended upon their cook for such mundane things. They were running out of "snack" food, and they were still wearing the same clothes. Rachel Roxanne at least had become a bit more stable. In addition, the hospital sent MJ and Todd home, that is, to the Raven Compound.

As usual, R³ took charge. "Look, we need food and clothes and some computer stuff for Felix. How do we get them? We're going to need to use Rachel's ID card."

"Oh, I have lots of credits. We should go to the EE women's store," she spoke up. "I must look my best. I can't, not wearing the same dresses. Come on. Let's go shopping."

"What about food?" R³ asked.

"Oh, that's Selma's job. Oh!" she just remembered Selma had been killed too.

"So how do we hire a cook?" R³ inquired.

Poor Rachel Roxanne looked perplexed, trying hard to "think" about this detail.

Trevor spoke up hastily, not wanting her to have a relapse. "Maybe you can ask at the EE women's store. They might know."

Rachel Roxanne brightened up; her face returning to normal.

R³ was very pleased to see Rachel Roxanne had the store entered into the EMAC database, though she figured her mother, Regina, had probably entered it. A half hour later, the women were browsing. Fortunately, they did carry a very limited selection of men's apparel, fine suits. Trevor and Felix had to make three trips carrying out all their many packages to the EMAC. None of the clerks noticed the nearly identical looking women. R³ took the opportunity to inquire about a cook, since Rachel Roxanne wasn't coherent enough to deal with this. One of the shop's EE women said that she would see if she could locate a cook for them.

Finally, nearly dragging the three women out of the store, R³ got directions for a food mart. The group again bought sacks of "snackable" foods. Satisfied, they headed home to the Raven Compound. At least, Felix had found a new laptop. Surprisingly, the EE women's store sold them as well.

While the young women took charge sorting out their new clothes and arranging themselves into three guest rooms, Felix began digging into the Medical Center's records. All along, he feared many of the ODs would be removed from the wards, sent off to have their body parts donated to any number of recipients. Until now, he had no way of really being certain. With his new laptop, he quickly gained access to the records the way he would when they lived in Ward 4. This time, he widened his search to include all the ODs in the facility. There were close to a hundred of them, which is why before he'd always chosen to look only at Ward 4.

"My god. There's a little me in there!" he exclaimed.

"What's that?" Todd looked up from he was doing, experimenting with the microwave machine, trying to make something for Mary Jane.

"On Ward 5, they had an eight-year-old me, but he's gone now. There is still a little Rachel Roxanne, Mary Jane, and Rhianna there too. And even a little Todd and Trevor too. Wow. They have eight-year-old versions of us. This is really strange. There's an eight-year-old Able too."

"What's going on here?" Todd asked. "Why have an eight-year-old me?"

"Dunno yet. Going to see who is in the other wards now," Felix answered, growing more curious.

A bit later, he sat back alarmed at what he discovered. Among the many adults, there were twenty-one-year old versions of the adults who had been murdered! So far, none of them had any orders to be taken away for organ donation operations. Felix breathed a sigh of relief.

Just then, Trevor joined him. "Okay hot shot. I have a job for you."

"Huh?" Felix replied, annoyed at the distraction.

"I found a safe in Mr. Raven's private study. I can't open it. I need your hacking skills, sir," he teased him.

Standing before the wall safe that Trevor found, Felix replied, "Now this is a challenge!"

"Can you open it? Rachel Roxanne doesn't know the combination. I asked her," Trevor said. "She did say she thought it contained really important stuff."

"Just give me some time with it," Felix answered. Trevor left him to work his magic and continued his thorough explorations of the entire complex, arming himself with one of the many guns that he uncovered in the armory room—his word for the room with all the guns, ammunition, and bombs. He wanted to protect everyone should the black-clad assassins return.

Felix was observant. Four of the number keys on the keypad were quite worn. Obviously, these were used to open it. Lacking any other data, he began trying sequences of these numbers. An hour later, he hit upon the right combination. The door opened.

Inside, he found a worn journal and a stack of papers. Trevor was disappointed, for he expected to find all sorts of valuable things. Felix, the job done, took the stuff to Rhianna, Mary Jane, and Todd, since Rhianna was their historian, and returned to his computer hacking of the Medical Center.
***

"Glad to see you four all home at last," Chan-Petra

said, grinning ear to ear. The four had finally been allowed to leave the hospital. However, they were under orders for two weeks of bed rest. As usual, Juan took care of them, always their protector, a job given to him by the professor. However, now two Trikuza men watched over them just outside their penthouse suite.

"Look. They work fine, but our shoulders are still real sore and stiff," Beth explained, wiggling her hands a little.

Tilly added, "It is a miracle, that's for sure! I feel like a human again."

Chan-Petra smiled. "I'm very glad and thankful you are whole." She clapped her hands together and stated businesslike, "Now then, we've still not been able to get into those files—the ones of the murdered families. Any chance you could use your feet to lend me a hand with them? There are almost no leads on this one. Technicians are trying to unravel some encrypted emails, soon I hope."

"I'll bring her laptop," Juan said, knowing there would be no stopping the Weasel. He placed it by Beth's feet and opened it up for her. "Remember, you aren't supposed to be using your hands yet." Beth glared at him and then broke into a smile.

It took her two hours to crack the Total Care security around these files. "My god, Chan-Petra—that's some of the best security I've ever seen! Anyway, I'm into this first one, Randal Raven. Relaying the contents to your system now."

"Weasel strikes again," Chan-Petra teased him. All five chuckled.

When she left the four that evening, all the nine files had been relayed to her computer in her Feds office. Although it was late, she headed to her office, entirely too curious to let it go until the morning. Knowing it was going to be a long night, she ordered in a pizza.

She opened the three older men's files, tiling them on her large monitor. All three were Cabal members, though of lower rank. Each man had a normalized net worth in the tens of billions of credits. Each man listed their now deceased sons as their immediate heirs. What also caught her attention was some additional, confusing listings. One page held this:

Randal B 21	Ramani Chicago Medical Institute
Regina B 21	Ramani Chicago Medical Institute
Roy A 20	Ramani Chicago Medical Institute
Roy B 9	Ramani Chicago Medical Institute
Rachel Roxanne A 18	Ramani Chicago Medical Institute
Rachel Roxanne B 8	Ramani Chicago Medical Institute

In other files, she found similar pages for the other two families, Waberly and Michaelson. None of this made any sense at all. Further, all had an entry that read:

Total Care Case A.

Chan-Petra made printouts of these, forwarding a copy to Tilly. The other she took with her. Tomorrow, she decided, she'd pay another visit to the sole survivor and see if this made any sense to her. Besides, she was annoyed that, as yet, those six friends of hers had not sent in their ID numbers. If nothing else, she intended to accompany them to their homes and get those numbers. Chan-Petra hated loose ends.

***

That same evening, James Buffett received an emergency, secure call from Henry Koch, who ran Total Care International. "James, we have been hacked, breeched! Someone has gotten access to the secure files for Raven, Waberly, and Michaelson. It's confirmed that those men have died. Now the Feds are on the case and that spells trouble."

"Thanks for the warning. I told you eventually the Feds would get at those records. Won't do them any good, mind you. I suggest you increase your security twofold. We've quite a mess on our hands this time, but I'll see what I can do to put an end to this. Good evening, Henry."

He hung up, knowing that he'd put off this visit as long as he dared. It was most troubling. Nothing like this had happened in over a century. Three Cabal members dead and only one legitimate heir, a worthless EE wife. For the tenth time, James reviewed the old documents and then the recently arrived ones that showed the two marriages. No question, Rachel Roxanne Raven Waberly was heir to both the Raven and Waberly fortunes, but no woman, let alone an EE woman was ever allowed to be a Cabal member! (The last wealthy woman had been "eliminated" centuries ago.) Worse, the Waberly's Mary Jane had married Steve Michaelson, making her the heir to the Michaelson fortune as well as the Waberly fortune. He rubbed his temples. There wasn't any way out of it. This meant the Michaelson's fortune legally fell to Rachel Roxanne as the sole survivor of the Waberly and Michaelson families. The three fortunes had to be merged into one, now controlled by this worthless EE woman!

"Well, that won't last long," he muttered. "Just as soon as this news becomes public knowledge at the full Cabal meeting on January 1, half of the Cabal families will send a man to try to marry this Rachel woman. One of them will do the deed and take over the fortune. At least, the Cabal numbers, ninety-nine, are reduced by another three members. That is something positive. There are still far too many Cabal members for my liking." He stuffed the formal papers into his briefcase, locked it, and then turned in for the night, fearfully dreading the morning's trip. He hated to go out into the world. The only safe place really was his own secure compound here in France.

Around ten the next morning, his EMAC landed at the Raven Compound. After making sure his appearance was immaculate, he stepped off, heading for the main doors. Trevor answered his knock, but James saw he wore a gun strapped to his side. James' nervousness increased ten-fold. Why wasn't this young man on Pytalon, he wondered. The only good men were those on Pytalon and implanted as well. "I must see Mrs. Rachel Roxanne Raven Waberly."

Trevor saw a nervous older man, certainly not threatening, holding a briefcase. "This way," he said, leading him into the living room where everyone was currently sitting. As he entered the room, he saw four EE women, but was quite surprised to see two EE women who were nearly identical! Trevor pointed, "That's Mrs. Waberly. Sorry, I didn't get your name."

"Ah, Mrs. Rachel Roxanne Raven Waberly? Correct?" James said politely.

"Yes. Who are you? You're quite handsome," she replied, noticing how nicely he was dressed and wondering if she should flirt with him. He was so much older than she was, but then perhaps she should. Her implant suggested so. She batted her eyes at him and smiled.

"I'm James Buffett." He had a French accent, R[3] noticed, but Rachel Roxanne missed that detail entirely.

"I've come to settle your inheritance, Mrs. Waberly. You're officially a Raven, so you inherit Randal's estate. Married to Scott Waberly and with the untimely deaths of that family, you inherit the Waberly's estate as well. Further, since their daughter, Mary Jane married Steve Michaelson and since the Michaelson family is also deceased, their estate also falls into that of the Waberly's by virtue of Mary Jane's marriage. That estate now belongs to you. Therefore, Mrs. Waberly, you have inherited all three family's estates. The net worth as of yesterday amounts to thirty-three billion normalized credits. Here are the formal documents so stating." He handed her a stack of papers from his briefcase, emptying it.

Poor Rachel Roxanne took them but looked completely ignorant of what he'd just told her. She knew this was somehow important, but in her Pytalon haze, she could only smile demurely at him.

"I would suggest you remarry one of the suitors who will be coming by for a visit early next year," he added sternly. "You should marry a man truly worthy of you."

He couldn't think of any way to tell her to marry another Cabal member, not with these six strangers present, none of whom was on Pytalon. That alone bothered him enormously! Worse, he couldn't shake the eerie feeling that something wasn't right here. This other EE woman looked almost identical to Rachel. How could that be? He certainly didn't know and was very eager to get away from these most threatening people. Let the younger Cabal men make their plays for this young EE woman heiress and sort out this mess.

Hastily, he rose and bowed, leaving as quickly as he dared. Only once onboard his EMAC did he finally relax and wipe the beads of sweat on his forehead. The world still wasn't right, not after all these centuries, but there was hope, he thought. Another half-century and all would be right, for all people would be implanted and on Pytalon, except those in the Cabal. That was the long-range Cabal plan anyway.

"He didn't smile at me. I don't think he found me attractive. I wonder what I'm doing wrong." Rachel Roxanne whimpered, silently repeating her implant script and wondering if her appearance was somehow flawed this morning.

No sooner had Trevor returned from seeing him out than he brought another person to see them. They recognized Chan-Petra. She wore a bright red gown with matching six-inch pumps. She looked every bit the stunning EE woman that her body was. "Hello everyone. I'm Chan-Petra, head of the Feds. I see everyone is here and looking well. Good. I've some more questions to ask. I'm afraid the investigation is going much too slowly for me. May I sit?"

R^3 indicated a seat across from them, and Chan-Petra sat down, bringing the papers she held forward. "Now then, I've finally gotten access to your parent's files. It seems you're a very wealthy young woman, Mrs. Waberly," she began politely.

"Rachel, please. I don't want to be reminded of that—well you know what I mean," Rachel Roxanne managed to say.

Felix was glad Rachel was rather coherent right now, but wondered how long that would last. If it got bad, he decided he'd make up some excuse to get her up and walking around so she'd get a big dose of pleasuring. That might work.

Rachel thought, *Humm. . . She's like me, an EE woman. I wonder if she wants to pleasure me? She's around my age maybe and very pretty. Maybe I should make the first move.* She batted her eyes at Chan and smiled demurely.

Chan-Petra continued. "Now then, I've come across the detail that all three older men were part of something called the Cabal. Do you know anything about this?"

Mary Jane flushed. She'd been reading and sharing the details of the Raven Journal with the others.

Rachel had some memories coming back to her. Didn't her father take them to some kind of meeting each year? "Exotic places," she muttered.

"Yes?" Chan-Petra encouraged her, realizing this was going to be a very difficult task to get useful information from the young teen.

"New Years. Trips. Meetings. Fancy places. I sort of remember. Terribly hard to recall," Rachel muttered, trying desperately to force out the words—if only the Pytalon wasn't so interfering with her mind.

"I see. Never the same place? Big meeting?" Chan-Petra encouraged her.

"Yes. Yes," was all Rachel could vocalize.

"I take it that you don't know what these meeting were about?"

"No." Well that one was easy, Rachel thought.

Time for a different approach. "I also came across this listing. I was hoping you could shed some light on its meaning?" She held up the Randal printout so that she and the others could read it.

Randal B 21	Ramani Chicago Medical Institute
Regina B 21	Ramani Chicago Medical Institute
Roy A 20	Ramani Chicago Medical Institute
Roy B 9	Ramani Chicago Medical Institute

Rachel Roxanne A 18   Ramani Chicago Medical Institute
Rachel Roxanne B 8   Ramani Chicago Medical Institute

Rachel stared at it, trying to make some sense of it all, but simply could not. On the other hand, the other woman who looked almost identical to Rachel flushed. Chan-Petra didn't miss that detail. So when Rachel shook her head no, she looked directly at R^3. "Miss? Do you know something about the meaning of his list?"

Oh no! We've been discovered! Our freedom is shot! Ah well, she's going to find out soon enough. R^3 looked at Felix and sighed. He too picked up her thought. *The game was up; their freedom, gone.*

"Yes sir. I believe that I, er, we do know what it means, mostly anyway," R^3 said hesitantly.

"Please. Anything you can tell me will be greatly appreciated," Chan-Petra encouraged the young teen, observing she wasn't on Pytalon and that her implant wasn't as overwhelming as it was for Rachel.

"I—I think that one is me, Rachel Roxanne A. That's what they called me in the ward at the medical institute."

"Huh?" Chan-Petra blurted. This made no sense at all and took her by complete surprise.

"We six here are ODs. I was called A, but Felix has discovered that there is another me, or rather Rachel Roxanne here, who is eight years old and is called B," R^3 answered.

"I'm sorry. OD?"

R^3 explained, "Organ donor. All of us on Ward 4 and now other wards are organ donors. We had no parents, not like Rachel Roxanne. She is supposed to be my host, so if she needs an organ, then they take it from me. They did that with Mary Jane here. Her host was the woman who was shot in the head, but before that, she was caught in the bombing at the EE Women's Store at the Medical Institute. Her arms were shredded by flying glass, and so Mary Jane Waberly-A here had to donate her arms to the real Mary Jane, but then the real one was shot and dying, so we cleverly got them to transplant Mary Jane's arms back."

Chan-Petra was shocked! "What? Oh my god. You mean these people on this list are all being raised as organ donors for the members of this family?"

"Yes, but some of us don't want to be organ donors. We here want to live. We want a life. We want freedom, so we escaped a few weeks back, escaped from Ward 4 that is. But then in the bombing, we were in the EE women's store, and they got Rachel and me confused and brought me back here, thinking I was the real Rachel, and Rachel got put in Ward 4. My friends just had to escape and bring the real Rachel back to her home and rescue me before they found out. Please, don't send us back there. We don't want our bodies cut up and given to other people. We want to be free and live like real people, even though we're not really real people. I don't know exactly what we are, other than ODs."

"So that's why none of you have an ID card," Chan-Petra began putting these ghastly pieces together.

"No, we don't, but we really do need them. Felix has been trying to figure out a way for us to get them, but we don't have any credits. Rachel Roxanne has a lot, and we figured she could give us some. Please don't send us back there. Besides, Felix and I want to be married. So does Mary Jane and Todd and Rhianna and Trevor."

"Don't worry about that! No way will I send you back there! This is just incredible. We've never heard of this organ donor thing. It looks as if there is a whole lot that I don't know," Chan-Petra declared.

Felix was encouraged by her response. "Excuse me. You should know something else. If one of the hosts dies, then they take all their remaining ODs and cut them up, giving their parts to many other people. We saw that happening already. I've been monitoring the Medical Institute, since everyone was murdered. Eventually, all those on your lists, their ODs, are going to be disposed of, except us since we escaped, but they'll cut us up too if you take us back. They haven't done that to the other younger versions of us, maybe because they don't yet know the nine are dead."

"Oh good god!" Chan-Petra exclaimed. "What have I stumbled into this time?" Suddenly, it struck her. "My god. You're clones, clones of your host people! I thought that was science fiction. That explains why you look almost identical to Rachel here."

"Yes, we all look exactly alike our hosts," Felix agreed with her. "What's a clone?"

R3 added, "But aren't we people? Just like everyone else? I know I look exactly like Rachel Roxanne, but I'm me. I like many things. I'm very smart. So are all of us. Felix is a computer whizz. Mary Jane and Todd are into medical things. Rhianna knows a lot about geography and history, while Trevor knows a lot about fighting, guns, and stuff. We aren't dopes, as many ODs are. Admittedly, some are pretty dumb, sitting around all day playing dollhouse and video games, just waiting for their turn to donate some organs, as Able did. He donated his right arm and leg."

"Clones. Well, as far as I know, you are people. Okay. We have a very serious situation here. First, I will get you six an ID card. Since Rachel here has billions of credits, I'll take some of her funds for your accounts, especially since you six are looking after her. In addition, I'm going to send some very competent guards here to protect you, just in case those assassins should try to finish the job. Then, I'm going to look into this whole organ donor mess. It has to be highly illegal or should be. If you need anything, give me a call. Here's my card. Also, I agree it would be wise if you were married, because that will make it more difficult for anyone to put you back in Ward 4. I'll send someone to marry you later today. I'll have your ID cards ready by then."

R3 exclaimed, "So we *are* real people anyway? Thank you! We'll keep on taking care of Rachel Roxanne here."

"Sure you're a real person." *At least I hope so,* Chan-Petra thought to herself. "Now, if you'll excuse me, I best get all this going. I've got to stop them from cutting up more of those people." Chan-Petra rose and saw herself out, leaving the teens excitedly chatting.

Just outside, she assigned her two Trikuza guards to watch this place, until another half dozen could arrive. Then once inside her EMAC, she placed a hurried conference call, joining the professor, Lady Persephone, Beth, Tilly, Amanda, and Jessica. "My god! You won't believe what we've just stumbled into!" Chan-Petra exclaimed, and calmed down, explaining what she'd just learned. She ended with, "So a clone is a person too, right?"

The professor replied first, "I don't know. Bloody mess. You say the clone is identical to the host?"

"Yes, Rachel and the other who calls herself R3 are identical. You can't tell them apart, except they're wearing slightly different dresses and that the real Rachel is heavily under the influence of her EE implant and probably a massive dose of Pytalon. It would also seem to me of the two women, R3 is vastly smarter than Rachel is. The six seem quite bright and aren't on Pytalon, though the three women have undergone the EE implant. However, R3 says some of the other organ donors are more like morons. We have stumbled upon a huge mess."

The professor replied, "Bloody well have. If their DNA is identical, then maybe their fingerprints will be too. Crap. We would have no way to identify one over the other. Bloody interesting."

"Let's hope they aren't criminals," Chan-Petra teased him.

"Certainly, these six deserve to have a true life," Lady Persephone spoke up. "I think you made the right call. Of course, their names will be problematic, but then there are many people with the same names."

Beth barked, "What a crappy time to be laid up like this. Juan, get me my computer, Jessica's too. We'll use our feet, so don't worry."

Tilly inserted, "We've never factored in a cloning process. What bothers me is this is something major with the Total Care program and we know nothing about it."

Amanda added, "And what is this Cabal thing?"

Jessica took another approach, "Chan, we should get

those four women's implants desensitized and get Rachel off Pytalon as soon as possible. If you can bring them to our penthouse suite, we four can at least work on desensitizing their EE woman's implant."

Chan-Petra replied, "Good idea. If we can get Rachel off Pytalon, she might be able to recall more of what happened. So far, I've no clues of the assassins. I'm hopeful the techs can decrypt the computers we recovered. Beth, Jessica—I rather wish you two were able to lend a hand. Still, I've faith in my techs eventually working it out."

Around four that afternoon, Chan-Petra had the three couples officially married, six new ID cards made, each backed with a million credits from Rachel's nearly unlimited account, and had all four teens at the penthouse suite in the capable feet of Beth, Jessica, Amanda, and Tilly.

With her two Trikuza bodyguards and a half dozen Chicago Feds, including Captain Lech, she headed into the Ramani Chicago Medical Institute. At the reception desk, she asked, "Get me the person in charge of this entire facility. Now," she barked. She just couldn't believe the inhumanity this medical institute was apparently fostering.

"That would be Dr. Hamal Ramani. I'll send for him," the glassy-eyed receptionist replied, thankful this was another easy one to handle.

Chan-Petra didn't like how long she stood there waiting before the man of Indian descent appeared, walking slowly towards her. He was middle-aged, but very well dressed, a rather smug look on his face. He wasn't on Pytalon, she noted immediately. "And how may I help our Feds?" he asked overly politely.

"I want to examine the ODs you're keeping on several floors above here, specifically Ward 4, for starters. Human trafficking is illegal, you know," she stated very pointedly.

"I'm sorry. Those floors are off-limits. Security reasons. Is there anything else that I can help you with?" he said rather covertly.

"Either you take me to that floor this instant or I will go there myself."

"Those floors are restricted. I'm sorry. Only authorized medical personnel are allowed onto those floors. No exceptions. I can't expose our patients to outside germs. Now is there anything else?"

"So you aren't voluntarily going to show me Ward 4 and the other organ donors?" she countered.

"Of course not. Restricted access. You don't qualify. Sorry. Mind you, we take our security around here very, very seriously," he added. "Most definitely, you Feds aren't allowed on those floors."

"Okay, have it your way. I will be back in force. If I find you're dealing in human trafficking, keeping humans for the sole purpose of their organs, growing humans for that purpose only, I will hang you out to dry by your balls, if you even have them."

"Excuse me, but where could you possibly have gotten the idea we are trafficking in humans? I'll admit we have a number of volunteer organ donors here at the institute."

"I believe the proper term is clones, doctor. For example, you have a twenty-one year old clone of Mr. Randal Raven somewhere up there," Chan-Petra probed a bit, since he had volunteered a bit of information.

"I assure you, a clone is not a human person, merely a cloned, physical body, solely used for medical purposes. A clone isn't a person," he replied authoritatively, as though looking down upon a mere Feds and one who was a pathetic EE woman at that.

"I have big news for you, buster, a clone is just as much a person as you or I."

"Hardly. Mere human-like vegetables, good for organ transplants. Have been so for nearly two centuries. Now if that is all, I have work to attend to," he said dryly, turned, and walked away, leaving Chan-Petra fuming. Right now, she had no choice but to leave, quite irritated by the man's arrogance.

As soon as Dr. Ramani reached his office, he placed a secure call. After outlining what just happened, he was put on hold and another secure call made. Eventually, he was reconnected. "You'll receive some transfer orders within the hour. Goodbye." Dr. Ramani smiled. Problem solved.

***

R[3]'s comment when Felix and the others picked them up from Beth's penthouse suite that evening spoke volumes, "Wow, Felix. I now don't have to keep on reciting those damned words. None of us do. This thing Jessica invented really works!"

She, Rhianna, Mary Jane, and Rachel Roxanne were very pleased. Beth's group had gotten two of the implant script's sentences desensitized this first day, namely the repeating it line and having always to look their best. Still, Rachel Roxanne was glassy-eyed, but R[3] explained they even had a way to get her safely off Pytalon.

Todd had news too. An older woman had come by asking for the cook's job. He'd hired her despite the fact she only had one hand. "She's not on Pytalon and seems to know what we need. Juanita used to work as a chef at a fancy restaurant, but was the victim of a Pytalon accident. The drugged man mistook her hand for a side of beef and chopped it off. After that, no one would hire her, but I didn't see any reason not to."

When they got home, Juanita had dinner waiting. For the first time in many days, they ate a nourishing meal. R[3] praised Juanita's cooking, bringing tears to the older woman's face. Somehow, against all odds she now had a paying job doing what she loved to do.

After eating, Felix again checked on the ODs in Ward 4. "Oh no, I was right! They are scheduling them for the chopping block!"

R[3] dropped everything and rushed to him. "What? They are going to kill them?"

"Yes, all those who had a Raven, Waberly, or Michaelson host! I have to call Chan-Petra right away,"

Felix declared.

"Let me do it," R³ intervened. She quickly dialed her, explaining what Felix found. She heard an explicative-filled tirade in response.

Felix added, "Tell her they're being transferred to Cook County General tonight via EMAC bus. One had been scheduled to arrive at the Medical Institute around ten tonight. Maybe we can stop the bus before it gets to Cook County." R³ relayed that to Chan-Petra as well.

Chan-Petra was annoyed and overly emotional when she heard what the teen told her. She calmed down, realizing her hormones were acting up. For the tenth time, she regretted having decided to start a family so soon. Peter was dead, and she and Yan both had newborns to care for. At first, she thought it wouldn't interfere, but now she wasn't so sure.

"Okay. I'll arrange for the EMAC bus to be stopped in transit. We can board it and see for ourselves if they are taking them to be used," Chan-Petra replied, regaining her composure. "I'll send someone to pick you and Felix up shortly. We'll need your identifications of the personnel on that bus, since they won't have ID cards."

"Hey tell her that we can put them up here," Todd called out to R³. "There are plenty of rooms."

R³ did as he asked, after which she told Todd that was a very good idea.

After hanging up, Chan-Petra made another conference all. The professor made an astute comment that caused her and everyone else to pause a moment. "Look," he said, "some of these clones may have almost no education and may have being an organ donor as their life's purpose. It wouldn't be right just to force them to give that up. I have a hunch, and Tilly can back me up on this one, that some of them will be bright like R³, while others will be barely functioning. Take that into consideration, Chan."

Shortly after ten that night, R³, Felix, Captain Lech, three Trikuza members, Chan-Petra, and a dozen other Feds stopped the EMAC bus six blocks from Cook County

General. Besides the driver, there was only one security guard present, and he didn't offer any resistance. Chan-Petra, Captain Lech, Felix, and R³ entered the bus and found fourteen men, women, and children onboard. The nine adults, that is, the clones whose ages were twenty or more, were mostly zombies and really didn't grasp what Chan-Petra was offering them, freedom and a new life. They kept saying they wanted to give new life to their new hosts. Five children, eight and nine-years-old, were bright and were eager to have "real" lives in the big new world. Thus, they removed the five children and sent the bus on its way.

R³ had already figured out they would call these children their little brothers and sisters. She escorted her little eight year old "sister" to the waiting EMAC. "You're my little sister, but since all three of us sisters are Rachel Roxanne, we're going to call you just Roxanne so we don't get confused. You can call me R³. Now you get to come live with your big brothers and sisters in a big, fancy house."

They rescued nine-year-olds Roy, Scott, and Steve, and eight-year-olds Roxanne and Mary Jane.

As they headed home, Captain Lech commented, "Well boss, rescuing a third of them isn't bad. These children can have a chance at a good life."

Chan-Petra flashed him a big smile, for those were her thoughts precisely. The next morning when Chan-Petra arrived at her office, already a strange man was waiting to meet with her. As she passed by the receptionist, he told her, "A Fred Koch is in your waiting room to meet with you." She thanked him and headed on up to her office suite. Sure enough, she found a strange man sitting patiently in her reception area. He wore a dark blue suit, an expensive cut, she noted, nearly as well dressed as Mr. Buffett.

"I'm Supreme Commander Chan-Petra Delius. I'm told you wish to see me," she said politely, moving to shake his hand. He didn't offer his, but his eyes scanned her from her tall heels upwards to her giant bosom, finally lighting on her face, though his eyes failed to meet hers. It was impossible for him or anyone to miss the fact that she was a new mother. She did note he was doped up on Pytalon.

"I've come to deliver these documents to you. Per United Nations Law 21345 of 2050, a clone is by definition not a person. Here," he handed her the proof. He went on, "Since 2050, cloning has been a proven medical method of providing quality, compatible organ donors and continues to be today. As head of the Illinois branch of Total Care, I hereby order you to cease interfering in the organ donor program. If you don't cease at once, I'm told all Total Care funding for the Feds worldwide will be terminated and that you'll be removed from office, as your previous leader, Peter Delius, was. Good day."

He finished his well-rehearsed speech, rose, and left her office, not even waiting for her reply. As a Pytalon case, Chan-Petra realized he wouldn't really be hearing anything she had to say in rebuttal anyway.

She looked over the documents and then did a quick search to prove their validity. After satisfying herself, she placed another conference call, relating the latest turn of events. The professor promised to make her a "new law" making clones real people, but Lady Persephone became even more worried about the hornets' nest that had been stirred up. She suggested Chan take a maternity leave.

In fact, the next day, Chan received a new law from the Professor, though she now wondered if they'd cut off the funding of the Feds.

Continental Congress Declaration 42

1 November 2272

Human clones are hereby recognized as real human beings and are accorded all the rights and privileges any human being has. From this day forward, all clones, especially those in the Organ Donor program are to be treated as normal people and not medical objects.

Chan-Petra smiled and then sent the email to all known Total Care offices worldwide. *That should shake them up some,* she thought. After that, she decided to take Lady Persephone's advice and take a maternity leave. Dealing with her newborn baby and trying to run all the Feds was just too much to handle. She appointed Captain Lech to take her post as temporary head as Supreme Commander, impressing him.

Chapter 7—Moves and Countermoves

November 4, 2272, Franco Helu was forced to call yet another emergency meeting of the Camarilla, something that had not happened in at least fifty years—two emergency meetings within three months! It was held in an ancient castle-manor in Luxemburg.

"Gentlemen, I don't have to tell you why I've had to call this meeting. Somehow, a number of things have gone off the rails. We must put them back on track and before the January meeting. First, James wishes to bring us up to date on some Cabal issues. James," he began politely.

The nine men wore immaculate suits, and they were clearly more than a little worried. Fearful would be a better adjective, if not outright terror.

James rose, cleared his throat, and began. "Yes, as you know three closely related but lesser Cabal families have been eliminated. Raven, Waberly, and Michaelson to be precise. Worse, due to their intermarriages and the lone survivor, Mrs. Rachael Roxanne Raven Waberly, the EE woman has legally inherited all three family fortunes."

Several gasped, knowing that would put this new Cabal family upwards within the Cabal member hierarchy. A net worth of thirty billion would certainly displace over half of their members moving them down a slot.

He went on, "Yes, I've had no choice but to deliver the appropriate merger documents. However, I point out this pathetic woman is only eighteen and is on a heavy dose of Pytalon, barely able to function at all. After the January meeting, I'm sure one of the younger sons will put this right—marrying her."

"But that's not all. Gentlemen, I fear other Cabal members have already heard of this most unfortunate event, and frankly, I believe some may entertain similar ideas."

"Here, here!" Lord Henry Koch broke in testily. "Surely, you aren't suggesting other Cabal members will start eliminating other Cabal families. There is always the inheritance angle to keep them in line."

"Yes, well the Raven, Waberly, and Michaelson families certainly wiggled their way around the inheritance laws," James pointed out dryly. "I'm convinced others will try something similar. Ben, I urge you to take swift action. After all, this Rachel woman holds all the remaining stock of your companies. It would be ideal if you controlled one hundred percent of the EMAC and Air Liner corporations worldwide, not just your eighty percent." Ben Michaelson-Waberly grinned; that was his plan ever since hearing about the tragic deaths. That these deceased men had tried to get back at him for having absconded with most of the engineers' fortunes entered his thoughts.

James finished up, "I would suggest we beef up our security arrangements."

Franco called upon Henry Koch, who ran Total Care Worldwide. Henry rose, feeling more nervous than he had felt for a century. "Gentlemen, I bear terrible news, though perhaps it isn't as bad as it first appears. It seems somehow our highly guarded cloning organ donor program has come to the attention of the Feds! So far, it's contained to the Chicago area and has affected only five children clones that were scheduled for termination anyway. Still, I can't tell you how serious a breech this is. If news of the cloning project becomes widely known, that can lead them to the Cabal families."

"Next, there is this matter of some kind of Continental Congress rogue group that's pretending to make up new laws for the world—in this case, claiming clones are real people. We know nothing about this rogue group, but we should annihilate this group as soon as possible!"

Visibly upset, Henry continued, "Then there is the significant security breech in our Total Care computer systems. We're taking every precaution known as I speak. I trust we have sealed our systems down tightly. If not, I can't begin to tell you the damage that could be done to our extensive program! It could set us back a century!" All eight others grimaced and grew even more fearful with this news.

"Finally," Henry continued, "in the small matter of a number of Chicago high school graduates who were allowed not to get their implants, Pytalon dosages, and their Total Care defined employments, I'm happy to inform you the situation has been remedied. All those who 'missed' their appointed Total Care appointments have been found, implanted, put on a heavy dose of Pytalon, and assigned proper employment. That has been handled in Chicago. So far, the Feds who supported this move haven't discovered what I've had done. At least, we've won one small battle."

He sat down, relieved only a little bit. The rest was just too scary to contemplate. He imagined a world of non-implanted, non-drugged people running around the world and shuddered visibly. Hideous, just hideous.

Franco was just as unnerved as the others were, but rose. "Now, I call upon Al Rumani for his report. Al." He sat down as the head of the Medical Facilities Worldwide rose.

Emulating Franco, Al cleared his throat. He was from India, but spoke with the typical accent. "Gentlemen. We have successfully received two complete sets of the Lin brothers Transference Machines and supporting pods. We have verified they are in working condition as promised. Thanks to the tireless efforts of Thomas Goode of St. Louis, we know the location where the Lin brothers are being kept. As I speak, a rescue team is en route to retrieve them. Once we have them and they verify their machines are complete, work will begin on fabricating more of them. For the first time in history, we will not be utterly dependent upon those brothers for our 'new' bodies." That brought a round of applause, since each man here had received at least one of these "new" bodies in the past.

"So yes, one of the conditions of their rescue will be to assist us in the manufacturing process. At this time, I can report the four EE women that were given total arm transplants in order to obtain these two machines for us have fully recovered. However, I've done some investigations of my own. It seems these four EE women are close confidants of the late Peter Delius and of Chan-Petra. Also, Chan-Petra has recently given birth, so if we need to send her further encouragement, we might do so with these four EE women associates—that is, unless you decide Chan-Petra must be replaced."

"Now before anything gets decided, I have additional and very disturbing news, particularly about one of these four EE women associates. It has recently come to my attention that this Jessica woman has been instrumental in discovering a way to virtually undo physical implants!" Al paused, listening to the startled gasps from the eight men.

"Indeed. This is terribly shocking news. Horrible, just horrible. I don't have any other words to describe this horrid development. I don't have to tell you the ramifications of this!"

All eight began talking at once, expressing their horror at this startling news, but Al wasn't finished. "Wait. There is more. Someone has figured out a way not only to get someone safely off heavy doses of Pytalon, but also to remove all lingering physical effects. In short, gentlemen, we're facing a crisis of unimaginable proportions! This could wipe out two centuries of our very hard work."

"Hell, Al, all our plans!" Franco butted in, quite shocked. Thus began a lengthy discussion of just what had to be done.

A half hour later, Al received a text message. He looked up very annoyed. "Excuse me. News. The Lin brothers have been rescued. They are on their way to Mumbai, India now. However, the Feds have gone too far. Not only have they somehow used their own Transference Machines to put both brothers into young female bodies, but they also turned them into EE women, heavily implanted and on Pytalon. They made both utterly helpless by removing their arms and their eyes! Such butchery of our most brilliant scientists! Outrageous! We cannot stand for such treatment! We must act. Send these people a strong message!" Al was livid and more frightened than he had been for over a century!

In fact, at this meeting, all nine men were more terrified than they had been for close to a hundred twenty years! Just when they had become complacent believing they had the entire world totally under their control, everything seemed to be coming apart at the seams! These Camarilla men were terrified. Franco also realized that when the other Cabal members learned of this, they would be just as mortified and more importantly, they would be demanding swift, powerful action to remedy these horrific alterations to the Total Care program.

***

That same day, Captain Lech paid a personal visit to Chan-Petra and Yan at their penthouse suite. "Boss, I've just had the most alarming news. One of those high school counselors came by to see you. I told her you were on maternity leave, and I got her to tell me what was troubling her. She claims every one of the recent graduates that we allowed not to be implanted and put on Pytalon have been kidnaped. Each one was implanted, put on Pytalon, and given Total Care jobs. She is irate that you lied to her and the other counselors about this. I told her this was news to us and that we'd take action. Just what, I surely don't know. Boss, how did they get to all those graduates?"

"Damn! Okay. We must make this right. Find my list of them. Double-check it against all the Chicago-land high schools. Then, find them and get them to our new Rejuvenation Center at once. Wait; assign a dozen Trikuza members to guard that center. Make sure they're fully armed with whatever they wish as weapons. I've a bad feeling about all this," Chan-Petra ordered.

Lech smiled and left to carry out her orders,

thankful he hadn't had to issue them. Just as she was about to email this startling development, she got a conference call, this time setup by the professor.

"Bad news. The safe house in Flagstaff was raided and the Lin brothers taken away. We're going to go over all our security arrangements. Somehow, we have had a serious leak. All isn't lost. Greg had put his locator chips in their shoulders. It seems as though they're en route to India. Do we go after them?"

Lady Persephone answered, "No, leave them to me. I'll do some legwork this time. I have a feeling we should batten down the hatches as they used to say on ships entering a storm. These new developments are most troublesome. We have encountered something far more sinister than we ever dreamed possible."

"I've increased security at our Rejuvenation Center here in Chicago," Chan-Petra added, then explained what she'd just learned.

That only added to their worries. The professor suggested all the other centers around the world also beef up their protections, and Chan-Petra agreed to see to that detail, firing off an email from her laptop to that effect to the other Feds leaders worldwide.

That evening, Beth, Tilly, Jessica, and Amanda finished desensitizing the four young women's EE implants. Now they only had to get Rachel off Pytalon and had her scheduled to report to the Rejuvenation Center tomorrow to begin her detoxification program.

As they finished, Rhianna volunteered, "Say Amanda, I'm into history too. You should see the Raven Journal that we found in Randal's private safe. Some of the things in there are beyond description, if they're actually true. Want to come by tonight and I'll show you? Something about a Cabal, but they have to be very evil men."

All four suddenly looked at Rhianna. The mention of that word caught their total attention.

Amanda exclaimed, "Absolutely! We've been trying

to find out what this Cabal is all about and have gotten nowhere at all. You bet we would love to see this journal! Lead on, historian Rhianna!"

Rhianna was extremely pleased they were interested. Perhaps, they could make more sense of the rambling narratives. The eight women, plus Juan and two Trikuza members arrived at the Raven Compound, where Juanita had dinner waiting, but not for so many.

"Don't worry," R³ consoled her, "We should've let you know that we had guests. We only figured that out just before we left. We can make do just fine."

The four were too excited about the journal to eat, so Rhianna brought it out, and Tilly began reading it aloud to everyone while they ate. "My god, this is utterly invaluable information, Rhianna," Tilly praised her.

R³ then suggested, "You know, if Mr. Raven kept this journal, perhaps Mr. Waberly and Mr. Michaelson did too."

"Brilliant idea," Beth exclaimed. "We should go search those homes for secret safes tonight. Where there's one of these, there's bound to be more."

All four simply had to explore this immediately. Here was so much missing information over the last two centuries! After dinner, Rachel Roxanne volunteered to take them to the other two complexes, because she knew she could operate the EMAC's destination menu. Felix, Rhianna, and Trevor insisted on coming along as well.

"Hey, I cracked the safe's combination," Felix explained.

By ten that night, the four had their hands on two more similar journals, along with volumes of other documents of greatly lesser importance, mostly dealing with the running of the many corporations the deceased men had owned. Around eleven, Juan landed their EMAC on the roof of their skyscraper. Four tired women, Juan, and the two Trikuza men stepped down, heading for the elevator to take them down to their penthouse suite.

Just then, a dozen black-clad men rose up from their

concealed positions and rushed the group. Juan dropped the bag containing the books and engaged two men, while the bored Trikuza men flew into action. Three against twelve wasn't good odds, particularly when four of the twelve had specific orders. They fired dart guns at the fleeing women. The knockout drug took effect swiftly, dropping all four, but not before Tilly reached the elevator doors and pressed the alarm button.

Behind them, the Trikuza were deadly, dropping seven men before they were darted as well. Juan got two men before he too was dropped with the powerful darts. One of the remaining five attackers was severely wounded, so one of the four put a bullet into his head.

"Leave them. That bitch managed to signal the Feds. Here comes our EMAC now. Get the four EE women onboard. That's our orders. Leave the others," he barked his orders.

As soon as the EMAC landed, the four picked up a woman each and carried her to the bay ramp, just as it touched the rooftop. They marched inside, closing the door behind them, while the vehicle slowly lifted off, heading for Cook County General.

"The knockout drug won't last too long, so we have to get them in there fast," he explained to the others, though he need not have. All knew precisely the drug's effect. While extremely fast acting, its drawback was its relatively short duration, thirty minutes more or less.

After landing, a doctor met them. The leader barked, "You got your orders for these four EE women?"

The glassy-eyed doctor replied, "Yes. Right here. Put them on the carts." Four orderlies walked slowly up to the doctor, mindless men, ready to push them inside. Minutes later, the EMAC lifted off, heading back to clean up the mess on the top of the skyscraper. However, they veered off. Already the rooftop was swarming with Feds. Hence, they headed far away from the location, while the leader fired off a text message.

Done. Lost Seven.

Juan came too rapidly, because the dart had only grazed him. He got up, rubbing his head, while looking around. "Shit. They've been abducted again!"

Hastily, he dialed the professor and told him the bad news. Within a short time, Greg activated their locator chips, and the professor relayed their location.

"Juan, all four are in Cook County General Hospital. That can't be good. See if you can get to them before anything bad happens," the professor advised.

By now the Trikuza were rousing. Hastily, they retrieved their throwing stars from the dead men. A Feds EMAC came in for a landing. Juan wasted precious time explaining the kidnaping, but he was able to takeoff within five minutes, leaving the Feds to examine the dead men for clues. They also called in for a strong backup force to head to Cook County General.

Juan and the two Trikuza landed on the rooftop emergency dock. The receptionist walked out, looking for the patient.

"Four EE women were just brought here minutes ago. Where are they?" Juan barked at the drugged man. That confused him, and Juan wasted precious minutes waiting for the man to regain enough sense to try to find out about the women.

"They are in surgery bays five through eight," the man finally answered, greatly relieved. *If only people wouldn't be in such a hurry.* "Sanity is doing a good job," he whispered.

"What floor?" Juan asked.

The beleaguered man fumbled with his screen for a moment. "5. But you can't go there. The waiting room is on Floor 2. They'll notify you when the patients are in recovery," he added his well-rehearsed reply to such queries.

Juan and the two men charged into the building, wasting more time trying to find an elevator that would take them to Floor 5. All the ones that did required a key card. They were only allowed up to Floor 2.

Angry at the rebuff, Juan punched out a man who appeared to be a doctor and stole his key card. The two men smiled and joined him in the elevator. Juan punched 5, hoping they were not too late. When they stepped off the elevator onto Floor 5, two security guards jumped up from their chairs. "You aren't allowed on this floor. Delicate surgery is ongoing. Please go back down," one said with glassy-eyed emphasis.

Both tried to stop Juan as he pressed forward. Two throwing stars flew, connecting with the guard's foreheads, dropping them instantly. The Trikuza pulled them out as they passed by the guards, following behind Juan, who raced down the hallway looking for the right rooms.

He barged into the first operating room, startling the various personnel, several nurses and a doctor. He saw Beth unconscious, her arms inside some giant medical machine. "Stop this operation at once!" he demanded.

"Who are you? You shouldn't be in here. Contamination. Germs. Unsterile. Besides, the machine is now operational. It can't be stopped mid-operation. If you will just return to the waiting area, I'll notify you when she is in recovery. How did you get past the guards?" the glassy-eyed doctor finally registered he had unauthorized personnel in his operating room.

Juan ran out and into the next three rooms, but all three other machines were also mid-operation. Juan sighed. He was too late. Whatever they were undergoing, he was helpless to prevent it! He swore. Hastily, he dialed the professor to tell him the bad news.

"Okay. We're getting them out of here as soon as the operations are done. Have them to you as soon as possible." He hung up. "Men, stand guard. We're taking them out of here the moment the surgery is done."

Both Trikuza nodded and headed back to the elevator, cleverly jamming it open, preventing anyone from using it. Then one headed off to find other elevators to take them out of service as well.

A half hour later, the befuddled doctors stepped out

127

of the rooms. "It is done. Now they must be taken to recovery. They'll need to spend a week in the hospital before they can be released."

"Put them on carts. We're taking them with us now. Be thankful I haven't killed you!" Juan cried out, trying hard not to do just that! One by one, the unconscious women were wheeled out. Their lower arms had been removed at their elbows, which were heavily bandaged. Carefully, Juan positioned the women on a cart. While he and one of his men pushed them, the other took up a position in front of them. They headed to the elevator and pushed the top floor button.

"We might have to fight our way out of here," Juan advised.

One answered him, "More fun!"

Juan didn't think this was fun at all. The four had been mutilated yet again. He swore vengeance on whoever had ordered this hit!

When the doors opened onto the roof, six armed guards were waiting for them. Throwing stars dropped two before they could even react, Juan fired his gun, dropping another, while the Trikuza men took care of the other three. A minute later, they carried the four women into the EMAC and lifted off.

Juan dropped the Trikuza off with the Feds, picked up the precious sack with the three journals, and then punched in the coordinates for Phoenix, setting the throttle to maximum, hoping to get there before the anesthetic wore off and trusting the professor had doctors standing by when he touched down. He needn't have worried about that though. He calmly placed a conference call, notifying every one of the damage done.

Late that night, Chan-Petra had her own problems. She and Yan retired for the night, while their babies slept between feedings. A silent EMAC hovered just beside the windows of her penthouse suite. The bay door opened and a man attached a suction plate to the window. Then, he used a laser gun to cut a large circle around it, man-sized.

One gentle tug and that section of window broke away. He pulled it on inside the EMAC. Next, two men dressed in black jumped from the vehicle through the hole. At this point, the alarm finally sounded, rousing the women.

The masked men rushed from room to room, finding their bedroom just as Chan-Petra had gotten to her feet to see what was going on. Both men held guns with silencers on them. One said, "This is your last warning. Stay out of our business." The other shot Yan in her head, just as the terrified woman was sitting up.

"Damn you! You'll pay dearly for this!" Chan-Petra screamed, figuring she was next. At least, she had yelled back at them before she was shot. Instead of firing, both backed out the way they'd entered, keeping their guns on her. Once out of her sight, they raced to the window hole and leapt into the EMAC, which then lifted up, as its door shut. A few seconds later, it vanished in the late night skies of Chicago, leaving a screaming Chan-Petra behind.

She came to her senses and called Lech and emergency services, but she knew Yan wasn't going to make it, not with a large caliber hole in her forehead. They'd executed her—of that she was certain! Soon Feds and emergency responders swarmed her penthouse suite, waking the two infants. After reciting what had happened, Chan-Petra broke down, bawling. Poor Yan had paid the price, and she had been powerless to prevent it, just as she'd been powerless to prevent the killing of her Peter body.

It took all of Lech's people-skills to get Chan calmed down and to handle the crying babies. Once she did, she called the professor to relay what had happened. She'd barely hung up when she received a covert text message telling her about her four EE women associates, again warning her to stop meddling in affairs she knew better than to. She cursed wildly, swearing to bring them all down, whoever "them" was.

An hour later, the professor called her back. "Listen. I want you to come to Phoenix immediately. Bring the babies with you. That's an order!"

Early the next morning, she complied. She realized it wasn't just herself now; she had two babies to care for and her four friends. What was happening? Had the world gone completely mad?

Late the next day when she was nearing Phoenix in her EMAC, she received word from Lech that an attack on the Rejuvenation Center had been foiled. The Trikuza had eliminated a strike force of a dozen men. Lech promised some answers soon, because he now had a goodly number of dead bodies. "Bodies have tales to tell," he relayed to her.

"Well, that was short lived," Beth greeted Chan-Petra, who had just landed and was brought to the infirmary to see her four friends. Beth waved her bandaged stumps around. "At least they left us some of them," she added in disgust.

Tilly added, "Thanks to Juan, they didn't get to do anything else to us. It doesn't hurt."

"Heavy pain killers," Amanda muttered morosely.

Jessica added, "Sorry about Yan. She was a good person."

Chan-Petra broke down and sobbed again. Tilly broke in on Chan's grief. "On the bright side, we have uncovered three journals that are yielding a tremendous amount. I think we're beginning to have a handle on just what has actually been going on for over two centuries! As soon as Amanda and I are up and about, we're going to pour over those journals, though the professor is already on it. We will get them. I promise you. Anyone heard from Lady Persephone?" None had and Tilly wondered about that, in spite of the dopiness of the painkillers.

During the coming week, Jessica began running each of them through this recent operation, using her new technique that she'd figured out with the pony women of London. By the end of the week, their trauma had been pretty much erased, Chan-Petra's too. More importantly, they were off all pain medications and only had small wrappings on their stumps, compliments of the marvels of modern medical techniques, though grossly misused in this case.

However, one detail continued to bother Tilly, who didn't say anything about it yet. That was, why? Why hadn't these evil men gone ahead and just executed the four and Chan as they had with Yan? If the five were being seen as such a serious threat, why not kill them instead of removing their lower arms? In her mind, execution should have been their orders, not mutilation and execution of a close friend, Yan. So why had they been mutilated and not executed? Tilly couldn't figure this one out and vowed to spend more time restudying her many behavior formulas. She knew she must be missing something vital.

However, at this time, Captain Lech sent Chan-Petra the best news yet. The Feds technicians had finally cracked the three Cabal men's computer systems. He forwarded a copy of the recent, relevant emails to her.

"Wow! Listen to this. Raven ordered the hit on the Waberly family. Waberly ordered the hit on the Raven family and the Michaelson family."

"So who did it?" Beth asked.

"Thirty million credits. That's what it took to kill off three entire families. Mary Jane was supposed to be the sole survivor, so she would inherit the three fortunes. Guess who executed the hit?" Chan-Petra teased them.

Tilly glared at her, so she added, "The MMS, Marshals Militia and Security men. Now we have them."

"Crap!" Tilly exclaimed. "We knew they must be up to no good last May or was it June, when we went to those high schools."

"Right dear, but we haven't had any time to pursue them or much else since then," Amanda pointed out the obvious.

"Well, it's time to get justice. Only I don't want anyone to know who is doing this. I've had enough of these men," Chan-Petra declared. "Excuse me. I've plans to make."

In her new temporary room, Chan-Petra placed a

secure call to China. "Master Yao Bing? Hi. This is Chan-Petra Delius. No, I'm not fine." She relayed recent events. "I have a mission for your group, one that must remain a total secret, but a very honorable one that is going to be invaluable in bringing justice for many victims. My people have pinpointed the main location of the MMS group, but perhaps on the ground, your people may be able to obtain the location of others in this organization." A bit later, she added, "Yes, this organization must be eliminated in total. No survivors."

When she hung up, she had a smile on her face. The one advantage the Feds had that other militia groups didn't was total access to the countless spy satellites. It was a relatively simple matter for Lech to locate their headquarters. It's hard to hide such a large para-military organization from the birds in the sky.

On December 1, one hundred fifty Trikuza infiltrated the main headquarters of the MMS, Marshals Militia and Security men. Five hundred militia men died, though ten Trikuza were injured. After ransacking the headquarters and confiscating several Air Liners filled with guns, ammunition, and bombs, they also found three smaller installations and removed them the next day. The Trikuza were efficient and left no clues. If the Cabal checked up, they would find no Feds involvement in the mysterious attack. Chan-Petra wanted to send a message to those who would commit such atrocities.
***

Meanwhile, Al Rumani had his hands full overseeing the recovery of the precious Lin brothers. They were brought to his facility in Mumbai, the Rumani Medical Research Foundation, where he had the two Transference Machines and life pods set up and ready for operations. The first problem he faced was the accurate estimation of their state. True, they were EE women, complete with implants and maximum Pytalon doses, but they also had to wear the debilitating ballet boots. They lacked arms and eyes. His initial assessment was grim. Both were babbling idiots.

Step One, he decided, was to get them into fresh bodies that were not on Pytalon, in hopes that in a brief while the effects of Pytalon would be eliminated. He decided against giving them male bodies. Their EE woman implants would probably cause them to go completely insane. Hence, he sent word to some of his usual "helpers" to acquire two eighteen year old women, pretty ones, lowest caste, ones that wouldn't be missed, and more importantly ones that were not yet on Pytalon.

Two days later, his helpers brought him two specimens for his approval. Both were unconscious, of course. Both were pretty with rich, long black hair, typical rural Indians, he thought. He gave his consent and had them turned into EE women, physically that is. They didn't undergo the usual EE woman implant, for the Lin brothers already were enduring that part and would be brining that along with them. The next day, he personally ran the Transference Machine, unwilling to risk any error, hoping that he remembered the operational details well enough. Bo Lin had once shown him how it was done when he'd visited Peking, many years ago.

Bao and Huan woke up in the new young Indian women's bodies, while the unsuspecting Indian women were in the helpless bodies. Bao's first reaction upon coming out of the process was to strangle her old body personally. Shortly after that, Huan followed suit.

Dr. Al Rumani spent several days watching the behavior of the two. He had to know their mental state. Could they even be saved? He wanted to salvage them, if possible. Both were brilliant men and had the potential to offer so much more to the cause, if only. . .

After a few days, the Pytalon drug mass seemed to go away, probably because these new bodies had not yet been exposed to the drug. Still, they frequently recited the EE women's litany, but he expected that. Would they calm down? From long experience with EE women, he knew in time, they would cease repeating their implanted scripts.

However, he also knew a shortcut, a proven one. He had his own wife step in and assist the two women. She provided the very latest in vaginal stimulation devices for the pair. Now they only had to press a button to get their bodies fully satisfied.

It worked well. A week later, both Bao and Huan were lucid much of the day. More importantly, he learned that Beth, Tilly, Jessica, Amanda, and a Lady Persephone Briton had been heavily involved in the mutilations of the Lin brothers, twice in fact! Al was frankly dismayed at the stories the two told him of their two captures, escapes, and failed revenges. Both Bao and Huan were somewhat mollified to learn that the new arms of the four had been removed at their elbows. Still, both could think of little else except to get revenge on the five. Al hoped in time the two could put that aside and get back to work. At least, the two decided to help him begin manufacturing these machines of his, for a hefty price that is. He agreed since the Feds had already confiscated all the Lin brother's centuries of accumulated wealth.

Of course, Al relayed what he learned on up the line to the other Camarilla members. In turn, he learned the five had vanished, though the deeds had been accomplished. The four were crippled again, and Chan-Petra had been sent the strongest possible warning. Nevertheless, both Al and the Lin brothers were very uneasy that the five had gone into hiding. Revenge would be far harder to obtain this way. Still, Al reported the Lin brothers were being patient about their revenge—a good sign he thought.
***

Lady Persephone was patient. She arrived in Mumbai and found the research facility, but it was heavily guarded. Greg confirmed the Lin brothers were being held inside the facility. She parked her EMAC at the main landing. She donned a disguise, including darkening her skin to look like a native. Satisfied, she headed off to the facility using the MET. She took up an observation point across the street from the main entrance in the early morning. She watched and saw her way inside.

In any facility this size, occupying an entire city block, countless maids and janitors were needed to keep the place clean. She spotted an implanted and Pytalon doped female janitor leaving and quietly followed her, taking her out. While she hated to kill an innocent, helpless woman, there was far more at stake here. She then disguised herself to look like the woman's image on the ID card. The following morning, she entered, swiping her card to gain entrance. Now her real work began. She dutifully scrubbed all the hallways on the first floor, using the time to check each side room off. Each day, she move up one floor, but there were many floors!

Two weeks passed before she reached the fourteenth floor. Her diligence paid off. She spotted Dr. Al Rumani chatting with Bao and Huan. He called them by their old male names even though they had new Indian women's bodies. She continued mopping the floor until the two women were left alone. Then, she came into their room, pretending to mop the tiled floor. As she drew close to Bao, she appeared to slip, but her fingers latched onto a key pressure point. Bao went down like a rock. Huan looked up startled. She circle kicked her, knocking her out too. Then, she quietly held her fingers on a very critical pressure point. Bao died shortly thereafter. Then she did the same to Huan. Once satisfied, she deposited an Ace of Spades on each dead woman's head and continued mopping the floor.

Two rooms down, she found the two Transference Machines. Again, pretending to mop the floors, she quietly deposited a pair of bombs and left the room. She took the stairs down a floor and continued mopping. When no one was looking, she pressed a button and smiled. Above her, the two bombs detonated. Bits of ceiling dropped down onto the floor, causing panic everywhere. She joined a group of other workers who frantically began descending the stairs, afraid the building was going to collapse. Once outside, she disappeared onto the MET, joining the throngs using it. Later, she arrived at her EMAC and quickly lifted off. Once the course was set, she took a long overdue and much needed bath. That done, she placed a secure conference call.

"It is done. No more Lin brothers and no more Transference Machines in the hands of the enemy. That is all." She decided to go to Phoenix to discuss everything that had happened and to work out a new strategy. She also knew her place in London wasn't safe to return to—the enemy would be on to her, just as they were with Chan-Petra and the four EE women.
***

"Look, our new friends have done an awful lot for us," R3 suggested. She and the rest of her Circle of Six had just learned of the assassination of Chan-Petra's Yan and the abduction and mutilation of the four women who had selflessly helped them overcome the effects of their EE woman's implant. "So I think it's up to us to continue the fight for freedom, since they can't right now, if ever again."

"I agree. We have lots of guns and stuff. I say we fight back!" Trevor declared, impressed with the tremendous changes in his wife, Rhianna, and the others. He just didn't have a target in mind.

"Well, we aren't the Feds," Rhianna cautioned them. "We don't know anything about the world, excepting the ODs."

"I think that's what we should focus on, doing something we know about," R3 pointed out. "It's great having sort of a family now." She was referring to her new little sister and her "twin" sister. Others nodded.

"Well, we could clear out all the others in the Medical Center, the rest on our ward and all the others too," Felix suggested. "We know the layout and all that."

"But what do we do about those that don't want to be anything more than an OD?" Mary Jane countered. "After all, Chan-Petra let the adults go when she stopped the EMAC bus. We can rescue the kids, most likely. What if there are babies there too? We don't know anything about raising babies, but perhaps we can learn, don't you suppose?"

"Hey, and just how many other places are they keeping ODs? That's what I'd like to know too," Todd spoke up. "We haven't seen more of me or Trevor or Rhianna yet. Maybe there are some little versions of us there too."

"Hey I know. We could put those that still want to be organ donors in one of those other mansions Rachel Roxanne now owns, the Waberly place or the Michaelson place," R³ suggested. "We certainly don't want to kill them or turn them over to be chopped up. We could house them there, and they'd not be the wiser if we said this was a safer place, what with all the bombing and stuff. We can keep the children here with us and any others like us who want to be real people."

"Good idea," Rhianna declared. "That could work. We could get everyone out of the wards, sort them all out, and give them a safe place to live for now. Probably have to hire a cook or two. Oops. We would have to get them some computers so they could keep on playing their silly video games."

"Okay. The first thing is for me to hack in there and get a listing of everyone still on our Ward and then find the other wards and who is on them," Felix suggested.

R³ declared, "Cool. We girls will see about getting the other places fixed up to hold those who still want to be ODs."

A couple days later, Felix had all the information on their Chicago center. There were two other wards, 5 and 6. Ward 5 held the older adults, while Ward 6 held the younger children. He found adult versions for the Kingmann, Goode, and Winslow families, that is, six more adults, each of which was at least twenty-one or more years old. Further, he found eight-year-old versions of Todd, Trevor, and Rhianna there as well. Curiously, the Winslow family had no sons, only Rhianna. Even more interesting, Felix discovered the home cities of these families. The Kingmann family lived near Detroit; the Goode family lived near St. Louis; the Winslow family lived near Kansas City, Missouri.

Additionally, he discovered six other "families" present as well, whose residences were around the central mid-west area. Evidently, this Chicago center served as the hub for this geographical area. Before they went any further, R3 suggested he try to find the locations or names of the other places where the ODs were being kept. Her reasoning was that if they struck the Chicago facility, they might lock down their computer systems so he couldn't get in again. Dutifully, Felix continued his sleuthing and discovered nine other centers, scattered around the world. Each contained no more than a dozen separate "families." There was one in LA, New York, and Florida. The other six were overseas, specifically in Paris, Mumbai, Peking, Berlin, Taiwan, and Moscow.

R3 realized they couldn't do anything for the ones overseas, primarily because of the language barrier. Armed with this data, which Felix sent off to Captain Lech for Chan-Petra, the Circle of Six began working out their Rescue Mission Plan, the RMP, as they referred to it. R3 decided getting the children out of there was top priority, and Felix came up with a workable plan, based on their own escape.

On November 10, they put his plan into action. They parked their EMAC close to the fire tunnel chute exit doors. Trevor used stun guns on the lone guard patrolling the exterior of the complex. Felix hacked into Ward 6's control center and created a fake fire drill. All the children were to be sent down the tunnel chute for a practice emergency test. The Pytalon drugged staff were very willing to follow the orders being displayed on their monitors.

Soon, the seven, eight, and nine-year-olds came sliding down the chutes. Each was excited and wanted to do that again. This was the most fun they'd ever had. R3, Rhianna, Mary Jane, and Todd were there to help them out of the fire escape and into the EMAC, telling them that next they were going to go for a fly around the city. Trevor, his stun gun in hand, kept guard, though no one was the wiser this evening. Within minutes, the dozen youngsters were safely onboard the EMAC. A minute later, Felix lifted off, but did do a fly over of Chicago, giving them their promised view of the Windy City. Then, they took them to their Raven Compound, where they were given new rooms, new clothes, and a new start on life. They were very happy to see little Roxanne, Mary Jane, Steve, Scott, and Roy. The teens happily chatted with these newcomers, making them more than welcome to live in this new, exciting, real home.

Unfortunately, the Circle of Six ran out of bright ideas to get the others out of the medical center. However, Felix continued to monitor any orders sending anyone from the wards to Cook County General. Early December, he discovered an order sending six members of the Johnson family. He alerted Captain Lech, who again intercepted the EMAC transport, rescuing six children and two teens. The others, he let continue on their way to donate their bodies.

Only much later did they learn that the Taylor family had launched an attack on the Johnson family, wiping them out, except for their daughter who had married into the Taylor family so that the Taylor family now inherited the Johnson family's estate. Word had already spread of the Raven-Waberly-Michaelson event. That gave other Cabal members ideas, some of whom executed them.

With their grand rescue scheme temporarily blunted and while waiting for fresh ideas, Felix continued messing around with the Medical Center's older records and came across the ODs that had given their arms to Beth, Tilly, Amanda, and Jessica. Of course, those young teens were now armless but alive. They'd come from New York, Florida, and LA. Checking further, he found young children clones of these four as well. He fired this information off to Lech as well, asking him to forward it on to Beth.

Chapter 8—Explanations But No Plan

"Good thing I taught you how to use your feet," the ever-bubbly Lisa teased the four. It was late November. The four had fully recovered from their recent surgeries.

"True. But Lisa dear, we can do lots more with these," Jessica teased her back, waving her stumps about. All five chuckled, as the professor walked in, sobering the women.

"Hate to break this up, but now that the doctor has released you, it's time we took a very, very close look at those three journals. I've gone over them, but I want you four to do it as well, and then we can compare notes. Honestly, prepare yourselves. Much we did not know, and frankly, I'm having nightmares over all this. Mind you, there are conflicting reports between the three journals, so who knows which one, if any, is an accurate representation of history."

Coming from the professor, Amanda felt very worried. He had been the one who always seemed to know what was and had been going on. To hear him talk like this more than worried her. What was in those journals anyway?

"Hey, at least we can carry them and even mostly page our way through them," Tilly noted. "See Lisa, stumps have some uses, though not a whole lot." Lisa managed to giggle again and left them.

Tilly read only a few pages before she gushed, "Amanda! We're going to have to rework every last one of the prediction formulas!"

"No kidding!" she exclaimed. "This is horrid."

"Makes sense," Beth grumbled.

"Crap! I can't easily take notes," Jessica complained. Juan quickly got their laptops up, positioning them at their feet. "Thanks, Juan. Have you seen these?" Juan nodded that he had, but his face grimaced. She knew it must only get worse.

Three days later, they and the professor met to discuss the contents of the journals. The four had their laptops up, their notes at the ready, while the professor handled page flipping when needed.

"Well, finally history makes sense," Amanda declared. "Hideous, but it makes sense."

"Bloody right it does," the professor agreed with her. "What I'd like us to do today is to create a readable summary of these journals so we can get it to all of our friends and allies around the world. The Truth shall set us free, or so I bloody well hope and pray."

"Let me take an initial stab at this," Tilly spoke up, "seeing how this affects my prediction formulas the most. Amanda, hop in if I miss anything. Keep me on the right track."

"I'll jot it all down," the professor said, relieving the incredibly slow typing of the four, who looked very relieved with his suggestion.

Tilly began, "It all begins nearly three centuries ago in the US, primarily. Back in the 1990's, ninety-nine of the world's wealthiest men and women decided they wanted to control the world. Why they did is currently unknown to us. There is some hint about their being terrified, but about what isn't clear just yet. These billionaires formed a secret society called the Cabal."

"At that time, the US had a huge middle class, men and women who were making hefty salaries and were living very well. The Cabal's first action was to pressure the giant corporations they owned into moving these middle class, prime jobs overseas. Instead of paying a computer programmer nearly $50 per hour in the US, they could pay an Indian or Chinese programmer $2 per hour. Within a decade, vast numbers of these prime jobs were lost."

"During this massive job exodus, they manipulated the financial housing market, allowing huge home loans, often worth more than the homes were valued, and to uncredit-worthy homeowners. The Big Financial Collapse followed, which required a gigantic government bailout to keep the markets afloat."

"In the 2010's, the US discovered the middle class was becoming extinct. The number of people in the unemployment or underemployment lines reached double digits. The sheer number of poorer folks who were on the then existing welfare rolls increased dramatically. One of those programs was called food stamps, though we don't precisely know what that was about, since you can't really eat stamps. At this time, the Cabal and their giant corporations funneled gigantic volumes of money into the election campaigns of the country's main rulers, the president, senators, and representatives. They succeeded in getting a great orator elected, but one who only followed their orders, since it was their money that got him elected, though he claimed otherwise."

"In his first term, he played the victim card well. The cost of health care had skyrocketed. Very large numbers of citizens couldn't afford basic care. A trip to the hospital emergency room for something as simple as a tetanus shot ended up with a bill over two thousand dollars, for example. Adding to the problem was the aging of the Baby Boomers. Apparently, after the end of World War II, there was a giant spike in the number of children born. In 2010, many of these were now sixty-five or older. The care for the aged was unbelievably expensive and threatened to wipe out health care entirely, overwhelming the assisted living centers. Hence, the president then got the Cabal's next step implemented, often called Obama-care, a supposedly Affordable Health Care Plan."

"The Cabal knew this plan was doomed to utter failure within just a few years, but that was their intention in the first place. With the almost total loss of the middle class, whose members now dropped down into the poorer lower class, they were now guaranteed proper health care, whether or not they could afford it. On paper, it looked as if everyone would be covered and get the health care they needed."

"The Cabal played to human emotions and reactions very well. Given the economic assistance just to stay alive, given free health care, these people, who now represented the vast majority of the US population, continued to demand more. Those who used to command larger salaries now found themselves working in the service arena for a small fraction of what they were earning. Thus, they too needed these government handouts."

"As the Cabal expected, the financial drain on the government soon became staggering, particularly so since the US and most other countries of the world had long ago gotten off the gold standard so their money now had no real value backing it. Those first eight years of that president saw the US rack up many trillions of dollars in debt, numbers beyond anyone's comprehension. Common sense says one should not spend more money than one makes or has, but apparently, those in power ignored this detail or didn't care. The record isn't clear why. Anyway, the healthcare drain pushed the country into a near runaway inflation, anticipated by the Cabal, who now stepped in with the next phase of their very long range plans."

"Here is where the Total Care Program got its start. You see, at that point, a handful of US citizens had billions of dollars, while the rest were in dire straits. The Total Care Program promised jobs for everyone and a new monetary system, the credits. It promised every participant they would have a job, receive enough credits to pay for their food, clothing, and shelter. Into the chaos of those times, the population jumped at this grand chance for survival. Who wouldn't? No matter what your Total Care job was, you were guaranteed food, clothing, and shelter."

"The Cabal had one small stipulation. Those accepting Total Care had to begin a regimen of anti-psychotic drugs, the predecessors to Pytalon. Within a few years, Pytalon was invented, turning normal people into almost zombies. At the same time, the PDH implanting

143

machines were invented. Here was an entirely new way to force a person to act and behave in very specific ways. Soon, implanting became a requirement, along with Pytalon. The population, long being supported by Total Care, went right along with the new orders. After all, the alternative was to starve to death. Few had other viable choices."

"By 2100, most of the US was completely on the Total Care program. Only the police, army, company leaders, and the official rulers were not implanted or on Pytalon. Around that point in time, Total Care moved into their next phase, the elimination of the police and army, replacing them with the AP-cops and the Feds. Mid-century, the official rulers were no longer needed, since Total Care, from the Cradle to the Grave, ran everything like a well-oiled machine. Crime had all but been eliminated, thanks to Pytalon and the implants. Since Total Care had spread to the other major countries of the world, there wasn't any need for armies or rulers."

"True, there were still what the Cabal calls 'hot spots' around the world, usually very remote areas, such as the nuclear wasteland of Iran, the jungles of Africa and South America. These were minor and posed no threat to the rest of the world. By today, 2272, the Cabal has pretty well gotten the entire world implanted and/or on Pytalon."

"True, they were aided by several engineering breakthroughs that reversed Global Warming, namely the EM motors and their use in the MET system, EMACs, and Air Liners, all of which wiped out the oil barons, since fossil fuels became antique relics. The elimination of Global Warming is an obvious great benefit to mankind everywhere, but that was brought about by two women inventors, not Total Care. However, please note those were invented and broadly implemented in early 2100's. Since then, there has been virtually no change. The society engine under Total Care keeps running along with no significant changes. Men spend their lives polishing the same door knobs or opening the same doors every day."

"Now let's shift the story over to those ninety-nine behind these changes. What of these Cabal members? Great advances in medicine and surgical techniques were made in the late 2000's, including the breakthrough in India, which began large scale cloning of human beings, in secret of course. Who was cloned? These Cabal family members. Why? What isn't widely known about Total Care is their Case A classification, which only applies to the members of the Cabal families. They get the very best health care and procedures, which included organ transplants. With cloning coming to fruition in India, these Cabal families had themselves cloned. Later on in life or when they had an accident, they were given renewed life via organ donations from their clones, who were perfect matches. Thanks to the new medical machines, organ transplants became extremely easy and safe to do."

"The result was simple. These Cabal men used their clones to keep themselves alive. Literally, any organ could now be replaced, except for their brains. Hence, while ordinary men and women grew old and died, these men who were controlling the world became nearly immortal, as long as they received timely organ transplants."

"That changed when the Lin brothers developed the Transference Machine, which allowed any person to be transplanted into another physical body. Here in 2272, this is the usual means by which the Cabal men continue to live. When their bodies get too old, they steal another young body and make use of the Transference Machine, giving them twenty-one year old bodies once more. So yes, many of these top Cabal members are well over a hundred fifty years old, and perhaps some are even older. We just don't know all the facts yet. While pure speculation, it's possible some of today's Cabal members are the very same men who began their Grand Plan back in the 1990's!"

Tilly finished her summary. "Now on to the more important aspects for us. Armed with this information, we can make some reasonable assumptions about these ninety-nine men. We know all them are men. The journals state all women billionaires have been replaced. My key assumption is these men are terrified of normal people, fearing they're out to destroy them somehow. Given what these men have done to the world, today that is an accurate assessment! We're dealing with terrified men who will stop at absolutely nothing to continue to exert total control over the human race. They have no morals as such. Any action that will further their goals or keep human kind under their control is possible. A conscience is foreign to these men. Look, they had the entire Raven, Waberly, and Michaelson families murdered."

"Further, there isn't any reasoning with these men. If we approach them, they will see us as their vicious enemies, to be destroyed by any and all possible means. What we see as greatly beneficial, such as the desensitizing of implants, the detoxification and removal of Pytalon from bodies, letting high school students have a choice of jobs and not to be implanted—these men see such things as heinous attacks on themselves. Hence, they act accordingly, as witnessed by the murdering of Peter and Yan, and the mutilations of us four, several times now."

"What makes matters worse for us is that they control Total Care, which provides the credits that run the entire world, including the Feds. We have no idea of just who these Cabal members are, except those who have been killed recently. At this point, the Cabal knows about us, while we know nothing about them. Well, perhaps with a few exceptions, thanks to Chan-Petra, who has met a couple of them, perhaps, unless they sent lackeys to meet with her. The odds, gang, are stacked heavily against us! Unless anyone has any disagreements with these observations, Amanda and I will rework all our prediction formulas and see where we're at and what avenues we can potentially explore."

She ended. Silence. Beth sighed, "It's hopeless, isn't it? That's what you're saying?"

"Bloody well hope not or I'll fire her and Amanda," the professor replied. "Writer's cramps." He shook his hands wildly, bringing a flash of a smile to the other faces. "Look. This pretty well defines what the situation is and how it got that way. I point out we have come a very long way in the past year. A year ago we knew nothing about how to lessen the impact of an implant, how to get anyone safely off Pytalon, let alone get it out of their bodies. We've doubled the number of free and able people here in Phoenix. We have total control of the Feds and the Trikuza. Don't lose sight of what we have done and against steep odds, Beth. Not to mention we now know about the Cabal and what they have done to the entire world. We've taken the Transference Machines out of their hands as well. That alone dooms them, eventually."

"True. I'd forgotten about that. We have made progress. Well, the Weasel and Shifty Eyes have a whole lot of new work ahead of us, but we're only able to proceed at a snail's pace compared to before." Beth waved her stumps about as though no one realized this detail. Yes, she was annoyed, but still determined.

***

Early December, Lady Persephone arrived, reuniting with her friends she hadn't seen for several months, while she was in India. She planned to check up on them after they returned to the States to see if they were still adapting well to the loss of their arms. However, they had new arms transplanted and then had their lower arms removed almost as soon as they'd recovered. She was more than a little worried about them, as well as how Chan-Petra was doing, having lost her Peter body and her dear friend Yan.

After hearty welcomes, Tilly commented, "Well, My Lady, we now know these beasts have no conscience and will do absolutely anything to stop us."

"Well, you don't have to worry about the Lin brothers anymore. I've killed them, and blown up the two Transference Machines we sent to Mumbai, India," she explained again, hoping this reminder would comfort them a little.

Tilly grinned and teased, "Hope they have an Ace of

Spades on their bodies."

"Naturally," she cracked a broad smile. "Now how about filling me in on those three journals."

"First, look over the professor's copy of my summary," Tilly replied. "Then, you can read them yourself and correct any of my conclusions. This information changes nearly every damn formula Amanda and I've been using to predict events. We have to rework everything from the ground up."

Amanda broke in, "Don't forget the clever work Felix and R^3 have been doing in Chicago with the ODs. They keep on getting us interesting data."

She laughed, "They have a vested interest in it. Have they figured out who the organ donors were for your arm transplants? At the medical center in Mumbai, I only inspected the lower floors. I did come across hints the OD cloning was taking place on higher-level floors. On my way back, I had the idea of sneaking in there and inserting your DNA and requesting four clones be made, then absconding with them." All four looked up at her, curiously. "But then, the downside is they would be tiny babies. You'd have to wait at least ten years to get the transplants, unless you wanted very tiny lower arms and hands. Besides, we'd then be no better than the Cabal men." Faces fell.

"Not too workable," Beth pointed out. "Wait. I see what they're doing with the clones. With the adult members, they keep a younger version around. Their personal clones are in their early twenties. That way, if they are injured or need medical help, they have a perfect clone ready for them. On the other hand, with their children, they make a clone shortly after the birth of their real child. That way, as the child grows up, if troubles come, they have a perfect clone waiting in the wards. Later on, since that clone will soon also get into its twenties, they launch a new clone—the eight and nine year old ones. That way, when the real person ages enough, they dispense with the first OD, relying on the younger one. Clever scheme."

Tilly sighed, "Yes, always be one step ahead.

However, from all indications, during the last century, they have been relying more on the Transference Machine, but only using it on the Cabal family head, never on their children."

Amanda added her speculation to the mix. "Have any of you thought this all the way through? Look, say the male head is twenty-one and gets married. Soon, he will have a family, but what happens to the children and his wife when he, at age fifty or sixty, gets a new twenty year old body? I bet anything we'll see him getting rid of his current wife and children, taking a new wife and having more children. Wives and children are expendable commodities, kept around for fun and minor uses only. Beasts. We're dealing with real beasts."

Tilly added, "Odds are you're right. We'll probably find a drastic drop in the number of clones being made, say during the last century to century and a half, when the Transference Machine went into full production."

"Does that mean now that I've blown up their machines, they'll make a bigger push on their clone method, increasing their ODs?" Lady Persephone asked. She shuddered.

Jessica volunteered, "The wrong people are being made immortal; that's for sure."
***

December 8, a strange man knocked on the Raven's front door. The children playing inside games on this cold morning spotted the bright sunlight reflecting off the descending EMAC and sounded the warning.

R³ quickly took charge, "Get the kids into a back room. Keep them quiet. The rest of us, hide, but keep your guns ready. We aren't expecting anyone, so stay alert. Rachel Roxanne, you're up, since you're the only one who is supposed to be living here."

"I can do this, I think," she said hesitantly. Each afternoon, she had been taking the EMAC into the Chicago Rejuvenation Center, sweating out the Pytalon in their sauna. While her EE implant was stable, she was still a bit foggy in her thinking, but was getting better with each day in the sauna. The vitamins were also helping her.

She answered the door and saw a handsome man, perhaps in his middle twenties, immaculately dressed in an obviously expensive suit. Sunlight reflected off his polished shoes. He wasn't carrying a gun, not a visible one, and she relaxed a little. "Yes?"

"Mrs. Rachel Roxanne Raven Waberly?"

"Yes, can I help you?" she asked, thinking that was a very silly thing to say. She was terrified of strangers these days, paranoid perhaps. She'd seen too much evil.

He grinned, showing his very white, perfect teeth. "Allow me to introduce myself. I'm Benny Michaelson-Waberly, a very wealthy man. I live in a fabulous resort, where dancing and good times are had each and every day. I've heard about the awful tragedy you've endured. My condolences on your recent losses. I've come by to attempt to enliven your world, to show you a good time—that there can be fun and enjoyment in this very boring, mundane world. A beautiful EE woman such as yourself shouldn't be locked up, like a flower in some vase. Oh no. You should be out there dancing, having a fabulous time. I'll drop by on Friday, around six to pick you up and take you to one of the finest dances anywhere in the world. I promise you that you'll have the time of your life! I won't take no for an answer. Please, dress up. This is a formal dance, filled with fun and much enjoyment. I look forward to our dance-filled evening. Until Friday night, Rachel," he finished, bowed, turned on his heels, and walked back to his EMAC. *Oh she's absolutely ideal. Perfect.*

Poor Rachel. She was more than a little confused. *If only the Pytalon was totally out of my system, then I could—well I don't know what.*

She was brought out of her temporary confusion by R³, who said, "Who was that? What did he want? Is it safe for everyone to come out now?"

Rachel Roxanne repeated what he'd said, as best she could remember, something she still found slightly difficult, though vastly better than before she'd begun the sauna treatments and stopped taking the nasty pills.

"Oh this can't be good, Rachel," R[3] declared, putting her hands on her hips, thinking hard. "We don't know this man at all. Felix, see if you can find out anything about him. I don't think you should go with him."

"Dad kept me almost a prisoner in this house all these years. Honestly, a dance sounds wonderful, don't you think?" she tried to explain how excited she felt. Not even Scott had danced with her, but those days were still rather foggy in her mind. "Oh look at the time! I best hurry up. I don't want to be late for the sauna."

While Rachel was gone that afternoon, Felix was unable to find anything on this man. Frustrated, he sent an email to Beth, asking for her help and advice. When Rachel returned, her skin quite pinkish, she felt more alert.

"Look, if I go with him and if he is one of the bad men, I can bring back lots of useful information. I want to help too. I don't know anything about the OD program, so I can't really help you, but maybe this will give me an opportunity to find out more good stuff. Maybe he will know more about the OD things," Rachel insisted.

"But we don't know anything about this man," R[3] protested. Still, she saw Rachel desperately wanted to find a way to help too. Her intuition told her she shouldn't blunt Rachel's reach. She had Felix fire off another email to Beth, asking her what they should do.

Beth grimaced. She knew this wasn't a wise move on Rachel's part. Still, she also knew that insisting she not go would ruin her feeble grasp on her own self-respect, her own self-worth. It was human nature to want to help others. Rachel was now reaching out, offering such help as she could envision. While this was a bad idea, Beth knew it would be a severe blow to Rachel to deny her this opportunity. As a precaution, she chatted with Greg, Lisa's husband and inventor, about it.

Greg was insistent, and the two took a quick, high-speed trip from Phoenix to the Raven Compound. There, he injected one of his tiny locator chips into her neck before she headed off for her next sauna round. The two chatted briefly with R³ and Felix and then returned at top speed to Phoenix. Greg was being overly cautious, having seen more than enough brutality to last him a lifetime.

Friday afternoon, Rachel Roxanne spent hours getting herself dolled up and ready. She was very excited about going out and with the wonderful prospect of a formal dance. If nothing else, she was going to see more of the world, a bit of freedom. R³ and Mary Jane helped her get dressed and ready, though she insisted she wear a bit of makeup, certainly some cherry red lipstick to match her red satin gown.

"Thanks everyone! I feel like a million. I've never felt so excited before, but don't worry. I'll get all the information I can."

R³ advised, "Look, he could well be another one of those nasty Cabal members. So you be careful, Rachel. These are really bad men."

"Yes, but if he is one of them, I can find out where he lives and all that. After all, nobody knows any of the other living Cabal members yet. That's what Chan-Petra was saying, though she thinks some have visited her," Rachel Roxanne pointed out.

"Okay then. You know this could be very dangerous for you, but do your best. I know you look your best, so that's something," R³ replied, unable to think of anything else to suggest.

"Thanks. I do look my best. Even if I'm killed, you won't have to worry, because Chan-Petra made me a will. I'm leaving everything to you, because I know you and Felix will take care of all the children properly."

"Thanks, Rachel, but you had better not get killed," R³ declared. She hugged her identical sister. "I'll be worrying the whole time you're gone," she whispered in Rachel's ear.

"This is so cool—to have sisters, like we are," Rachel replied.

As the hour approached, Rachel waited alone in her front room, near the door, while everyone else hid from sight. The man was precisely on time. At six, he knocked on her door. "My, you are an amazing flower, Rachel. Allow me to pin this corsage on you." He presented her with a beautiful flower, pinning it onto her left chest. That it was December and all the local flowers had long faded away didn't quite register in her mind. This was an orchid. Later, she learned it came from his estate in southern Florida. He put his arm around her waist, leading her to his EMAC, and they were off.

Flying at top speed, they reached his "regal kingdom" around nine that evening. Rachel, however, didn't see it. He'd poured her a glass of berry juice shortly after taking off, having set the autopilot. Soon after that, Rachel drifted into unconsciousness. Upon arrival, he stopped at Miami County Hospital and carried her inside, where everything was arranged for her. Benny was quite thorough and efficient. Always keenly observant, at their first meeting, Benny saw she was off Pytalon and that her EE implant wasn't working well. Hence, she was first given another EE woman implant, but modified slightly. All the women in Benny's harem wore ballet boots. Hence, the line, "I must always wear my ballet boots" was added. The second added line went, "I am absolutely the perfect model of beauty, perfect in all ways."

From trial and error, Benny knew this last line was needed, because once the implant was finished and she was injected with a goodly dose of Pytalon, she was then taken up for minor surgery. Her lower arms were removed at her elbows, just as all his harem women were. Benny knew with the modern surgery techniques, after the first full day in heavy bandages, she'd only need light bandages for the next week. Hence, he kept her unconscious for those twenty-four hours, until the doctor removed the heavy bandages.

"Yes, healed up nicely. Now we use the light ones. Remember not to let her get them wet for the next week," he advised Benny, but then he'd told him similar things many times, but he couldn't remember exactly how many. It didn't matter. "Sanity is doing a good job," he muttered, unaware that Benny heard him.

He set about removing the many tubes from the woman's body. She was still wearing the same fancy gown but her heels had been removed and new cherry red, patent leather, knee-high ballet boots put on her feet. Benny wheeled her out to his waiting EMAC, carried her onboard, and put her in the exact same seat she'd been in when she first went unconscious. He found it less upsetting to the women this way, for he had much experience with this.

He landed in his kingdom, his giant, ultimate mansion and retreat, far off the beaten path. Here palm trees surrounded the outer walls, ten feet high with razor wire atop them and security cameras covering the entire mile perimeter. Inside the marble columned and tiled floors of the multi-million dollar mansion, the dance and his ever-growing harem of perfect women awaited him. Now came the delicious part. Benny never ever tired of these next, few precious minutes. In fact, these minutes made life worth living for him. How long had he gone without such a moment? Far too long, perhaps a year now.

He felt a wonderful rush of ultimate power, ultimate control over this woman, who sat unconscious in the very seat she'd been sitting in when he picked her up. He waved his smelling salts beneath her nose, rousing her.

"What happened to me?" she muttered, raising her hands to her face.

They all had similar a reaction, at first. He'd seen this before, many times—the realization of no hands or lower arms. Delightful.

For a moment, she panicked, realizing she'd somehow lost her hands and much of her arms. Nice white bandages encircled her stumps at her elbows. However, her new EE implant also kicked in, her mind completely befuddled with the large dose of Pytalon.

"Oh! I'm perfect now. Oh, I'm absolutely the perfect

model of beauty, perfect in all ways." She noticed her ballet boots and added, "I must always wear my ballet boots." She tried to scream; she felt utterly freaked, but the Pytalon haze prevented those thoughts from being executed by her body. Instead, she began reciting the entire EE woman script. With a sadistic grin, Benny watched her confused reactions and her recitation of the script that he so carefully altered.

He noticed she repeated the two additional lines. Satisfied that all was correct, he said, "Indeed, my beautiful Rachel, you are a rare flower, just perfect in all ways. Now it is time for that formal dance I've promised you. Come; let us join the dance; shall we?"

"Oh yes, let's. I'm so perfect now, aren't I?" she exclaimed.

"Indeed, you're absolutely, stunningly perfect in all ways," he replied, punching in her implant solidly.

As she tried to stand in the ballet boots, she lost her balance, swinging her arms wildly. "Oh! I can't seem to stand properly." A crushed look replaced her gorgeous smile.

"Allow me. You're so perfect like this." He put a steadying arm around her and helped her out of the vehicle. He knew the other women had little difficulty walking on his marble tiled floors, but he also sensed just how utterly helpless Rachel felt deep down beneath the implant and drug. He reveled in that sense, for he now had the ultimate control over her, just as he had with his harem.

He thoroughly enjoyed her unsure wobbling, as she tried to walk elegantly in the extreme heels, failing miserably, all the while attempting to flirt with him, begging for pleasuring, and insisting she was indeed the perfect woman for him. Benny was extremely pleased, leading her into his master living room, filled with every luxury that he could find worldwide.

Sitting on couches and awaiting his arrival was the rest of his harem women-wives, all dozen of them. All were dolled up and all looked the same as Rachel, missing their forearms and wearing the ballet boots. Various colors of hair, satin gowns, and ballet boots greeted his eyes, as he took in his world of perfect women, every one under his complete and total control. Such a feeling, he could not get enough of.

"Everyone, this is our new perfect woman. Meet Rachel. She's come for our formal dance and a fun time. Doesn't she look just perfect, my dears? Come on; get up and welcome her. Make her feel at home, while I start the music."

Awkwardly, the dozen women got to their feet. Each was a perfect EE woman to begin with, long, lush hair, massive bosoms, thick lips. His servant staff had their makeup done just right, he noted. Leaving Rachel standing alone for the first time, wobbling wildly, but trying to look regal, elegant, and perfect, as her bandaged stumps moved about in a nearly useless attempt to help her keep her balance, he turned on the music system. Music had all but died out centuries ago. The few selections he had were all that anyone could scrounge up, but they made for nice dance music.

He watched as the dozen women, now quite accustomed to walking on their toes, moved slowly up to Rachel. "Oh, you do look so perfect, just as we are all just perfect," one blonde woman complimented Rachel, moving close to give her a fleeting hug with her stumps.

As the waltz began playing, Rachel grinned. Only once before had she ever heard music. In the back depths of her mind, she truly wanted to dance, but only confusions were reflected in her physical body. Benny came up to her and put his arms around her, forcing her to take a step or fall down.

"I don't know how to dance," she finally got her body to speak.

"You're doing beautiful, my gorgeous flower," he whispered in her ear, relishing how helpless she was feeling right now. He could sense it coming from her, somehow.

Oh how he reveled in this sensation. *This must be how a god feels.*

Rachel's feet cramped in intense pain, but he kept on making her move in time to the music. "You must continue to be perfect in all ways. Ignore the pain. It's just pain," he whispered. "You dance divinely."

"Oh, I do? That is good then, because I must be perfect in all ways," she found herself replying, most unwillingly. She had no idea her feet were being crushed and brutalized, or that she should have long since taken the boots off.

Finally, he stopped. The waltzes had been repeated ten times and had become boring to him. "It is time for your medication, Rachel. Please stand here while I prepare them for you. My wonderful ladies, watch over our new perfect woman, please."

A lovely brunette complained in a teasing manner, "But Benny, we're all so desperate for pleasure. How much longer must we wait like this? You're tormenting us. Come on; we must pleasure you now."

"Soon, my beauties, soon." He left the room and found the pill bottles. He took out a heavy-duty painkiller and the daily dose of Pytalon. He poured a glass of water and brought them to Rachel. After seeing that she took them, he said, "Okay, my darlings, my perfect women, it's finally time for your pleasuring. Lead the beautiful Rachel to our bedroom."

The dozen women gushed various complimentary words and rather pushed Rachel out of the room and down a long hallway. At least one woman pointed out the bathroom as they passed by, and Rachel desperately tried to remember where it was located.

The bedroom was huge and held a dozen satin-sheeted beds. Here a few dazed servant women undressed the women, leaving their garter belts, hose and boots on them, but nothing else. A brunette pushed Rachel hard, and she fell onto one of the beds, unable to keep her balance. The brunette knelt down along with a redhead and began pleasuring Rachel, who moaned and fell into a deep, satisfied sleep.

The next day, the servant women handled their morning needs, dressed them, and then led them to the kitchen where they then fed the thirteen women. After that, Benny ordered them to go for a walk around the mansion. He then fired off an email to his father, Ben, telling him the mission had been entirely successful.

Ben Michealson-Waberly had long known about Benny's plan to add Rachel to his harem. He'd suggested it weeks before. Ben knew all about his son's perverted ways. It was the price he had to pay. Over a hundred years ago, he saw an opportunity to gain another ten billion net worth to his fortune. If he acquired that, he would displace a member of the Camarilla, taking his place as one of the nine in control of the whole Cabal. That had been his single-minded goal for almost a half century.

An old Cabal member was in dire need of a new, youthful body, but Ben also knew of the man's desires, thanks to spies in his household. Ben made him an offer. "Take my son Benny's body. I'll give you my Florida mansion and unlimited funds, where you can do whatever you desire."

The Cabal man signed over his fortune to Ben, stipulating Ben would forfeit the fortune should he, Ben, make any attempts on his, Benny's, life. This way, Ben could not and dare not touch Benny, while Benny had free reign to do whatever pleased him. This was Benny's third new body now.

Ben looked on Benny's ways with his harem women as disgusting, but valuable, in that the women were completely under the man's control in all ways, just as it should be. Still, he wanted to get rid of this thorn in his side, who spent lavishly while giving nothing back to him.

At the emergency Camarilla meetings, Ben was fully aware things were rapidly falling apart. That terrified him immensely, giving him sleepless nights ever since the last emergency meeting. Then came the terrifying news from Al

Rumani. Not only had the two new Transference Machines been blown up, but also the Lin brothers had been assassinated. Yes, the Camarilla knew it had been an assassination. There were the undeniable Ace of Spades cards stuck in their heads: Persephone, the Assassin! This giant loss truly shocked and terrified Ben. No longer could they easily obtain a new youthful body when needed. While he left that detail up to Al, he began to speculate.

He knew this Lady Persephone Briton of London was somehow mixed up in this incredible Feds mess. However, no one knew precisely how. Yet, this recent assassination by Persephone, the Assassin, got him thinking. Were these two women one in the same?

Then, it struck him. They'd kidnaped the Lin brothers from their mostly unknown enemies. Not long after that, Persephone, the Assassin struck back. Would she do that again? A plan slowly formed in his devious mind. If it worked, he could get rid of Benny and his harem once and for all. True, periodically, Benny dumped all his harem women, beginning all over again. As he frequently said, "They are getting too old and had to go." Currently, Benny was working on his fourth set of harem women. At least, it didn't cost much to make one of his harem women, Ben mused.

Still, if this plan worked, he would be rid of Benny forever, and he might well capture Persephone, the Assassin, as well. For a time, he mused about what should be done with this assassin. Then it struck him—Benny's harem women—perfect end result for this Persephone, and even better luck if she was also that Lady Briton person.

With his plan solidified, he sent a lengthy email to Benny, telling him about the incredible beauty that was Rachel, that she was eighteen and widowed after being married only a few days, a prime harem woman. He spiced it up some, enticing Benny to strike.

Once Benny decided to add Rachel to his harem, Ben set the rest of his plan into motion. If no one came to rescue this Rachel woman, nothing lost. At least her huge fortune wouldn't fall into another Cabal family, but would join with his fortunes, perhaps even raising his position within the Camarilla. And yet if the assassin did show up, eliminating Benny for him, his people would be there to strike from behind.

He researched all the reports of her assassinations, trying to work out how best to take her when she didn't expect it. She was deadly, no doubt about that. Plus, she'd probably have many others with her. One thing he was certain about: he couldn't hold on to her, as Benny did with his harem women. That was just asking for trouble. No, it would have to be a quick snatch and grab, do the deed, and release her. How much time was needed?

After consulting his favorite psych man, he knew the implant would take thirty minutes. A check with his doctor yielded an hour for the operation, but if everything was prepared in advance, it could be done in a half hour, especially if no attention was given to the patient's care after the medical machine finished up and the bandages applied. Could the two operations be done simultaneously? After consulting both men, yes they could. Ah, the time was down to a half hour now. Allowing for a five minute flight from Benny's to the facility in Miami and five minutes back, that came to a total of forty minutes that she would be missing, hardly time for anyone to react, at least he hoped so.

Still Ben worried. Forty minutes was a long time, considering the vicious criminals he was dealing with. Could it possibly be shortened any? He paid the doctor another visit. "Look, time is critical here. Can the operation be done any faster than thirty minutes?" The doctor hemmed and hawed, but agreed to do everything possible to speed it up. If they eliminated part of the healing cycle, the time could be shortened, but her recovery would take far longer and be more painful.

"Plan on that," Ben ordered. He cared nothing for her pain or how long it took for her to recover, only that she'd never again be a bother to any of them. Besides, she might later be useful to them, especially if she could be used to bargain for more Transference Machines. If he could pull that one off, the others in the Camarilla would owe him big time.

Ben knew the total layout of the mansion. It had been one of his residences in the distant past. He called in his best men, outlining precisely what must be done. First, when they detected the attack, text him. He'd alert the psych man and the doctor, who would drop everything and get ready for these fast operations. Second, they were to bide their time until they got a clear shot at her with the dart gun. Yes, they were to use the super-fast knock out drug on the tiny darts. Third, they were to remove her body as fast as possible, putting her into the EMAC, which they had concealed nearby, where Benny wouldn't see it, and make for the Miami facility at top speed. Once the operation was finished, they were to return her to the scene. Ideally, no one would miss her in the heat of the battle. With so many harem women to handle afterwards, with luck, she'd not be missed. By the time they searched the expansive grounds for her, they'd find her where they dumped her body.

Upon further reflection, Ben felt he should leave specific instructions on her body. He didn't want her to die. That would defeat his ultimate plans. She had to be alive. Carefully following the doctor's orders, he wrote out a lengthy care and handling document and gave it to his men. "Make sure she has this on her body when you drop her off. Under no circumstances is she to be killed. If she dies, then I'll see that you die as well. Am I clear?"
***

R3 grew worried when Rachel didn't return Friday night. When she hadn't come back by Saturday night, she had Felix text Beth, fearing the worst had happened to her sister.

"Crap. Just got a text from Felix. It seems our fears might have been well founded. They've not heard from her in over a day," Beth barked.

"That's not a good sign," Tilly replied. "Come on. Let's see Greg and have him locate where she's at." The two headed off to find him.

"What's she doing in Florida?" Tilly griped. "That's a hell of a long way from Chicago. She has to be in serious trouble. I best alert everyone."

An hour later, Chan-Petra decided, "Look, we can't take any chances. She might be in very serious trouble. We haven't any choice but to send someone down there, see what's going on, and extract her if we can."

"I agree. They don't know me," Lady Persephone spoke up. "I can lead the raiding party."

"Let's use the Trikuza again," Chan-Petra insisted. "That way, the Feds won't be involved. So it looks as if this Benny fellow may be another one of our Cabal members?"

"It's beginning to look that way," Tilly answered. "Look, Rachel is worth billions now. I bet many of the Cabal men would like to get their hands on her fortune. Greedy bastards," she added disgustedly.

"Shouldn't one of us go with you? You've never met Rachel," Beth asked. "It's kind of my responsibility, since I gave my okay for her to do this, even though I had my doubts."

"Hey dress for battle, but stay in the EMAC until it's safe. We can't afford to have anything else happen to our Weasel," Lady Persephone replied with a wry smile.

"Well, we can't afford to have anything happen to you either," Beth countered. "Still, once it's over, I aim to search the place for clues."

It took them another day to arrange to meet with a dozen Trikuza men in Chicago. Late the fifth day, Lady Persephone set her EMAC down just outside the walls of his compound. It was just after dark, and the thirteen fanned out to reconnoiter the place. Going over the walls would be problematical. The barbed wire and cameras would alert the enemy at once. Instead, she opted for a bolder plan: sit the EMAC down on the ground inside his compound. However, first she had to know Rachel was here and needed rescuing.

Greg handled the first one. He reactivated the chip he put in her neck and got a GPS reading, then turned it off to save on its battery life. He brought up a detailed map and confirmed she was inside this marble mansion. With Beth's assistance, they hacked into the IR surveillance spy cameras. Within an hour, they had zoomed in on the mansion. The humans appeared as reddish images on the screen. Once more, Beth had to use her feet to control the display, secretly wishing Lady Persephone would step in and do it for her. She was so pathetically slow using her feet, but she didn't make the offer.

As she worked the controls with her toes, she suddenly realized that originally as Ben, he'd wanted to play this game of hack the universe and fight the bad guys. Back then, he'd been insulated, protected by the cover of anonymity, and hiding in his secret underground safe house. The reality of "fighting the bad guys" had become a serious threat to his body's well-being. After all the abductions, mutilations, and humiliations he'd endured, including the forced sexual change and now the deliberate loss of her lower arms and hands at the whims of these bad guys, she found herself desperately not wanting to play this game of hack the universe and fight the bad guys. That reversal of her desires, her original game, was causing her intense frustrations.

Beth mused. *Well, I wanted to play that game, but now I don't want to. I wonder if Ben had a change of mind just as he drove that Air Liner into the Pytalon company skyscraper. He was going to stop the production of Pytalon in Chicago, but at the last minute before he smashed it into the building, I wonder if he had a change of mind. Well, maybe not, since he ran it on remote control. Still, this is goofy. I'm making the bad guys responsible for my loss of hands, and for the second time. It wouldn't have happened if I weren't going after them; so really, I'm responsible for my own loss of arms and hands. It was just a part of this deadly game.*

Well, hell, I like this game. You can't stop Weasel. When I get back, I'm going to voice-activate everything.

"Ah, I have them, Lady Persephone," Beth spoke up. The IR scanner zeroed in on what Beth wanted. "I spot a dozen guards roaming about the complex. Five outside. I have what looks like a bunkhouse with another dozen sleeping, two to a room, nice and orderly. That far building to the right of the main marble building."

Beth went on, "Okay, inside, I've got five others in a back room. Looks as if they're in bed too. Ah, there's one person prone in a central room, next to a larger room with lots of beds. I count thirteen sleeping there. Wait a second; something's not right with their IR images. What were the precise coordinates Greg sent for Rachel's position?" Lady Persephone read it back from her cell phone.

"Bingo. Got her located now on the scanner. She's with this group of thirteen. Here, have a look at their IR forms. Compare them to that lone one probably in the next room," she asked.

Lady Persephone looked over her shoulder. "Kind of looks as if their arms are shortened or something."

"Like mine, perhaps," Beth speculated.

"Okay then, the raid is on. Everyone, check your comms. Beth, check yours too. You're our eyes. We want to go in as quickly and silently as possible. Avoid gunfire if we can," Lady Persephone ordered. She then took over the controls of her EMAC, gently setting it down in an open area close to the other EMAC, presumably belonging to Benny. The five outside guards came running towards the ship from various locations around the giant estate and buildings. In the process, they must have alerted those who were sleeping. Beth saw movement among the dozen sleeping men and alerted her group.

The instant the doors opened, the battle was on. The dozen Trikuza swarmed out of the EMAC, followed by Persephone, the Assassin. All were dressed in black, wore night vision goggles, and were heavily armed with the tools of their trade. A few gunshots flew by from the five guards who had reacted first; their guns had silencers on them. Beth heard soft popping sounds and the occasional ding of a ricocheting slug off the EMAC. More importantly, she kept her eyes glued to the IR scanner, alerting her forces to the rapid movements of the enemy.

Suddenly, Beth saw another dozen images coming from some distance away. They were outside the complex walls! Where did they come from? Who were these men? She alerted the group and kept close tabs on them. What were they doing? As she observed the small red images, they were scaling the walls! She couldn't see they had come prepared and had a bridge device that flopped up and over the walls in two locations. She could see the red images scrambling up and down over the walls in those two locations. She relayed this to her group.

There were now so many red images on her scanner that Beth couldn't tell who was who any longer, frustrating her enormously. Even the dozen guards were now engaging them, having scrambled out of their beds. She focused on what must be Benny, who was still in his bedroom, though he was up and moving about, presumably securing his room. Then, she saw the dozen newcomers backing up. No, only nine of them. Up and over the wall. Weird, she thought. She wanted to follow them, but the action just inside the marble mansion forced her attention there.

"Yes, the room to your left. Benny must be in there," she directed two of the Trikuza men. "On down, take the next room on your left. The women are in there, we think," she advised another Trikuza man.

She saw the red form of Benny dropping into a peculiar shape; a moment later, a Trikuza man reported, "Benny down." That was followed quickly by another's report, "Found the women. Positive ID on Rachel. My god! What has he done to all these women?" Beth's heart sank. Another reported, "Found the service personnel. Zombie women."

"What's the women's status? How bad are they? Can we get them out to the EMAC?" Beth asked.

165

"They are like you, missing their lower arms. Wearing the exotic toe boots. Naked. All are implanted and on Pytalon. Massive confusion," the man reported.

"Okay. Wake the servants and have them get the women dressed," Beth ordered. "That will calm them down some. Search the place. We need his computer installation found and retrieved. I'll join you now." Seeing no signs of the nine who retreated back over the wall, she rushed down the ramp, across the lawn, noticing dead guards here and there, and headed on into the fancy mansion, marveling at how exotic and expensive this place actually was.

"But I'm perfect now. I must look my best. Please hurry up and get me dressed and my hair brushed out," Rachel Roxanne protested to one of the Trikuza men guarding the group of thirteen women, while four Pytalon drugged women mechanically went about getting them dressed properly. Beth walked in and cursed viciously. Since there wasn't anything she could do here, she backed out and joined the two men who were searching Benny's room.

"Boss. He was working on his laptop. It's still running. What do you want to do? He's got other things in here, but we're boxing them up now," one explained.

Beth sat down at Benny's desk and looked over his laptop. She simply couldn't resist and began exploring it. Before long, she was into his bank account! *Stupid man, leaving his computer running when he's being attacked. My god! Billions of credits! Well, that's going away right now!* Quickly, she entered a simple bank account transfer, leaving one credit in his account before turning the computer off and having it packed up too. *Time enough to explore its contents later on.* Already, some of the women were being moved into the spacious living room.

As she joined the confused scene, she saw the women trying to seduce the Trikuza men! More chaos, but Beth and the others quickly realized that under the circumstances, these women were just acting out their implanted behavior patterns. Rachel Roxanne finally came out into the living room, joining the others. Right away, Beth saw that the other dozen women were very adept at walking in these boots, while Rachel wobbled about wildly, annoyed at her pitiful appearance. That meant the others had been wearing them for a long time, and she suspected their feet were badly damaged, grim.

Meanwhile, a few of the men gathered up the guns from the eliminated guards and searched them. That's when one noticed a difference between some of the bodies. A few wore entirely black outfits, similar to those of the Trikuza men, quite unlike the guards who wore normal clothing, except for those who had been roused from sleep. The conclusion reached was that these were the unknown men who had come at them from behind. These dead men were very carefully searched. Most carried a small dart guns!

Finally, Persephone was missed. Several Trikuza tried to contact her to come and check these unusual men out. "Where's Persephone?" became the cry echoing around the complex. At once, Beth raced from room to room looking for her, while several others dashed about the grounds, double-checking the fallen. Beth had a sinking feeling; her stomach knotted.

One by one, the Trikuza reported in—no sign of Persephone anywhere. That's when they reported the discovery of the dart guns to Beth, the second in command.

"Start getting the women onboard the EMAC now. I'm going to call Greg and get a fix on her location!" Beth ordered, her heart sinking. Lady Persephone was taken on her watch!

Fumbling with her cell, she finally punched the speed dial button with her nose. "Greg. Persephone is missing. I need her location now!" She fought back from tearing up while she waited, fearing the worst.

Minutes seemed like eternity to Beth as she sat there waiting to hear back. "She's in transit. Moving. Close to you, getting closer. Probably in an EMAC," Greg spoke up. Even his voice sounded quite shook up, trembling a little.

"What's going on? The professor wants to know."

"Don't know. She's missing. Wait! I see an EMAC descending now! Call you back! Everyone, emergency. EMAC is landing beside ours! Battle stations." She wondered if that was the right word, the right order. Slowly, the EMAC descended, coming to rest upon the lawn some fifty feet from hers. A Trikuza forced her back inside out of the line of fire, while ten of them took up a defensive position, expecting the worst, but ready to defend with their lives.

When the door opened, a white flag fluttered before a black-dressed man appeared holding it. Slowly, he stepped out onto the ground, followed by two men carrying a half-naked female body, her arms heavily bandaged at her elbows. "Persephone!" Beth gasped. The men laid her on the ground, dropped a paper on her chest, and rushed back inside the EMAC, which took off rapidly.

Beth hadn't ordered the men to attack. Instead, several rushed to Persephone. They carried their boss into the EMAC and laid her in the back on the floor, covering her with a blanket. One brought the paper to Beth, but laid it on a nearby chair.

"Boss, it appears to be medical instructions. She's unconscious," he explained.

"Okay. Get the women onboard. Load up the stuff and let's get out of here fast," Beth ordered, moving to the pilot's seat. Using her toes, she activated the menu and selected Phoenix, ready to hit the Go button with her nose when everyone was onboard.

Minutes flew by in a flurry of action, but Beth couldn't see well. Her eyes were drenched with tears. Lady Persephone had been brutally mutilated, just as the others had. She wore similar ballet boots, knee-high, but her now mammoth bosom was fully exposed. She had obviously been turned into an EE woman as well! Beth simply bawled, unable to contain her racing emotions. Someone pressed the Go button for her and made the call to Phoenix, reading off the medical instructions to those there.

"Damn! They hurried up the operation, Beth," the professor reported to her.

Upon landing, men rushed Persephone to their hospital, helped the rescued victims off, and even carried the confiscated items into a storage facility. Jessica helped Beth off, joining Tilly and Amanda in the hospital waiting room, where Lisa, Greg, and several others were already waiting. Wisely, Jessica insisted Beth tell them what had happened. By the time she finished up, the professor came out with the doctor's report.

"Yes, a rush job. They shortchanged her on the healing time in the medical machines, so our doctors have put her back into it in hopes they can finish the process. We know she was turned into an EE woman, but her feet are fine. She's not even stood on them, since she's been unconscious the whole time. She's also been dosed with Pytalon, but that will likely be out of her system before they bring her around. They're planning to keep her under for several days at least, making sure the arms heal properly. There isn't anything more we can do for her just now, so let's get together and figure out what the bloody hell happened here and what you found at Benny's place."

The group headed to the main meeting room, where kindly staff had an early breakfast waiting for them. The sun was just rising, and it had been a very long night for all. Once more, Beth and one Trikuza member went over the entire action event.

Beth added, "Well, if Tilly can check for me, I believe I was able to transfer thirty billion credits into Rachel's account from Benny's. That should help some." That brought a round of hearty cheers and a brief smile from Beth.

With breakfast and the after-action reports done, one of the other doctors joined them, reporting on the thirteen women. "We looked at Rachel first. Her toes are broken and we've set them. She'll be in a cast for a week, but her feet should be okay after that. She's otherwise healthy. She should remain in bed for a week after that surgery though. The man must have been nuts to have gotten her up and about after only a day or so after the surgery."

He went on. "The other women's feet are pretty well smashed up, healed or fused might be a better statement, Beth. Much like yours were months ago. Not much hope there, unless we take them to the Wolf's fancy foot doctor over in Germany. All are heavily doped up and their EE implant is quite alive. Since there are so many of them to handle, could we possibly borrow Beth, Jessica, Amanda, and Tilly to help us with desensitizing their implants as soon as possible? Once that's done, we're going to put them into Lisa's sauna. After that, who knows?"

Tilly then took over the discussion. She was fighting mad. "Okay, we have our work cut out for us. When we aren't working on the victims, let's go over everything they brought back from this Benny fellow. We need clues, gang, clues to just who these Cabal men are. Their locations would be helpful too. Let's get cracking."

Back in Chicago, Felix and R³ felt bad that these beasts had also mutilated Lady Persephone. She stated, "We have to find a way to help all five of them, no six of them. After all, Felix, if we hadn't escaped, I'd be donating my arms and hands to Rachel Roxanne now. We have to find a way to help them. What about finding more ODs for them?"

"I agree. Let me do some digging. The four had it done at Cook County General. I'll start there. You see what you can find about where it could have been done down in Florida," Felix suggested.

Thus began several very long days for the two sleuths. Bit by bit, Felix began making some headway. He discovered the four women's DNA was on file at Cook County and at other Total Care locations. Further, he traced their initial full arm transplants and discovered some of the organs the four donors gave were still in "cold storage," preserved for future use within the next six months. Preservation techniques allowed organs to be kept alive artificially for that long and still be viable.

Curious about this aspect, he checked further, following the trail of the four specific DNA patterns on file. He discovered a startling fact. When they had their lower arms and hands removed, those appendages were also put into "cold storage" as well. The idea was for potential future usage by other needy recipients. They were being stored in their old Medical Center!

Armed with this insight and R³'s location where the surgery had been done on Rachel and Persephone, Felix discovered that their amputated appendages were also put into "cold storage!"

Given this data, R³ declared, "Felix, I wonder if we can get them re-attached somehow."

"I don't know, but I'm going to see if I can get the Miami center to send Rachel's arms up here to the Medical Center. That has to be the first step," Felix declared. "You find out if Phoenix has the capability of performing the transplants, dear."

A day later, Felix had confirmation from the automatic system that the lower arms and hands in question were on their way to Chicago! "Amazingly stupid system they have. Anyone could hack into it," he declared.

R³ added, "Phoenix can't do the operations, though. So now what?"

"Cook County General can. I wonder if I can get all the arms sent over to them?" he questioned. After a bit more hacking, he knew he could get them moved to Cook County. Armed with these results, he sent a lengthy email message to Beth.
***

Meanwhile back in Phoenix, Jessica knew the next day that something was very different about the implants of these thirteen cases and that another way of handling them was going to be needed. They all acted as though they were sex-starved, "perfect" EE women, demanding nearly constant attention. It drove everyone around them to exasperation. So while Beth and Jessica attempted to find the "scripts" the implanting psych had used, they decided they would try to get them off Pytalon.

"But we have to look our very best," Rachel insisted, trying to go into the sauna wearing her complete outfit, as did the twelve others.

Only with great difficulty was Lisa able to get them into the sauna while wearing only their boots, which they had no choice but to wear. Except for Rachel, these dozen had been on a very large dose of the drug for a very long time, years in some cases. Lisa found the process very slow going, filled with all manner of protests, complaints, and desires, with particularly strong insistence on being pleasured frequently, in spite of nearly passing out from heat exhaustion.

The second day, one of her helpers came up with a workable solution, putting the special panties on all thirteen. As long as they moved around, they sent themselves into sexual heaven for a time, but it made a mess of their sauna times. Each woman had to be watched like a hawk for heat exhaustion or stroke. Rachel finished up in around ten days, now only dramatizing her unusual EE woman's implant, laid in on top of her earlier one, making it more like a double whammy. The others took nearly three weeks to rid their bodies of the Pytalon toxins, but they too then constantly dramatized their implant.

Only at this point could the group begin to work Jessica's methods to desensitize the implants. Beth found the logged scripts that had been used. Armed with this data, they and Lisa's helpers set to work on the thirteen women.

Meantime, the doctors kept Lady Persephone under heavy sedation for a week, guaranteeing a full recovery. When they finally revived her, the bandages had already been removed, revealing tender, pinkish healing skin. The surgery was done well by the Medical Machine leaving very little physical scarring. Mentally, that was another story, just as everyone anticipated.

As Persephone gradually became fully aware, she screamed loudly, her alto voice jarring Jessica who was currently sitting beside her bed. As soon as Persephone ceased screaming, Jessica helped her into a sitting position on the bed, struggling a bit to get the pillow behind Persephone.

"What did they do to me?" she sobbed, fighting to regain control. As she did so, she also saw her bosom was now as monstrous as Jessica's and her three friends. Likewise, her hair was a bit thicker and had been grown an additional two feet so that her blonde wavy locks touched the small of her back, instead of her shoulders. Her hair was the least of her worries, rather her two stumps were her main concern. Then, helplessly, she began reciting the implanted script, shocking her further.

Jessica waited patiently until Persephone finished her automatic recitation. Then, she quietly said, "I want you to go back to the start of the attack to free Rachel and the others. Okay. Now go through what happened and tell me what you are seeing, what you smell, what you are sensing, as you go along."

"We landed. I'm racing out," she began, but quickly ended with, "I am dodging this man's gun hand, circle kicking it out of the way. I feel a pin prick in my neck. Blackness. I woke up here in this bed. That's all."

As Jessica expected, the vast majority of what happened to her was buried beneath the drugs and anesthetic used in the operation and implant session, as well as the sedatives administered while here in Phoenix. She said, "Okay, let's go over it again. Tell me about anything more that you can see or feel or smell." Thus began a very long day for Jessica.

Juan dropped by and fed Persephone her lunch, while Jessica managed to use her feet as usual, causing Persephone to break down in tears again, realizing she too was as crippled up as her friends were.

When Juan returned with their supper, both women were quite tired, but he could see a marked change in

Persephone already, even though Jessica wasn't done with her. "You look much brighter, My Lady. Your face looks vibrant again."

"That's about all that's vibrant. The rest of me isn't so good at all," she waved what was left of her arms a little. *I have to steel my will. I have to present a proper demeanor, if only for Jessica's sake.* She was able to fight having to recite the implant words, a tiny victory.

"Give yourself time to adapt," Juan encouraged her. "I think you've made great progress today. I do like your longer hair. Looks good on you."

She flushed slightly at the compliment. She found herself saying, "You are welcome to share my bed tonight, Juan." Her face flushed even more. *Now why did I say that? Oh, the implant.*

Juan grinned, "Oh, I'd like nothing more than to do just that, My Lady, but not when it could be that nasty implant talking. I know you need pleasuring and I'm willing to help you with that, if Jessica thinks that is what we should do. Wait on the other until you're fully recovered."

Damn him; he's bloody right, but I do so want him. "I think I have to have something done. I can't believe how powerful this implant thing actually is. I had no idea it was this bad."

Jessica chuckled. "That's an understatement. You should see how Rachel Roxanne and those thirteen other women are faring. God, it's really bad for them."

"We, we do have to find a way to end this whole PDH implant thing," Persephone whispered. "Jessica, I don't know how to thank you for finding ways to reduce their effects," she gushed. "Without your help, I'd be totally lost, just as the billions already are. I guess my cover is blown. Like this, I'm pretty much useless now."

"Oh I wouldn't be so hasty, My Lady," Juan countered. "Let's give it time."

Time was what she needed. For another two days, Jessica worked Persephone, going over and over the abduction, operations, and implanting, until she was sure she had wiped it all out. Beth provided her a copy of the psych man's script that he used on her. Armed with that, Jessica punched in each of the lines, until there were no further reactions on Persephone.

"Yes, I can still sense the implant is there, but it doesn't seem to have much of an impact on me now, Jessica. I can't possibly tell you how much I appreciate what you've done for me," she said sincerely. "And all the others too," she added. "I guess now I have to do like I kept working with you four to do. Take your time and use your feet and toes." *God, this is so impossible, but I simply bloody hell have to do it as I forced those four to face it. If I don't, I'm lost forever.*

"Well, the professor wants another conference when we can all get together," Jessica reminded her. "I'll have Juan work with you and your feet until supper. We're all meeting right after that."

Chapter 9—December's Discoveries

"Thank the gods Lady Persephone is back with us!" the professor began his evening meeting.

"Not so sure what bloody use I'm going to be now, professor," she retorted, still fighting how terrible her life had become.

"Well, we have to sort out what happened there at Benny's place," he went on. "First, Tilly wants the floor." He nodded to her.

"Okay. Amanda and I have been giving this whole thing a good study, applying our new formulas and simple deductions," Tilly began. "I think it's more than likely this whole thing with Rachel was carefully orchestrated by someone as yet unknown to us."

"Why do you say that?" asked the professor. "I mean Benny has obviously been doing this to young women for a bloody long time. Janine was there for six years."

"Oh, quite true. Benny's been at this women mutilation and harem thing a long time. No doubt of that. From the records that Beth and the Trikuza recovered, he's been at it over a century," Tilly went on, rather shocking everyone. "We think he's had four such harems over the years, dumping them all periodically, probably when he tires of them."

"Look, the other men who were totally concealed and who abducted Persephone—those men are what leads us to conclude it was orchestrated by another person, probably another Cabal member, whose motives are as yet unknown to us," Tilly explained. "Ninety percent certain of that."

"Why didn't they kill me?" Lady Persephone asked. "Did they know they had Persephone, the Assassin?"

"Ninety-five percent chance they knew they had Persephone, the Assassin," Tilly replied. "Based on the fact you personally intervened in Florida with the Lin brothers and the Transference Machines. I think you were set up. Look, they laid in wait, spotted you and you alone, drugged you, mutilated you, and returned you back. They were totally after you, probably in retaliation or revenge," Tilly pointed out.

"Well, I see what you mean," Lady Persephone replied, biting her now thick lips. "But why didn't they just kill me? They had every chance."

Amanda answered that one, "Based on our assessment and profile of these Cabal men, they have no conscience, no morals, no sense of shame, or even remorse. They think all society, all people, are totally against them, hostile to themselves. They deal wholly in the suppression of everyone, everywhere in the world. They surround themselves with messed up people, such as the five of us and the thirteen rescued women. Their wives are always EE women, and they implant their own children to get rid of them, except for the possibility of a single male heir, whose body they have taken over at least one time that we know of—Mr. Michaelson's journal says so. These people support only the most destructive actions to society. They are totally out to stop us, as we try to free everyone. They certainly are fighting us wholeheartedly. Even their Total Care Program shows us they have a twisted sense of ownership, since no one in this program now really owns anything outright. They control everything in society."

"More to answer your question," she went on, "in their twisted state, they attack wrong targets, take wrong actions. Yes, the correct action would have been to eliminate you, as Persephone, the Assassin, and Chan and us too. Instead, they mutilated your body, leaving you still a formidable threat, though they certainly don't think so— again a wrong action. You can use that to your advantage. Actually, I think this aspect of attacking the wrong targets with wrong actions is going to be our best weapon against them. Finally, our predictions suggest that if we can show them we're still trying to help people, it will drive them berserk. Tilly and I think that might be the proper course to follow. As they go berserk, they'll make numerous mistakes, allowing us more chances to stop them in their tracks."

"But why are these Cabal men like this?" Lady Persephone asked.

"Their basic motivation is they are intensely terrified by people," Tilly replied.

"I think I see. If they are terrified of someone, then that person will seem to them to be their bloody worst possible enemy—an enemy to be utterly destroyed," Lady Persephone suggested. "Still, I can't see why they didn't simply kill us. I certainly would have done that to my enemies."

"Precisely so," Tilly validated her, "but they're so terrified that they simply can't directly attack, but will have to use all manner of covert means to do their dirty work, such as sending in those flunky men to kidnap you. They couldn't possibly get up enough courage to attack you themselves, unlike us, who led the attack to free the women."

"Bottom line," the professor summarized, "is we keep on openly helping others. We'll get more of the detoxification centers opened up this coming year and get more implant desensitizing people trained, as well as trying to expand our high school program of not having everyone graduating being implanted and put on Pytalon. That should continue to scare the crap out of these Cabal men."

"Next, I have some key news uncovered by our organ donor friends in Chicago. It seems when the doctors amputated your lower arms, they preserved them, ready for other organ donor transplants. According to what Felix found out, they can be preserved for up to six months, before becoming unusable. In addition, he found out you four have yours being stored at the Chicago medical institute where they were being preserved for a time. Persephone and Rachel's are—or were rather—being stored in the Miami center. He's cleverly gotten them to ship both sets up to the Chicago facility."

"What? Are you saying our arms and hands still exist? That it's possible to get them somehow reattached?" asked Persephone, who suddenly had a ray of hope. Already, she was planning to use one of the Transference Machines on herself.

"According to Felix, all that's required is the medical operation. He's discovered quite a bit. These automatic Medical Machines are gigantic, occupying half of a ward's floor. It's unlikely we could get our hands on one of these beasts," the professor answered. "However, there is hope, if we can find some way to secretly get some doctor with access to them to do it for the six of you. We're working on that possibility."

The professor changed topics. "Now back to this Benny fellow. Thanks to Beth's fast action, we're in possession of his thirty billion credits. I think it wise to donate ten million each to the thirteen other victims. We have no way of getting their hands back. I've sent x-rays of their smashed, fused feet over to Wolf. We've not yet heard back from his podiatrist on whether their feet are salvageable. Our own doctors aren't holding out much hope since the damage that their feet suffered began years ago. Hence, the funds should help them get by. How are their therapy sessions going, Jessica?"

"Well," Jessica reported, "it's slow going. They're unable to contact their trauma time directly. Desensitizing has been put on hold until Lisa gets the Pytalon out of their bodies. They were so heavily doped and for so long that it's interfering with all else. She certainly has her feet full with those women. She hopes to have them done with the sauna treatments before the New Year. Hopefully in another week after that, we'll have their implants desensitized enough for them to get by. Honestly, professor, their lives are going to be miserable at best. With that much money, they can at least afford someone to care for their needs."

"My thoughts precisely. Another matter. Felix has discovered the locations of all the other organ donor facilities." He outlined where they were. "According to R³, the children are salvageable, but probably only a third of those in their late teens will be. The rest have no goals or purposes other than to donate their organs to their hosts. It's a grim situation. I can't imagine being raised from a baby with my only goal being to stay healthy so my organs can be harvested. Bloody hell!"

Tilly spoke up, "So she and Felix want to rescue those they can?"

"I think so, but the how is eluding those two at the moment. Oh, I got side tracked again. Have we learned anything else useful from this Benny fellow?" the professor inquired.

"Actually, I think so," Beth spoke up. From what we've studied of his stuff, Benny was mostly on his own, doing his own perverted harem thing. Yet, he was once one of the Cabal members. I think he has ties somehow to a Mr. Ben Michaelson-Waberly. If so, this other man has a high position in the Cabal. Location? Not sure, but from the account transfers, I think London is likely. Jessica and I have a new idea about how we might possibly track down these Cabal men, but it's a very long shot."

"Oh yeah? How?" asked a curious Tilly.

"We're launching a long running web search of ancient records, looking for lists of billionaires," Beth explained. "Of course, many could well be dead by now, but then maybe not, what with the ODs and the Transference Machine."

"Keep us posted, Beth, Jessica. Any other news?" the professor asked.

"Oh, Lady Persephone," Amanda spoke up, "this India connection has me intrigued. I did some checking. They're using the older implant models in the smaller towns in India, just as in China. From what I've dug up, there are quite a lot of accidental deaths during implanting there as well. Barbarians."

"Interesting," she replied. If only I wasn't helpless now. Damn, damn, damn.

"Okay then. Here are my proposals for the coming year," the professor continued with his meeting. "Since the Cabal no longer has the Transference Machines, let's focus on their OD program and see if we can knock it out too. Hit them where it surely hurts. That's target one. We need to fully investigate the Total Care program and get a handle on just what they are doing. After all, they hinted to Chan-Petra they could end all funding for the Feds. That would cripple our ways and means."

"What are we going to do about Chan-Petra?" Beth asked.

"It's too dangerous for her to go back to work just yet. Besides, she's looking after two babies now," the professor answered.

"Still, I know she wants to get back there," Amanda protested.

"Hey, it isn't safe for us to go back to Chicago either," Beth pointed out. "I think the smartest move would be for us to go to our place in East Peoria. I think there we could be safe enough."

"I'm still going to have to do my part too," Lady Persephone added.

"I agree with both of you," the professor sighed, wondering how he could handle their security.

Beth glanced at Juan and Persephone, and then said, "Look, we don't really need Juan with us now. It's pretty darn boring for him there. He could be far more helpful to Lady Persephone now, but we'll need someone to help us though."

"I know," the professor had a bright idea. "We've rescued another EE woman named Julie. She's only eighteen, but wants to help. She's gone ahead and had her breasts shrunken down to the size they were before she was implanted. She really wanted to become a chef before she was turned into an EE woman in Flagstaff. Working with you four would be a golden opportunity for her—give her back some of her self-respect."

"Fine with us," Tilly replied.

"Okay, then let's see about getting things rolling. I know Captain Lech has had all your things in your penthouse suite boxed up and stored in the basement of the Feds building. It'll be a simple matter to get them secretly shipped to East Peoria," the professor explained. "Juan, I'm releasing you from your protection duties of these four and assigning you to be Lady Persephone's full time bodyguard from now on."

Both he and Persephone grinned. "Aye professor," Juan teased him.

As the meeting broke up, Lady Persephone wanted a word with Jessica. When they were alone, she explained, "I'm immensely better, but I still get slight headaches if I don't get it, well you know what I mean, and if I wear pants, I also get a touch of one. Is this normal?"

"Yes, we four still do. That's why we often continue to dress like EE women. Keeps the low grade headaches away," Jessica answered her honestly. "The more time passes, the easier it gets though. Just give it time. I wonder how Julie is managing with her reduced breasts. I'll speak to her, but I bet she has low grade headaches all the time, since she can't dress as we do—lacking the giant curves," she teased.

When Juan joined Lady Persephone that evening to help her, he asked, "Okay, My Lady. Would you still like me to join you in bed?"

She flushed. "Yes! I really do love you. I've wanted to kiss you for some time, but well, I was embarrassed to try. Besides, you had to watch over those four who desperately needed your help. But really, Juan, I'm not much of a woman anymore. Look, my stumps are hardly longer than my boobs. I'm more helpless than those four who have picked up some skills from Lisa."

"You aren't your body, My Lady," he whispered back. That night, Lady Persephone had the best night's sleep since her abduction and with no trace of any headache, much to her relief.
***

R[3] wasn't idle either. While Felix continued his explorations, she continued to work out how they could rescue all the OD children from around the world, emboldened in her thinking, because Felix was able to get the Florida people to send the two pairs of lower arms up to Chicago. If the Medical Ward people were that easily manipulated and if they took their orders from Total Care higher ups, then could she somehow use that to get at the OD children? And what about the teens? From their Chicago experience, she suspected only a third of the teens would want to be "rescued." Still, they should have a chance at a real life.

Sipping a cup of tea while the kids ran about the house playing tag, Mary Jane assisting them, R[3] bounced some ideas off Rhianna. "You know, perhaps the way to approach the rescue of the children is financial."

"How's that?" Rhianna asked. "With these people, money is god."

"Right. Money is god. What if we convinced them the way to save money would be to house all the children in one facility, like Chicago? Put the teens in another facility. After all, we know they don't have many organ donations each year. We saw hardly any in our years in the Ward. Able was the first I can recall having actually seen," R[3] explained.

Rhianna smiled. "Now you're on to something. It would be more cost effective to house only children in one location. I can think of a zillion reasons why, such as maintaining only one set of baby care givers and not dozens of sets. Besides, with the Air Liners, they could transport the needed OD to the right facility where the transplant is needed in less than a day. Since there aren't many of those, the cost savings would be substantial. Come on; let's write up how this could be."

The two spent a couple of hours writing up a document outlining their ideas and just why it would be drastically more cost effective. Over supper, R[3] showed Felix their attempt and explained her reorganization ideas.

"Super idea, R³! If we can get the children moved here to Chicago, we can rescue all them. If the teens are in one facility, I think I have a way I can find those who want to be rescued—secretly mind you," he replied, growing animated.

The next day, he took R³'s document of cost-savings rationale and uploaded it to the computer of the head of Total Care Worldwide, putting the document on the man's desktop and labeling it "My Bright Idea for Saving a Fortune in Costs." Now they could only wait and hope the implanted-Pytalon drugged man would respond to it. If he didn't, then Felix intended to take it further, issuing a slew of fake orders to get it carried out. That was very risky, so he hoped this approach would pan out.

***

"Well, Juan, I knew life was going to be really hard for Beth and the others, when they were staying at my castle in London, but I had no idea just how awful and difficult it really was for those four," Lady Persephone admitted to Juan, while he was getting her up in the morning.

"Walk a mile in my shoes. Isn't that the old saying? Well, if anyone can rise above this, it's you, my incredible flower," Juan replied, brushing out her now much longer hair. "Still love your longer hair, though."

"Glad you do. I can't really manage it now myself. I can see having those four always working together allowed them to get by somewhat. I'm wholly dependent on you, Juan. God, I hate this feeling, this situation," she admitted to him. There wasn't any reason not to open up to him, not anymore, not since last night in bed.

"Quite true. Okay, what do you want to wear today?"

"I don't have a choice anymore, Juan. I have to wear an EE woman's outfit or deal with low-grade headaches. I need a clear head, so put the off-white dress and heels on me please. God, the heels are darn near impossible. I don't know how they manage."

"Give yourself time. Where are we off to today?"

Juan changed the subject, having finished dressing her and giving her a passionate kiss.

"India. I want to check on those accidental Indian deaths. I've an idea. We simply can't afford to lose one of us freedom fighters, which we almost have several times. Beth's discovery of being able to run two bodies at the same time is critical. Now that the Cabal has killed the Chinese bodies we were using, I'm checking into the possibility of everyone obtaining Indian bodies as their second body. Er, that is, we are checking on it. Running two bodies at the same time worked out well for Beth, Peter, and the others, especially when one set of their bodies were at my place in London and their Chinese ones were there in Chicago. I'm hoping to get that going again, a little safety precaution. Remember, the young men and women 'died' while undergoing the PDH implants, so we're merely salvaging their bodies."

"Ah, plus you're getting one extra body for yourself too, I take it?" he teased her.

"Absolutely, but Juan, I'll let you pick her body out. How's that?" she teased him back. "Crap. I guess you have to work my computer. I'm never going to get my toes to do anything. I can't use the stumps for much of anything. Damn those Cabal men anyway." Her frustrations grew.

Hours later, the pair arrived in Mumbai and browsed Total Care operations there. Looking over his shoulders at her monitor, she declared, "Well, we're in luck. The psychs are taking the teens when they turn eighteen or when the graduate, whichever comes first. All right. We need to locate six remote towns where they're still using the older implant machines, the Model I's, and pay them a visit. Around one in ten die during the implant process from these ancient machines. Then, we have to make a quick trip to London so we can get the stasis pods. We best land by my castle at night, because it's likely being watched, since they got to me. You're going to get a workout moving six of the survival modules, those stasis pods, into the EMAC."

It took Juan and Lady Persephone two days to obtain what they needed and to return to India. Another day was spent in visits to remote village psych men, giving each her card and making arrangements similar to those she'd made in China last year—to be notified of unexpected deaths during implants. Their timing was good. Near the end of December, a number of high school students graduated or turned eighteen and were forced into the Total Care program. As expected, ten percent perished during their implants. Thus, by the end of the year, all six stasis modules held recently deceased Indian EE women. The two felt somewhat like undertakers and joked about it. From the number of EE women they saw just from observing the streets of Mumbai, they realized in this country EE women were quite popular. Most of the upper caste women were EE women, interestingly enough.

Vaani, Aasha, Bahiya, Faizah, Mahala, and Sameera were their original first names. All looked remarkably similar, slightly darkish skin, oval faces, and rich, thick, black hair, reaching their knees, quite typical for this country. Juan chose Faizah for Persephone, since this body looked the strongest and fittest of the six. They headed back to Phoenix on the last day of the year with a present for many. Cleverly, Persephone already issued shipping orders for one of the Transference Machines, and it had already arrived there.

***

The last day of the year, Felix noticed that there were an alarming number of new OD transplant orders being issued, nearly all were being sent to local hospitals and not being done at the various OD medical centers. He spent hours exploring what was happening worldwide. Many existing OD men and women were being discarded and their organs being utilized for salvage operations at many local hospitals.

With so many transplant orders circulating, Felix had a bright idea and sent in an order to his old medical ward, following that up with six orders to Cook County

General hospital. Each order listed a fake return email address, all of which were routed to his own. No sense in getting the hopes of the six women up, he wisely thought, for they might not go along with his plan to have the hospital re-attach their lower arms and hands. What were six more operations out of nearly a hundred others?

January 1, Felix let out a cry of joy. "I did it, R3! I did it." She rushed to his side, looking at the monitor and grinned. There were the orders for the six to report to Cook County General to get their arms reattached.

"Way to go my hotshot!" she declared. "Best send Beth and the others the good news right away! I guess they can take care of the hospital reimbursement money."

During the first two weeks of January 2273, Cook County General received nine ODs, whose organs were being transplanted into dozens of recipients. Some of the donors were children, meaning some ordinary children were being given a precious gift from Total Care. Felix discovered that when an OD was scheduled for termination, Total Care tried to donate all his or her organs to needy recipients. In fact, four ODs were shipped to Cook County General from New York, since the donors had to be compatible with the intended recipients.

Thus, Felix cleverly slipped his six transplant requests in among the hundred plus operations that were being scheduled. The six were scheduled for six successive days, beginning January 12. Beth quickly transferred the sixty million credits needed to Cook County General, the funds coming from those "donated" by Benny.

Beth awoke from her surgery and found her lower arms were attached but that she had thick, huge bandages wrapped around them. Though her arms were immobile, she was told to continue to wiggle her fingers as much as she could. After a week the size of the bandages were reduced. The surgeon explained that mobility in her elbows may well be limited, but with stretching and use, she was expected to regain much of her flexibility, but she was under orders not to lift more than two pounds for the next two months. According to the surgeon, she could expect to recover between fifty and eighty percent of her previous functions of her lower arms and hands.

When queried, he explained that with the relatively small area of connection, this was about the best that could be hoped for. Right now, she had far less than fifty percent though, but at least her fingers mostly worked. One by one, the others were handled. However, Rachael Roxanne fared less well; the surgeon explained if she was lucky, she might regain fifty percent. Still, even that much pleased her, since she wouldn't be completely helpless, unlike the dismal fate the other thirteen harem wives faced. She shuddered even thinking about them.

Rachel had a lot of time to think about those thirteen women, and, when she finally was allowed to return to her mansion outside Chicago, she invited the thirteen women to come share her mansion. They could help watch the large number of children. These women felt wonderful after the detoxification and implant desensitizing actions were finished, even though nothing could be done for their feet, and they accept her offer. In Phoenix while being detoxified, they felt very useless and in the way of everyone. Besides, all thirteen really did want to have their own families, but now felt that was blunted, so being around and helping with children would be a substitute.

On the other hand, Rachel Roxane saw this as an opportunity for the many younger girls to have a way to help out, to contribute by helping these thirteen women with their many daily needs. She hoped it would work, though she too needed a good deal of assistance, because in all likelihood her lower arms and hands would never be the same.

Chapter 10—The 2273 Cabal Meeting

January 1, 2273, the combined Cabal met in a rustic castle in Luxemburg for their traditional New Year's Day meeting, which typically lasted several days, depending upon what needed to be handled. Their EE women wives and eligible daughters attended, spending their days showing off the latest in EE fashions and flirting with each other and all the men. The male heirs, eighteen and older, attended the opening session, but weren't allowed to attend any meetings beyond that. The initial session was mostly an introduction of new heirs and identification of the members. After that, the heirs roamed the castle, drank, played card games, flirted with the EE women, and such. A few men also brought along their EE women daughters, in hopes of marrying them off to some of the unmarried heirs. These young women did their very best to enthrall any of the young men, as dictated by their relatively recent implants.

Once the introduction session was over, this time lasting but twenty minutes, the real session began. Franco began the closed session. "As you can tell, our numbers are down considerably since last year. It began with the attacks of three greedy men. We now know that Randal Raven, Ace Waberly, and Alan Michaelson took out contracts on each other. By sheer accident, only Rachel Roxanne Raven Waberly survived. By our own laws, she inherited all three fortunes, worth around thirty billion." He allowed the gasps to run their course.

"Obviously, she wasn't invited to attend this meeting. So I encourage you to see if your sons can manage to reel in this really big fish." Several older men chuckled. Franco had to make this announcement. It was either that or lose forever the thirty billion net worth from the Cabal. He was half-inclined to do just that, but didn't dare do it on his own, fearing the other Cabal members would disapprove of throwing away that much net worth.

He then continued, "At this time, a number of other Cabal members have died and a number of you have already inherited their fortunes. Specifically, we are down another ten members. With the three that I mentioned, the full Cabal now numbers eighty-six, though if someone acquires Rachel Roxanne, then we might rise to eighty-seven, depending on the circumstances. We've lost the Ichan family, the Mars family, the Knight family, Mikhelson family, and the Melnichenko family." He rattled off five more. "As you may be aware, these were all lower echelon members, whose net worth was less than fifteen billion. Cleverly, all their assets have been assimilated into other Cabal members' portfolios, quite unlike that fiasco stateside around Chicago."

"I have dutifully logged the revised net worth of these members. However, these new amounts have not yet affected the Camarilla members—hence, no change in our ruling council. I've sent you all a new ranking list. So much for those formalities. Now to the true problems we face."

"Let me be up front right here at the start, gentlemen. We are facing the worst crisis in over a hundred fifty years! Our mighty efforts are crumbling left and right. Your Camarilla has been holding emergency meetings attempting to handle some of these situations as they arose late last year. Now it is time to spell out everything for you. Together, we must take effective actions before we lose the entire world. I call upon Dr. Al Rumani to begin relating the terrible news we face."

Al rose, cleared his throat emulating Franco. "Grim. That's what we're facing today. Earlier this past year, the Feds got under the control of one Peter Delius, who appointed himself Supreme Commander. He raided the Lin brothers in Peking, twice actually, and confiscated all their precious machines. Yes," he punched in, listening to the collective gasps of utter shock, "we've lost the Transference Machines."

"Worse, they used those very machines on the Lin brothers, placing them into armless and blind EE women's bodies! It took some doing, but your Camarilla discovered where they were being held prisoner, rescued them, and brought them to India, under my care in Mumbai. We approached this Feds leader to try to get our precious machines back. Peter and a Chinese woman, Chan-Petra, were sharing the leadership position. We killed Peter and threatened the EE woman, who then took over for Peter, if you can believe that—an EE woman leading the Feds!" He paused to allow the men to guffaw loudly.

"We then investigated further and discovered four of her close friends were involved in the kidnaping and theft. They were armless EE women. Lord knows how they managed to lose their arms. We used them to get to her. We offered them new pairs of arms in return for two Transference Machines and got them."

"What we didn't count upon was the appearance of Persephone, the Assassin!" Again, he paused for dramatic effect, for this "assassin" was world-famous. "Yes, somehow, she infiltrated my own medical facility, assassinated the two Lin brothers, who were in their new bodies, and she blew up the two Transference Machines!" More gasps and cries of dismay forced him to halt again.

"So we have lost two of those precious machines and the two men who invented them. Our only avenue is to obtain more machines from the Feds or from whomever the Feds gave the machines. Ben Michaelson-Waberly wants to add to this a bit." He sat down and Ben quickly rose.

"We've been doing a lot of digging and correlating of information. It is my belief that Lady Persephone Briton of London has these machines and that she may well be this most wanted criminal Persephone, the Assassin. I laid a trap for her, and I believe we did get her. If so, she's now an EE woman, heavily dosed on Pytalon, in ballet boots, and with her lower arms removed. She won't be a threat to us any longer. She's not been seen around London for quite some time, so we believe they are one and the same."

Someone shouted, "So can't we force her to give us back our critical machines?"

"We are proceeding along that route, once we know for sure that Lady Persephone has them. As of now, Chan-Petra is on maternity leave. We had her close friend, another Chinese woman who lived with her, killed, though we didn't harm her baby. Thus, this Chan-Petra has had the sternest of warnings. I don't believe she'll reappear in the Feds, but she can be forced to tell us who has our Transference Machines, if Lady Persephone isn't involved."

Franco turned the meeting over to the head of Total Care, Henry Koch. He discussed the alarming action taken by the Chicago Feds in not allowing the new high school graduates to be implanted and dosed on Pytalon. Again, gasps echoed. He explained that each of these graduates was rounded up and handled appropriately.

He went on, "In lieu of our massive loss of the Transference Machines, the OD program is once more extremely vital. However, one of my subordinates has come up with a cost saving new approach. We're going to group all children at one or two facilities, moving the teens and adults there to other facilities. However, some of the adult ODs for you men will still be housed in their current facilities so they are close to you, just in case you need them. The other adult ODs, such as those for your wives, sons, and daughters, will be housed in together in several facilities. By combining like-aged ODs into one center, we anticipate saving close to a half billion a year—all this without compromising your personal ODs. However, we will be increasing our cloning cycles."

"By that I mean we'll be requesting a new baby clone for every Cabal man here. Just as a safety precaution, mind you. What I need to know is whether you wish others in your families to have additional baby clones made. I know some of you are partial to your EE wives." None desired that extra cost for their wives, and Henry was quite pleased at how well this went over.

Next, Delius Pogs rose. He discussed the alarming news that someone had found ways to get people off even the heaviest doses of Pytalon, as well as somehow eradicate the effects of implants. That brought a very loud reaction, as he suspected it would, shaking the very foundation of their centuries of work. "No, at this time, we don't know who is behind this atrocity of enormous magnitude. However, we have some suspicions and will be exploring them in the near future."

"Take heart. We haven't been idle. As you may have heard, midsummer, we came up with a far stronger version of Pytalon, which we're calling Pytalon-Ex, for extra strong. Production has just begun using this new formulation. By the end of the first quarter, anyone taking Pytalon will be taking this new, improved formula. That should take care of these meddling people's attempts to get them off it."

"Further, we've also redesigned the PDH machines to deliver an even more unbreakable implant. We're going to begin replacing all the older models with this new version, just as fast as they can be manufactured. Of course, there's a downside to this vastly more powerful one. The casualty rates are as bad as the very first models invented; one in ten die from unknown causes during the implant. Still, the benefits far outweigh the few deaths. After all, with this new version, I defy anyone to disobey their implants, let alone undo them. It's really quite powerful indeed. So I think we have beaten the people who are trying to undo our many centuries of diligent work."

Ben Michaelson-Waberly decided to toss his opinion. "If I might make a suggestion for our troublesome EE women." Delius nodded, knowing what he was going to propose. "Since obviously some of the EE women are causing or have a hand in these monumental troubles, I would like to make some recommendations regarding our future EE women. All those who are found to be, shall we say, 'troublesome,' should be re-implanted a new way. My late son pioneered some of these suggestions, which were found to be most beneficial. He had *total* control over his

EE women at all times. Besides, with these new modifications, they'll need to hire personal assistants to assist them with everything, except satisfying our sexual needs." He passed out a brief document outlining the proposed changes, and they were accepted.

"But you are still going to try to find those who are undoing our work, right?" one member asked.

Franco answered, "Of course. They must be handled, via our new machines. Now then, there's more sad news. Jacques," he nodded to his fellow Camarilla member, whose fortune was in armaments.

Jacques talked only briefly. "Sad news. The entire MMS, the Marshals Militia and Security, has been wiped out by some surprise attack of great magnitude. Hundreds were murdered. The Feds were definitely not involved. I don't think they even knew about the MMS. We simply don't have any clues about who did this heinous act. I'll begin a new recruitment cycle, obtaining fresh high school graduates to form up a new militia, but it will take time to get them trained and up to speed." He failed to mention that he didn't know how they would be trained, since the existing MMS members were dead. He sat down, thankful that he had nothing else to have to report. The news had never been this bad that he could recall.

"So just who is behind all these horrible crimes?" another Cabal man asked. "Are we getting closer to identifying them? What is our Camarilla doing about it? This is a huge setback, in my opinion, a disaster of monumental proportions."

Regrettably, Franco rose to handle this one, seen as a direct attack on the Camarilla. "We have suspicions, but nothing concrete as yet. We know Chan-Petra was directly involved, but she is an EE woman, hardly capable of masterminding these monumental crimes. Her four EE women associates probably are also involved, but just how we don't know. Obviously, EE women can't be our main enemy in this. Whoever is behind it is probably just using these EE women. With the mysterious slaughter of the

MMS, we must be cautious. Whoever these men are, they are certainly well armed and deadly. I urge all to beef up your own security arrangements."

Someone called out, "Why not bring those five EE women in and get it out of them? There is always the Truth Drug-A. Then subject them to the new improved implant and EE woman's appearance."

"We could and have thought about that, but right now, the five seemed to have vanished without a trace. Chan-Petra is officially on maternity leave. Where? We don't know. We do know the Feds in Chicago went to the penthouse suite the four EE women associates were living in and packed up all their possessions. Our inside person has told us the crates are being stored in the basement of the Feds building. So our attempts to follow their possessions have yielded nothing as yet," Franco pointed out.

"Shouldn't we just kill them all and be done with it?" another asked.

"Oh don't be silly. They're only EE women. If they were men, then of course we would have to execute them," Franco declared. "After all, we all need our sex dolls." Many laughed at that, for implanted and drugged men and women were not seen as a threat, but as providing manpower or sex dolls.

Franco opened the meeting up for suggestions. He explained, "It's time for you Cabal members to speak your minds. Please, we're all waiting to hear your ideas about what we can possibly do to handle this disaster. I assure you that your Camarilla will be listening carefully to your suggestions. Fire away."

One man rose and suggested, "I too have seen Benny's EE women. I've also seen those two incredible top European EE women who have vanished while on a trip to the US. I think we should modify this new EE woman's appearance, which you've proposed for the troublemakers, and call it the Fetish EE woman. Give all our existing EE women the option of becoming one of these new Fetish EE women. Then promote this new style to all those new candidates who are to become EE women in the first place. It'll create many new jobs for other flunky-women. I'm tired of having to dump so many high school graduates into the catchall Garbage Collector Twentieth Class or making them wash the same windows or polish the same door knobs every day for their entire life. We should make better use of our population. After all, there's only so much trash that can be collected. So many have almost nothing useful to do as it is. Being a personal assistant to a Fetish EE woman would give these young graduates an actual working job to do."

His idea was accepted. Another offered, "Why don't we disband the Feds? They aren't truly useful any longer, are they?" Many thought this was a terrible idea.

Someone suggest raiding this Lady Persephone Briton's place in London and see if the machines were there. This wasn't taken seriously because the person couldn't suggest who would lead such a dangerous mission.

Another complained, "Look, I don't disagree with the new Fetish EE woman and trying to make them widespread in popularity, but why all this emphasis on EE women? Obviously, they can't be the ones behind this uprising. Men are involved and men who aren't on Pytalon or implanted. We should be going after them. Can't we go over the world's male population, find those who aren't handled and get them implanted and on Pytalon?" However, no one could suggest how this could actually be done.

One Cabal man from LA spoke up. "Look, as it is, we have a terrible shortage of real jobs for men in the greater LA basin. It's commonplace for desperate men to get full sex change operations so they can be gainfully employed by Total Care's offered jobs. Why not turn some of them into these new Fetish EE women and then make them available to local bachelors? We'd then be able to hire a care giver as well, handling two problems at one time." Many like this idea, since they had similar problems in their very large cities. Even wilder ideas were voiced, before they broke for supper.

After supper, Franco pointed out to James, "Amazing. So far, no one has noticed the singular detail that somehow these 'unknown men' behind the attacks always seem to know just where these five EE women are at, and even Rachel Roxanne, who was abducted by Benny. I certainly hope no one raises that question. We'll look like complete fools. I'm amazed no one has taken offense with the obvious killing of the other Cabal families. I had anticipated that would raise the ire of many, but we've swept that under the rug with this new Fetish EE women action, I do believe."

"Let us hope so, James. Let us hope so," Franco sighed. All this was taxing his brain far more than he was willing to admit to James. Further, he dare not mention that he was growing more terrified each day—certainly not to the number two Camarilla member.

Meanwhile, several Cabal men approached their wives about the new improved Fetish EE woman program. By the next day, word of this wonderful new Fetish EE woman look and program had spread through all the EE women present. By the start of the morning session, over fifty had begged their husbands to get them converted into this new and powerful appearance.

The next morning session, after Delius Pogs took down the names of those who wanted to try out this new Fetish EE woman modification, Franco again asked for more feedback and suggestions from the members at large. One suggested, "We should re-establish the army and have them smash these horrible idiots who are trying to destroy what we have worked so long and hard for. Honestly, we're just now coming down homestretch in the whole darn project. We can't let some fools ruin everything." Many agreed with him, though not the army part. No one mentioned how these "idiots" could be found.

Others backed the idea to scrounge through the entire world database and find any man, who wasn't implanted and/or on Pytalon, and see they were handled. Another suggested the handling should be a sex change followed by this new Fetish EE woman implant. "Hey, if this man is behind the destruction of our world, then that would fully handle him." This won total approval from all the members present. Hence, the Camarilla had to accept this plan of action. They passed a resolution that any man so discovered would have their sex changed and would be turned into a Fetish EE woman.

Jacques spoke up, "Look, there are likely men who aren't in our databases. We've come across some who are living off the grid. Our Feds in Chicago first discovered their presence last year and then had other major cities investigating them too. I think it is a safe assumption that there are men in most major metropolitan areas who are off the grid. Perhaps our unknown attackers are some of these men."

"Okay," the originator countered, "let's amend our plan to also include citywide searches for all men. Find those not in our databases and handle them the same way—turn them into Fetish EE women." That quickly passed unanimously.

"So just how do we do this?" asked Henry Koch, head of Total Care Worldwide.

"Send your desk people out to check," someone suggested.

"That's asking a zombie to think," someone else pointed out the fallacy of that.

"So have our Feds do it for us. They are supposed to be working for us anyway," the original Cabal man countered. That too passed.

Henry then pointed out, "Look. If the Feds are run by this Chan-Petra woman, then they may well avoid doing this, once they know what we're going to do with the men we find."

"So don't let them know what is done with the men," he countered. Henry accepted that idea. He could work with that.

Even wilder ideas were tossed about, but none was agreed to, and the 2273 Cabal meeting adjourned. All but the Camarilla members left for home, with many rather excited about this new Fetish EE women plan.

Ben Michaelson-Waberly took Tom Walton aside before the Camarilla formally met. In a low voice, Ben said, "Okay, I've given your suggestion considerable thought. You're right. It's time my Jana gets married. I've not come up with any better deal than this one. I'll agree to marry her to your Lyle, as long as you keep Lyle from interfering in my Preston's plan to snatch that Raven heiress."

The two men shook hands, sealing their private deal. Ben then sent a quick text to his son Preston, before the nine members officially met.

"Okay," Franco opened their meeting, "I assume you have a plan to rollout your new machines and procedures, Delius?"

"Yes, the first thousand of the new PDH machines are already shipping. I've sent along script changes to the EE woman's implant as well as medical instructions. Major cities should have them later this week. My companies are shifting into full production mode. We should have most all of the existing current models replaced by the end of the year. After that, we'll take these replaced units and ship them off to the boonies, replacing their original models, which are totally obsolete," Delius replied. All eight men nodded their approval.

James volunteered, "I'll visit the Feds and arrange for the citywide searches for all untouched men. We'll need to ship them somewhere the Feds don't know about, get them turned into the new Fetish EE women, and then brought back and given to deserving men."

"Or women," Ben teased him. The men chuckled.

"That too," James agreed.

"I'll handle that aspect. You have the Feds get them and send them to the New York Total Care office. We'll take it from there," Henry volunteered, satisfying James.

Franco then said, "Our real problem is how to find

where Chan-Petra has gone, along with those four EE companions of hers. They and perhaps this Lady Persephone Briton are our only real leads to those behind this heinous plot against us."

"Don't forget she may well be the person we need to get our hands on to get us another Transference Machine," Henry pointed out. "We know she's been gone from her castle estate for quite some time now. We could go to the Feds Supreme Commander and demand to meet with her to discuss this. I can use Total Care force on her, if needed."

Delius suggested, "Say, whoever she put in charge for her during her absence must know where she is at and likely the others as well."

"It's a Captain Lech, head of the Chicago bureau," James volunteered. He'd kept close tabs on that position.

"There you have it, fellows," Henry smiled covertly. "We snatch him, force their location out of him with the Truth Drug-A, then send him off to become a Fetish EE woman as the Cabal men suggested. Problem solved. Clean and neat."

Franco hadn't said anything much yet. Now he chose to speak. "You know, we followed the incredible mess the Feds had last year with the renegade Field Marshal fellow, what's his name?"

Jacques answered, "Oh, you mean Grand Field Marshal Hans Gudrunda. Yes, I see your point. Our true enemy could well be another one of those insane men. Well, he and his band were certainly off the grid. We could have the Feds do an extensive search for other such groups."

"Needle in a haystack," Delius grumbled. "Hell, that nutty man went undetected for over twenty years. Lord knows how much damage he inflicted on us."

Francisco, who had been mostly silent, explained, "Massive damage in major cities. His men infiltrated the Pytalon manufacturing plants and caused those faulty pills, which resulted in that massive insanity outbreak last year."

That sobered the men even further, but they continued to outline their next moves. As they broke up, Franco punched in, "It's amazing we can't find six EE women!"

Chapter 11—Escalation

January 3, 2273, with Juan's help, Persephone began working her Transference Machine miracles once again. Aasha-Beth, Mahala-Jessica, Bahiya-Tilly, and Sameera-Amanda became the second bodies of the four, much to their great pleasure. "I do like this one better than the other one," Beth commented, "and I especially love my Mahala-Jessica. You are hot, dear," she teased, pleasing her mate.

Next, she did the same for Chan-Petra, who now also ran Vaani-Petra. "I'm going to keep Vaani-Petra here with the babies, when I go back to the Feds," she pronounced.

Finally, Juan felt confident enough to handle the Transference Machine himself. He worked the controls on My Lady. Shortly, Persephone had her second body, Faizah-Perse, as she chose to call herself. Of the six, she had the most difficulty with this, since she hadn't yet had the incredible experience of running two bodies at the same time. Fortunately, she had nine more days to learn to deal with seeing, feeling, and moving double-like.

Beth's idea took firm hold with her. "Let one sleep in the day and work at night and vice versa. It works well for us, and we get twice as much done, more or less." Faizah-Perse agreed and began sleeping during the daytime hours, rising at night, while getting used to her strange, new body. She realized the Cabal men who had swapped bodies in the past thereby prolonging their lives, possibly for more than a century, didn't know about this aspect. *My god, if they knew they could run two bodies at the same time, we'd be in double trouble!*

Chan-Petra ended her leave on January 7, a Monday, walking into her old office, but Captain Lech wasn't there. She buzzed others and learned he hadn't yet been in this morning. It wasn't until late morning that she got worried. This wasn't like him. When he hadn't shown up by lunchtime, she sent men to his apartment. Fifteen minutes later, Chan-Petra was on the scene, along with their entire CSI department and the emergency medical team! His door had been smashed in. There were signs of a struggle, including a bit of blood on the rug, later identified as his. He'd been abducted. His wife, Mary Lyons Smith, had been given a knockout drug and the medical team brought her around. However, she had been asleep when the attack happened and really didn't know anything. Chan-Petra wanted clues immediately, hounding everyone there until she was asked to go back and check his current case files for clues.

She fell back into her chair and took off her tall heels. What happened to him? Okay, check his case files, she told herself, finding it hard to distance herself from this crime. He had been her very close friend for years. She entered his codes and brought up his files. *Damn, he wasn't working on anything.* He'd pretty much cleared everything out before the holidays. The only ongoing action was trying to track down all the missing high school graduates that had been abducted from their new jobs—the ones that had been found already had been implanted, put on Pytalon, and given new, menial jobs. These, he had cleverly removed from the system, taking them to the relatively secret detoxification-desensitization unit to be helped.

Before too long, she received a text stating it was Lech's blood that they found. Nearby surveillance cameras picked up four hooded men coming up the MET. Later, they retraced their steps, carrying what appeared to be a drunken man between them. Even from the fuzzy video, she recognized Lech. He looked pretty beat up. What did they want with him? By the end of the day, the Feds finally reviewed enough video from many other locations to know that he'd been taken to an EMAC that ended up at New O'Hare. There, they lost all trace of him and the abductors.

The four men didn't appear to leave the airfield on any video from any nearby location. The only presumption was that he had been put on some Air Liner, of which a dozen had left since the approximate time the men had arrived. Many had destinations overseas. Poor Mary, she kept calling Chan-Petra for news, but she had so little to report.

By suppertime, Chan-Petra knew she was stumped on this one. She alerted all the other Feds worldwide to be on the lookout for Captain Lech, sending along a recent photo of him. She asked them to check videos of arriving passengers for signs of him. Now all she could do was wait.

Chan-Petra took a new approach upon her return to work. Since the assassins had invaded her penthouse suite, she opted to set up house there in her Feds office. She had other Feds bring her clothes and sundries from her old suite here, and she arranged for one Trikuza member to watch over her office suite during the night, figuring the sheer number of people in the building during the daytime was enough protection.

The next day, she sent a text message to everyone else back in Phoenix, alerting them to the abduction of Captain Lech. In return, she received many suggestions to beef up her own security precautions. Then around noon, she received a kidnap ransom call. A distorted voice said, "We've kidnaped Captain Lech of the Chicago Feds. Proof of life is being sent. Deposit one million credits into this account by Thursday noon or we will kill him. Click." The caller hung up, but the photo appeared shortly afterwards, showing a drugged Lech sitting in a chair.

Between Tuesday and Thursday, the Chicago Feds worked on this case, exclusively. They attacked the kidnap and ransom from all angles, but uncovered absolutely nothing, except the photo was taken on a disposable cell phone, purchased in Bohn, Germany, months ago. Reluctantly, Chan-Petra executed the funds transfer before the deadline arrived. Now all she could do was wait on the kidnapers. Already Beth was monitoring that account, but it was registered to a Garbage Collector Twentieth Class in

Hyderabad, India, which made no sense, particularly when the Feds commander there, Hana Rumanana, checked the man out. He was just what he seemed and had no idea what a million credits actually amounted to. The account was a total dead end. Why? This abduction was making no sense at all.

***

Captain Lech Smith was rudely awakened by someone breaking his door down. He jumped out of bed and was able to get in a number of solid punches before one of his four assailants hit him with a stun gun. He didn't feel the needle being injected into his neck or being carried to the airport. Nor did he know that he'd been flown over to Europe.

He awoke, sort of, in a stone-walled room, strapped to a chair. His mind was fuzzy and someone took a photo of him. Then a very well dressed man walked in and injected him with something. After a time, questions were fired at him, rapid fire. He fought hard to keep from answering them, but the truth drug was stronger. At some point, the man seemed satisfied and injected him with something else. All went black. He awoke screaming in a soprano voice, not his own, he swore.

***

"Yes, as soon as you get all fancied up as one of these brand new Fetish EE women, we'll be married, my love," Lyle smiled lovingly at the tall brunette Jana Michaelson-Waberly. Secretly, he lusted for her since he first met her at a Cabal party some six years ago. He monitored her as she grew up, even sending her flowers on her birthday. For the last two years, he had pestered his father, Tom, to find a way to convince Ben to let him marry his daughter. Then only two months ago, Tom had taken him aside for a private chat.

"Son, if you're serious about wanting Jana, then here's what you have to do. Send Preston Michaelson-Waberly some threatening emails telling him to stay away from Mrs. Rachel Roxanne Raven-Waberly—that she's yours," Tom explained.

"Why dad? Who's this Rachel anyway? Why would I want a married woman?" Lyle countered. This made no sense.

"Moves and countermoves, son. Trust me. You want Jana, and I want her in our family too. This is a way to make it happen," Tom replied, but said no more. *Stupid kids. They haven't brain one. Well, one day, he can play CEO for one of my major outlets. He's not bright enough for much else.*

Lyle wanted Jana, at least he thought he did, and so did as his father asked, sending Preston, who he barely knew, several emails. Preston didn't reply, for which he was thankful.

Then as the Cabal meeting in Luxemburg wrapped up, Tom said, "Okay, Lyle. I've gotten Ben's okay for you to marry Jana. She'll be one of the first of our new Fetish EE women. After she gets that done and accustomed to it, you two can be married."

Lyle was elated and sent Jana even more flowers. He was able to meet her briefly as the Cabal members began departing. That's when he'd said, "Yes, as soon as you get all fancied up as one of these brand new Fetish EE women, we'll be married, my love." He thought she too seemed very pleased, and he dreamed of her for days afterwards.
***

Ben explained to his wife, Emma, and to Jana, "Well, we're implementing a brand new Fetish EE woman's line, based on the two top fetish EE women of Europe, who have been setting the fashion craze over there for years. Many of our other member's wives are demanding to have this new appearance. I do believe you'll be even more attractive than you now are, my dear Emma."

"Oh, I do so hope so, Hunny Bun. I do so want to please you so very much. You know that. Jana, dear, you must do this too. After all, you want Lyle to love you truly, so you must look your very best," Emma chatted away, without having the slightest idea of anything fetish or what was planned.

"Dad, will I truly be as gorgeous as mom is? I mean, will Lyle really love me lots?" Jana asked nervously.

"Of course, my darling Jana. Already you've blossomed into a beautiful young woman. Soon, you'll be married to a wonderful man and enjoy the fruits of love, just as your mother always has. Hasn't she just been truly happy every day?"

Jana could only agree and felt a bit more relaxed. She didn't bother to ask why they were going to Luxemburg to get it done.

That was because Delius Pogs had gotten the first of his new PDH machines operational there, the Model III. Further, he had the medical facility primed for a flurry of women, anticipating many Cabal members' wives and daughters. They deserved only the very best. Besides, if there were any foul ups, they'd have his head, unless he could prove it was an accident, which he was always prepared to do.

His setup was in another of the old castles of Luxemburg, one that had been restored about a century ago and later used to house this fine PDH and medical center, which served this tiny country and surrounding lands. Beginning on January 5, a steady stream of customers flowed through the medical and implant center, well over a hundred of them. That only added to the confusion of those first days of the new Fetish EE Woman project.

The new script that was played to the patients contained only a slight alteration and a quartet of new lines: I must wear my ballet boots at all times. I must wear the tightest corsets possible with my fetish gowns. I am a model of feminine perfection. I must walk elegantly and gracefully at all times.

However, the script was punched in with a far heavier dosage of both the headache-delivering pain electrodes and the accompanying drug, in hopes the implant would be rock solid, unable to be cracked.

However, following the Benny model, the women's lower arms were also removed. In addition, if this was their first time being implanted as an EE woman, they had their breasts enlarged to the usual G-cup size, their lips thickened, and their hair both thickened and lengthened so it at least reached the small their backs.

Delius, working with Tom Walton, had also assembled the whole new Fetish EE Women's wardrobe, consisting of either a satin or latex, tight-fitting gown that ended at their knees, an inner, severe waist-reducing corset, an outer matching or contrasting corset, and of course, the calf-high ballet boots, which matched the gown. With so many things being standardized on these EE women, there weren't that many different sizes actually needed, just lots of them in many colors and materials. His staff used the famous two European top fetish EE women, who had somehow vanished over a year ago, as their guide in the choice of fashions. His only worry was running out of a particular one before this first rush of women were handled. After that, there was enough time to restock all stores worldwide, as the new fashion craze expanded as the Cabal planned.

Because there were so many women being made into or converted to the new Fetish EE Woman model, the patients were being doubled up, two to a room, along with their original or newly hired helpers. Delius Pogs created a new position for women: Fetish EE Woman's Assistant. These heavily doped women had to be trained to handle their charges and were to live with them, making a total of four per room at the castle, only adding to the confusion level.

The assistants were first trained on how to dress their new charges. To prevent chaffing, they were instructed to put a chemise on their charges before putting on the inner, very tight, highly metal-boned corset. This had to be tightened down in stages. Next, fine black seamed nylons were fastened to the eight garters of the inner corset. The calf-high ballet boots were then put on and tightened down. To prevent accidental untying, a flap of leather then wrapped around the knot and was locked in place with a tiny padlock. The assistants were reminded never to lose the little keys. The assistants were instructed to next put on the special latex panty with the pleasure-giving device carefully inserted so that merely by walking, their charges could pleasure themselves.

The assistants were drilled that from this point on, when their charges went to bed, they were to put a nightgown on over all this, but in the mornings, they were to remove the nightgowns and proceed with dressing. A slip came next, followed by either a satin or a latex gown; lastly, an outer contrasting or matching corset was secured. This one had no garters and was decorative. These implanted and Pytalon drugged assistants had to be repeatedly drilled in order to get all this down pat. Then, it was on to their other duties—the brushing of hair, donning of makeup, feeding their charge, and handling their bathroom needs. All this was an awful lot for these newly implanted and Pytalon drugged young women to grasp, far too many sequences to be followed, which also added to the overall confusion of these first few days.

Those EE women who were getting an "upgrade" to this new model standard were first put unconscious and underwent the surgery to remove their arms at their elbows. They were then kept sedated for several days, while the advanced medical healing was handled. When the heavy bandages were removed and thin, light ones put on, they were ready for the next step.

At this point, their assistants stepped in and got them fully dressed. Still unconscious, they were put into wheelchairs and taken to the PDH implant station, where they were given the newest treatment, which lasted a half hour. This was the operation Delius worried about the most. In trials, a few didn't survive the electrical shocks the machine delivered. However, Delius was far more terrified of normal people than he was of having one of these women accidentally perishing during this new implant. He had to make certain these new implants couldn't be undone by the mysterious people who were doing just that.

Once all these actions were completed, the women were wheeled into their new bedrooms, doubling up with another Fetish EE woman and her assistant. Once they awoke, their assistant was instructed to help solidify their adjustment by getting them walking, which, with these special panties, should pleasure them as dictated by and help to re-enforce their new implants. However, from previous experiences, Delius was aware of just how difficult people found learning to walk properly in these boots. Most experienced a good deal of foot cramping and pain. He wanted to minimize this by giving them painkillers, but decided against that out of fear that such would dampen the implant headaches that were needed to help ensure compliance with the implant's orders. However, after the first few women were done, he had to begin giving them some painkillers, both for their aching feet and throbbing elbows. True, he was learning how best to handle this new process. Later on, he found even better ways of hiding their initial foot cramping and pain—severing key nerves in their feet.

In actuality, none of these hundred plus initial women had any real idea just what this new Fetish EE Woman actually was, other than some had seen images of those two top European women a few times. Those who were already EE women, struggled to breathe, then screamed a little as they saw their missing lower arms and hands, but rapidly the new and more powerful implants kicked in, forcing them to recite the revised litany, which calmed them down almost at once. They had been perfect women before and now were more than perfect. Quickly, they settled down and allowed their often life-long assistants to help them learn to walk, though they constantly harped about their having to walk elegantly and gracefully—and were they doing so? Of course, most weren't.

On the other hand, those new to the implant fared

far worse. Jana awoke from her implant with a splitting headache, aching elbows, and intense pressure around her chest, making breathing almost impossible, and aching breasts. Even her lips felt strange. Jana had fought a horrid battle with the intense, grey pain shooting through her body's head. At its peak, it seemed as if she was apparently being driven out of her head some three feet behind it, so intense was the pain. Just as she was about to conclude she was dead, the electrical shocking subsided, and she seemed to fly back into the pain-filled head. Only later would Jana realize she'd come a hair from dying! Right now, her head throbbed, and she tried to rub her head, but saw stumps where her lower arms and hands had been. It took a moment to register that they were gone. Then, she screamed and promptly fainted from lack of breath.

Three more times, this cycle was repeated before she fully regained consciousness. At this point, her implant script kicked in, and she began reciting the litany. "My body is hypersensitive to sensual touches. My body needs sexual sensations and stimulations several times each day. I exist to provide elegant and sensual experiences to men and women of power. I am a Fetish Exotic Escort woman. I must look my very best at all times. I must wear my ballet boots at all times. I must wear the tightest corsets possible with my fetish gowns. I am a model of feminine perfection. I must walk elegantly and gracefully at all times. I must be ready to flirt at any time. I must be ready to engage and satisfy the sexual fantasies and satisfactions of both men and women at any time. I am a super-sexual, hypersensitive woman. I must wear only the finest and exotic gowns and heels. I must look absolutely perfect at all times. I will repeat to myself these words several times each day. I must not forget these words."

Somehow, after saying all this, she felt better and allowed her new assistant, Anne, to help her sit up and then stand precariously on her toes. "Oh, I simply must learn to walk elegantly and gracefully," she gasped for breath. She'd never worn a corset before or worn such heels, though she'd always admired her mother's tall heels and had even played dress up in them when she was younger.

Anne helped her walk around the small bedroom, but before long, the special panties did their job, and she swooned in an unreal ecstasy, caused for the most part by her response to her own implant, which dictated she was now hypersensitive. This led to her reciting the whole litany again, while Anne recited her own implanted script.

Jana was in a complete daze. She had no control over her own thoughts. Deep down, she tried to fight this whole thing. It wasn't what she had wanted or expected. She was a helpless cripple now, but all those thoughts were so deeply buried beneath the pain and drugs that they simply couldn't be vocalized. Instead, she continued to rattle off her litany. In fact, she had even forgotten her own name. Her newly made assistant Anne, barely remembered her own name and had also forgotten Jana's name as well, but at least she had a paper somewhere, on which she'd written her charge's first name, if only she could remember where the paper was. All that Jana knew was that she was in total misery and in an unreal ecstasy at the same time, that she was utterly perfect in all ways, and that she needed to pleasure men and women. In her confusion, she couldn't figure out if that meant she was also to pleasure Anne. Anne kept refusing her advances, so perhaps not. That was the height of her new reasoning abilities: to decide that Anne wasn't to be pleasured, though why wholly eluded her thinking. Yes, this new powerful implant, combined with Pytalon-Ex nearly wiped the recipients out, burying their observational and reasoning powers extremely deeply, beneath monster walls of pain and drugs.

With so many here, quarters were tight. Another unconscious woman was brought in, along with her helper, Emma, who was also eighteen. This new woman was somewhat older and had very thick, strong legs. However, when she regained consciousness, her soprano screams chilled Jana to the bone.

The last thing that Lech Smith remembered was sitting in a chair and being asked all manner of questions, to which he more or less answered. He hadn't wanted to answer them, even tried hard not to, but the strange chemicals flooding his body made it impossible for him to resist answering. After that, all went dark again. He was flown to Luxemburg. Once there, he was handed over to the surgeons, who changed his sex, adjusting his body accordingly. Since no one had told them whether "she" was to be able to have children, they went ahead and made sure that was possible as well. That done, they also altered "her" form into that of a proper Fetish EE woman, per the orders, but had to extend her "treatment" time another hour just to get "her" black hair the requisite length, to the middle of her back. They kept "her" sedated and under for several days, while the advanced machine healed the body up to the acceptable standards. Only then did they execute the PDH implant operation. Like the others, only much later did Lech come to realize just how close he'd come to calling it quits, allowing his mutilated body to die during the implant. Had he known what they'd done to his body, during the implant he would certainly had left it, causing it to die. Unfortunately, he didn't know at that time, and thus fought the implant all the way to its end.

That done, they brought in her assigned, new assistant, the eighteen year old Emma, who had also just received her own implant and heavy dose of Pytalon a day ago. She was drilled on the proper care of her new charge, getting Leah properly dressed. Lech was now going to be called Leah; they'd even changed her ID card properly, though he had no idea all this was going on. Properly attired, Emma waited patiently for her new charge to awaken from the implant drugs, hoping she could remember all the proper sequences she was ordered to follow while caring for her new charge.

Meanwhile, Anne was still walking the very confused Jana around their shared room. Jana was even more confused when Lech roused and finally grasped what had happened to him. His shrill scream pierced Jana to the bone, but barely registered with Anne and Emma, for they were completely enmeshed in the fog of Pytalon-Ex. After passing out from lack of breath, Leah awoke and screamed again. Jana finally realized Leah was reacting as badly as she had, though she couldn't find any way to get that thought from her mind out into the world around her, both frustrating and confusing her further.

Eventually, Emma managed to get Leah sitting up in the bed. "Leah. I'm Emma, I think. You're supposed to walk now. You're perfect. I'm supposed to say that. Sanity is doing a good job."

"I'm Lech, Lech Smith," she stopped. *That isn't my voice! Oh god, what's happened to me?* At that instant, his implant kicked in. Leah began reciting the same script that Jana had been reciting, causing her to recite it along with him, several times. Finally, Emma managed to get Leah onto her toes, though madly waving what was left of her arms around, knees bent, barely standing, gasping all the while. Emma pushed her, forcing her to attempt to take a step. After several steps, Leah began to insist she had to walk elegantly and gracefully. Then the waves of pleasure swept over her new organs. Leah nearly collapsed from the strange sensations flooding over her body. It was all that Emma could do to keep her upright.

Somewhere amid all this sensory overload, Leah asked, "Where am I?" Neither Anne nor Emma had any idea.

Jana thought she should know the answer to that question and tried to think. Nearly ten minutes later, she said, "Luxemburg," but by then no one knew what she meant by that. Several recitations of their litany had already passed by the confused four.
***

Meanwhile, Beth, Jessica, Tilly, Amanda, and Persephone had their lower arms reattached. Beth was looking forward to being released in another day, while Persephone was barely in her second day of recovery.

Today, they were doing Rachel Roxanne. While the four laid around their hospital beds, their other bodies were hard at work, setting up all their equipment in their old underground hideout in East Peoria. The Feds had moved the crates of their things from the basement of the Feds building up to the back freight doors. At night, Juan and the four loaded them into their EMAC and brought the stuff back to their old haunt.

For the last five days, the four worked hard on integrating all the newer equipment into the existing setup. Space was at a premium, but their new cook, Julie, was working out. Their small kitchen was filled with food and the odor of fresh baked breads, Julie's specialty. Juan had added more beds to the rooms for the nine, removing some of the older furniture, replacing them with compact, tall wardrobes designed to hold the women's fancy clothes. In two days, Beth would be returning, followed shortly by the others, so Juan wanted everything ready for them. After they got back, he and Lady Persephone were getting married and heading back to London to sort things out there.

A bored Beth lay in bed, allowing herself to focus on running her other body, which was putting the last minute touches on her new electronic systems. An orderly entered and came up to her, pretending to be examining her chart. She still had immobilizing bandages on her arms, though. Suddenly, she felt a pin prick in her neck. Then blackness flooded over her. A transfer notice was placed on her chart and her body placed on a pushcart. In the next room, an unconscious Jessica was added to her cart. Both were pushed to the elevator.

Shortly, another man pushed up another cart carrying Tilly and Amanda, both unconscious as well. Then, a third orderly arrived, pushing Persephone on a third cart. They took the elevator to the roof, where they transferred the women into the waiting EMAC, and signed off on the official transfer papers that the guard held for them. As far as the hospital was concerned, the five were being transferred to a St. Louis hospital, though later checking showed this to be an erroneous set of papers. They too had been abducted. No one was the wiser, since they were using their new Indian bodies and these were simply unconscious bodies. The abduction wasn't actually detected until that evening, when Chan-Petra stopped by to check on the five.

By nightfall, the five were across the "pond," and being wheeled into the Luxemburg castle. Delius took no chances with these five. He had his team standing by and began the conversions to Fetish EE Women immediately. Since all five were already EE women, they had merely had their newly attached lower arms removed, but this time, the lower arms were not worth saving and were pitched. Additionally, they had their hair lengthened, since the five had trimmed it back to a more manageable level of shoulder length. Once more, their hair would fall to their lower backs.

That done, Delius allowed the healing process of the medical machines to work on them overnight before wheeling them into the new PDH implant machine. By noon the next day, their five new assistants had them fully dressed and were waiting further instructions. It was at this point that things got very confusing. They were then temporarily moved into the same room where Jana and Leah were staying.

Why? Because Delius was terrified someone would discover these women had been kidnaped and brought here. He fully expected enemy men at any moment would come into the castle with guns blazing. After all, this Leah was a Feds leader! He'd been kept here far too long for Delius's comfort! He wanted them shipped back to the States as soon as possible.

The five new assistants, totally confused themselves, headed off to find the kitchen and bring back supper for these five. However, they got lost in the maze of castle halls. Meanwhile, zombie guards arrived and took everyone in the room out into a waiting EMAC, including Anne and

Emma, who were trying to help Jana and Leah walk so that they didn't have to be wheeled out, even though they had to pause for several minutes while their exploding sensations subsided enough to allow them to continue trying to walk.

The EMAC trip was short, dropping them off at the airport in Amsterdam, where they were taken onboard an Air Liner. Once in the air and seated for a bit, Leah finally managed to get a coherent thought expressed, "Where are we?"

Jana attempted to work out the answer, but was unable to do so. Everything was just too confusing. Besides, she found herself reciting her litany again. Anne did figure out they were the only passengers on the ship, but simply couldn't work out why this was so. By now, the drugs wore off the five women, but as it was dark, they slipped into a deep sleep instead of rousing. Soon, Jana and Leah drifted into slumber as well, leaving Anne and Emma confused. Should they wake them up and put them into nightgowns? If so, where were the nightgowns? Where were their beds? Even more confused, they too fell asleep.
***

"Yes, they've been kidnaped again!" Chan-Petra barked angrily into her phone. "Juan and some of my Feds are still at Cook County, but it's confirmed. Three men using fake transfer orders took them out of there. Juan is furious too, but we've no clues, except they've been transported by an Air Liner, just like Captain Lech Smith. Have Greg locate them for us. I'll stand by and send every damned Feds after them!" She was quite angry and hung up to await news.

Unknown to her, another EMAC landed on the Chicago Feds rooftop, apparently showing credentials of the New York Feds. When the masked men disembarked, they took the two Feds guards by surprise, downing them with tranquilizer guns. Swiping their badges, three of the men used them to open the elevator doors. When it opened onto Chan-Petra's floor, one stayed behind, holding the doors open and pressed the rooftop button, while the other two headed for her office.

"Yes? Oh crap!" Chan-Petra reacted to the two men charging into her office. Her Trikuza guard sprang into action, but he too was taken by surprise as well. While he managed to eliminate one of the men, the other hit him with a tranquilizer dart, dropping him. Chan-Petra had drawn her service gun, but he dove for cover before she could shoot him. After exchanging fire, Chan-Petra was also hit with a dart. The locked open elevator prevented other Feds from reaching her quickly. The man then lifted her up and raced for the elevator. A minute later, the two raced for their EMAC and lifted off the instant the door closed, just as a swarm of Feds finally came rushing out onto the roof, guns blazing. Too late. Chan-Petra was unconscious and abducted too.

Taking no chances, the EMAC went to Philadelphia before landing. There, the men climbed into their Air Liner and headed off to Luxemburg, dropping Chan-Petra off at the castle near dawn. Once more, Delius had his staff ready and a few hours later, she was handled completely. However, he did allow for a day's healing to occur via the medical machine, before sending her back to the States on another flight. However, he didn't send along her assistant, though Delius had the assistant fully dress Chan-Petra before her departure. The men were under orders to keep her sedated until she was dropped off.

When Greg called Chan-Petra back, a Feds man answered her phone. "Yes, she's just been abducted right here from her office!" He described the attack and Greg hung up. He then contacted the professor and Juan to relay the bad news, which just seemed to come pouring in. Shortly after that, Vaani-Petra left the two babies in Phoenix and took an EMAC to Chicago, flying at top speed, but kept in communications with the Feds who were still scouring the site for clues.

Vaani-Petra knew the other body was out, but it wasn't interfering with her operations of this body. Hence, she picked up where Chan-Petra left off, coordinating the

Feds' response. According to Greg's locator data, the kidnaped women were somewhere in Luxemburg, of all places. Hence, Vaani-Petra began making calls to Wolf, working out a rescue mission. However, before they could even finalize their plans, Greg reported the five were being moved again, though Chan-Petra wasn't.

That they were heading towards the US gave Vaani-Petra hope. Once back on US soil, the rescue would be far easier to coordinate and pull off. All she could do was wait until they landed. Each hour, Greg turned on their locator chips, got a fix on their position, turned them off, and texted Vaani-Petra their current location. The last call she received indicated the Air Liner was over New York City, heading westward. She didn't answer the subsequent phone calls, again alarming Greg, who made additional calls.

Juan headed over to the Feds building and was escorted up to her office, where six Feds were standing over Vaani-Petra's body. She appeared to be unconscious. Juan picked up her phone, texting Greg that he was here. He then texted Julia, the women's new chef and received an alarming return text. The four there too were unconscious. Now Juan became extremely worried!

At four in the morning, Greg texted that the Air Liner was probably landing at New O'Hare. Juan reacted, relaying word to the other Feds in the office. One took charge, and they took an EMAC over to New O'Hare, arriving within fifteen minutes of Greg's call. When the men swarmed onto the field, they saw an Air Liner rising into the sky, but there standing forlornly on the tarmac stood four women, while five more were in wheelchairs.

Juan recognized the five immediately and rushed to the group. It was obvious even in the dark that the five were unconscious, but they and two who were standing precariously on their toes had their lower arms gone. The lifesaving operation had been undone on the five. Juan breathed a huge sigh of relief, since Lady Persephone was sitting in one of the wheel chairs.

"Who are you?" a Feds asked the four standing women. From her fog, Anne said softly, "I'm Anne, a Fetish EE Woman's Assistant. Sanity is caring for my charge properly." Both Anne and Emma were eighteen-year-old teens from London.

Hearing her speak, a very confused Emma whispered, "I'm Emma. Sanity is caring for my charge properly."

"And who are you?" one asked Jana, who continued to wobble to keep her balance on her toes, valiantly trying to suppress the shooting pains from her crushed, cramped feet and toes.

Who am I? I should know the answer to that question, but I can't seem to remember. Instead of answering, she began reciting her implant words, feeling that was the right thing to do. Leah followed suit, unable to get his confused answer vocalized. Instead out came the litany words instead.

A Feds man saw his ID card on a chain around his neck and looked at it. "It says that you are Captain Leah Smith. This can't be. How did you get his ID card?" The question filtered into Lech's mind, but he simply could not answer it. He had no idea. Hadn't it always been his ID card?

"Come on; let's get them back to headquarters," Juan suggested. Fifteen minutes later, they were back on the rooftop, where their medical technician was waiting.

Under the good lighting, they examined Lech's ID card. Sure enough, it held an image of this strange looking woman. At this point, the medical technician, who was very familiar with Lech, pulled up the satin gown, revealing more of his upper leg. "This must be Lech. See, there's the bullet wound he got last year. I know, cause I handled him. What the hell have they done to our boss?" he exclaimed.

Unfortunately, lifting up the gown caused Leah to react, once more reciting the implanted script. "Now what do we do?" the technician asked.

The lieutenant who had taken charge suggested,

"Well, we have to notify his wife, Mary Lyons. I suppose the best thing to do for now is to return him to his home and wife. We can sort this mess out later on."

"But I have to go with him. I'm his assistant," Emma protested. The lieutenant shrugged and took her along with Leah, heading to the Smith's home, not far from the Feds building.

Juan made a decision. "I'll take these five and the other pair with me. I'll leave Vaani-Petra here. With luck, she will be awake by morning. I'll keep in contact with you."

The Feds were more than glad to be rid of these strange and helpless women, as sexy looking as they appeared. The medical technician continued to watch over the still unconscious Vaani-Petra.

Several hours later, Juan landed outside the abandoned warehouse in East Peoria and carefully nudged the vehicle inside before setting down solidly on the concrete floor. The early morning sun was just coming up, as he began wheeling the five unconscious women inside their secret hideout, where Julie had breakfast waiting. Finally, he put an arm around Jana, helping her walk inside, Anne following along behind them. He had to pause twice, finally realizing what was happening with Jana as she walked some. He could sense her body's wild reaction to the stimulus she was receiving just by walking.

Once inside, he got the five lying beside their Indian bodies, covering them up. He, Jana, Anne, and Julie then sat down for breakfast and a very strong cup of black tea. Juan needed it. "So who are you," Juan asked over tea.

Jana again tried to figure that one out. The best she could do was mutter, "I'm a Fetish EE Woman." He did guess she was from England, as her accent was similar to Lady Persephone's.

"But what is your name? Where do you live?" Juan tried a different approach.

Watching her carefully, he realized she was so heavily implanted that she couldn't respond even if she wanted to. Frustrated, Jana could only recite her entire implanted speech, but this time, Juan was alert enough to jot it down, noticing mostly the slight alterations to the usual script with which he was familiar.

***

Back in Luxemburg, Delius Pogs knew something had gone wrong. He fired Chan-Petra back to the States, but personally began going from recovery bedroom to bedroom in search of the missing Jana Michaelson-Waberly. She was nowhere to be found. Delius fought his rising panic. What could he do? He dare not admit he'd lost an EE woman! In a flash, he had his answer. He sent a quick, urgent message to the London Medical Institute. Two hours later, the eighteen-year-old OD Jana arrived at the castle, looking a bit confused, but ready to help her most valuable host woman. He told Lyle, who had been waiting patiently for his "love" to be brought out to him, that she needed another two days to better recover. Lyle griped about the delay, but went horseback riding in the picturesque countryside to pass the time.

Already Delius Pogs had to make similar substitutions for six other women, none of whom had survived this new implant. He'd cleverly brought their OD backup bodies in from the Medical Centers, replacing the "lost" bodies. Their husbands and family members wouldn't know the difference, since the women's memories were so heavily buried beneath the new implant and Pytalon-Ex dosages. Still, that Jana had gotten lost bothered him. His assumption was that she'd died, but where was her body? The next day, he even took a walk around the castle grounds, looking for her body. Perhaps she'd taken a bad fall somewhere around the maze of corridors and halls and stairs. He found nothing and later forgot about her disappearance.

In two days, Jana was carefully walked out to meet Lyle, with her new assistant, Jane, holding on to her. Delius explained, "Lyle, you can expect Jana to be a bit confused for a time. Be patient with her, and she'll work it out. They're disoriented after the implant, but I assure you, there isn't any way for her to break this one down. I'm sure she'll provide you with years of pure pleasure and enjoyment."

"You're even prettier now, Jana," Lyle whispered to Jana, who replied by reciting her new litany, most confused, but her short arms did stroke his face, lovingly. Lyle only thought, *what a knockout sex doll!*

Chapter 12—Recovery Attempts

January became a very scary month for all concerned! Beginning later that first morning, the five women woke up, dazed, very confused, while reciting identical implant scripts! Juan had his hands full. While he was used to handling the half-armed women, their new implants caused enormous troubles, much of which he didn't understand at first. Jana and Anne only added to the confusion. Into the chaos, the six needed to go to the bathroom. Since Anne couldn't handle them all, Julie and Juan helped out, discovering their special panties and eventually their restricting corsets.

More importantly, Juan saw the flaw in Lady Persephone's grand plan of running two bodies at the same time. The five were spiritual beings, not their bodies, as demonstrated by the Transference Machines. To his dismay, Juan discovered it really had been the beings who were implanted via their bodies. Thus, their five Indian bodies reacted the same way as the five half-armed bodies and Jana did! That is, all eleven women recited the same implanted words, which only added to the overall confusion of that first morning. Try as he might, he couldn't get the Indian bodies to respond in any other way! Worse, they continued to insist they simply must have the tight corsets and the ballet boots as well.

The only redeeming aspect was that the five Indian bodies fed themselves, while Julie, Anne, and Juan had to feed the other five. Nevertheless, Juan simply had to bring some order. His plan was simple. Get half of them sleeping during the day; the others, during the night. After breakfast, he got the six walking around the complex, practicing their walking and thereby getting their sexual stimulation cravings satisfied, while he watched the other five Indian bodies using their fingers to satisfy their needs.

Before long, the six were tired and exhausted and were put to bed, leaving him with the Indian versions.

Juan took Mahala-Jessica aside and tried to desensitize one phrase, just as Jessica had always done. He discovered this new form of implant was drastically stronger than the normal one. One by one, he tested them: Faizah-Perse, Aasha-Beth, Mahala-Jessica, Bahiya-Tilly, and Sameera-Amanda. Each had identical implants, which he found comforting, but each woman continually demanded they be given proper apparel and boots, when they weren't trying to seduce him or pleasure themselves or each other.

Since he couldn't get anywhere with the desensitizing process, he tried Jessica's alternate therapy, choosing to try it on Mahala-Jessica, since in this body she had experienced no pain. "Okay, Jessica, I want you to close your eyes and return back to Cook County General, where you were lying in bed. Now come forward and tell me what you are seeing and feeling as you move through what happened to you."

Soon, she was doing just that. The entire incident was live in her mind. Unfortunately for Juan, the other four overhead them and began reciting what had happened to them as well. Juan grimaced, realizing he was working all five at one time! The only thing that saved the day was the five had nearly the same identical traumatic incident, without any perceptible differences.

All day long, Juan kept them at it. By suppertime, he felt some progress was being made. He had to stop because the other bodies had woken up and needed help and supper. Another round of massive confusion resulted. By this time, Juan was exhausted himself, having gotten little sleep in over twenty-four hours. He had to sleep, but he also needed the six half-armed women to stay awake all night. He convinced Anne to help them spend the night learning to walk well. That she could do, and Julie pointed out snacks she'd prepared for them to eat.

As it turned out, this plan worked out well. The six

were driven by their new implants to ignore the intense cramps and pains in their feet and the intense compression from their corsets, and to learn to walk elegantly and gracefully. Naturally, wearing their special panties also triggered their cravings for sexual stimulus, which continually interrupted their walking practice. Still, it kept them occupied all night.

The next day after the massive morning confusion died down and the six were put to bed, Juan continued working the five women via their Indian bodies. He picked up where they'd left off yesterday and continued to run them over and over their nasty trauma. Many days later, he'd finally accomplished the miracle! The five erased the bulk of the implant and its overwhelming force on them. Finally, some semblance of normalcy returned.

What shocked all five of them was just how close they had actually come to dying during the implant. Lady Persephone was the first to realize what had happened to her and to her friends. She described it to Juan.

"I was fighting the drugs and the intense pain in my head, but I was losing the battle. It's so weird, but it felt as if I was being pushed out of my head. At the end, I was seeing the back of my head from three feet away, and it was encased in this white, intensely painful energy. I think a second longer and that would have been the end of me and my body, but at that instant, the energy, the pain, the whatever, seemed to be subsiding, and I was pulled back into my head. Juan, I think I understand now what happens to those who mysteriously die when being implanted on those older Model I implant machines! They get pushed out of their body's heads so far that they believe their body is really dead. Bloody hell, I was a hair from that point myself!"

Hearing her explanation, Beth quickly added, "Right, Lady Persephone! That's exactly what it seemed like to me too! A hair from giving it all up! Wild!" Amanda, Jessica, and Tilly agreed with both of them.

Tilly added, "A hair's breadth from tossing in the

towel! Hey, what would have then happened to our Indian bodies here? God, this is so confusing! Would we have lost these bodies too? I was so disoriented!"

No one had an answer for that one, but Lady Persephone suggested, "We might not have, if someone could have tried to rouse us in these bodies, but I'm not sure. This transference thing is highly suspect. I don't trust it too far, but I'm sure these psych men don't have a clue about what is truly going on, that we are spiritual beings and not just some bodies and minds. Bloody hell, we're bad off enough anyway." She sighed and added, "But this is better than being dead."

While all the effects weren't completely eliminated, at this point, they could operate their Indian bodies well. Thus, during the succeeding nights, Jessica began working on Jana to help her over her intense implant, while Amanda did the same with Anne. Sure enough, Anne recovered within a day, because she had received her implant from one of the older machines. By now, the Pytalon was out of her system, though she would need a complete detoxification soon, since she still had frequent hallucinations. She was certainly confused to discover she was in the States and not London. However, Jana presented the same difficulties as the five had.

Jessica discovered it took around six to seven days of her special therapy to eradicate much of the intense force behind these new implants, a six-fold increase in the time needed! Jana was quite confused, but by the sixth long night of Jessica's therapy, she finally reduced the implant's effects on her, as well as that from Pytalon-Ex. Now she was again confused, discovering she was in the States and not married to Lyle.

Thus, by February, none of the six needed to continue to wear the tight corsets or the ballet boots, though they all still needed to wear the fancy apparel, substituting their usual six-inch heels for the boots. Yet, there were still strong residual aftereffects present, dramatized by both the half-armed women and their new

Indian bodies as well. At this point, they dove into their researches with a newfound motivation! In her spare time, Jessica also continued to work with each for many days after this point, trying to get rid of the powerful after-effects that still plagued them at random times, desensitizing phrases that popped up randomly.

***

Chan-Petra was returned to Chicago two days after the six were dropped off. Her case played out differently. True, when she awoke to find herself re-implanted and when she was operating that body, she had no choice but to react as all the others had. However, the Feds kept her sedated, per Vaani-Petra's orders. When operating Vaani's body, she was able to keep the implant under partial control. Why? What had been done to her old friend, Lech, as well as her dear friends caused her necessity level to rise higher than it ever had been in her entire life. The result was that she merely periodically recited the litany silently to herself. At other times, she was able to focus and keep things running, though only with a Herculean effort on her part.

Clues were slowly developing, in part from a thorough investigation of the dead men from the several crimes. In fact, an even more significant clue came her way the very day her Chan-Petra body was returned.

A man entered the Feds building, announcing himself to the receptionist, "I'm John Harms, the newly appointed Supreme Commander of the Feds."

"I'm sorry. We have a Supreme Commander. I'll send you up to see her," the man replied, signaling Vaani-Petra, who ordered six other Feds to come rushing to her office, joining the two Trikuza men watching over her.

The well-dressed man walked in and saw Vaani-Petra, an EE woman from India, sitting behind the desk. "Excuse me, but I have been appointed to be the new Supreme Commander of the Feds. You will please vacate this office. We don't allow EE women in the building."

Vaani forgot being Petra for a moment. "The hell I

will. I'm the Supreme Commander, taking over for the kidnaped, mutilated, and implanted Chan, until she recovers. You, sir, are an imposter. Check his ID card. Take his fingerprints and DNA at once!"

"Where the hell did you come from? You weren't appointed to this position. I was! Stop that," he tried to avoid the Feds carrying out her orders. "You haven't any authority over me. Arrest her. She's the imposter. Chan-Petra is now one of those new Fetish EE Women, wholly incapable of being anything more than a helpless sex doll. Unhand me now!"

"Who sent you? Who appointed you? Who told you about Chan's situation? Better yet, arrest him. We'll subject him to Truth Drug-A immediately!" Vaani barked viciously.

With broad grins, her Feds did just that, very willingly. After all, they'd witnessed the horrific treatment of their beloved Captain Lech and then the debilitating attack on Chan-Petra, to say nothing of their own building having been raided. They wanted payback!

Within hours, they learned the head of Total Care Worldwide, a Henry Koch, had personally briefed him on this post and had appointed him the new head. Whoever this illusive leader was, he had intimate knowledge of just what was being done to Chan-Petra before it even had occurred! Vaani fired off text messages to everyone outlining her suspicions that this Henry Koch was a Cabal member. They didn't get much more useful information out of this imposter, other than he was to put an end to the Feds constant interference in world affairs. With Lady Persephone currently out of the picture, Vaani took justice into her hands. She ordered the imposter to be implanted as a Garbage Collector Twentieth Class and heavily dosed on Pytalon.

They all continued to follow the clues from the dead men. The kidnaping men that had been killed were identified as members of a New York group called The Righteous. Vaani sent off a dispatch ordering the New York office to launch a full-scale investigation of this group and ordering the apprehension of their entire group and to use Trikuza if needed. "Now we are getting somewhere!" she declared to her Feds.

"Right on, boss!" several men chanted, punching their fists in the air, as if that would somehow lessen what had happened to Captain Lech.

Later, when the location of Luxemburg was unraveled during Juan's marathon therapy sessions on the five women and later Jana, Vaani ordered Wolf to search that entire country, find that castle, and shut it down, arresting everyone there. A few days later, the Wolf reported they found the castle, but it had been very hastily evacuated, probably a day before. Still, he found numerous signs of what had gone on here, including quite a pile of discarded lower arms and hands! Grim.

Unknown to Wolf, Delius suspected this castle would be found, and he'd arranged for it to be evacuated after the last of the current women were handled. Later on after the situation died down some, he planned to reopen this center, which served the greater Luxemburg area only. It reopened in April, but by then the Feds had forgotten about it, just as Delius thought.

Additionally, the Feds beefed up their security around their building. They added four more guards on the EMAC rooftop platform and changed their key codes. Now none of the guards up there could open the elevator doors. Instead, someone on the inside had to verify visually what was going on via new security cameras and open the elevator doors for them. Two more Trikuza men joined her in her office, adding to her sense of security.

A week later, Mahala-Jessica arrived to work her magic on Chan-Petra. As with the others, it took her six days to get it mostly dormant. During that time, she remained in the office, sleeping in the back room with Chan-Petra. Once she finished up, she left, taking Chan-Petra with her. Following the orders of the professor, Chan-Petra went back to Phoenix, where she once more began looking after the two babies, leaving Vaani-Petra in

charge of the Feds. That done, Mahala-Jessica returned to Chicago and went to Captain Lech Smith's home to see what could be done for him, that is, her.
***

The Feds dropped Leah Smith and Emma off at his home. The lieutenant explained, "Mrs. Mary Lyons Smith, we've retrieved your husband. The enemy has done quite a job on him, I'm sorry to say. As you can see, they've turned him into a woman and then implanted him, er her, as one of their new Fetish EE Women, just as they've done to the five close associates of Chan-Petra and are very likely doing it right now to Chan as well. We're closing in on their operation, and soon we hope to shut them down. Meanwhile, this is Emma, who is supposed to be Leah's assistant. Leah—that's what they are now calling him. She's in a very bad way, but we'll send help for her as soon as we can get any kind of handle on this new implant."

He turned and left Leah and Emma standing in the doorway, and Mary staring in total disbelief at what used to be her loving, kind husband.

"Lech? Is this really you, honey?" Mary struggled to say and keep her voice from shrieking.

Seeing his one handed wife, the brilliant organizer, standing before him finally reached Lech. This time, the implant couldn't keep the emotions he felt from reaching his body. A tear formed, then two, then a stream. He tried to speak, but the litany attempted to take over his voice. Lech fought harder than he ever had in his life. His soprano voice barely whispered, "Yes. It's me. I'm so sorry. I'm ruined now." After that, his will power was overwhelmed by the massive headache that resulted from his disobeying of his implanted behavior, and he found himself reciting the damnable litany.

"She can't stand up very well. Can we come in?" Emma whispered, wholly confused. What were they doing in this strange woman's home?

Mary's voice cracked. "Come in. Come in." She rushed forward, throwing her arms around Leah, who tried to reciprocate, but her giant bosom was in the way; her stumps barely touched Mary, but that didn't matter. Mary squeezed them tightly for the both of them.

Mary led him to their living room sofa. Leah mostly fell into it, pulling her hair some. Emma hastily got Leah's long black hair out of the way, while Mary finally recovered from the shock. "Well, Leah is it now? They certainly turned you into a shapely woman, but how can you even walk in those boots?"

"I have to walk elegantly and gracefully," Leah tried to answer, but was able with some effort to add, "I haven't mastered it yet."

Emma added, "Walking provides the pleasuring she needs. Many times a day, I think. It's dark out; time to get her ready for bed. This is so confusing. I don't have her nightgown anymore. I must have lost it. I can't find her bedroom. It seems to have vanished, just like that strange castle."

Of course, Mary didn't understand what Emma was trying to convey. Instead, Mary helped Leah up, and Emma followed them into their bedroom. A half hour later, Mary now understood fully what Leah was enduring and why. Via the implant words, which Leah kept repeating frequently, and seeing her undressed down to the tight, heavily boned inner corset, and the latex panties, Mary finally grasped the situation.

Hastily, she fixed up the guest bedroom for Emma, and then left her to fend for herself, while she slipped into bed beside Leah. "I understand honey. We can make this work out." She leaned over, gave her a passionate kiss, and felt Leah's passions exploding. A half hour later, Leah fell into the first solid night's sleep she'd had since the abduction.

The next day, Mary's keen organizational skills took center stage once more. Already, she'd proven her worth to Captain Lech by helping him organized the Chicago Feds after he was appointed their leader. He had always "brought" his work home with him. That is, he'd kept Mary fully informed on nearly everything that had gone on, keeping no secrets from her. Also, she knew what would happen to Leah's toes if Leah continued to ignore the intense cramping and pains in her toes. Already, they were black and blue, a sure sign that toes were broken, most likely compression fractures, she guessed. If Leah ignored them and continued to attempt to wear the boots and walk in them, Mary knew Leah's feet would end up like the thirteen other rescued women. Leah would still be crippled up and forced to continue to wear these boots even if by some miracle Leah's implant could be desensitized and if the effects of Pytalon could be removed. Knowing her husband well, she knew that alone would totally demoralize him or her, once her reasoning faculties were restored. That, Mary could not allow to happen. Thus, she slipped a heavy sedative into his breakfast juice.

When Leah finally drifted off, Mary placed an emergency assistance call. An hour later, she and Emma had Leah in the emergency treatment center of Cook County General. X-rays confirmed her suspicions, compression fractures. Several hours later, the still sedated Leah had both feet in plaster casts. She was sitting in a wheel chair. Mary ordered Emma to push it, while they made another stop at the pharmacy to stock up on sedatives before taking the MET back to their home. During these hours, she ignored the nearly constant confusion boiling off from poor Emma.

Once home, she dosed both Leah and Emma on the sedative. Soon both dozed off in her living room. Finally, Mary had some peace and quiet in which to plan her next move. She knew both needed to be detoxed, Emma more so than Leah. Thus, she placed a call to Chicago's new center and arranged for someone to come, pick up Emma, and handle her. An hour later, Emma was whisked off to the center. They did give Mary a follow up phone call the next day. After that, Mary relaxed some. Emma's implant was the normal type, and she hadn't been on the drug for very long. They expected her to be finished in about ten days.

Meanwhile, Mary had to deal with Leah herself. She suspected Leah would have a horrific time trying to obey her implant while her feet were in casts. Thus, her plan was simply to keep Leah sedated for as much of the time as possible. She hoped in six weeks when the casts came off that someone would be able to help her get Leah's implant under control. If not, then she planned to contact Chan-Petra and ask for additional help.

Her burden was lessened some ten days later, when Emma was returned to her. The young English teen was bright, vibrant, and very alert, eager to help Mary. The detox program had salvaged her life, but she was still confused about being in the States and not London.

"Once we get Leah recovered, Emma, we'll see you get back to London. Since you want to help others, I think maybe we can get you a position in their new detox center." Emma loved that idea! She could do something of immense worth for others.

***

"Wow, that was a brilliant move, Mary," Mahala-Jessica complimented Mary. She'd finally gotten back to Chicago and had come to see what could be done for Captain Lech or Leah. She found Leah sitting on a couch, mostly relaxed and sedated, though the casts had been removed yesterday. "Perfect timing, Mary. This new implant machine's effects are six times worse than the current models. We've discovered it takes at least six times longer to get that damnable implant destimulated, but it will have strong, lingering after-effects. We're still working on those."

"Please, I'll give you anything if you can get my Lech back," Mary pleaded.

"Of course, I'll start on him or her today. By next week, we should be done. If you want, you can sit by me and witness how I do it," Mahala-Jessica suggested, knowing that was precisely what Mary wanted to do. She had a stake in seeing this through.

It took eight days. Mary had been giving Leah strong

painkillers during this period as well as the sedation medication. She'd also removed the tight corset and merely keeping Leah wearing a nightgown all these weeks. Of course, her implant did its best to force a behavior change, yielding migraines. Hence, the strong painkillers Mary gave her. Those slowed the process down some. Still, Mahala-Jessica got the result she desired: implant and trauma incidents destimulated. Just as she finished up, the OD group paid them a call.

***

R³ and Felix took the news of the kidnaping and mutilation of their new friends and benefactors hard. Because of those actions and what had happened to Rachel Roxanne and the other thirteen harem women, the two decided to act on their own. As a result, Mary Jane and Todd took over caring for everyone, while Rhianna lent them a hand. Trevor took their protection onto his shoulders, installing all manner of defensive measures using many of the weapons he found in storage on the three estates.

Felix suggested, "Look, R³, it's up to us to get everyone's arms back. You see if you can find or get everyone's DNA samples located. I'm going to do more digging into the OD situation. I wonder where they found the ODs they used to get their lower arms back. Something seems a bit fishy to me. Mary Jane says the donors have to be compatible with the recipients. That's obvious with us and our hosts, but what about everyone else? I'm going to do some more sleuthing, dear."

"Okay, we just have to do something to help them," R³ replied. "Look, we should consider whole arm transplants this time. Remember what we learned? There is a higher success rate with whole arm transplants than there is with only lower arm transplants. Even hand replacements have a better chance of success than lower arms. Look into whole arm transplants for all them this time, Felix."

"On it. My thoughts exactly," he replied, typing

away, following up on a hunch he had. Two days later, he knew he was onto something big. "R³. Come look at this. Universal Donors. What the heck have I uncovered this time?"

Looking over his shoulder, R³ read the document on his screen.

2050 Ramani Institute for Advanced Research, India

Today, the Ramani Institute announced their development of Universal Transplant Donors. A group of twenty-four donor clones, each with a specific DNA code, can provide compatible organs for an estimated ninety percent of the world's population. The researchers are calling these the UDs or Universal Donors. This medical breakthrough is a major breakthrough in the medical transplant arena, providing compatible donors in a timely manner.

With sufficient funding, the Ramani Institute hopes to begin full production of these UD clones. They expect to have donors ready for life-saving operations within eighteen years. A spokesman for the institute suggests that within twenty years there will be no waiting lists or waiting times for those in need of life-saving transplants.

"Wow! Felix, if this is real, I wonder if the program is still in operation?" R³ gushed, her mind racing with possibilities.

"On it now, dear," Felix replied with a smile. "This could be the break we've been looking for." His fingers flew over the keyboard.

A bit later, he exclaimed, "Incredible, R³! Right under our very noses! Ward 14! Oh, this is weird. They grow them in vats?" R³ dashed over to his side to see what he'd found.

"Good god! Those them? The UD clones?" she asked, shocked at the image he'd pulled up from a surveillance camera on Ward 14, ten floors above their original home Ward 4. She saw tall, fluid filled cylinders, with a confusing array of tubes and wires going into them. There floating suspended in the fluids were human bodies, unmoving, probably comatose she thought.

"Yep. There are the UDs, dear. Unlike us ODs, they're only sort of alive, I expect. According to the manifest, there are thirty adults in there and thirty teens and thirty smaller children, if those are the right words for them," Felix replied, uncertain of just what to call them. They looked human enough, though.

He pointed out one particular adult and fiddled with his computer, zooming in on it. "See, it is missing its lower arms. I wonder if this one was the donor for our people." He went on, "Anyway, we can see if we can't get enough UDs together to provide full arm transplants for everyone."

"Incredible, Felix. Okay, you see about that. I've got all the DNA samples isolated. Sending you a listing of them now. I'll email all this information to the professor. Felix, we just have to pull this off. We just have to get everyone their arms and hands back, somehow, someway," R3 declared.

Felix smiled, for that was his intention all along. A week later, Felix had worked it all out: twenty-one women were being scheduled to get full arm transplants, spread out over the last three weeks of February and over six different hospitals scatted about the mid-west, namely St. Louis, Minneapolis, Kansas City, Des Moines, Indianapolis, and Detroit. To disguise this whole operation further, Felix also scheduled as many other recipients as he could find in those areas who needed other organs, such as a kidney or liver or lungs. All told, he finagled a hundred transplants. Beth paid for all the operations from the confiscated funds from Benny's massive bank account, depleting it of approximately a hundred million credits. Nearly ninety other people would be benefitting from this as well, pleasing Beth enormously.

The professor insisted on tight security. Two Trikuza members and two Feds accompanied each woman to the hospital. This time, the four never left the sides of the patients, much to the doctor's dismay. By the end of March 2273, the twenty-one had fully recovered, their lives restored.

However, Felix and R^3 weren't done. Rather in February, they discovered their suggestion on the reorganization of the ODs had been implemented. Some fifty children were now being housed in their old Ward 4 and Ward 5. In a St. Louis facility, they housed some fifty teenaged ODs.

While they were awaiting on the massive UD transplant operations to commence, they set about rescuing the fifty children. This time, Felix became craftier in his hacking. While all fifty were rescued in the same way as before, an exhilarating trip down the emergency fire exit slide, he installed numerous fake transportation logs into a number of these facilities. Anyone checking on the location of these fifty children would discover that some had been transferred to this and that center, and transferred again to another center, all ending in dead ends. Thus, these fifty children, none of whom was over nine years old, seemed to have simply vanished from the Total Care system. In fact, they joined the other children at the Waberly compound.

At this point, Rhianna took over. She set up a "private school" at the mansion, hiring teachers, equipment, clothing, computers, and cooks for the ever-growing number of children. Rachel Roxanne provided the funds from her huge account.

Once she had her arms back, she and the other thirteen "harem" women chose to watch over and take care of these children. She wanted to make sure they had a fighting chance at a real life and a real education. She called it the Waberly School for Promising Children. Further, since R^3 figured other Cabal men might come after Rachel Roxanne, R^3 volunteered to take her place, leaving Rachel Roxanne free to work on running the new school and caring for all the children. Rachel Roxanne readily agreed, since her experiences with these men had been devastating to say the least. She wanted nothing more to do with them or even the running of the corporations she now owned.

With the children handled, Felix next turned his attention onto the teenaged ODs. He wanted to reach those who were like the Circle of Six, those who wanted to escape their hopeless OD situation. This was a far trickier situation to handle. From his own experience, he knew many teens were totally into being ODs and certainly didn't want any other life. Somehow, he had to find a way to reach only those who wanted a real life.

His lengthy project began simple enough. He hacked into the general network that hosted the teens' computer systems. One day when they logged onto their OD Ward computer, they found a tiny link that said: Freedom. Clicking it took them to a web page that Felix had copied, one that showed the reader just what the whole OD program actually was. From there, he had additional links for them to follow. Felix was intentionally leading the reader down the very path of discovery he'd followed. The ending link was one that sent him a secure email. Now all he had to do was wait and see if any of these many teens actually made it all the way through.

During these weeks, Trevor wasn't idle. While he found many guns and bombs in the various arsenals of the three Cabal member's estates, he knew he needed to provide far better security. Thus, he began an extensive web search for automated security weapons. That was the best description he could think of to describe what he wanted. Right now, there were very few men to guard all these children and women—just the three of them. He couldn't even protect one of these estates from the simplest of attacks. He had no idea how he could hire security men, and besides, Pytalon-dosed men would be next to worthless as security guards.

After a week's searching, he found entries that described the Automated Security Gun System, called ASGS. He studied the specifications in detail and particularly how to set them up for a good defense. The pdf files were very explicit and gave him many valuable ideas. Next, he researched how to acquire them and met a dead end. They had been abandoned back in 2100, though most had been confiscated by the Feds and put into cold storage. The questions Trevor had were: where were they and could he get his hands on a bunch of them?

The first question was the easiest to answer. A day later, he found their location: an underground facility in Colorado, a secure facility. He spent some time trying to invent a way to get into it, but gave that idea up. He then sent a detailed email to the professor, outlining his security concerns for these three estates, his proposed solution using the ASGS systems, their location, and asking for advice on how to proceed.

A day later, Vaani-Petra sent him an email, suggesting he submit a formal request for them with the Chicago Feds. He did as she asked, requesting thirty of them, along with a goodly supply of ammunition. To his amazement, a week later, he received an email with instructions to follow.

A Feds man picked him up and drove him to the facility in Colorado, where they were met by four local Feds from Denver. Together, they entered the facility. Trevor was impressed. Here was a huge arsenal of weapons! The four local Feds used small EM forklifts to haul the thirty boxes to the entrance area, while Trevor and his driver began storing them in the EMAC. He was also given an extra three crates filled with ammunition for these fifty-caliber guns, pleasing him. No one asked him why he needed thirty of these ASGS systems, which he thought unusual, but Trevor didn't complain.

The Chicago Feds man spent three days helping him set them up at the three estates. Around the perimeter of the Raven estate, they installed nine of these monster guns in such a way that they provided covering fire for each other. They were targeted to fire upon anything coming over the outer walls, but nothing beyond about ten feet from the walls. The tenth was setup centrally. It was programmed to fire upon any landing vehicle that didn't respond with the "clearance code." Trevor installed that code into all their EMACs and gave it to the Chicago Feds man, who promised to give it to the local AP-cops as well. That way, they hoped no innocent EMAC would be accidentally shot at.

Trevor and the Feds man then held a demonstration for R[3], Felix, Mary Jane, Todd, and Rhianna, along with Rachael Roxanne. While everyone watched from a good distance away, the Feds man tossed a crash dummy over the wall. Instantly, two of the ASGS systems opened fire, their large caliber shells ripping the dummy into small pieces.

"Ta da. Now we have some protection here!" Trevor declared. "If they try to come over the walls, they'll be stopped." Even the glassy-eyed Feds man was impressed with the system.

Trevor explained, "We'll arm them at night, once everyone goes to bed, and turn them off in the morning. That way we can't easily be taken by surprise."

"Well, I'll sleep better now," Rachel Roxanne declared, recalling that terror-filled night when the three families were attacked. Felix and R[3] also felt safer, particularly with all of the children now their responsibility as well.

Chapter 13—Decisions, Adjustments, and Actions

"Mary, I don't have any words to thank you for putting up with me these many weeks and saving my life," Leah explained to her wife. She'd just been returned from Detroit where she had full arm transplants from some UD. She wasn't supposed to lift more than two pounds for the next month. After that, she had an extensive exercise and rehab program laid out for her by the doctors there. "I can finally hug you again," she added. "But we have to talk, Mary."

"I'm so happy to have you back and whole again, dear," she replied. "Besides, you rescued me from my misery at Southend. I'm glad I had a way to truly pay you back for that too."

"Yes, but Mary, I still love you more than anything in this world, but we have to be practical. They've made me into a woman now. I can't possibly satisfy you any longer. I have no right to make you stay with me now. I mean, you should find another husband, a man who can. As I am now, I'm hardly worthy you," she admitted.

Mary pulled back from her and stared hard at Leah, before replying. She intuitively knew this day would come, known it would from the moment the Feds had brought Leah back to her and she saw him in their doorway. Mary sighed.

"Isn't this just like a man? Captain Lech, haven't you learned anything from our marriage? You think you aren't worthy of me anymore, but what about my feelings when we first met? I didn't think I was worthy of you, not with my stump here. I got over that and so can you. You've already told me everything that means anything to me. Love. I love you and you love me. Love isn't about our bodies. Haven't you learned that yet? Now come here. I need a big hug. Besides, we have to get you back to your post at the Feds. Vital work has backlogged."

"But how can I face going back there? Like this? An EE woman no less?" Leah protested.

Mary pulled her tightly to her. "Together, we can face it. After all, Petra had to do the same thing. If she could do it, so can you. Now enough of this. We need to work out what you're going to wear, dear. We both know you're going to need to dress as I do, at least most of the time. We'll take along your boots and pants too. When you need to go out into the field, change into them. Now come on. Chicago and the whole Midwest need you, now more than ever. Besides, you and I need to find out just who did this to you, and then we'll get them. I'll strangle them with my one hand if I can."

Leah sighed. Relief. She felt as much relief from what Mary had just declared as she had when she awoke to find she had hands again. She gave Mary a very passionate kiss, before declaring, "Mary, I'm going to get you trained to shoot a gun. Together, we'll shoot the damned bastard who did this to me!"

An hour later and wearing a light blue satin gown and matching six-inch heels, Captain Leah Smith and his assistant, Mary, walked into the Feds building. When they reached his or her old floor, a dozen of his fellow Feds stepped out of their offices and began clapping. "Welcome back, boss!" one yelled and several others hollered as well, embarrassing her slightly.
***

Jana Michaelson-Waberly sat around the underground bunker of Weasel and Wart, looking just as confused as ever. True, Jessica had finished her special therapy, drastically reducing the effects of the new Fetish EE Woman implant on Jana, and the Pytalon-Ex drug had weeks ago left her system. However, Jana was still very confused. She was somewhat attractive, particularly so she believed, since she'd gotten her childhood dream of becoming an EE woman as her mother was. Her wavy brown hair reached her waist and her curves were impressive in her own mind, though her breast size was the same as all EE women.

Tilly accurately pegged Jana, though not in front of the eighteen-year-old. "She's even dumber than Rachael Roxanne. To be blunt about it, she's not too bright."

"Maybe it has something to do with how she was raised," Amanda came to Jana's defense. All five were willing to get to know Jana better before writing her off. During the ensuing days, they got a good understanding of Jana and at the same time helped remove much of the confusion the young woman had. In the process, the five gained valuable insight into just how the Cabal members raised and educated their children.

Jana's home schooling had been marginal at best. She could just barely read and write. Her math skills ended with basic arithmetic. She had no knowledge of history and certainly none of science. At least, she had some knowledge of the world's geography. Rather, she'd always admired her mother, the EE woman Emma, and wanted nothing more than to be married to a nice man and be loved. She had no real goals in life other than to be a loving wife, giving and receiving pleasure, a sex doll. That's all she'd ever known. All the women she'd seen during her eighteen years had been other Cabal EE women. She knew nothing else, though she had some vague ideas about having a child or two for her husband.

Jana knew she was supposed to be marrying Lyle Walton, but he wasn't anywhere around this strange series of rooms. Anne, her Personal Assistant, came from London and was just as confused about their situation. True, she regained her thinking abilities once her implant had been destimultated by Beth, but she too had had very little education and really had wanted to be a personal Lady's Maid. Both before and after having her arms transplanted, Jana continued to insist on wearing the Fetish EE woman's outfits, as restrictive as they were. Anne was quite pleased to assist her in dressing and even walking. By now, Jana had learned to walk reasonably well in her ballet boots. Why? Tilly worked it out. By looking like a proper Fetish

EE Woman, Jana still hoped to find a husband.

Thus, Tilly spent many days "educating" Jana on the true situation the world was in, opening the young teen's eyes considerably. That Jana knew she'd very nearly died during the nasty implant and that she'd been completely helpless without her lower arms and hands, combined to make Jana keenly interested in just what was going on in the world. Thus, by the time she returned from the arm transplant operation, she accepted the fact that her father and the other Cabal families were the "bad guys," as she put it. However, she still clung to her goal of being married and being a loving sex doll, much to everyone's disgust. Hence, in early April, they moved her in with the other OD teens that Felix had been systematically rescuing. There, she might well find a "husband."

All this wasn't to say that Jana wasn't able to give Tilly critical information on her Cabal family and several others. Rather the opposite. Jana was a mountain of information. She even sketched in detail the layout of Ben Michaelson-Waberly's secure compound on the outskirts of London. Tilly knew just what this top Cabal member did and that he was one of the nine Camarilla leaders!

Jana told them all about Tom Walton's family. Of course, she was to marry his son, Lyle. She knew they lived somewhere around St. Louis, just not precisely where. Before Jana left for the Waberly estate, Beth brought up some web pages for Jana, dispelling the last of her notions that she could still somehow marry Lyle Walton. The page showed a "Jana" had already married Lyle. Further, the image of this "Jana" looked exactly like her, less lower arms and hands, completely shocking Jana.

Via some clever hacking from Felix, Beth pointed out this married Jana was in fact her OD clone! However, Lyle had been implanted and put on Pytalon-Ex. Now he was the CEO at one of the Walton Corporation headquarters in Memphis. Those images finally convinced Jana that she'd never be able to marry Lyle as she had planned.

Thus, as the group got back into their sleuthing in early April, they knew about two of the nine Camarilla members, including the precise location of Ben Michaelson-Waberly. In addition, they had some other names to look into, among them a Delius Pogs, Henry Koch, and Al Rumani. Further, Chan-Petra added a few other names, including James Buffett.

During the early months of 2273, Felix and R³ also decided to take other preventative measures. Rachel Roxanne was not exceptionally bright, and after her horrid experience with Benny, she wanted nothing more to do with her entire heritage. All she wanted to do was to help the children now being housed at the Waberly estate and the Michaelson compound. She and R³ knew from Beth and Tilly that other Cabal men were highly likely to come to court Rachel Roxanne, probably to marry her and abscond with her impressive fortune that approached thirty billion credits. Thus, R³ decided from now on, she should pretend to be the billionaire heiress. Rachel Roxanne eagerly gave her wholehearted consent to this.

However, R³ had other reasons for wanting to take over being the heiress. These reasons, she simply couldn't put into words, not even to Felix. They were mostly strange feelings, as if she knew far more about all this than she ought to know. Further, she felt downright hostile when anyone spoke of Ben Michaelson-Waberly.

This proved to be a wise decision. Mid-February, Trevor's advanced warning system alerted everyone at the Raven compound of an incoming EMAC. Felix activated his new security cameras and ducked out of sight, while R³ headed to the front door. She watched as the EMAC settled down on top of the snow-covered lawn not far from their own EMAC. She took a deep breath and steeled herself, as a strange man stepped out, carrying a bouquet of red roses in one hand.

"Hello," R³ said formally, when he'd reached the door. Beneath a heavy winter parka that was unzipped, she saw a tall young man, perhaps in his mid-twenties, but very well dressed in a black suit. He had a small black moustache and goatee as well. His cropped black hair was partially hidden beneath a stocking cap.

"Ah, Rachel Roxanne Raven-Waberly. You are prettier than I was led to believe. I'm afraid these roses I've brought for you pale compared to your beauty," his bass voice broke the stillness, his breath quite visible in the cold, winter air before the door. His English accent was unmistakable. She accepted the roses, as he stepped inside past her.

"Thanks. I'm afraid I don't know you. You have me at a disadvantage," R³ countered.

"Preston. Preston Michaelson-Waberly. Surely, you've heard of the London Michaelson-Waberly's. Ben is my father. We own the rest of the EMAC and Air Liner companies," he explained.

R³ felt a surge of outright hostility, but couldn't figure out why. Thus far, the man was polite and pleasant enough. "Ah yes. Wasn't Ben Michaelson-Waberly the one who stole most of the EMAC and Air Liner companies from their original owners?" she asked pointedly, recalling some of what she'd recently learned of ancient history. Could that be why she felt so hostile towards him?

"Ah, well, yes, that's true, Rachel, but golly, that happened over a century and a half ago. 2022 to be precise. I know my history pretty well, Rachel. Originally, two female engineers applied the EM technology to build them. Joanne Waberly invented the EMACs, while Jena Michaelson created our Air Liners. Between the two, they amassed a fortune worth close to fifty billion, but then they divided their estate among their children. That diluted everything. Honestly, it doesn't make good business sense to have the EMAC companies divided among different owners, or the Air Liner companies either. So yes, back in 2022, my dad tried to bring common sense back into the business by marrying Jana Waberly. We've a portrait of that stunning EE woman in our living room. Surely, you can see the extreme merits of having these two companies being run by one person and not divided up piecemeal."

R³ retorted, "Well, yes, that makes a whole lot of sense. It's also my opinion all the EMAC and Air Liner companies should be under one leader. That way, you get consistency of production."

"I'm glad you see this too. That's why I'm here, my lovely Rachel. I want to marry you, and then we can get all these companies back together under one roof, so to speak. Soon, you're going to get many other fellows from other Cabal families wooing you, just to get their hands on your vast fortune. That will never do, since our companies would still be split under two or more owners," Preston explained the obvious.

R³ replied, "No, I agree. That will never do at all. Don't worry. I've no intention of marrying into some other Cabal family. After all, how could a man running the Consumer Goods companies know how best to run EMAC and Air Liner companies? Hardly."

Preston's face broke into a huge grin, obviously greatly relieved. However, he jumped the gun, "So you are interested in marrying me?"

"Not exactly. I'm interested in merging the ownership of these two companies under one roof. Mine," R³ declared.

Preston raised his eyebrows in disbelief. "But you're an EE woman, though I must admit, you aren't quite what I expected." She wore a red satin gown with matching tall heels, accentuating her long black hair.

R³ grinned teasingly, "So what did you expect?"

"Well, I was led to believe you were a Fetish EE woman, I believe that's what they are being called now. Weren't you kidnaped and added to Benny's harem? That must have been awful for you."

"Well, as a matter of fact, yes I was, but I've put that behind me now," R³ replied.

"But you still have your arms. I take it you didn't like wearing the sexy, exotic boots? Mom has become a Fetish EE woman, and she looks positively stunning! Dad just can't keep his hands off her. They've never been as happy as they have been these last few weeks. I was expecting to see you had also become one of these incredibly fantastic looking women," Preston admitted and hinted that was his preference for her appearance too.

"Just had my arms replaced. ODs. Sorry to disappoint you, Preston, but I certainly don't want to be a helpless person, dependent upon others for everything. Hardly." R³ retorted.

"Well, as far as I'm concerned, you look fabulous as you are. So can we get married soon?" Preston continued.

"Preston, you seem like a nice fellow, but I've never seen you before. I'm certainly not in love with you. How can you even think of marrying someone you've never met before, let alone someone you don't love?" R³ countered.

Preston flushed, "You look beautiful. I figure that after we're married and live together, love will follow. Say, you don't seem to be following the proper behavior EE women have. You're really on the ball, as we say."

"Oh, I assure you the implant is there. It's just I have control over it and don't have to be mindlessly acting all that crap out or reciting the script endlessly. I'm hardly a zombie, Preston."

"I see. So your implant was somehow botched? I've heard that sometimes does happen. I could see about getting it redone properly this time for you. It must be hard for you to be an EE woman when your implant isn't working right," Preston suggested.

"No, I'm perfectly happy just the way I'm now, thank you very much. If all you want in a wife is a sex doll, please look elsewhere. I'm my own person, Preston."

"I can see that. Still, you agree we should get our companies under one roof. So I take it you aren't wholly ignoring my marriage offer?" he asked, growing curious.

"Not as such. No. We should get to know each other better," R³ replied, thinking ahead of what more she could learn from Preston. If she could learn where this Cabal family lived, their compound layout, their business organization, and so on, she could let Beth and the others know this invaluable information. (It was February, and Jana had not yet been salvaged.) Acting on pure intuition and a hunch, she added, "I would sure enjoy a tour of the main EMAC company research laboratories."

Preston grinned, "Golly, Rachel, I'm sure dad would be honored to show you around. I think the main research lab is in northwest London. Want me to arrange a tour?"

"I'd like that, but I'd want to see everything there. I'm really very curious about it." R^3 didn't know why she was so incredibly curious about the research lab, only that she was. She added, "But then I'd be afraid you would drug me as Benny did and then turn me into a Fetish EE woman again. What with the unknown men murdering my whole family and also all the Michaelson's and Waberly's too, you can understand my hesitancy."

"Oh yes. That was just a terrible thing to have happened. Have they even found out who did it?" Preston feigned sympathy, not missed by the observant R^3.

"In part. It seems some evil men called the MMS or Marshals Militia and Security did the murders, but the Feds told me someone murdered those men too. We still don't know why our families were murdered," R^3 lied.

"I don't think anyone knows why that happened," Preston replied. "Well then, my pretty rose, let me see if I can arrange this tour for you. Would you feel more comfortable if some Feds accompanied you on the tour?"

"Yes, that would put me more at ease about it, Preston."

"Great! I'm sure glad you too believe that the control of the two companies should be under one leader," Preston added.

R^3 smiled. "Yes of course, but it probably should be under my leadership. After all, my IQ is in the high genius category," she added with a smirk, knowingly teasing him. She watched his reactions carefully. He flinched and that told her all she wanted to know.

"Okay then. Let me see what I can arrange with dad.

I best be going. It's a long flight to London from here." He bowed and kissed her hand before turning and leaving. R³ watched from a window, sounding the all clear once he was airborne.

"You can't be serious about going to London, can you?" Felix gushed the moment it was safe for him to reappear.

R³ bit her red lips. "Well dear, actually I have a feeling I really do need to see that research lab. I think there's something very important there. I can't put my finger on it. Call it a hunch. Let's see if there is anything unusual on their company web pages. It's only the EMAC companies, not the Air Liners," she added.

Satisfied a little, Felix headed off to do just that for her, while she headed to the kitchen to make a cup of tea and ponder why she was sticking her neck out like this. Something was there; she just knew it, but what? Felix was thorough, but he found nothing of note on their company web pages, and R³ agreed with his findings.

A couple of days later, Trevor had their new automatic security system installed. Nine auto-firing cannons guarded the outer walls, while the tenth battery as centrally located, ready to shoot down incoming, raiding EMACs.
***

Preston returned home and gave his father a complete report. "Look, I'm certain Rachel has gotten Benny's Fetish EE woman's alterations undone, presumably using her OD. Further, Rachel's implant is completely faulty. She's acting like a normal person, just as Jana did before she was converted and married to Lyle Walton." He explained Rachel's comments on joining the companies.

"You've got to be kidding me, Preston," Ben exclaimed. At first, Ben was highly encouraged that Rachel believed their EMAC and Air Liner companies should be merged under one person's leadership. However, he made his exclamation when Preston reported Rachel thought that person should be her.

"No, I got the distinct impression she felt that she should be the one controlling and running the businesses, dad. Isn't that just the silliest thing ever? An EE woman running the companies?"

"Son, it's preposterous, beyond laughable," Ben replied, growing more fearful than ever. So many things were going squirrely these days. "Obviously, her implant was totally botched. Probably because of Benny's screwball harem thing. Well, that can easily be rectified. Turn her into a proper Fetish EE woman and the problem will be solved in more ways than one, son."

"My thoughts precisely, dad. I mean, she looks good now, but she'd be even sexier if she were like mom and Jana," Preston admitted.

"Okay then," Ben decided, "we'll take care of her by the old tried and true snatch and grab. I'll take care of it. You check with Delius and see when his new procedures will be ready here in London."

Delius expected to have the London office ready to go with the replacement Model III machines and the necessary Fetish EE Woman accessories by mid-March. Hence, Ben delayed taking action for a week. Considering how simple this snatch and grab would be, he hired six Locki's Freedom Fighters to pull it off.

R^3, Felix, Rhianna, and Trevor were rudely awakened around midnight on March 12. Gunfire erupted from their central cannon! Trevor grabbed several guns and dashed to the windows to see what was going on. The fancy system had floodlights shining up into the sky, reflecting off a black-painted EMAC. Its operator was frantically swerving wildly trying to avoid the spray of high-caliber cannon shells. Finally, it gave up and vanished from sight. Once out of range, the lights turned off and the automatic system shut down.

"Wow! It sure works!" Trevor gushed to the others, who had rushed to join him. "It sure drove those invaders away!"

"I think you should stand guard in case they come back," a worried Rhianna suggested. He did just that. High on adrenaline, he couldn't sleep anyway. The next day, Felix reported these new systems were working well, and he sent a lengthy message to Beth to be relayed to the others.

When Beth realized she couldn't talk R³ out of making this trip into the lion's den, so to speak, she had Greg fly up from Phoenix and implant one of his trackers into her neck. "Best be safe, R³," she explained.

The professor then called R³ directly. "My dear, this is a terribly dangerous thing you're proposing to do. Bloody hell, these Cabal men can't be trusted in the slightest. What is so darn important that you need to visit the EMAC research facilities?"

R³ bit her lip. "It's a hunch or feeling. I get hostile just thinking about this Ben Michaelson-Waberly man and how he stole the companies, but it's not just that, professor. I think somehow it's vitally important for me to visit that lab. Why? I've no rational reason, no believable explanation, sir, just a gut feeling."

The professor chuckled, "Sorry R³. I've never understood this bloody female intuition thing. I remember when Jessica and Amanda landed on my doorstep in Joliet. I went along with them, so I guess that's the closest I can come to this feeling thing. All right then. Make darn sure you have trusted Feds men with you, and do be careful. We can ill afford to lose you, R³."

She promised, and he hung up, knowing that for good or ill, this was something important that Rachel Roxanne Raven just had to do herself. *Life's bloody well like that, and you just have to let them do it. It'll ruin her self-determinism if I didn't.*
***

"Damn! Damn! Damn!" screamed a highly annoyed Ben. His hired men reported their failure, due to the installation of some kind of powerful weapons system! Ben's orderly world was coming unglued. That a lone EE woman no less was doing this seemed completely unbelievable.

Preston grinned, "Dad, I told you she told me she was incredibly smart." Secretly, he was rather pleased the snatch and grab had failed completely, that Rachel had outsmarted his father. Rachel would make an incredible sex doll wife—of that Preston was certain.

"Okay, looks as if we'll have to give her this tour of hers," Ben calmed down a little, but his armpits were drenched with terror-caused sweat. "What does she want a tour of?"

"The main research labs, dad. That's what she said anyway. I can email her for more specifics if you like," Preston answered, hiding his mirth over his dad's upset.

"Okay, do so. I'll work on the arrangements. Let's set the date for March 25. That will give me time. We'll need to contact our local Feds and get her a couple of Feds guards."

"But how will we take her when she has Feds guards around her?" Preston asked.

Stupid kid. He hasn't a clue. Well, he'll make a good CEO once I get them married and get her fixed up the way she should be. Then, I'll have one hundred percent of the EMAC and Air Liner companies and the MET as well. Plus, I just might end up leading the Camarilla. "There'll be some kind of accident," he said, but didn't explain further.

As the date approached, Ben had the formal papers taking over control of her companies prepared. Of course, once Rachel was married to Preston, her signature wasn't needed to join their fortunes together. As far as the Cabal rules went, merely having married his son was sufficient. Ben's plan was simple. Once the "accident" occurred, Rachel would be taken to the Implant Center and turned into a proper Fetish EE Woman, and as soon as she regained consciousness, a priest would marry her to Preston. The formal papers would then be sent off to James Buffett, sealing the deal. Rachel wouldn't even know what had happened. It was a perfect plan. Nothing could go wrong. Ben even splurged, drinking some very old wine the night before the tour.

As the day of the trip drew near, Felix complained, "R³, you can't do this. They're likely to kidnap you, torture you, implant you, and turn you into one of those Fetish EE women. I love you. I can't stand you being hurt. Besides, you know this Cabal Ben just wants to get his hands on your fortune, or rather Rachel's."

"I love you too, Felix, but I have this gnawing feeling that I just have to see this research lab. For the life of me, I can't say why I feel this way or even remotely what I expect to find there. It's just a strange, weird feeling in my stomach, and yes, I do expect this Cabal Ben fellow will try something, but I have a plan. Here's what I want you to do if I get captured," she whispered her ideas into his ear, bringing a broad grin to his face.

He chuckled. "So it's about justice and getting even, belatedly. I like that, but are you sure? The price could well be too high."

"Ah yes, but it can only be paid by one of us ODs," she pointed out. "No one else could pay it. Honestly, Felix, I think I can outsmart them, because I'm sure he doesn't have a genius IQ, and according to Tilly, he's terrified of us," R³ added.

"I still don't like it. I'd rather take your place," Felix lamented.

"I know, but there isn't anyone I trust watching my back besides you, dear," she replied, giving him a passionate kiss.

Around nine the next morning, a Feds EMAC hovered over the Raven estate. After giving the proper code, Trevor lowered the defenses, and the EMAC landed briefly, picking up R³. Two Feds accompanied her to New O'Hare, where they boarded a public Air Liner, arriving at London Heathrow that evening. Here, two London Feds met them, escorting them to a local hotel.

When R³ entered her room, she found Lady Persephone and Juan sitting on chairs waiting for her.

"Room is clear," Lady Persephone whispered. She pinned a small broach onto her red gown. "We've got your back," she added, "so get some sleep. I hope you know what you're doing," she added. "But I know what it is to have a hunch that just doesn't go away."

R³ nodded and smiled, giving both a hug.

Preston knocked on her door around nine in the morning. She'd already used room service for a breakfast. R³ checked her appearance in the mirror. Satisfied she looked like a proper EE woman, she opened the door. "Morning Preston."

"Morning my beautiful rose," Preston replied gallantly, presenting her with another red rose, which he pinned to the shoulder of her dress. Offering her his arm, he led her to a waiting EMAC, prominently displaying the company logo. Two London Feds moved silently in behind them, but she noticed they were a different pair than had met her yesterday and stood guard around her room last night. She also saw that Lady Persephone and Juan had also vanished, but suspected they weren't far away. So far, so good, she thought.

It was a ten-minute flight to the huge EMAC research facility on the northwest edge of sprawling London. As their ship landed, R³ spotted dozens of other company EMACs parked in the lot. The building was only a single story tall, and R³ reasoned that most of the facility was underground. As Preston led her up to the building's entrance, Ben Michelson-Waberly stepped out to greet them. R³ rightly guessed his body was in its early fifties. He'd probably used the Transference Machine, likely more than once.

"Welcome Miss Rachel Roxanne Raven-Waberly," Ben said, his eyes scanning her form, noticing she had a proper EE woman's form and dress. She was attractive, he noted, halfway wishing he could marry her. *Well, once she is properly implanted, she'll cop off with me just as readily as she will with Preston.* "Preston tells me you're keenly interested in merging all the EMAC and Air Liner companies under one leader. I wholeheartedly agree with that. Not only does it make sound business sense, it is financially beneficial as well. I do hope we can reach some agreements in this area before you return home."

R³ replied, "Yes, it certainly does make sense. Of course, I also feel strongly the companies need female leadership, much as they did when they were founded centuries ago, but I'm eager to see all the research labs here. It's so exciting to see them with my own eyes. I don't expect you'll reveal any corporate secrets, so don't worry about that."

"Yes of course," Ben countered. He changed the topic as they entered the building, "I do hope you will marry my Preston here. He so has his heart set on you. Now that I've met you in person, I can see why he is infatuated with you, Rachel. Ah, here is the main office. I've got visitor ID cards for you and the two Feds." He clipped one onto her dress, while handing the others to the two Feds. R³ saw that beyond this office the vast above ground building contained numerous EMACs and servicing stations for them. As she anticipated, the real facilities were underground.

More importantly, as R³ entered this office portion, she had an intense feeling that all this was familiar, intimate somehow, as though she had been here before, not once, but many, many times.

Ben motioned, "Here we take the lift down to the rest of the facility."

As they took the elevator down, these feelings only grew more and more intense. "This is called Lab One," Ben called out, very much bored with this whole trip.

Though the space was huge, perhaps seventy research stations, only five were manned, but R³ first saw hundreds of men and women in white lab coats bustling around these stations. She blinked and saw the many empty stations and the five men who were actually there.

Ben took them on down to the next floor, growing more bored. What did Rachel see here? Why had she insisted on seeing these unused labs? It made no sense, but then perhaps it was because Rachel was already an EE woman. Ben chalked this unreasonable visit to just that. "This lab and the ones below us are no longer in use," he said dryly, hoping the Rachel had seen enough.

As the elevator doors opened and the small party stepped out into Sub-lab 2, once more, R³ saw a bustling lab before her, but blinked and saw the wholly empty facility. *How weird is this anyway. I keep seeing what isn't here.* Then it struck her. *Can this be what it used to have been? If so, that had to have been well over a century ago.* She managed to say, "Cool. What's below us?"

Ben sighed quietly, becoming more convinced Rachel really was both implanted and a bit divvy or even a nutter. There wasn't anything down here to see. He'd even taken a quick trip through these labs two days ago, on the off chance that there was something here that had been missed. "More of the same," he replied in a monotone and stepping back into the elevator.

Sub-lab 3 and Sub-lab 4 were just as abandoned, but still R³'s first glimpse was of hundreds of workers, though a blink revealed the emptiness of the lab. Still, as they continued to descend, R³ became more and more excited, convinced this was somehow vitally important. "Well, this is the last one, Sub-lab 5. I'm told our ancestors Joanne Waberly and her daughter, Jana, used to work down here. As you can see, it's empty, unused. Now, that's the end of the tour. Let's take the lift back up. I've some light refreshments for us."

"May I walk around this lab, Mr. Michaelson-Waberly?" R³ asked politely.

"Oh don't be a prat, Rachel," Ben replied, growing more annoyed with this whole episode. "There's nothing down here."

"Humor me," she replied and began walking out into the spacious room, filled with desks, lab stations, and various machinery. Ben refused to budge from the elevator, but Preston hastily moved to her side, taking her arm in his.

She headed for the far-back end of the facility, several hundred feet from the elevator. R³ noticed at once that this room was half the length as the labs above. She smiled, realizing that meant there was a concealed, secret lab ahead of her! Standard construction would have all the labs the same size. It made no sense to have the bottom floor suddenly half the length of the floors above it. No, something was hidden down here. Her mind suddenly saw a section of the apparent wall sliding back, revealing Jana's secret laboratory. She knew once there had been something secret, vital, and perhaps revolutionary being built in there. R³ guessed whatever it was, it was still there, since these labs had obviously been long abandoned. Dust was thick on the floor; she could see their footprints as they turned around to retrace their steps.

"Fascinating, Preston, just fascinating," R³ finally commented. "Thanks. I really did need to see these facilities for myself." She knew it was vitally important for her to find out just what was hidden behind those walls for so many years. She had images of a young woman working on something in secret, but R³ couldn't quite tell what it was.

"Glad you liked it, my rose," Preston poured it on, eager to get on with it, imagining Rachel soon fawning all over him.

Countless small steps later, the two rejoined Ben and the two London Feds who held the elevator doors open, drumming fingers on the side walls and tapping a toe on the floor though there wasn't any music playing. "I've tea and biscuits waiting us in the main office floor," Ben said dryly, pressing the G button, for ground level, but with some gusto. The doors closed and the elevator began to rise.

R³ heard a faint hissing sound buried among the elevator noises. She wanted to sound the alert, "Gas attack!" She didn't, but bit her lip instead. R³ dared not foil Ben's plans, not just yet, not until he had signed the legal documents. She knew now this trip, no matter the personal cost to her, was beyond priceless! "What's happening?" she heard her voice faintly calling out.

Her legs felt weak. The two London Feds slumped to the floor of the lift seconds before her legs gave out, but Preston held on to her, preventing her collapse. The world went dark, but she heard Ben say, "It is done."

"Dad, I think it's affecting me. . ." Preston's voice trailed away. Now R^3 felt her body slumping down along with his.

"Of course, Preston. You didn't think I was doing all this for you, did you? Stupid prat!"

Lady Persephone and Juan sat in her EMAC about a mile from the lab facilities, monitoring the live video feed from the embedded spy camera in the broach on R^3's gown. They saw the two Feds collapse. "It's happening, My Lady, just as R^3 said it would. Come on; we have to rescue them now, before they cut her to pieces!"

Back in Illinois, Felix was also watching the live feed via a hook up with her EMAC. Over the secure line, Felix heard Juan's suggestion and quickly called out, "Juan. Wait. It has to be done. R^3 was very specific. Keep on monitoring them. She knows what they are likely to do. It's critical. Keep watch for those documents. That's the only thing that is important right now! Trust R^3."

"But he's going to mutilate her," Juan protested.

Felix swallowed hard. He knew that was highly likely. Even R^3 had said Ben would do this to her. It took all his will power to reply, "I—I know, but R^3 expected it would happen. Those documents are what this is all about." He swallowed hard again. He never thought he'd be allowing his precious R^3 to be knowingly mutilated and implanted, but here he was doing just that. Faith. That was all Felix had left, a complete faith in that R^3 knew precisely what she was doing. Without that faith, Felix knew he'd go berserk about now, ordering an all-out charge, busting in there to rescue her.

R^3 wasn't stupid or unobservant. She anticipated

Ben would somehow stage an attack, knocking her unconscious. That done, she'd likely be turned into one of the new Fetish EE women and then hastily married to Preston. She figured the odds were fifty-fifty that Preston would also be implanted and put on Pytalon-Ex as well, farmed out to being one of Ben's CEOs somewhere in London. She was prepared for this, at least she thought so.

As soon as she felt the blackness of unconsciousness seeping through her body, she focused her mind, all her thoughts, solely and only upon those strange images that she had had of this lab and all the hundreds of workers. She kept her attention on those images, drowning out all other sense perceptions. R^3 had no idea if her plan would actually work, but it was the only thing she could think of doing. Everything hinged upon Ben signing those formal documents, everything.

Juan, Felix, and Lady Persephone watched as the elevator doors finally opened on the ground floor. Ben barked his orders, "Okay. Take the Feds away and dump their bodies in the Thames or anywhere. Let's get these two into my EMAC." Several glassy-eyed men lifted R^3 and Preston up and carried them into Ben's EMAC. The last they saw, the men were heading back to take care of the two Feds.

The three saw little else, and Ben said nothing more, after he placed a secure call, "I'm on my way. Ten minutes out."

Only when hospital orderlies carried Rachel out of the EMAC could Lady Persephone positively identify where they'd taken R^3. London General. Hastily, she fired up her EMAC and headed there rapidly, unwilling to be far behind R^3. Meanwhile, Juan continued to monitor the live feed from the spy camera. R^3 was placed on a Gurney and wheeled into the hospital. Shortly after that, she was fully undressed, and he lost the feed at this point. Now R^3 was on her own; he could only guess what was happening to her.

R^3 continued to focus only on those strange images

she had in the lab. Around her, the doctors put her body into their giant medical machine and performed the relatively simple operation, removing her lower arms at her elbows. That done, they wheeled her still unconscious body over into the attached implant station, where Delius Pogs had recently gotten his new Model III installed and ready for operations. The Pytalon-dosed psych man then followed his orders to the letter, reading from the new Fetish EE Woman script. The machine injected her body with the powerful drug. Then, the hellish electrical pains coursed through the electrodes attached to her head, causing massive pain, a pain so great that one in ten succumbed, abandoning the body, believing it was dead. Over this pain and drug combination, the psych man's voice drolled on, reciting the new Fetish EE Woman's command script.

She began to sense this massive pain, but did her best to ignore it completely, focusing her mind on the weird images she had. *I will not resist it. I will not resist it,* she continued to think. Previously, she had made an observation that when a person felt pain, their first reaction was to resist it, to fight against it, to tense up and hold it still. R³ hoped a total non-resistance to it would lessen its impact on her. That's why she focused on these other images, not allowing the slightest resistance on her part to the flooding pain over her body's head.

Later, she didn't even sense her newly made Personal Assistant, eighteen-year-old Nana Worthington, fumbling to dress her in her new fetish outfit. At least, Ben picked out a cherry red latex gown for Rachel to wear, one that more or less matched the satin one she had been wearing.

Two days later and with only light bandages now wrapping her elbows, Nana wheeled the properly dressed Rachel into the elegant front room of the Michaelson-Waberly mansion, just outside London proper. There, a glassy-eyed Preston stood waiting, dressed in an expensive suit, waiting to be married, all sexually-oriented urges gone. His thoughts were on getting this done so he could go to his new office and run a business, following his implant orders.

Ben also wore a fancy suit, black. He had his arm around his wife, Emma, who wore her Fetish EE woman's outfit, a bright blue with a blue and white striped outer corset contrasting with her gown and knee-high ballet boots. She had her left stump resting on Ben's shoulder, a broad grin on her face. Nearby, her personal assistant stood, glassy-eyed as well. Ben nodded and Nana waved a small vial beneath Rachel's nose, finally rousing her from the entire ordeal.

R3 felt the pungent odor and finally let go of her strange mental images, fluttering her eyes and becoming aware of her surroundings and body, though she had no idea how many days had passed. Breathing was very difficult. Her waist felt intensely compressed; the pressure nearly too much to endure. Slowly, her eyes took in the scene. She was in the fanciest room she'd ever seen, but recognized Ben and Preston.

"Ah, awake at last, dear Rachel. You're just in time for your wedding to Preston. Oh yes, I'm to tell you to take shallow breaths. Now then, this is your new Personal Assistant, Nana Worthington. Nana, if you'll help Rachel to rise, we'll conduct the wedding ceremony at once."

As expected, R3 waved her short arms about trying desperately to get her balance, as Nana forced her up onto her toes and then to take clumsy steps toward the two men.

Ben added, "Don't worry. After a few weeks of practice, you'll be walking quite elegantly, just as my lovely Emma does."

Emma nodded and smiled reassuringly, though reciting her implant script softly to herself. Even though it had been months since she had gotten her new implant, this ultra-powerful one from the Model III still totally controlled all her thoughts.

In the back of R3's mind, the implant script began rolling along, but she didn't vocalize it, but focused on trying to breath and somehow walk without falling down. She forced her mind to focus on one word: document, as though it was the most important thing in the entire world. It more or less worked. Minutes passed by her in a sort of haze, but she heard the priest say, "I give you Mr. and Mrs. Preston Michaelson-Waberly."

She felt Preston's lips touching hers, felt her body reacting with a wild flood of sensations and emotions, but R³ continued to keep all of her attention on that one word: document.

Ben dismissed the priest, while Emma walked elegantly up to her and gave her a sort of hug, trying to say "welcome to the family." She got part of it said before she halted to recite her implant script. R³ found herself involuntarily reciting the same words. It took all her will power to get her attention back onto that word: document.

"Bring Rachel and Preston over to the table, Emma," Ben called out.

I hope I can soon walk as gracefully as Emma, R³ found herself thinking, noticing how clumsy she was walking or stumping rather alongside Emma who continually used her right stump to push her towards the mahogany table, Preston following aimlessly behind them. R³ ignored the cramping pains in her feet and stood beside the table and Ben.

"Ah. Good. As we both agreed, the companies should be merged into one and lead by one person, not split up as they have been all these years. So today, dear Rachel, we both have our fondest wishes. I've prepared the documents that officially merge the Raven-Waberly-Michaelson fortune and estate into mine, the Michaelson-Waberly estate. As you can see, I've already signed them. Preston, you sign here." The zombie son did so. Ben continued, "So now it is official. Of course, Rachel you should read it too."

R³ did so, though it took everything she had to focus solely on doing just that. She was able to comment, "Oh, I see Preston is your current heir, and I am too after him.

Thank you."

Ben couldn't resist a chuckle over his perfect plan of reunification. "Yes, of course, Rachel." *Prat. As soon as possible, Preston and you will meet with an unfortunate accident and then it all falls to me.*

R^3 smiled. Perfect. The document made it complete! If only she had a way to let Felix know that the document was signed now. She wondered where her special broach had gone. *All I have to do is wait now,* she thought, but then she felt the implant taking over her body once more. She barely heard Ben saying, "Okay Nana, walk her around. Show her the place and get her walking properly."

"Yes, my charge must walk elegantly and gracefully. Sanity is doing a good job," Nana whispered and began forcing R^3 to begin to walk, ignoring her gasps for breath and complaints about pain in her feet.

Ben hastily sent one copy of the document off by courier. R^3 wiggled about and followed him to see what he was doing with the second copy, confusing Nana a little. She saw him duck into his private room and figured he had a safe in there somewhere, just as Mr. Raven had. R^3 finally relaxed. All she had to do now was survive until Felix and the others took action. However, she needed to let Felix know the document was signed. Where was her broach?
***

"Okay, so now what do we do?" Juan asked. They'd lost track of R^3 in the huge hospital facility.

Over the comm center, Felix answered him, "Let me do my thing; after all, this is a hospital." Already, he had hacked into their system. Before too long, Felix reported on his wife's situation. "She was right. Fetish EE Woman. She's in recovery now and scheduled for the implant in a few minutes."

Juan relaxed a bit. At least Rachel wasn't being killed, just mutilated and implanted. He looked at his new wife, Lady Persephone, and saw that in spite of all Jessica's therapy, she was still a little bothered by the implant, fidgeting with her feet. He sighed, wondering why R^3 would ever have willingly put herself in this position. It made no sense. The physical ramifications were hideous and the lingering aftereffects were still visible in Lady Persephone. Whatever this new Model III machine did, it certainly made far more debilitating implants.

The only positive thing Juan could think of was that they were going after a very powerful Cabal member. In fact, according to the information Beth and Tilly had relayed from Jana, Ben was a member of their inner circle, this Camarilla group. They didn't know they were going up against the fifth most powerful Cabal man! Juan sighed. *R³ must have her reasons.*

"Tilly's complete layout of Ben's compound is coming in now, thanks to Jana," Lady Persephone announced. A bit later, she commented, "My god! This man is within a veritable fortress. We're going to have to plan this one very carefully. Juan, head to the Feds headquarters now. Felix, keep us posted. We probably have a few days."

Felix replied, "Right. Remember, we have to give them time to get the documents signed and delivered."

He felt he just had to remind them. R³ had been very insistent about that detail, claiming that was the only thing that was critical about this whole affair. He recalled his wife's whispered explanation to him.

R³ knew the others would soon be going after Ben, eliminating that Cabal member, probably as they had done with the MMS group. She'd pointed out with these Cabal men, inheritance was everything, since they did everything possible to extend their own lives. Likely, this Ben was several hundred years old now and certainly had used the Transference Machine at least once. R³ had told Felix they needed to remove his massive fortune from the Cabal, making those billions of credits work for the resistance, to help free the world from these men. While Felix had bought her offered explanation, he also sensed there was something more than just what R³ was telling him. He knew her well and suspected even R³ didn't know precisely what that other reason was.

"Fifteen foot walls topped with razor wire," Lady Persephone explained to the Feds and Trikuza members at the London Feds headquarters.

Captain Lark, who led the London Feds, his relatively new assistant, Martha Bettingham, a rescued EE pony woman, and the Trikuza leader, Cai Cheng, all groaned.

She added, "He has fifty security guards living on the grounds, but according to our informant, they're on Pytalon. Damn, of all the bloody times for me to be laid up," she said very much annoyed with her own physical body. She was still recovering from the total arm transplants and had not yet even begun to retrain her arms in her martial arts. Worse, she also still had aftereffects from the implant that occasionally appeared, forcing her to continue to dress at least as an EE woman.

Captain Lark commented, "Well, I can have the Feds ready to come onto the scene to 'pick up the pieces,' making it look officially as if we're on top of this 'crime.' How are you going to take out this stronghold? It seems impregnable to me."

"I can hover above it and use the IR scanner to locate the guards and direct your men," Lady Persephone replied. "The motion detectors are going to be hard to disable from the outside. Ordinarily, I'd suggest dropping me onto the roof and let me infiltrate the place so I can disable their motion sensors and other electronic warning systems."

"You can't do that, dear. Doctor's orders. You're still recovering," Juan protested.

"Worse, they have motion sensors on the roof," Lady Persephone countered her own idea.

"Let's go over everything you know about this place again," Cai Cheng suggested.

"Right. We must be overlooking something," Martha added. She'd already risen to become Captain Lark's top analyst. Having to always dress as an EE woman, she was unsuited to being a field agent, but her sharp mind had already proven its worth. "There is always a weakness."

Cai grinned, "Aye, she's right. There's always a weakness. Observe and find it. Please, Lady Persephone, let's go over everything you know about this place one more time."

"Excuse me, Captain, but we've just had a report of an EMAC crash outside London. We've an anonymous tip someone important was on that flight," another Feds broke in on their conference.

It was April 1. Nana was slow in getting her charge dressed and her makeup done. The lengthy script that the Fetish Woman's Personal Assistant had to follow was almost more than Nana could handle in her dazed state. Still, she got the job done. R³ was up and finally dressed for the day. Carefully, she led her charge out of their bedroom, heading towards the dining room where she was expected for breakfast with the family. Whispering her new litany, R³ made her precarious way to the table, wishing Nana had not put the damnable panties on her, but then changed her mind partway there. It did have its use, she lamented.

As she sat down, she noticed Preston wasn't present. Ben spoke up, "Well, dearest Rachel, I've some bad news for you today. It seems my over-eager son, Preston, took off early this morning to get to the office. I've just gotten word there has been some kind of terrible accident. I'm so sorry to have to tell you this, but once more, you are widowed. Preston was killed in the crash."

She sensed not the slightest remorse in his emotions; rather she sensed it was more like relief.

Ben thought. *The prat. The idiot. Whatever came over him to have to go charging off to the office early this morning? He was supposed to wait and take Rachel here with him. Two birds, one stone. Ah well, the stupid prat is gone. That'll give the Feds something to do.* "I'm so sorry for you, dear Rachel, but don't worry. You're part of our family now. You can pleasure me when you need to, just as Emma does. We'll get over this somehow."

R³ needed a way out of this mess and decided her litany would do nicely. "Oh dear, I must look absolutely perfect at all times. I must walk elegantly and gracefully at all times. Am I walking elegantly and gracefully? I don't think so, but I must. I must practice more, don't you think?" she asked innocently, as though the death of Preston meant nothing to her. Well, it actually didn't, it just saved her dealing with that detail. She silently went over the remainder of the script in her head.

"Yes, yes, practice dear. We must walk elegantly and gracefully at all times," Emma answered her automatically. "I don't think I did, not at first, but I do now, don't I, Ben dear?" she asked him, sounding as though she doubted she did walk properly.

"Yes, yes, practice. Nana, you make sure darling Rachel here gets plenty of time to practice her walking today," Ben ordered her. *Perhaps, this is just as good. I don't really need Rachel dead, not just yet. Besides, she's gorgeous. I should get my money's worth out of her before I eliminate her. Still, she's barely walking. Best give her time as I did with Emma.*

"Yes. Practice walking. Sanity is doing a good job," Nana replied.

***

"Well, that's encouraging," Captain Lark replied. He had just received confirmation Rachel was not onboard the EMAC, only Preston Michaelson-Waberly. As required, he ordered his Feds to carry out a full-fledged investigation of the "accident," and returned to the others with the encouraging news.

"We're lucky she wasn't onboard. It's obvious Ben is trying to consolidate his newfound wealth," Lady Persephone replied.

Martha spoke up, "Cai and I think we have a way to get in there. It'll require your guidance, My Lady, using the IR system." Hastily, she explained the idea the two had come up with.

"Okay then. D-day will be midnight tonight. I'll

coordinate with Wolf over in Berlin. The surviving security men will be taken there for re-implanting," Captain Lark ordered.

Close to midnight, Lady Persephone handled the IR scanner, while Juan hovered her EMAC high above the fortified compound. Below her, six other EMACs loaded with fifty Trikuza members waited for her directions. Carefully, she analyzed the reddish images on her monitor, relaying the precise location of the guards who were patrolling the compound, six of them. The many others were asleep in their barracks, some twenty feet from the main complex proper.

Ropes descended from the hovering EMACs. Six Trikuza silently slipped down them, eliminating the six guards without raising the alarm. Then, they froze in place while another batch slipped down. Only when all their forces were down did they move out, which then activated the alarm system.

Most charged into the barracks. The roused guards had little chance against these alert, highly skilled fighters. Meanwhile, the others raced through the giant mansion, directed from above by Lady Persephone. They found the servants quarters, but left them alone. Then they swarmed into the master bedroom, where Ben had just gotten up to see what was happening. He fired his gun, wounding the first Trikuza who entered his room. The second one tossed a throwing star, striking Ben in his forehead. The Cabal man dropped like a rock, while Emma struggled to sit up and see what was going on. Her implant didn't allow her to react other than to say, "You must wait until I get properly dressed. I must look my best at all times."

While a third black-dressed man helped the wounded man out, the other retrieved his throwing star, picked up Ben, and carried him out to the EMAC, where Lady Persephone had him put into a stasis pod. Meanwhile, Emma's assistant came into the room to help her get properly dressed, and the Trikuza left them to it.

"Rachel?" a masked man asked, entering her room,

which she shared with Nana. Both women roused.

"Yes. Help?" R³ asked, fighting from reciting the implant script.

"Yes, get her dressed," the man ordered Nana, who obeyed as though nothing unusual was happening.

Finally, Lady Persephone heard the magic words over her headset, "All clear."

"Okay, sit it down and let's get to R³," she ordered her husband who did as asked. Holding her securely, Juan helped her down the ramp. She had little choice but to continue to wear her tall heels and fancy gown. She dared not let a migraine affect this mission. Together, they headed into the mansion, while watching the Trikuza carrying unconscious guards out to other landing EMACs.

"R³, it looks like we got to you in time," Lady Persephone said, as she entered her room. Nana had R³ dressed and was just finishing tying the laces on her right boot. "How are you doing?"

R³ fought hard against vocally reciting the implant script. "Document. Safe. Study." That was all she could vocalize. With Nana supporting her, she led the way out of her room and to his private study. "Here," she finally added, but that was all, since she simply had to go over the implant words, though she did it silently.

"Search for a hidden safe, Juan," she ordered. The two began tearing the place apart and soon found the hidden wall safe behind an otherwise drab painting. Now came the hard part, cracking the combination. Because she was still under orders not to lift more than a pound or so, Juan carried her small backpack of gear.

"I need the Cracker, dear," she explained. Although he had no idea what that was, Juan began rummaging through the pack until she spotted it.

"That's it. Attach it to the safe there," she pointed, and he did so, noticing it was magnetized and stuck securely to the safe's door. "I'll take over now," she said demurely, flashing him a big smile.

Minutes later, the combination was visible on the

red led display. She punched in the ten-digit combination and the safe opened. Many documents and journals were inside, but the one she was looking for was on top. "Ah, this is what we're after, R³. Let's have a look at it." She laid them out on the man's table.

R³ moved in close to read them herself. She forced herself to say, "Heirs."

"Right. Looking for the heirs clauses now," Lady Persephone explained, making sure R³ understood she got her message. Reading legalese is challenging, and it took them several minutes to find the proper section. Everything hinged on this section. Just who was officially Ben's heir or heirs?

The Trikuza had the fifty guards loaded and sent off before the three found what they were looking for. "Ah here it is. Preston is the designated heir, followed by his wife, Rachel. Looks as though Emma gets nothing," Lady Persephone explained. "Just like a man, cut his loving, devoted, helpless wife out of everything." She spat on the floor.

R³ visibly relaxed. "Me. Perfect. Home, please." After that, she again had to recite her script.

Cai then joined them. "My Lady, what is to be done with Emma and her assistant? Has that been determined yet?"

"Yes, Ben left her absolutely nothing. I'll see she gets an account with a million credits in it. Put her on an EMAC for London's Heathrow. I know where to find a good man for her." They exchanged bows, and he left to carry out the order, while she placed a secure call.

"Master Yao Bing? Sorry to disturb you at this hour, but I've a small situation here that may interest you." Lady Persephone explained the situation with Emma, and Master Yao was pleased to accept her, promising to find her a kind, loving new sponsor. Master Yao also promised to "take care" of the prisoner. Lady Persephone then placed another call to Captain Lark, who arranged the Air Liner flight and set up a new credit account for Emma and her assistant.

Meanwhile, Juan packed all the safe's contents into a large bag. Then, he and several other Trikuza searched the entire mansion, retrieving a few other items that were potentially important, such as computers and phones. Around three in the morning, they left the compound. They made a short stop at Castle Briton, where Juan and a Trikuza man moved the stasis pod into Lady Persephone's concealed workroom. A half hour later, the Trikuza took Ben's lifeless body back to his compound and put a bullet into the man's head, thereby disguising the throwing star's deadly wound. The stasis pod now held Ben, who had been transferred into one of the few remaining "dead" Chinese EE women that Lady Persephone had confiscated from the psych men. The pod was sent to Master Yao along with Emma. Everyone else then left Castle Briton, catching an Air Liner at Heathrow, arriving back home at the Raven compound around four that afternoon, thanks to the time zones.

R3 slept most of the flight, while Lady Persephone and Juan went over the pile of confiscated documents. They had a treasure-trove of information on other Cabal members, just not their locations. Still, Lady Persephone wondered if all R3 had endured and would be enduring was worth it? They could just as easily have gone ahead with the planned attack anyway. There wasn't ever any doubt they would be wiping out Ben Michaelson-Waberly. Patience, she told herself.

When the EMAC from New O'Hare landed, Felix rushed out to meet his wife, knowing she now needed all kinds of help. "My god, R3, you look incredibly sexy!" he gushed as he finally saw what they'd done to her. "Are you okay otherwise?" He put his arm around her, rather displacing Nana's hold on her, leading her down the ramp.

"Hard. Implant. Love you," R3 fought to say before having to silently recite her programmed words.

Felix gave her a loving kiss, which she desperately needed. He felt her body relax in his arms. By now, R3 had adapted to the overly tight corset and was walking fairly well in the boots. During these past days, Ben had been injecting her feet with a local twice a day. He was following Delius Pogs' orders to numb their feet for the first week, to remove the intense cramps and pains these women usually faced. At this point, her body had adapted somewhat and the sharp pains were mostly gone, unless she was on her feet for longer periods.

Once inside and sitting around the kitchen table with hot tea provided by Rhianna, Lady Persephone outlined what had happened and what they'd found. Tilly and Jessica were there, as well as Mary Jane, Todd, Trevor, and Rachel Roxanne, who was now very, very glad that she'd abandoned her position and inheritance to R³! Still, she wanted to hear what had happened. It could well have been her!

Everyone kept a sharp eye on R³, and Nana to a much lesser extent, fearing the horrid effects of this new and very vicious implant. She was obviously fighting it, but was doing amazingly well in that she wasn't vocally reciting the words nor was she acting out the script continually. Still, she was only barely able to communicate with them.

R³ said, "Documents. Me inherit all. Must inherit. Join companies."

Lady Persephone repeated back to her to make sure they understood what R³ was trying to say. "So yes, the documents prove R³ here inherits all of Ben's estate and fortune. All of it. Are you saying you simply must inherit it? That you want to control all these corporations? Unifying them as they once were over a century ago?"

R³ nodded rather than fighting to say anything else. "Make public," she struggled to say.

"You want us to make all this broad, public information? That you're the new heiress? Oh, so the Cabal men know about you and it?" Again, she nodded vigorously.

"Okay, let me call Captain Lark. He'll put up a full news story on the attack. I sure hope this doesn't bring down further Cabal attacks on you, R³," Lady Persephone replied and placed her call.

"Must get to labs," R³ then tried to say, but couldn't get more vocalized.

"Okay then, but first, we have to get that implant and destimulated," Jessica volunteered.

No one argued with her, since they could see that R³ was only just barely in control. They wouldn't get much more out of her until Jessica worked her miracle on R³, assuming that it would work as before. The others contented themselves to studying all the documents and journals they'd recovered, looking for more clues. Tilly began making a listing of all known Cabal members, and in addition, she now had a complete list of the other Camarilla members. Ben's private laptop would undoubtedly yield far more clues, but she'd have to take that back to Beth and let the Weasel work her magic on it.

After feeding R³, Jessica took her into her bedroom where it was quiet and began her therapy on Rachel. When she later joined the other, leaving Nana to get R³ ready for bed, her comments spoke volumes, "This is the strangest case yet! Weird is an understatement. R³ has somehow found a way to nullify the implant partially, but she has some strange memories too. I don't understand what she's saying, but we're definitely making progress, but it's going to be slower than it was with the rest of us."

In fact, it took her eight days to get R³ squared around—the implant desensitized, at least as much as she had with all the others who had this new, more powerful one. Neither she nor R³ really had a good explanation for the many strange, apparent memories that R³ had. Yet there was no denying those memories were vivid in detail, almost as though they were real, with the only conclusion that R³ may have somehow been the legendary Jana Waberly, the daughter of the incredible EMAC inventor herself. At least R³ could now better explain why she did what she did.

Around the table and while sipping her tea through

a straw, R³ explained, "I had this overwhelming hunch or intuition about this whole thing. I just had to see their underground research labs in London. That triggered all these strange memories, if that's what they are. Anyway, I know there's a hidden, secret room in the basement lab, and something of immense value to us all is inside. I'm speculating here, but I think Jana Waberly was inventing something beyond the EMACs that her mother had, but it wasn't quite done or somehow wasn't released before Ben got to her and wiped her out by making her into a mindless EE woman. I have to go back there and find out."

She went on, "There is another reason for this too. I knew the resistance would soon be taking out Ben. They had to do that, but I also know he has a vast fortune, since he's one of the nine Camarilla members. I simply had to get myself as the sole heir to that fortune. Why? I want to take all that money out of the Cabal's hands and be able to use it to help support the resistance movement. If Total Care pulls the plug on the Feds worldwide, now I can step in and back them financially and anyone else who needs operational funds that they cut off. I accomplished several vital goals here. I'm still alive, so we're in business."

"I need to get word out to all the various CEOs and companies I now own, letting them know I'm in charge," R³ added. "Plus, I should announce to the world I've married Felix here. That should end the Cabal's attempts to try to force me to marry one of their sons and put this entire fortune out of their hands permanently."

"Unless they then assassinate Felix here and try again," cautioned Lady Persephone, sobering everyone at the table.

"We'll cross that bridge when we come to it," R³ declared stoically. "Plus, I'll let the companies and CEOs know that Felix is now my Operations Manager and to take their orders from him. I think we've an awful lot to learn about our huge companies. Still, as soon as feasible, I need to get into that lab."

"Damn, R³. Your plan was brilliant indeed," Tilly

complimented her. "In one action, you've made something like ninety billion credits available to the resistance, to say nothing of the entire EMAC and Air Liner corporations. Very well done indeed. On behalf of the entire resistance, thank you!"

R3 beamed proudly. She added, "All ODs are not dummies." Felix roared with laughter, joined by the other Circle of Six members.

Felix then asked, "Shouldn't we get you scheduled for full arm transplants soon, dear?"

R3 bit her lip before replying, "No, not just yet. I think I need to continue to appear as a Fetish EE Woman for a while longer. After all, the other Cabal men know Ben turned me into one. It would play along with the deception if I continue to look the part for a while yet. I'm getting by well enough, as long as I have you and Nana with me. It's more important for the Cabal to let go of all notions of regaining the fortune and companies than it is for me to have my arms back. You know wherever old Jana Waberly is at, I bet she is very pleased her estate is totally whole once more." Several nodded agreement with her thought.

Later, Lady Persephone placed another secure call to Master Yao. He said, "Ah yes. We have found a good sponsor for Emma. We have followed your orders with Ben. Jinjing is now being cared for in the secret Lin Foundation underground facility. We're ready to care for more of these evil men."

Lady Persephone chuckled. She was loathed to kill these Cabal men outright. If the professor was right and if Ben and these others were truly immortal spiritual beings, then if their bodies were killed, they'd just get a new baby body and be back causing trouble in less than twenty years. This way, imprisoned in teenaged, but helpless EE women's bodies, they wouldn't be causing more trouble for at least a half century, maybe more if needed. In the back of her mind, she saw in time this facility housing all these Cabal men.

***

"My god, Franco, it's all over the London news!" James Buffett barked over his secure connection. "Yes, I've gotten the documents from Ben. He did pull it off, getting Rachel Raven to agree to sign over her fortune to Preston and marry him, becoming another proper Fetish EE Woman as well. Yes, Ben followed protocol and left his estate, all of it, to Preston and then to Rachel, should she survive him, but how did this mysterious attack happen? Preston and Ben are both gone. I suspect Ben arranged for the accident that killed Preston. I know I would have done just that, but who the hell wiped out Ben and his entire garrison?"

"What have the Feds to say about it?" Franco replied, a note of terror in his voice that he failed to conceal.

"My spy inside the London office says the Feds questioned Emma and Rachel extensively. All those women could tell them was that a number of black-clad men attacked the place around midnight. All wore masks. Since Ben left nothing to Emma, the London Feds found her a new sponsor over in China, so she's out of the way. Honestly, Franco, the Feds don't have a clue. All fifty of Ben's guards have simply vanished and are presumed dead and buried. We'll probably never know who was behind it, but we can rule out the Feds. This kind of an attack isn't remotely their style, as you well know. Just look at how the Feds handled the Peking attack against the Lin brothers— an all-out, massive daytime strike. No, this was a covert operation. Ideas?"

Franco squirmed. "Hell no. We must have some as yet unknown but powerful enemies. This is most unfortunate. Any chance we can marry this Rachel to someone fast and recover the lost fortune?" He asked what he most wanted to know.

"No, apparently some other man has already married her, probably to get a hold of her fortune. Some bloke named Felix, who is now apparently her Operations Manager for the companies. Face it, Franco, we've lost the entire Michaelson-Waberly fortune along with the Raven-Waberly-Michaelson fortune," James replied.

"Couldn't we kidnap the pair, torture this Felix fellow until he signs over all the rights to this fortune to one of us, then kill the pair?" Franco asked the obvious.

"Not easily done, Franco. The Feds are all over this one. Hell, the Cabal specifically asked for intense Feds assistance. We don't dare touch them now, not for a long time. Maybe after all this quiets down for a year we could try something like that. For now, it's a dead issue."

"Shit. Well, do we have to move someone else up to fill the vacant Camarilla seat?" Franco asked.

"That's your department. I'll have to pay a visit to this Rachel and confirm she has sole ownership of the combined estates. God, I dread making that trip."

Franco replied, "Stuff it, James. She's just a stupid Fetish EE woman. I'm going to look over the list for a potential replacement of Ben, but I'm not going to act right away. Look, the mysterious person behind this attack may well be the Cabal member who is next in line. We must investigate him thoroughly before we admit him. Christ! We don't want to bring a murderer of us onboard the Camarilla."

That ended the call, giving James something even more worrisome to fret about. Was another Cabal member responsible for the assassination of Ben? A Camarilla member no less? The world was crumbling around him. James was convinced of that. Still, he had a duty to perform, and he steeled himself for the trip across the ocean.

The next day in his rented EMAC, James slowly descended onto the Raven compound ground, but was accosted by an automated message. "Speak the access code or state the purpose of your visit. Otherwise, the automated system will open fire on your EMAC."

Oh good god! James began sweating more so than normal. He opened the comm channel and said, "James Buffett here to meet with Rachel Roxanne Raven concerning her inheritance." Shortly, another voice gave him clearance to land. He set the ship down, noticing the very large gun pointing skyward.

He walked across the spring greening lawn to the main doors, where R3 was waiting for him, Nana at her side. James relaxed slightly. She was indeed a Fetish EE woman. One glance clearly showed him she was a quite helpless young woman, a damned attractive sex doll, but little more. *Perhaps this won't be so bad,* he thought, joining her.

"Please come inside, Mr. Buffett. If you don't mind, let's sit down. It's terribly hard for me to stand for very long. This is my Personal Assistant, Nana. Am I walking elegantly and gracefully, Mr. Buffett?" R3 asked demurely. "You have probably seen many of us Fetish EE women. Here, I'm the only one and I'm having a hard time knowing if I'm walking properly. I must always walk gracefully and elegantly." R3 cleverly punched in the idea she was what she appeared to be and detected some relief showing in his demeanor.

"Well, more practice will help, Rachel. Now then, I've come officially to notify you your inheritance is in order." He rattled on, but confirming what she already knew—that it was all hers. "By chance, did you receive a copy of the formal inheritance document?"

"Nana, can you get that paper thing for him, please?" Nana rose and headed off to find it. "You see, the assassins raided Ben's safe and took everything, but then one came back and gave this to me saying I would need it. Is this what you mean?" Nana returned with the precious document, and James said that was it. After a few other formalities, James finished up and left as quickly as he could, more than thankful this outing was finished.

As he lifted off, he thought, *Rachel is impressively attractive. I might like to make a play for her myself. She's completely helpless and would make one incredibly fine sex doll. Best not make any move for at least a year. I need to find out about this Felix fellow and how best to take him out of the picture. Still, she wasn't reciting her implant words, as I would have anticipated. I wonder what that means.*

***

Felix stepped out of hiding and snuggled up to R³. "You did a good job with him, dear. So how long are you going to continue to dress like this?"

"Aren't I the sexiest thing on two legs, dear Felix?" she teased him.

"You know you're driving me nuts just looking at you," Felix countered.

R³ laughed. "And our love making is indescribable now, dear. I don't mind being hobbled up. The rewards are fabulous for me. I can see I'm going to need to keep up this image for some time. Hope you don't mind," she again teased him.

He responded with a passionate kiss, but that quickly led them to their bedroom and a lengthy time out, after which Nana had to redo her makeup and brush out her raven locks.

For her part, Nana was quite pleased herself. Her own implant had been desensitized, and she would soon begin her detoxification program in Chicago to rid her body of the residual effects of the Pytalon-Ex drug. On top of that, she had a secure position here and a bank account of one million credits! Nana owed Rachel her undying loyalty.

Chapter 14—Discovery and Impacts

Felix and R³ spent the rest of April diving into just what the three corporations consisted of, namely the production of MET systems, EMACs, and Air Liners. The operations were spread out across the entire world with many subsidiaries providing a constant supply of raw materials. For a time, both were boggled by the vast size and complexity of the three industries, upon which the world now depended. However, by May Day, they had gotten a basic understanding of how the many pieces fit together.

It was at this point that R³ and Felix felt they could begin the next phase. The two, along with Nana, R³'s constant companion and vitally needed personal assistant, headed for Phoenix to meet with Greg. R³ had heard of Greg's invention of a very small EM powered vehicle, perfect for short trips around town for shopping trips. R³ had the notion these should be made available for everyone's use.

"Wow, you do look hot!" Greg commented when he finally met R³ in person after her abduction and conversion.

R³ chuckled, "Of course I do. That is supposed to be the whole point of this new Fetish EE woman thing. Of course, arms and hands would be most beneficial. Anyway, Greg, we're here to get your design mass produced."

"Great," interjected Lisa, "but you have to also produce the variant that I can drive and use too."

R³ chuckled, "Lisa, you can count on that! Heck, I could use one of them myself." Lisa looked pleased, and they discussed the details, one of which would make Greg very wealthy, assuming the invention sold well. "We'll make them readily affordable by everyone, including Garbage Collectors," she explained, satisfying both Lisa and Greg. She decided this new small vehicle would be called the GL shuttle, after the pair, pleasing them further. Greg sent two working models back with them, one of each type. Already, he had built ten of them for those in Phoenix, but had so many others wanting them that he had little time for further inventions. Now he could focus on inventing new things.

With that settled, R³ then brought up the second reason for her visit. "Greg, we're about to check out something in the basement of the research labs. I think we'll find something vitally important and perhaps even revolutionary there, but it might not be quite finished. If so, can we impose on you to come check it out and lend a hand with it, if needed?"

Greg was intrigued. "You bet! Just give a call, and we'll be there as fast as an Air Liner can get us there."

"Coolest. I was hoping so. Okay then, we best get on with it," she declared. However, the professor wanted to chat with them a bit before they left.

On May 4, Captain Lark and Martha met the trio at Heathrow. The professor insisted the Feds accompany R³ and Felix to this research lab. After all, it was there that Ben had abducted her in the first place.

"Gee, you look stunning, Rachel," Martha said cheerily, as Felix helped her down the ramp from the Air Liner, Nana following along behind her. "You still look like a Fetish EE woman. I kind of thought you'd not be."

R³ giggled, "I do look more impressive this way. Besides, it's how the Cabal expects me to look, at least right now. You look good yourself, Martha." Martha had also been abducted and turned into an EE woman and worse. Hence, she too had the enormous bosom and had to wear EE apparel, including the tall heels. Interesting enough, R³ had gotten fancy heels and gowns for Nana, who now looked very attractive herself, though she wasn't officially an EE woman.

Captain Lark added, "You're darn right, Rachel. We've an announcement to make. Martha has agreed to marry me. Isn't that just the greatest?"

"Congratulations!" R[3] said with enthusiasm, Felix adding his best wishes to hers. Martha beamed, her face flush with a happiness she never anticipated having, not in this zombie society.

"You go ahead with them, dear. I'll unload our special gear," Felix suggested, knowing R[3] needed far more time to negotiate the tarmac and get into the waiting Feds EMAC. Nana moved up and put her arm around R[3].

Martha commented, "Gosh, Rachel, it must be just horrid not having arms and hands. I can't imagine how you can manage."

"I know, but it's the desired image those men want. I'm lucky to have Nana and Felix looking after me," R[3] chatted away, slowly covering the distance to the waiting vehicle. "Felix is bringing along what he thinks we might need to get into this secret room."

Fifteen minutes later, Felix ran his ID card over the entrance scanner, and the door opened automatically for him. The group wandered into the research facility, this time on their own terms. A quick check revealed that the five research men, heavily dosed on Pytalon, were disassembling the EMAC that had crashed, killing Preston, looking for the cause of the crash, following the explicit orders from the Feds, namely Captain Lark in this case.

A few minutes later, the small group reached the empty, deserted Sub-lab 5. "See, it's less than half the length of the labs above us," R[3] pointed out.

"I see what you mean, now that you point it out," Captain Lark commented, "but I don't think I would have spotted that detail on my own."

"Oh sure you would have," Martha protested. "You probably would just need a bit more time to look, that's all, but Rachel, where is the door? The entrance?"

Felix spoke up before she could. "First thing, we need to verify that there *is* a hidden room behind that wall. That's why we brought along a Ping-meter." He setup the small device, explaining it sent out low frequency waves that would image what lay beyond. "First, let's ping the far wall where there should be nothing but ground or maybe solid rock." A minute later, everyone saw what that looked like on the small monitor, a dark mass.

Next, he positioned it at the middle of the supposed hidden section. A minute later, everyone gasped. On the monitor was a fuzzy image that looked like a vast chamber. "R3 is absolutely right. There is another room behind this wall," Felix proudly declared.

"Now comes the hard part," R3 explained. "We have to figure out how to open it up without smashing down the wall. Come on; let's inspect the wall for a key pad or maybe an ID card scanner or something like that." Slowly she walked up to the wall and began walking its length, some hundred feet. Felix, Captain Lark, and Martha followed her, but Nana didn't, since she had no idea what to look for. "I didn't see a darn thing. How about you guys?" R3 stated flatly.

"Nope, nada, but there must be a way inside," Martha countered.

"Look, if this was indeed Jana Waberly's private lab, she had to have an easy way to get inside," R3 reasoned. "So we only have to find it. Since we haven't found an ID card scanner or any visible device, I can only conclude the mechanism is either voice-activated or that there is a pressure sensitive spot on this wall."

Felix added, "If it's voice-activated, then we're out of luck, since we don't have any idea what should be said nor do we know what Jana's voice was like. So we're going with a pressure sensitive spot."

"Right. So look for some signs where one might apply some pressure," R3 explained.

Captain Lark and Martha began randomly pressing their hands on the wall, to no avail. Since she didn't have them to press, R3 stood back and observed the wall carefully. Before long the pair gave up, believing this was hopeless.

"Guys, if someone repeatedly pressed their hand on the wall, over time, they would leave a bit of oil behind.

That would collect dust. I think I see it," R³ called out, moving slowly on her toes over to a spot in the center of the wide wall. She touched her right elbow stump to the spot and pressed inward. She heard a clicking sound and stepped back a step to see better. A large section of the wall in the center moved inward a bit and then slid on out of the way, revealing a large opening into this hidden room. Everyone stood shocked and gaping at the huge lab facility dimly illuminated from the opening.

"I was right," R³ broke the silence. "Dear, see if you can find the light switch."

A minute later, the room was brilliantly illuminated, as was the rest of the lab. The group walked into Jana Waberly's lab, the first people to enter it in far more than a century. There was no doubt it was Jana's lab. On the main desk was a yellowing photograph of Jana and her mother. Several very old computers lay scattered about the lab, but what caught their attention was a strange, cylindrical, metal device in the center of the lab. It stood about eight feet tall and six in diameter. None had ever seen anything quite like it. Very thick power cables were fastened to it.

"Well, here it is, Jana's revolutionary new thing," R³ declared. "The question is: what is it?"

"I see some papers over here," Martha called out, while the others moved around the lab looking for what was here. "What's an EM Power Generator? I've never heard of it."

Felix dug out his laptop and was pleasantly surprise to have Internet reception this far underground. Hastily he did a search for it, but came up empty. "It doesn't exist," he called out.

Meanwhile, Martha continued to read over the papers. "Boys," she teased them. "It says here it generates clean energy, based on planetary lay lines. Ah, there's more here. It says earth has an energy grid system, following geometrical forms and with symmetry. The intersection points form a matrix and make extreme power points on the planet. Ah, it says this new EM Power Generator converts the raw earth energy into normal electrical energies. The proposal says that with enough of these devices at the intersections, the entire world's power needs could be met, extremely cheaply. Wow, if she'd have gotten this going, it could change the large number of power generation plants around the world."

"So that's what she was working on," R3 declared. "Now I can see why it is so vital. It would eliminate all the hydroelectric power plants, the nuclear plants, the coal-fired plants, wind farms, all them. This is indeed revolutionary. Okay then, we need to get it up and running, but we must keep it a secret until we have it working and can figure out how to implement it worldwide."

"So really, Rachel," Martha asked, "how did you know this was down here? I mean, as far as the whole world is concerned, this has been lost for a hundred plus years."

R3 flushed. "Honestly, Martha, I don't know. I have all these mental images of this place. When Ben brought me down here, I was literally swamped with them. So I focused on them all during the operation and implanting they did on me. It rather kept me from becoming a mindless zombie from the implant. Other than that, I have no idea at all, but this is vitally important. If we can generate almost free and unlimited power, then that will really help out the whole world."

"I'll gather up all the computers, dear. We can see if we can salvage anything from them. I can see that we've a lot of work ahead of us. I just wish there were more people around who could work on such a thing as this," Felix spoke up.

Even Captain Lark sighed. "Son, you are darn right about that. I sure am glad we're finally beginning to undo the god-awful mess the Cabal has made."

An hour later, they had the papers and computers packed up, the fancy door shut, and departed for Heathrow. R3 and Felix both knew they really had something to work on, something of immense value.

During the short flight to the Air Liner, Felix placed a conference call to many others, outlining what they found and its ramifications. More than one gasped at the magnitude of the find.

Back in Phoenix, the professor merely said, "Blimey, times like this make all of our efforts more than worth it."
***

"We must make all our efforts more than worth it," Delius Pogs of Hong Kong explained over his secure conference call to Dr. Al Rumani, Henry Koch, and Tom Walton. "I know for a fact Franco, James, Jacques, and Francisco don't trust us any longer. Why? It's obvious. Each of us is bumped up one slot within the Camarilla. Any newcomer will have a lesser fortune than you, Tom. The Feds still haven't a clue about who assassinated Ben, wiping his whole family out. Suspicions fall upon us, my friends, rightly so, since it is only us four who directly benefit from Ben's demise."

"Hum, point taken, Delius," Tom replied. "So you really think one of us was behind Ben's assassination?"

Henry broke in, "He's got a good point. Look, whoever was behind the attack knew the total layout of Ben's fortress and his defenses. They obviously had inside knowledge to pull it off. Notice, the Feds didn't say the fortress walls were breached or that there was a pitched battle. None of that. It's obvious to me they had inside knowledge. Of course, where did they get that? That's what we should be asking ourselves right now."

Henry continued, "And there's only one answer that is plainly obvious, Tom. Jana. Your Lyle married Jana, and Jana knows everything about her father's fortress and his security arrangements."

"Oh good God!" Tom exclaimed, a wave of terror seeping into his mind. "You don't think I had Ben assassinated?" He paused. "Christ, you do think that!" he added, shocked. "Listen, you can talk with Jana anytime you want. She's hardly coherent at all, a perfect Fetish EE woman, barely able to function. She can't remember much of anything about her former home life; she's a complete idiot now. She can't even tell you what city Ben lived in. Delius, your new implant is working to perfection, not the slightest trouble with Jana or my wife either, perfect sex dolls. No, while I can see what you're alluding to, the leak didn't come from Jana. I give you my sworn word on that, though I'll admit I did quiz her about Ben's defenses. Got squat from her. She didn't even know she and Ben lived in London. No, it's preposterous to think I had anything to do with that assassination."

Delius squirmed a little. He knew that somehow he'd lost the real Jana, who had completely vanished. He had substituted Jana's OD in her place, which was why Tom had learned nothing about Ben's security arrangements. However, there wasn't a chance in Hell that Delius would reveal that, not unless he was forced to do it. Rather, he steered the discussion along the lines he intended, now that he had all three men softened up. "Look, I've got a new proposal for you fellows. Last year, Al got his hands on the Lin Brothers Transference Machines, but as we all know, Persephone, the Assassin, destroyed them. What Al hasn't made public yet is that before they were destroyed, he attempted to copy the machines, at least their basic circuitry, right Al? He sent me a copy of the crude plans."

Al spoke up, "That's true, but for god's sake, keep that to yourselves. Technicians have yet to get a new working model up and running. I've no idea if they ever will, since the plans were not completed before the machines were destroyed."

"Now that is interesting, Al," Tom replied.

Delius continued, "I've been tinkering here in Hong Kong. I believe I've made a new breakthrough that we may be able to put to good use. No, I've not recreated the Transference Machines, but I've been able to make temporary transferences. In controlled laboratory situations, I put a man under and am able to put him in control of another body for a short time. After a few hours, it wears off, and the man returns to his original body. I can see a vital application of this, and it couldn't come at a more opportune time. Gentlemen, what if we had a large number of identical, powerful fighter bodies? Then, we take skilled soldiers, put them under my machine, move them over into these fighter bodies, and have them execute an attack. Once done or the few hours elapses, they move back into their soldier bodies. Even if the fighter body gets killed, it's only a clone. Plus, if several get killed, all anyone could say is that they are identical fighters."

"Hold on a second," Henry interrupted Delius. "Are you saying we could have our own private assassination squads?"

Delius continued, "That's one way of looking at it. We take a core group of highly trained soldiers and put them under. Move them into the prepared strong fighter bodies, have them carry out the mission, where losses are immaterial, and then wake up back in their soldier bodies, ready for the next mission. What do you three think of this approach?"

"I think it is positively brilliant, Delius!" Henry exclaimed, greatly relieved. Here was his own private assassination squad! "But where do we get these expendable clones? Where do we get the soldier volunteers?"

Delius answered, "Al, that is your area of expertise, the clone bodies. Henry, you are in the best position to find us the trained soldiers or assassins."

Tom broke in, "Shouldn't we let the other Camarilla men know about this? Surely, Jacques could provide all the weapons we could possibly use. Heck, he probably would know where we could recruit the soldiers as well. I, for one, always depended on the MMS, but they're history now."

Delius countered him, "I know that sounds reasonable, bringing Jacques in on this, but gentlemen, consider this. We don't know for sure that one of those top four wasn't behind Ben's assassination. After all, Ben did manage to get Rachel Raven and her newly combined

290

fortune under his control, albeit short-lived. Add another thirty billion credits to his total fortune and he could well displace Francisco or Jacques in the hierarchy."

"Good god! You don't suppose Jacques had Ben wiped out, do you?" asked Tom, growing extremely worried now. He'd not thought of this aspect either.

"Shit!" Henry exclaimed, letting Delius know he'd not considered that.

Al sighed, and then said, "Look, the UDs won't work. Their bodies are relatively weak, just barely alive, but provide viable organs. The ODs, likewise, won't work. Some of them are bright in their own right, though many are game addicts. Besides, you'll never get the Cabal members to donate their vital ODs—not until we get proper Transference Machines operational again. However, there is possibly a way to do this. If I remember right, a hundred fifty years ago, I developed a fighter clone program for the Department of Defense. It was canned when Total Care, the implants, and Pytalon eliminated the need for any armed forces. I mothballed the program. Give me a few weeks to see if I can bring that out of cold storage. With any luck, we might be able to provide burly fighter-types, but not in any large quantity, mind you."

Delius replied, "Excellent, Al, excellent. Henry, Tom, what remains for you two is to find or recruit us the volunteer soldier types who are willing to take over temporarily these clone bodies and carry out our missions. As you know, bodies are a dime a dozen in this part of the world. Already, I've done a bit of experimentation. What's interesting is that I had one of them shot and killed while pretending to carry out a mission. When that taken-over body died, the test subject simply returned to his real body. Of course, he had a severe headache, since I shot the taken-over body in its head. These soldiers of ours can attack with total impunity. Nothing can harm them, not even getting their taken-over body killed. A perfect fighting force, if I do say so myself."

Tom chuckled, "Delius, you old devil. Now I see

where you are heading with this. If it was Jacques or Francisco who was behind the assassination of Ben, with this program of yours in operation, we can protect ourselves."

Delius laughed. "Of course. I do value my own skin, rather highly, I might add."

"Okay, you have a deal," Tom replied. "I'll look into finding proper soldiers. Henry, you do the same. Let's you and I work on this together. This might be our very best route to survive this bout of chaos in our Grand Plan." That ended the conference call.

Delius Pogs sat back with a broad grin on his face, knowing he had sewn just enough doubt and confusion in his fellow Camarilla members to give him a wide margin of safety. After all, he'd not survived as long as he had without having many plans in the works. In fact, he was two hundred and twenty years old. His long complaint was that he had lost his Japanese body about a hundred fifty years back, when Bo Lin began transferring him into new bodies, Chinese ones, unfortunately.

That hadn't stopped Delius though. His fortune was extensive, had been for a very long time, which allowed him to purchase his own home in Hong Kong, the skyscraper that had once been the Playboy Club, filled with every luxury you could imagine. In addition, it boasted top of the line security features, which he added to over the centuries. The lower floors were his workshops and experimental labs, though one whole floor was his wife's research lab.

The current flower of his life was Dr. Akira Aki Pogs, a thirty-year-old Japanese woman with very long, thick, black hair. (He surrounded himself with Japanese women.) He met Akira when she was just eighteen, graduating from one of the many high schools in Hong Kong. She wanted to be a doctor and invent a cure for degenerative brain diseases. Of course, in truth, there wasn't any medical doctor program in existence any longer. All the doctors were implanted and drugged men who followed precisely written scripts, which if followed, resulted in the expected cure or organ transplant. One of the high school councilors had contacted him regarding Akira's desires; he'd met her, fallen for this incredible beauty, and made her an offer she could not refuse.

At eighteen, the lovely Akira Aki became an EE woman and married Delius, joining him in his exotic skyscraper, filled with nothing but absolute luxury. Part of his offer to her was that when her mind cleared enough, he would help her achieve her goal of finding a cure for the various degenerative brain diseases. Thus, a year later, she had her own entire floor and all the research material money could buy. Delius always had plans within plans. Besides having a new, stunning EE woman wife, she just might find those cures, which would handle the sole remaining organ transplant problem. Everything else in a human body could now be effectively transplanted, excepting the brain, whose complexity still eluded all such attempts. Hence, if she could find such cures, then the OD program would be complete, providing an alternative immortality to the Transference Machines.

They had one child, Ren, who was now twelve-years-old, precocious, and a splitting image of her mother. Delius also had kept around one son by his previous marriage, Chou Pogs, now twenty-years-old, though he was implanted and on Pytalon, serving as Delius's head of security.

Of course, Delius hadn't come up with the Fetish EE Woman plan overnight. When he released it at the January Cabal meeting, he'd already fully researched it, developing it into its final form, which he released to the world at that time. Here in his upper floor suites, he kept his own research harem. All were Japanese women, naturally, and all had the typical long, straight, black hair, which he so passionately loved. He'd begun this Fetish EE woman research three years ago with Tamiko, who was twenty-one today. Then came Mika, twenty, Hana, nineteen, and he'd added Keiko, eighteen, only this year. With four Fetish EE women in his private harem, which he shared with his wife, Akira, he'd been able to research fully and develop this new modification or trend.

Thus from practical experience, he knew each Fetish EE woman needed a personal assistant. However, here in his suite, he allowed Dr. Akira, Ren, and Chou to assist his four harem women. As an EE woman herself, Akira just loved to help and satisfy the four women, and he considered this excellent training for his young daughter, Ren, who was constantly begging him to make her into an EE woman like her mother, which he promised to do when she was older. Now he was experimenting with Ren, waiting to see if she would change her mind and desire to be one of these incredible Fetish EE women.

Since physical strength was needed to fully tighten the four's heavily steel boned inner corset, he had Chou assisting them. Of course, Chou was physically and mentally unable to respond in the slightest to the charms of the EE women. Pytalon completely buried such responses.

However, early on in the development process, Delius wondered about having a Fetish EE man around to help keep them all satisfied. While he did his best with them each evening, he couldn't keep five sex dolls contented, and focused mostly on Akira and Mika, whom he loved the most. Thus, he'd invented the Fetish EE man, using his youngest son from his prior marriage, Ken'ichi, who was now nineteen. Like the women, he had his arms removed at his elbows. He too wore the extremely tight inner corset that held up the same black seamed nylons and the requisite black, knee-high ballet boots. However, he was then dressed in the finest black silk suit, as befitting a male erotic escort. His job was to keep the four Fetish EE women and himself satisfied during the day, which because of the new Model III implant machine, he did perfectly.

In fact, the stark difference in behavior between Akira and these five was dramatic. While Akira now had a good deal of thinking ability and made a superb wife and research doctor and yet still being periodically a sex doll during at times during the day, these other five were wholly under the control of the implant. After four years, he could only begin to see a tiny amount of thinking power returning to Tamiko, minuscule compared to the lovely, charming, Akira. Still, he found the charms of Mika irresistible, as did Akira. Often, the two took Mika to bed with them.

What he found curious was Ren and Keiko had formed a strong bond. Here in May, Ren and Keiko often slept together, which Delius took as a good sign that perhaps Ren would soon beg him to make her into a Fetish EE woman. He also saw that Ken'ichi was often terribly frustrated, in that he needed to have someone undress him before he could obtain the pleasure he needed, though he was able to give it to the women in other ways while dressed.

Originally, Delius thought having Fetish EE men around a group of Fetish EE women would keep all them contented, but it hadn't worked out quite as he planned. Ken'ichi constantly flirted with him, which he found most annoying, since Delius was not remotely interested in men, only beautiful Japanese women with long black hair. However, they had to be at least EE women, for he was terrified of those not totally under his control. Thus, early on, he'd written Fetish EE men off as not being practical.

However, with the assassination of Ben and his entire family and security personnel, Delius rethought this aspect. He, like other Cabal men, had a fear of outright killing their enemy men. If asked why, none could really say. Somewhere in the backs of their twisted minds, they had the notion perhaps people were reincarnated upon death. If this were so, then their hated enemies would return, perhaps as soon as two decades. Since most of these men considered themselves immortal, this was positively terrifying to them!

Here in May, Delius began to see another approach. Rather than turning their enemy men into EE women, or now even better, Fetish EE women, he could turn them into Fetish EE men. As powerful as the new Model III implants were, these enemy men wouldn't ever again be a threat to them, not for at least seventy or more years.

These past four years, Delius closely observed his Fetish harem. He saw the women were highly satisfied, sex dolls, as long as they were given proper assistance. Yet, Ken'ichi was constantly frustrated, having few outlets to dramatize and carry out his implant's orders. Delius began to see making his enemy men into Fetish EE women wasn't totally the torture he'd desire, but that making them into Fetish EE men would work far better. They'd be utterly helpless, but also they'd be constantly frustrated, a much better long-term torture.

Thus, his next move in the Camarilla would be to present this new "cure" for their enemy men. He knew well just how much the other Cabal men feared outright killing of their most hated enemy men. Women had been always handled by making them into EE women. A few isolate cases of men having a sex change and being made into EE women were also studied in the past. While they underwent a tumultuous time with the drastic change, in time, they all adapted and did well, which wasn't precisely what Delius had in mind. No, this new idea was far, far better. He placed the call to the Camarilla members.

His Trans-assassins Project had been fully tested. His first experiment had been quite illuminating. He'd hooked Ken'ichi and Hana up to the new machine. For an hour, they had swapped bodies, confusing both of them totally. He found it hilarious. However, he needed a far better test. Over these many years, Delius always cultivated a symbiotic relationship with the Hong Kong Feds. Twenty of them now had EE wives, compliments of Delius. His main contact man, Sargent Dong Fa, had been one of his prime test subjects.

Six times now, Dong Fa needed to infiltrate and take down some criminals. Each time, Delius had temporarily transferred Dong Fa into the body of some random Garbage Collector Twentieth Class. Dong had used that body to do the infiltration and capture, though twice the body he had taken over had been shot and once even killed. After the sixth trial, Dong Fa was convinced of the total work-ability of this new procedure. However, Delius swore him to absolute secrecy, particularly since the Feds were now under the control of this renegade Chan-Petra and thus not to be trusted. Dong Fa went along with Delius, since he knew that if he didn't, Delius could send almost anyone after him and kill him.

Delius had another side, a romantic side, but only with women over whom he had total, absolute control. Within a block of the PB Skyscraper, was Central Park, some thirty acres filled with exotic formal gardens. While it had some darn Chinese name, which Delius was loathed to pronounce, being devoted to all things Japanese, he always used its English name, Central Park. Apparently, long ago it had been named after the famous one in New York City. Quite why, no one knew. The park was this family's favorite haunt.

After he made the revelatory call to the Camarilla, Ren found him. "Papa, can Keiko and I go for a walk in the park this evening? You and Akira can come too, please papa?" the twelve-year-old girl begged.

"Of course, dear Ren, I'd like to do nothing better. Fresh air is just what we all need, but do dress up in your finest gown, dear."

She giggled. "Of course, papa, but I would look so much better if I was an EE woman too, just as Akira is."

Delius grinned, "I know, sweet pea, I know, but you're only twelve. What about looking just like Keiko? Isn't she just incredibly beautiful as well?" He punched in this idea, knowing Ren had been spending lots of time with Keiko.

Again, Ren giggled, but also flushed slightly. "I do love Keiko," she admitted sheepishly. "I think she loves me too."

"Of course, she loves you, my sweet pea. Keiko is a fine young woman. Her figure far surpasses that of your mother, and that is saying something."

Again, Ren giggled. "I know, papa. I think she is just stunning." After a pause, she asked, "Could I be a Fetish EE woman too, just like Keiko? Could we be married, just like you and Akira?"

"Sweet pea, you can be whatever you wish. Certainly, you and Keiko could be married. I married Akira because I love her. There is no one more beautiful than she is. We are together always," he cleverly replied.

Ren beamed and then frowned, "But papa, I don't want to wait six more years. I love her now."

Delius grinned this time. "All right, sweet pea. I'll speak to Akira about it tonight while we walk. I can't promise you anything, so don't go getting your hopes up. Besides, Hana, Mika, and Tamiko also need your help getting dressed and dining."

That evening, Akira put her arm around Delius, who put his around her. In her ballet boots, she too needed support. She wore a red satin gown and looked stunning in his eyes. Ren wore a similar dress and had her arm around Keiko, who really did need her support, since she was just barely walking properly, having only had four months to adjust to her new life. Her Fetish outfit was done in a pale blue. The two followed behind Akira and Delius, as they walked slowly out of the PB skyscraper. Very carefully watching their steps, Hana, Tamiko, and Ken'ichi followed them, since they were on their own, having no steadying arm. Chou followed behind, armed with two guns, their protection man.

"Oh, the flowers are coming out, Delius," Akira gushed, smelling the many fragrances floating on the early evening air.

"Ah, I'm afraid these flowers cannot compare to the flower on my arm," Delius complimented Akira, who flushed slightly and gave him a quick, loving kiss. Soon, they broke up into smaller groups, wandering among the magnificent gardens. It was quite safe for them to do so, since they were the only ones in the gardens. While there were implanted-Pytalon dosed gardeners who cared for Central Park, very, very few others ever walked in the park.

Ren and Keiko purposely veered to the right, leaving Delius and Akira behind. Shortly, Keiko stopped, turned, and began rubbing her arms over Ren's dress. "I do so love to please you, dearest Ren. I really need you."

"I love you too, Keiko," Ren whispered back. Keiko's passions rose, and she began kissing Ren most passionately, while continuing to rub her short arms over Ren's youthful body.

Ken'ichi, Tamiko, and Hana fell behind everyone else and soon began kissing each other, while doing their best to rub their short arms over each other's bodies. Once more, Ken'ichi felt quite frustrated that he couldn't satisfy either his own urges or theirs, but he tried, just as did they. Always, he prayed for bedtime, when someone would undress him, at least enough so he could satisfy himself and the women.

"Dearest Akira, Ren has been hounding me to allow her to become an EE woman again," Delius broached the subject of this evening's walk, planting a loving kiss on her neck.

"I know she has; she's been on me about it too. We all do look our very best. She should too, you know—look her best. I try to see that she does. Dear, she's almost thirteen now, and she's become a woman. I spotted that yesterday morning," Akira explained. "Perhaps, it is time she too looks her very best, don't you think?"

"She's not eighteen though," Delius countered.

Akira sighed. "I know, but honey, she so wants to look her very best. Besides, have you noticed she'd smitten with lovely Keiko?"

"Ah my flower, yes, I've noticed. She told me they're in love. Could it be so?" he inquired, knowing Akira couldn't resist that word.

Akira squeezed him tightly. "Yes, of course. You know we love men and women equally, but my heart is yours, always." She gave him a passionate kiss, satisfying her implanted need to do so. She then sighed, "I so hoped Ren would want to be a doctor as I am, but then she's shown no interest in my work at all."

"I know. She's shown no interest in my researches either. We both are in the same boat. Yes, she wants to marry Keiko. Should we allow that? It might be a very good thing for both of them—being married. What do you think, dearest Akira? Both are Japanese."

Akira chuckled a little at that reference. She knew how passionate he was towards all things Japanese. "Yes, our marriage has been utterly heaven for both of us, hasn't it, my Delius?"

"But of course, my dearest Akira. Life would not be worth living without you at my side," he countered. *At least until you get too old, but then I can find another spring beauty to fill your shoes.* Again, Akira gave him a loving squeeze.

"Women should look their best. Ren should too. I think you should allow Ren to have what she wants, since she is a young woman now," Akira whispered. "Let her choose, don't you think?"

"But of course, my dear. I will discuss it with her tomorrow. It will be lovely having our married daughter under our wings."

"Oh indeed so. I just know Keiko will give her much pleasure, and Ren will be able to give Keiko her needed pleasure too. Everyone wins."

"So how is your research going, dear? Any new developments?" he changed the subject, satisfied he had what he wanted from her.

"I do believe at long last I'm making progress. My new antibiotic is definitely reversing the degeneration process. I believe that soon I should conduct field trials. Will you be able to help me with that?" Akira asked.

"Yes, of course. How many test subjects would you like to start with?"

"Oh, two I believe. They don't need to be kept in our labs, as long as I can make daily trips to observe them," she replied. "But enough of work. The gardens are so beautiful, just as you are. Kiss me, hold me, hug me," she whispered back, allowing her implant to control her body fully, relishing in his gentle touch, the soft feel of his lips on hers.

Much later that evening, Ren crawled into bed beside Keiko, having properly prepared her lover for the night. Their passions exploded almost at once. Similarly, Akira insisted Mika join them in a three-way round of love making, which Delius loved. Tomorrow, he thought, will be an important day.

He began by having a private chat with Ren, just as soon as she had Keiko dressed and fed. "Ren, my sweet pea, Akira and I have decided you should look your best too. We have only one question for you. Do you want to become an EE woman like Akira or to become a Fetish EE woman like Keiko?"

"Oh papa! Thank you! Thank you! I get my choice?" she asked, exuberant over the unexpected good news.

"Of course, sweet pea. It should be your choice. Plus, when it is done, we will see that you and Keiko are marred, but we do so want you to live here with us."

"Of course papa. I don't want to live anywhere else. Can I be like Keiko? Then, we would be the same," Ren replied without any hesitation.

"All right then, let's go see if Keiko agrees to marry you," Delius suggested.

Later that morning, he took Ren to the local hospital for the necessary medical procedures. Her lower arms were removed, her breasts enlarged to the proper size, her lips thickened some, and her hair lengthened so that it reached her knees. Ren was kept there for another day, sedated while the giant medical machine worked it healing magic. The following day, her elbows sporting light bandages, she was brought back to their skyscraper, where Delius carried out the Fetish EE Woman implant on her, using the Model III that guaranteed she would respond identically to Keiko. That done, she was then properly dressed, though her extremely tight corset made her waist far smaller than

Keiko's was. Still unconscious, Delius brought her into Keiko's room, laying her on her bed, giving Keiko orders to watch over her and help her when she awoke.

Next, he paid a visit to his Feds contact, Dong Fa, and made him an offer he couldn't refuse. Delius returned shortly bringing Tamiko with him. Dong Fa was now the proud sponsor of Tamiko. Delius had cleverly gotten rid of her.

Later that day, Ren awoke, gasping for breath and reciting the litany. Keiko joined her and began rubbing her arms over Ren's new, enormous curves. After passionately kissing each other, Keiko got Ren onto her feet, helping her learn to walk in the fancy boots, and Ren discovered the magic of the special panties, squealing with the sensual explosion, as did Keiko.

Next, Delius brought in a priest to marry the two couples. In a short ceremony, Ren and Keiko were married, as was Ken'ichi and Hana, much to their immense pleasure. After that, Mika became the constant sex doll of Akira and Delius. Now, he figured he had his own house back into order once more. Chou was assigned to look after Hana and Ken'ichi, while Akira looked after Mika, Ren, and Keiko.

That handled, it was time to present his Fetish EE man to the Camarilla. He led Ken'ichi and Hana up to the roof and helped them into his EMAC. As he drove to the airfield, he smiled, watching them rubbing each other furiously with their stumps, passionately kissing. While Hana had already been pleasured by her special panties while walking to the EMAC, Ken'ichi radiated constant frustration. Delius smiled; here was a perfect torture for men.

Thus on May 15, the other seven Camarilla men saw firsthand Delius's proposed new solution for their enemy men. Indeed, Ken'ichi was just as helpless as the Fetish EE women were. They watched as the young couple passionately kissed each other, while rubbing their stumps on each other, as much as they could reach, which in

Hana's case was very little, because of the enormous size of her bosom. More importantly, they saw she received her needed pleasuring just by walking, but saw that Ken'ichi was constantly frustrated, having no way to satisfy his own urges and needs, not until someone undressed him for the night. With wry grins, the Camarilla adopted this new solution of Delius Pogs, for they realized it was far worse than merely turning the enemy men into Fetish EE women. None wanted to risk killing their enemies and possibly finding them back at their throats in say twenty years.

Chapter 15—Moves and Countermoves

Henry Koch knew he had to get the Feds Supreme Commander under his control and soon. This Chan-Petra EE woman continued to defy his orders sent through the Total Care chain of command. She had four close associates, plus there was the mostly unknown connection Lady Persephone had with her, along with the possibility that she was also Persephone, the Assassin, and Delius convinced everyone that turning them into one of his new Fetish EE women would completely handle them.

Henry's wife Lela was certainly handled. True, she had been an EE woman for many years, but of late Henry had observed that she "thought" too much. When she returned as a Fetish EE woman in mid-January, all independent thought was gone. She was what Henry most desired, a true sex doll, nothing more. Further, he relished their romps in bed more than he ever had thought possible. Five months later, he detected no change in her behavior since she'd become a Fetish EE woman, quite unlike before when she'd become an EE woman.

Using his own means of spying along with his few covert agents in Chicago, he discovered two things. One, Chan-Petra and the others were apparently back to being EE women, but without displaying any implant behavior. Two, five Indian women had taken their places, with Vaani-Petra acting as the Feds Supreme Commander. Because Henry had used the Transference Machine several times, when he first visited this new Vaani-Petra, he knew at once she was Chan-Petra, ignoring the given name. She'd used the Transference Machine too!

This terrified Henry far more than he cared to ever admit, not even to his fellow Camarilla members. Rationally, he knew this Petra and her cohorts had stolen the Lin brothers Transference Machines, though they'd been forced to give back two of them. Thus, it was obvious they would use them, just as he and other Cabal men had.

While he had no direct evidence that Chan-Petra and the others had actually undone their new Model III Fetish EE Woman's implant or that they'd somehow managed to get an arm transplant, his spies suggested that this might be the case. Certainly, this was the case with the Feds Captain that they'd kidnaped and forced to reveal all the inner workings of this Chan Conspiracy. Delius had changed Lech's sex and turned him into another Fetish EE woman before returning him or her back to Chicago. His contacts definitely reported Captain Leah Smith was now back at work, running the local Feds from the same Chicago Feds office, but that she wasn't under the implant's behavior and she had arms. How could this possibly be? He'd given no such orders and never would have allowed such a thing.

Thus, he carefully researched all the various hospital logs, looking over the arm transplants. Several days later, Henry fumed. He'd found them, fake orders that had been acted upon, utilizing compatible UDs for the operations. Someone had cleverly buried those orders among the hundreds of other transplant orders. He sat back, his arms gripping his chair's arms tightly.

That someone had hacked into his Total Care system bothered him almost as much as the many others receiving full arm transplants. Combine all this with the hints that Delius had made, that one of the Camarilla had been behind the assassination of Ben, and Henry was confused, overwhelmed, and angry. Worst of all, he hated that someone was manipulating his very own Total Care system.

"Prioritize, Henry," he told himself. Calming down a little, he wrote out a list.

1. Remove the five Indians running the Feds

2. Find, capture, and re-implant Chan-Petra and her four cohorts

3. Establish whether Lady Persephone is the assassin

4. Force the Feds to obey Total Care regulations or cut off their funding entirely

5. Find and remove whoever is hacking into the Total Care system

6. Force Lady Persephone to give back another Transference Machine

7. Monitor Rachel Raven. Will she remain under the Fetish EE Woman implant?

As he looked these over, he realized Delius and his new Trans-assassin procedure was the answer to a number of these. Hence, he needed good soldiers, men who knew how to fight well. It was a shame the MMS was gone. Still, Locki's Freedom Fighters were around. He decided these men would be his best bet. He fired off an email to Eric Locki, outlining his request and the new method Delius had invented, assuring him that even if the fake men in the field got killed, the actual soldier running the body wouldn't be harmed. Then, he fired off an email to Al Rumani, asking when the mothballed project would be ready for operations. A later conference call between Henry, Delius, and Al produced results, as far as Henry was concerned. The action would take place on June 15.
***

Lady Persephone and Lord Juan returned to her castle in London, putting in a brief appearance. She dressed as a typical EE woman, not a Fetish EE woman, though. She filed a formal announcement that she had married Juan, that he was now Lord Juan, and that they'd just returned from their honeymoon. She hoped that would be enough to convince the Cabal she wasn't the Assassin they had presumed she was. It was bad enough they knew she had possession of the Transference Machines. If they also realized she was the dreaded assassin, then her cover would be irrevocable blown. She even toyed with the idea of having Master Lao drop one of her cards on the next victim, but such an opportunity had not yet appeared.

However, her arms were still weak. That plus her

now monster sized bosom combined to ruin her martial arts skills. Instead, she focused on trying to get her Faizah-Perse body up to speed. That failed miserably, frustrating her enormously. She realized what Master Yao had to deal with—a total retraining of his new body, and Persephone began to suspect she might never regain the former skills she had as Persephone, the Assassin. Complicating matters was that her implant still caused her frequent mild headaches, primarily because she refused to wear the highly restrictive corsets and the impossible ballet boots. If she wore either of those, she'd have no martial arts skills left at all, something she couldn't live with. Fortunately, Juan continued to support her in all things, offering hints, guidance, and constant encouragement, which she desperately needed.

Lady Persephone saw a new role for herself, intelligence gathering. The resistance knew the names of quite a few Cabal members, but they had virtually no other information on their locations. She decided to focus her efforts onto finding where their fortresses were located. She joined forces with Wolf over in Berlin to do just that. By mid-June, she still didn't have much new information though.

Weasel and Shifty Eyes fared little better. Searching the many databases for these Cabal men yielded little useful information, until Jessica suggested that they go back some two hundred fifty years, coming forward from there looking for traces of these men. By mid-June, that began to produce results.

Specifically, Delius Pogs was originally from Tokyo, but had moved to Hong Kong back in 2090. Emboldened by this discovery, the two sleuths began digging through all possible records trying to find out anything more about this illusive man. Shifty Eyes made the key discovery. She searched through ancient property purchase records, figuring that he had to live somewhere, particularly since he was phenomenally wealthy. Surely, there would be some property sale she could track down. After squinting at them for days, she spotted it. He'd purchased the entire PB Skyscraper!

Tilly then predicted they had a ninety percent chance of putting this top leader out of the game. However, since none of the four spoke Chinese, they decided to put Lady Persephone and Lord Juan on this one. Besides, they knew just how hard a time she was having adjusting to both the new Indian body and to her own restored body. Well, the four were having their own problems with this newest implant as well. None of the four wore the corsets or ballet boots and frequently had mild headaches, which Amanda cleverly traced back to this as the root cause. One day, she had Tilly help her into them again, though it took all three of them to fully tighten the under-corset. All that miserable day, Amanda had no trace of a headache, confirming her theory. The four groaned about her discovery.

Lady Persephone was very thankful Tilly had given her this job of gathering key intelligence on Delius Pogs. If nothing else, she intended to bring this man to justice, for it was his Fetish EE Woman's implant delivered via his new Model III machine that was causing their lingering problems. During early June, she and Juan scouted out the prominent skyscraper, piecing together details of the man's life.

The first thing they noticed was that unlike the other Cabal men, Delius was quite open about his life. He was helpful and friendly to the local Hong Kong Feds. In fact, he'd just provided a Fetish EE woman for one of their men, who married the woman. From the locals, they learned Delius was married and that he was often seen walking in Central Park of an evening, only a block away.

Rumors suggested his wife, Dr. Akira Aki Pogs, was doing some vital medical research, though she didn't have a medical practice as such. A bit of digging revealed she was working on a cure for degenerative brain diseases and had just begun her first field test on two patients with Alzheimer's disease. Carefully, they took up a spying position outside the hospital and spotted her one morning when she came to check on her two patients. Thus, they saw she too was an EE woman who chose to wear the ballet boots instead of the tall heels that most wore. Further, when she came out, they had a good look at her. She was an incredibly beautiful woman, in her thirties.

Further checking showed the pair had a daughter, Ren, who had recently become a Fetish EE woman, but was only thirteen. She'd had also married another such woman called Keiko. Next, the pair decided to hang out in Central Park to see if they could spot them. Mid-June after two days of patient waiting, they spotted the extended family group entering the park, but Delius wasn't with them. Dr. Akira Aki had her arm around another Fetish EE woman, whom they later learned was called Mika, supporting her as they walked. Behind them came Ren and Keiko, their short arms supporting each other. Both were shocked to see another pair following them, though at first they thought they were seeing another pair of Fetish EE women, but one was wearing a very expensive suit. As the pair passed by, they saw he was a man, a male Fetish EE, something completely new. Both gasped at the sight. Finally, another young man, armed with two guns brought up the rear.

From all the passionate kissing and arm motions, they concluded this was really a romantic walk in the park, hardly what Lady Persephone had anticipated from a Cabal family. The two decided to take a romantic stroll in the park, cleverly joining them. Crossing paths deliberately, Lady Persephone said pleasantly, "Hello. Fine evening for a stroll. Isn't this park just perfect?"

Dr. Akira Aki looked at the pair, noticing she was also an EE woman and was wearing similar ballet boots as she was. Visibly, she relaxed. "Why, yes it is. We just love the park. We always try to look our best while taking our stroll here. I've not seen you here before. I'm Dr. Akira Aki. This is my dear friend, Mika. You'll have to forgive her; she's still heavily under the influence of her Fetish EE woman implant."

Both looked at the shapely long, black haired young woman. Her face was roundish and angelic, but neither could miss the sense of anguish coming from her eyes. She wore a light blue latex gown, tight fitting, with an outer corset in matching blue and white stripes. Mika was mumbling her implant script, but managed to whisper, "Kill. Me. Begging."

Dr. Akira Aki grimaced. "Mika dear, you can't mean that. You'll have to excuse her."

"I understand, Dr. Akira. These new implants are far stronger than the old ones. I'm Lady Persephone, my husband, Lord Juan. We're here in Hong Kong on an extended honeymoon. Has she recently gotten the implant?"

Dr. Akira flashed a brief smile. "Congratulations. Yes, it is very pretty here. Mika? No, she had hers over two years ago, but she's still having an awful time adjusting. Delius and I really do love her, and she always shares my bed."

"Oh that is so very kind of you—to look after her. Is your husband here too? Was one of those others we saw briefly him?" she asked, knowing Delius wasn't here.

"No, he is off on another one of his business trips. The young one is our daughter, Ren, and her mate. She's just gotten married to Keiko. Both really do love each other. It is so hard to find good mates in this world, isn't it? You're lucky to have found each other, though I'm told we EE women are always able at least to find a sponsor. Me, I prefer to marry for love. So does Delius. That's why we allowed our dear Ren to marry so young. Besides, they're both Fetish EE women and do need each other," Dr. Akira Aki chatted away, before silently repeating her own implant script. She obviously had far more control over it, as expected.

While she was temporarily lost in her own thoughts, Mika again looked at Lady Persephone. Through her intense daze, she pleaded, "Kill. Me. Beg. You." Immediately, she began reciting her programmed script once more.

When Dr. Akira Aki's eyes returned to the present, Lady Persephone chatted, "So are you a real medical doctor?"

She smiled. "No, not really. I'm a research doctor. My life's goal is to find a cure for degenerative brain diseases. Alzheimer's took both of my parents when I was a young teen, and I swore I'd find a cure. It's taken me close to twelve years of constant research, but I do believe I've finally gotten a handle on it. I'm running tests on two older men, and so far, they're responding well. With luck, they'll be cured in a month or so."

"Why, that is just fabulous, Dr. Akira Aki!" Lady Persephone complimented her sincerely. "That would be a gift to all mankind."

She smiled. "Yes, it would be. I can't imagine why no one has found a cure before now, but I guess the OD and UD programs didn't see the need, but I certainly did. Oh, here comes my daughter Ren and her mate, Keiko."

The two Fetish EE women moved slowly up to the group of four, wholly ignoring the two strangers. Each was doing her best to stroke the other with an arm stump, while muttering, "Love you" repeatedly. Shortly after that, the other two joined them.

"Oh, this is Delius's son, Ken'ichi—by his previous wife who died—and his wife, Hana. My husband has created a new position, Fetish EE man. Honestly, I never could understand why there were only EE women and never any EE men. Surely, women like such dolls too. Now, the world can be more balanced. Those two are madly in love. Guess it's obvious though."

She began whispering her own script once more. Meantime, Ken'ichi and Hana recited theirs, while using their arm stumps to caress each other's bodies, at least as much as was possible, which was very little in fact. Like Ren and Keiko, both totally ignored the two strangers. They weren't even aware of them. Finally, the man with two guns walked up, looking both bored and glassy-eyed.

"Say, would you like to drop by our place for tea?" Dr. Akira Aki asked politely. "I so seldom have alert guests to visit with." Both could tell the doctor dearly wanted to chat with non-zombies, and they agreed, following behind the group as they headed back to the PB Skyscraper. Of course, the two had ulterior motives for the visit, noting the various security alarms that protected the family.

Gaily, Dr. Akira Aki showed them her research lab on the sixth floor, but mentioning the lower five floors were her husband's research labs. When they reached the top floor, their living suites, Chou led the other two couples off to their private suites, presumably to get them undressed and ready for bed and a chance to finally satisfy their implant needs. Meanwhile, Mika and the two sat around an elegant dining room table, while Dr. Akira Aki spoke to her chef, requesting tea and biscuits.

With Dr. Akira Aki distracted, Mika again looked at Lady Persephone and whispered, "Kill. Me. Please," before reciting her implant script once again.

She whispered back, "Are you sure you want to die?"

It took a great effort, but Mika managed to make her head nod "yes." That gave Lady Persephone an idea. They chatted for an hour over tea, which was an oolong that came from China, quite delicious.

"Please come back and visit me again, if you have time. I'm gone for an hour around ten to check on my two patients. Otherwise, I'm here. Perhaps, you can even meet my loving husband, Delius," she begged them. The two thanked her and promised to do so, if they could.

An hour later, Lady Persephone and Lord Juan compared notes. Neither saw vast security guards around the building nor did they see any signs of any inside, though they could only see a little bit. Certainly, there was a cook and two maids present, but no armed guards, other than his zombie older son.

Thus, Lady Persephone had Jessica research just what the ancient records showed for building security. Two days later, Jessica reported she'd found over a dozen such systems, including several that released poison gas if the proper codes were not entered. One of these had been installed on the elevator that led from the roof down to the top floor. Another was in the front entrance area, just beyond the main entrance. Conclusion: Delius depended upon electronic protections and not on the zombie security guards, except for the one guard, his son from a previous marriage, Chou. Moreover, they had discovered the new Fetish EE man implant; the first one was his son from a previous marriage, Ken'ichi, who had married Hana.

Complicating matters, when Lady Persephone checked with the local hospital, she discovered the two patients were responding well to this new treatment being delivered by Dr. Akira Aki. The doctor at the hospital showed a remarkable enthusiasm talking about it to her, even though he was obviously implanted and on Pytalon. He spoke English and chose to talk to her, because he recognized that as a Lady, she must be an important person. Hence, the members of Delius' family either were victims themselves or were doing very beneficial things for the world at large, that is, Dr. Akira Aki was. Lady Persephone knew whatever action they took to stop Delius, it must not interfere with the doctor's work and research. "Why can't it just be simple, Juan?" she grumbled, rubbing her aching forehead. Juan smiled.
***

June 15, Delius was in New York, having brought along six of his new, small, portable Trans-assassins machines. Henry kindly had him setup tha devices in his own fortress in upper New York, a totally secure location. Here, six members of Locki's Freedom Fighters arrived and were fully briefed on the required operation. The million credits were deposited in the indicated account, and they waited on the arrival of Al Rumani, who brought along a dozen of his identical, burly zombie men—men who had no minds, no personalities. They'd been grown in the lab, but they could walk and eat on their own, but little else. One might call them human vegetables.

Henry had already acquired a number of weapons from Jacques and had them stowed in an EMAC. He and Al watched closely, as Delius hooked up each of the fighters to his machine, attaching electrodes to their heads. Then, he hooked another set up to the burly zombie men. Satisfied with all the connections, he powered up each of the six machines. Two minutes later, the Locki men lay comatose on the cots, while the burly, identical fighters roused. Delius hastily removed the electrodes, while the six confused men felt their faces and bodies, then rose testing their legs and arms.

Delius reminded them, "Don't worry. Whatever happens to these bodies will not harm yours here in the slightest. When I pull the plug, you'll automatically return to your real bodies right here. If something goes terribly wrong, hit the emergency button, and I'll automatically transfer you back here. Henry wants to go over your orders now."

Henry gave them photographs of the five intended targets and the best layout sketch he had of the Chicago Feds building, pointing out they were all located on the top floor, just below the EMAC lot on the roof. That done, the six fighters checked over the supplied gear, including the explosives, which they would have to use. Then they took off in the EMAC. Henry brought up a monitor so they could watch the live action. "I sure hope this works, Delius," he commented.

"So do I," Al added.

"Oh it will work," Delius replied. "Any more clues about who wiped out Ben?" Both men shook their heads no, leaving Delius feeling uneasy once more.

Around noon, the EMAC touched down on the roof of the Chicago Feds building, four men hopped off, gunning down two Feds standing watch, but not before one shot back, eliminating one of the four attackers. The EMAC lifted off, but with its bay door down. Timed perfectly, explosive charged blew off the door, while the fifty caliber automatic gun on the EMAC began blasting away,

314

disintegrating the office windows surrounding the Supreme Commander's office. The three men charged down the stairs, guns blazing. Trikuza and Feds reacted and a blood bath ensued.

Four minutes from the initial shots, the battle was over, and the EMAC took off at top speed, leaving four identical attackers dead. Inside, the five Indian bodies were dead, execution style, except that Vaani-Petra's body was nearly shredded in half from the high caliber rounds. Three other Feds were dead as well. Four Feds and two Trikuza were wounded and were rushed to Cook County Hospital. Captain Leah Smith rushed up, too late to take part in the battle, but she took charge immediately, calling for the emergency crew and then placing the call to Tilly.

Back in Henry's front room, one by one, four of the soldiers suddenly woke up, startled. They'd just been shot and killed only to wake up back in their own bodies. Wild explicatives flew fast, as they finally grasped what had happened and that they were still alive and unharmed. Hours later, the EMAC driver arrived, along with the wounded gunner. Once the soldier was transferred back into his real body, Al put the wounded zombie down.

"Well, that was interesting. If you need us again, don't hesitate to call. Any way we can get our hands on this stuff?" one of the Locki fighters asked.

"Hardly," Henry replied and watched the six men board their EMAC and depart. "Well, that went perfectly. No more Indian Feds. I'll give them a few days to reorganize and then pay them a visit, installing my man as the Supreme Commander," Henry declared.

Delius smiled and left the six units with Henry, just in case another round was needed. Besides, the units were so easy to operate that Henry could do it himself. Delius was an expert at making a machine that even a zombie could operate. Both he and Al then headed for their homes.
***

Tilly placed a conference call five minutes after Captain Lean called her, giving Beth time to retrieve some of the Feds video surveillance footage of the massacre. Lady Persephone, Juan, the professor, Wolf, and Chan-Petra joined her and her three companions. The five of them knew their Indian bodies had been killed; they'd seen it, felt the pain of the gunshots, and watched their perceptions from those bodies fade away, as the lives expired, a very strange feeling indeed.

In silent horror, the others watched the awful footage that Beth replayed. Then, Captain Leah joined the call with further news, reporting on the casualties. "What is totally weird are the four dead perps! Look at them. I've lined them all up on the floor so you can see them. We have four identical men here. We're checking fingerprints now, but I'm guessing we'll come up empty on that line. How can there be four identical men? Even with twins, usually there are some slight differences."

Chan-Petra replied, "Captain, have full autopsies done on them. Compare their fingerprints and their DNA."

Beth interjected, "And send me their DNA results too. I'll forward it to our expert as well." She meant Felix.

Chan-Petra added, "Okay gang, I'm back as Supreme Commander again. This time, I'll run the Feds from an undisclosed location, Captain Leah. No one will know my precise location. When the office is repaired, setup a video conferencing system. I can conduct any office visits via the system. I have a hunch this Henry Koch fellow will be paying us a visit. This time, we'll be prepared for him. Here's what I want you to do, captain." She rattled off some orders.

Then, she said, "Okay. Next, go to the arsenal in Colorado and bring back some heavy weapons, ones that can shoot down EMACs. Get it installed on our roof in some kind of bunker. I'm going to have all the other major Feds installations also get prepared. These people could strike us again, and I'll not have more Feds killed on my watch!"

Wolf replied, "Now you're talking! I'll coordinate the retrieval of the arms for the European and Africa groups from here. I can also get them for our India units as well. Are you sure you five are all right?"

"Hey, just have phantom pains right now. Let me tell you, Wolf, that was really weird—seeing yourself get shot and killed, while you're in another body," Beth explained to her longtime friend.

Wolf laughed. "Just like you, Weasel. Always getting mixed up in some new kind of adventure." Everyone laughed, lightening the mood slightly.

Lady Persephone spoke up, "I think we're about ready to take down our next Cabal man, this Delius Pogs fellow. Juan and I have cased his place. I think we can do it with just a few Trikuza. I believe I have all the tools we'll need to circumvent his electronic traps. As soon as we can verify Delius is back there, we're going to strike. Since Delius is gone from Hong Kong, I'm starting to wonder if he played any role in this attack on us. Four identical men. Something isn't right about that. Keep us posted on what you find out Captain Leah."

Late the next day, Captain Leah reported their initial findings. The four men had identical fingerprints and DNA. Further, there wasn't any record of them in any database the Feds had. That bothered Beth and Jessica, and particularly Felix. Beth brought him in on the attack and sent him the DNA results. He replied, "Look, their DNA has to be on file somewhere. Give me some time to find it."

"What's up?" R3 asked when the call was done.

Felix told her about the strange situation with the identical DNA. She replied, "Sounds like clones to me."

Felix grinned, "Me too, hot shot. Let's see what I can find. Everyone's DNA is on file somewhere." He began searching through Total Care's extensive DNA database. The search ran for eight hours, but yielded nothing, no matches at all. Felix sat back and stared at the monitor, perplexed.

R3 commented, "Look, it makes sense someone somewhere has this DNA on file. If they are clones, and they simply have to be clones, then someone has it.

Obviously, it isn't part of the OD or UD Total Care program, so it's outside that. What's outside Total Care anyway?"

Rhianna overheard them talking. She idly said, "Well, historically, they used to have a military DNA database and a Department of Defense database as well, but those were centuries ago. I read that in a historical article when we were in Ward 4 last year."

"Rhianna, I could kiss you!" R^3 gushed. Both women flushed, realizing she well could because of their implants. "That's it. Felix, can you get into those ancient records?"

"Already hunting them," he replied with a big grin.

The next day, Felix hit pay dirt. He'd found the ancient records of the Fighter Clone Program for the Department of Defense, abbreviated the FCP project. He had a positive DNA match to those experimental clones! He captured the basic details of the apparently unimplemented project and emailed them to Tilly, the professor, and Chan-Petra. Of course, no one knew just where these clones were being manufactured or kept or supplied. Still, it was a solid first step.

Thus, when Henry Koch paid a visit to the Chicago Feds, bringing along a new zombie to become their new Supreme Commander, Chan-Petra was prepared. New and heavier glass windows replaced the shattered ones in her office. A fancy video conferencing system was operational, and Captain Leah led Henry into the old office. "Chan-Petra has resumed her post as the Feds Supreme Commander. Sit here. She is on live video feed. After this last attack, we take the security of our top leader quite seriously." She turned and left the zombie and Henry facing the big screen, which held Chan-Petra's image.

"Welcome to my headquarters. As you can see, they're still cleaning up the mess from the last attack on us. Now then, Henry, what can I do for you today?" she said politely.

"I've told you repeatedly, I'm your boss, and I choose who is to be the Feds Supreme Commander, and it's not you. I've brought my man along with me. He is to be the new commander. Cease this silliness immediately," Henry angrily barked.

"While that may have been true many years ago, that is no longer the way it is today. Sorry. I'm the duly appointed Supreme Commander, period. If you continue to press this man as the commander, I'll have him arrested just as I did the previous one. Now then, I have some questions for you. Just what do you know about that ancient Fighter Clone Program for the Department of Defense, abbreviated the FCP project? We have positively identified four of the assassins as being those very clones from that project. What do you know about it?"

She watched him carefully and saw a visible reaction when she mentioned it. Chan-Petra knew he knew about it.

Henry cleared his throat. His face reddened with anger. "All right. You leave me no choice but to cut off all the funding for the entire Feds organization worldwide. You'll not get one credit until you step down and allow me to install my choice for Supreme Commander!"

"Fine with me. We don't need your funding. We have our own, wholly independent source of unlimited funds, Henry. You can expect your Feds to find those responsible for these brazen attacks on the Feds and eliminate them. Of course, if Total Care is attacked, don't look to the Feds for assistance. It's your decision to cut us off."

Chan-Petra glanced at a small icon that had appeared at the bottom of her monitor. That was Captain Leah's signal that the tracking bug had been planted on his EMAC.

"That will be all for today, Henry Koch." She turned off the monitor via her remote control, abruptly ending the short conference. Henry fumed, rose, and left, leaving the confused zombie still sitting in the office. Shortly, a Feds man escorted him out of the building.

Captain Leah already had two EMACs airborne when Henry lifted off in his. The real question was would he fly home, implying that he lived in the States, or would he go to New O'Hare and take an Air Liner? If he took an Air Liner, following him back would be next to impossible, but Captain Leah had allowed for this and had several Feds at the airport ready to join any flight Henry might be taking.

Luck was with them. His men followed Henry back to a huge fortress compound in upper New York State! Bingo. Now they had the location of another powerful Cabal man.

Meanwhile, Chan-Petra called Felix and R³. "Looks as if we're going to need your funding. Henry just told me he's cutting off all funding for the Feds. Again, we thank you immensely!"

R³ replied, "Of course. Having unlimited funds was part of my idea when I went with Ben. This way, Henry's threat is harmless. Just let Felix know how much you need and when. He'll get it all automated. Sorry about the deaths of your five other bodies."

***

Lady Persephone had to prepare before handling Delius. After a not so quick trip home and back, she was ready. The professor also helped make some of the arrangements she needed. Finally, on June 22, she was prepared to strike. Knowing she dared not attempt to use her now pathetic martial arts skills, she hired three of Master Yao's Trikuza men; one was even one of his seconds.

That evening, Delius and his extended family once more took their evening stroll through Hong Kong's Central Park. The three masked and black cloaked men struck without warning! Poor Delius didn't even see the attack coming! With a touch on the right pressure point, he was out like a light, Dr. Akira Aki and Mika too, though the men kept the two women from falling. Two minutes later, the others were unconscious as well. Lady Persephone and Lord Juan stepped out of the shadows, verifying this was actually Delius Pogs. Four minutes later, the three men had carried Delius and Mika into her EMAC. She left one of the Trikuza behind to make sure none of the others roused until the operation was completed.

After landing on the roof of his skyscraper, Lady Persephone set to work. She had many alarms to disarm, some quite deadly. That took her a half hour. Once the protections were disabled, the two Trikuza carried Delius down to one of his labs, where he had his own Model III setup. She smiled; he'd even left the controls sitting on Make Fetish EE Woman. They strapped him in, and she followed the 1-2-3 script the psych men used to run the machine. She added one short sentence to the implant words. "My name is Mika." Then, she let the programmed script run its course, watching as the machine injected him with a powerful drug, then fired electrical currents into his brain via the lattice work of the headband, and listened to the script being played over and over into his ears. A half hour later, the machine turned off.

While this was going on, she had the men carry a large crate down from her EMAC and unpack the Transference Machine. It took them another half hour to get it up and running. During that time, they brought Mika down and put her on one side of the machine. Then, the unconscious Delius was laid on the other side. Carefully, Lady Persephone connected the various wires and finally activated the machine. When it was finished, she roused the Delius body, verifying it was Mika. Once more, she asked the woman if she really did want to die. Mika certainly did and managed to nod her head rather vigorously. Sadly, one of the Trikuza did the deed, painlessly though.

While she and Juan began packing up the machine, the Trikuza carried the deceased Delius body and Mika's body back up to the EMAC. An hour later, she landed it near the park. The two men carried Mika's body, laying it down beside Dr. Akira Aki's still form. That done, the three Trikuza bowed respectfully to Lady Persephone and departed. She then contacted the Feds, reporting an assault in Central Park. She lifted off and later dumped the dead body into a deserted street where it would certainly be found in the morning, and then landed at the hotel where she and Juan had taken a honeymoon suite.

The next morning, Lady Persephone and Lord Juan paid a call on the very distraught Dr. Akira Aki. "We heard about the terrible assault in the park last night! We came as soon as we could," she said feigning deep sympathy. "We're so sorry for your loss."

Sobbing, Dr. Akira Aki replied, "Yes, so awful. The men came out of nowhere. When I woke, my Delius was gone. They found his dead body this morning. It's just awful. Now whatever will we do?"

Lady Persephone allowed the grieving widow to talk for some time, before she began to make her carefully arranged proposals. Beth had already hacked into his bank account, removing his credits, all forty-five billion of them. She made a new account for Dr. Akira Aki, placing a billion credits in hers. She made accounts for the six others as well, placing ten million in each one. This way, no matter how it played out, Ken'ichi, Hana, Ren, Keiko, Mika, and Chou would have more than enough funds to survive well. The rest of the billions she split between the professor's account and R^3's account. Now it was in the hands of Lady Persephone.

"Akira, I've talked with others about your lifesaving discoveries and cures. Many others want you to proceed with your research at all costs. I made some calls this morning before I came here. The Raven Research Laboratories in London want to sponsor your continued research. They'll provide you with state of the art lab facilities and everything you could possibly need, including your own home—all expenses paid for life. They will cover all your moving costs as well, but they want you to bring your dear Mika along with you."

Seeing Dr. Akira's eyes brightening up, she continued, "I also found out each Fetish EE woman is supposed to have their own Fetish EE Woman's Personal

Assistant. Somehow, Delius didn't provide them, so I have several lined up for everyone here. They are Japanese, of course. The only question that remains is will they want to move to London with you and Mika or will they desire to move to Japan, perhaps to Tokyo? If so, I have some contacts there who can arrange really luxurious housing for them."

"But what about credits?" Dr. Akira asked.

Lord Juan answered this one. "If you will allow me to use one of your computers, we can check on just what your husband has left you and the children." A half hour later, Dr. Akira Aki was shocked to see that Delius had left her a billion credits in her very own account. Further, that each of the others also had their own personal accounts with very substantial amounts in them truly pleased her.

Around noon, the new personal assistants arrived and were introduced to their new charges. Chou, Ken'ichi, and Hana wanted to move to Tokyo, though it took some doing to get that out of them over their implants. Ren and Keiko wanted to stay with Dr. Akira Aki and Mika. Thus, during the next week, the skyscraper was a hive of activity. Movers came, packed their things, and moved the two groups to their new locations. Meanwhile, Lady Persephone confiscated the new Model III implant machine and several other devices, along with many computers and documents. The rest was merely common lab equipment, which was given to charity, and the PB Skyscraper put up for sale.

What of Mika or Delius? She awoke very confused, but was convinced her name was Mika. The new Model III implant was so powerful that Delius wasn't able to do anything to overcome its effects, just as all the others who fell victim to this new, improved implant couldn't. Unless someone applied Jessica's therapy to her, she'd be a mindless Fetish EE woman for a very, very long time. Considering Dong Fa's wife, Tamiko, had been implanted by this new model four years ago and she still acted as though she'd only just received it, everyone anticipated those who received theirs from the Model III would be acting this way for many years, quite unlike those who had it done with the older models, where after a number of years, some thinking ability returned to the person. Since Dr. Akira Aki did have a love for Mika, Delius or Mika was very content with being so close and intimate with Akira, which only reinforced the implant's impact upon her. That she also had an assistant to look after her needs was greatly appreciated by Akira who no longer had to deal with that extra work or that of Ren and Keiko.

Lady Persephone made sure their new home was very close to one of London's finer parks. Dr. Akira's new lab was the entire Sub-Level 1 of the Raven Research Facilities. Further, R^3 had Felix post an announcement that Raven Research Laboratories was now fully sponsoring the degenerative brain disease research of Dr. Akira Aki. Felix made a very nice press release presentation on their new web pages. R^3's idea was to let the Cabal men know this valuable research was going to be continued and held promising results.

In late July, Lady Persephone dropped by to see how Dr. Akira Aki was doing. She found the doctor was very anxious to have her as a close friend. No longer was Akira hold up in a skyscraper. Now she had a great deal of freedom, but no one to share it with. Thus, Lady Persephone and Lord Juan struck up a long-lasting friendship with her. About the only problem Akira had was Mika's incessant clinging to her, demanding almost constant intimacy, which she didn't get, excepting in the evenings. It also allowed them to monitor Mika, but she remained wholly under the control of the Fetish EE woman implant. Ren and Keiko kept her somewhat occupied during the daytime hours. Thus, Lady Persephone had firsthand knowledge of just how debilitating these new Model III's implants were, drastically worse than those from the Model II!

***

Henry Koch returned to the safety of his fortress,

angrier than ever! At once, he cut off funding for the Feds, much to the non-comprehension of the various Total Care Zonal CEOs. Then, he placed a conference call to the other Camarilla members, relating the news that Chan-Petra was back in control of the Feds worldwide, but that he'd cut off their funds.

"Relax, Henry," James Buffett spoke softly. "Surely, they don't have an independent source of funds as she said. Let's wait and see. I bet she'll be calling you, desperate for funds in less than a month."

However, he had his own frightening thoughts, which he didn't mention. What if that Raven woman who stole Ben's fortune along with her own began to support the Feds? That would make sense, since the Feds provided top-level security around the world. If this Chan-Petra hooked into her funds, then for sure they would lose complete control of the Feds! That terrified James. Money was his thing and he began to monitor what he could.

The next day, the Camarilla received even more shocking news. Delius Pogs was dead! An assassin had gotten to him and his whole family, though he was the only one murdered. This blow sent shock waves of stark terror through these remaining Camarilla members. Though it took them several days, they discovered his wife was doing valuable medical research. None was surprised to hear the Raven heiress was now supporting her research, which was fine with them. However, that most of Delius's vast fortune had mysteriously vanished shocked them as well.

James did point out Delius left no official heir behind. He'd not officially had one for the last fifty years. Stupid, foolish old man, James thought. After days of backtracking, he discovered someone had deposited the bulk of Delius's fortune into that Raven heiress's account!

"Look, this Raven bitch now controls more billions than even you, Franco. Some mysterious benefactor dumped Delius's money into her account. There's no legal way to get that undone, though. Stupid idiot didn't leave an heir or even a will behind," James pointed out, far angrier than normal. He always tried to maintain a soft-spoken demeanor and in the background. However, this shocking news hit him where it hurt, money.

Franco was also very terrified and upset. This situation was completely out of hand and only getting worse. In just a few months, they'd lost two of their Camarilla members along with their fortunes and expansive corporations. Well, Delius only had the implant machine manufacturing companies. Still. . .

He growled, "We must take strong and effective actions."

"But what? Damn it, Franco, we don't even know who is behind this mess," Henry protested. "True, Lady Persephone stepped in to assist Dr. Akira Aki, but we now know she isn't Persephone, the Assassin. She just got married and did the right thing, becoming an EE woman for her husband. He seems like a normal bloke. I agree; we need to strike a powerful blow, but against whom? We haven't a clue where this damnable Chan-Petra woman is at, and we have no idea who has been wiping us out."

Franco ran his hands through his hair, frustrated. "Oh hell, pick someone! Anyone! Who out there is normal still?"

"Well, that Raven's new husband," Henry answered. "He seems totally harmless though. She's running the show, not him."

"He'll have to do," Franco replied, suspecting this action was futile, but he had to suggest someone to fight. The others were depending upon him, after all. That Felix was a "wrong target" didn't even cross his mind. He was just another normal person whom he feared, since he wasn't implanted or on Pytalon-Ex.

"Hey, we should use Delius's latest modification, his new Fetish EE Man implant. Make him like his wife," Al Rumani suggested.

"Good. Make it so," Franco declared. "Say, I've heard rumors many aren't surviving the implanting from these new Model III's."

326

"Ah, yes. I've been tracking that for Delius," Al elaborated. "It seems about one in ten are dying. Perhaps, it's a bit too strong, but then from the results we're getting, the implants seem to be drastically more effective."

"I'll say!" Henry gushed. "My wife is totally into being a sex doll now. She hasn't had a clear thought of her own since we had it done early January. Damned near perfect. So what if we lose one in ten? Keeps the overall populations low."

Al chuckled. "Indeed, Henry. This new Model III is making unbreakable implants. I think we should begin a worldwide re-implanting of everyone. Make damned sure the implants are holding."

"Sorry, we've only got about a thousand of the Model IIIs delivered so far, Al," Francisco countered. "With Delius gone, I'll issue orders to ramp up production. Still, I like that idea. Henry, make it so through Total Care. Help fight sanity; renew your implant today."

Henry laughed. "I'll make you our marketing rep yet, Francisco." Several chuckled. "Seriously, I think taking out Raven's husband will send her a strong message not to mess with us, but I highly doubt she's behind anything. After all, she is a Fetish EE woman now. She still is, from all the spy reports I've received."

He didn't say he thought this was an excellent opportunity to advance this new idea of Fetish EE men onto the world. However, he also thought this was a silly response to such a deadly situation. He began to have serious doubts about these other leaders.

When the conference call ended, Henry joined Al and Tom. "Guys, I don't like this one bit. Delius is gone; Ben is gone. Their places aren't being filled. Not one clue about who is behind these. Franco is having us go after this Felix fellow. I smell a rat."

"I smell a lot of rats," Tom put in, quite nervously. "I'm beginning to think one of those four is behind this. What can we do?"

"Beef up your defenses. Take no chances, as silly

Delius was always doing. The world out there isn't safe. It's a war zone," Al pointed out. "Look, we know there are still many men who are neither implanted nor on Pytalon. We should be terrified of them."

"So what do we do?" asked Tom, more worried than he ever had been in a very, very long time.

Henry sighed, out of ideas. "Well, I'll take care of Felix for Franco, but guys, we damned well better come up with some ideas. Which one of us is next, eh?"

Quite nervously, Tom asked, "You really think they will go after one of us next?"

Henry smiled and replied, "Mark my words. This isn't over yet!"
***

On July 10, Henry's people struck. Actually, he made use of six of Locki's fighters and another half-dozen of Al's zombie fighters. Nana had R^3 dressed and ready for work in her research lab, giving her charge a little hug, as R^3 and Felix headed out the door of their plush new home in north London. Their usual two Feds and two Trikuza guards had already arrived and were waiting to escort them to the lab. Just then, another EMAC swooped down on them. Its bay door was open, and guns began blazing at them, while four men slipped down ropes to the ground.

The Feds returned fire, while the Trikuza men tackled the four men as they slithered down the ropes. The battle was swift and decisive. Within a minute, the four guards were wounded and out of the fight, but the four who had come down the ropes were dead. A fifth man, gun pointed at the shocked pair, slipped down the rope, while the EMAC landed. "All right. Felix, you're coming with us. Raven lady, he'll be brought back here to you in a few days. Watch who you're messing with." He forced Felix into the EMAC and it lifted off.

"Help Nana!" R^3 screamed, and her assistant came outside, hesitantly. "Call the Feds and the emergency rescue people. Now, Nana. Please hurry." R^3 felt frustrated. She longed to go help the wounded men, but knew she couldn't actually do anything for them. She chided herself. *Look, even if I had hands, I haven't a clue what to do for them.*

A swarm of Feds arrived around the same time as the emergency zombies. Captain Lark quickly checked on the four men and told R³, "They'll be all right. Through and through wounds—not life threatening. Now these others, they'd dead. Strange, they all look identical. I'm sending a pic of one back to HQ. I bloody well bet it matches those we have on file from that vicious attack on the Feds HQ in Chicago!"

It did. R³ had him relay the news of the attack to Chan-Petra, knowing she'd relay it on to the others. Now all she had to do was worry about what they were going to do to Felix. Had they found out about his computer hacking? Were they going to fill him up with truth drugs? What he could reveal was enormous, she thought, and had Nana attach her fancy phone to her ear so she could talk to the others. Chan-Petra joined her in a conference call to many others. R³ did her best to keep her wild emotions under control.

Tilly lamented, "Back in the old days, we were highly compartmentalized so if they got to one of us, they'd not get to the rest of us. Now there's a bunch of us who could be tortured into revealing nearly the whole resistance movement."

"Can't be helped, Tilly," the professor put in. "We must keep on doing the right things. Remember, these Cabal men don't think logically. They pick wrong targets. R³ did say they would be returning him in a few days. My guess is they're going to implant him or something. Still, let's double our guards for the time being."
***

Two days later, a medical EMAC from London General landed near the new Raven mansion. A dozen Feds were on guard duty. Captain Lark's idea was to capture the men when they returned Felix. However, Henry had out-thought them this time, using a routine medical transport.

One of the zombie technicians lifted Felix down the ramp, as another young woman followed along behind them. R³ gasped. Felix wore a very fancy suit, but his lower arms were missing. His shirt and suit coat were cut two inches above his lightly bandaged elbows, a rather strange look. His waist looked terribly small, similar to hers. His eyes were glassy. R³ went to him as fast as she could manage, while walking rather precariously on her toes. Yet, that was vastly better than Felix, who flailed his short arms about while taking awkward, stumping steps towards her.

When she got close, she heard Felix mumbling and tried to memorize what he was saying. "My body is hypersensitive to sensual touches. My body needs sexual sensations and stimulations several times each day. I exist to provide elegant and sensual experiences to men and women of power. I am a Fetish Exotic Escort man. I must look my very best at all times. I must wear my ballet boots at all times. I must wear the tightest corsets possible with my fetish suits. I am a model of masculine perfection. I must walk elegantly and gracefully at all times. I must be ready to flirt at any time. I must be ready to engage and satisfy the sexual fantasies and satisfactions of both men and women at any time. I am a super-sexual, hypersensitive man. I must wear only the finest and exotic suits and heels. I must look absolutely perfect at all times. I will repeat to myself these words several times each day. I must not forget these words."

R³'s heart sank. It was one thing for her to get this done to herself knowingly, for the rewards had been far greater than she'd even imagined, but quite another for poor Felix. When she reached him, he tried to put his short arms around her, but her massive bosom prevented that. Still he began passionately kissing her, and it took some doing to get him to stop.

"This is his personal assistant, Jenna. She's recently been implanted and is skilled at handling his daily needs," the technician read from a card. "You should have the bandages removed in a week and should get him more outfits soon. Sanity is making a good delivery." He turned and left.

R[3] looked at the glassy-eyed Jenna, who couldn't have been more than eighteen. Jenna was also whispering her own implant script, and she was heavily dosed on Pytalon-Ex. She was rather plain looking, quite similar to Nana in many ways, probably taken right out of high school. At least Jenna had the good sense to put her arm around Felix, steadying him as he tried to walk into the mansion, or perhaps she was trained to do that, R[3] thought. Most of the Feds quietly departed, leaving R[3] to deal with this mess.

By suppertime, Jessica arrived, accompanied by three Trikuza men. After seeing him for a few minutes and discovering he'd just been fed a good supper, though only a small amount, similar to R[3], she decided to start in on her therapy right away, much to R[3]'s great relief. As she expected, it was very slow going. The power delivered by these new Model III's was many times more than the older models, making the trauma extremely severe, painful, and deeply buried.

More than a week later, Felix was finally back to his new normal, and R[3] heaped tons of praise on her, thanking her over and over for saving her Felix. He'd been knocked out by some drug when he got onto the EMAC. He was first implanted and then taken to a hospital, probably in London, where the surgery was done. He'd been kept unconscious for over a day, enabling the medical machine to mostly heal up the surgery. When he finally awoke, gasping for breath, he was introduced to Jenna, his new personal assistant.

"Now what do I do?" he asked. "How can I run my computers like this?"

Jessica explained, "The professor and R[3] agree, Felix. You should stay as you are for a time. We don't want them to get overly suspicious of either R[3] or you. Obviously, they're going to be keeping a covert eye on you for the near future. Anyway, Beth has it all worked out.

Tomorrow, I'm going to put the voice-activated software on your computers for the both of you. That way, you can still do your work, Felix," Jessica explained.

It did take her an entire day to get it done on their many computers, though. However, in the process, they discovered a huge announcement had appeared on personal EE women's web pages as well as the Total Care pages. Emails had been sent to all existing EE women too.

"Oh dear god!" Jessica exclaimed when she found them. Everyone gathered around, looking over her shoulders.

Total Care is implementing a new program, the Fetish EE Man. All sponsors and mates of EE women are highly encouraged to become a Fetish EE Man as soon as possible. No excuses accepted. Total Care will provide each his own personal assistant. Yes, this means all CEOs as well.

All EE women must have their implants refreshed as soon as possible. At that time, all EE women will be highly encouraged to become Fetish EE women themselves and will be provided their own personal assistant. Again, no excuses accepted. Your local Total Care representative will be contacting each of you and arranging dates for you.

Further, Total Care will soon be launching a refresh implant campaign worldwide, refreshing everyone's implants. It is high time we stamp out the last vestiges of Insanity in our world.

"My god, Jessica, this is horrid—a nightmare!" R3 exclaimed.

"Well, I best see to handling Jenna now," Jessica sighed, emailing the alert to Beth, knowing she'd relay it to everyone else.

Jenna's implant had been done on the older model. Hers was desensitized in one long day's work. That done, both Jenna and Felix visited the Rehab Center in London, sweating out the residual drugs still in their systems. Jenna had only had two doses of Pytalon, so both finished that sweaty ordeal in just a few days.

Although he wanted to get out of the restrictive corset, R³ advised against it. "Honestly, you'll get used to it. If you take it off, it'll be murder when it's put back on in the morning. Remember all the trouble I went through when we tried that on me?"

Felix sighed. Jenna prepared him for sleep as always. He too wore black nylons attached to the corset and wore the boots to bed, as did R³. That way, if he needed to get up at night, he could stand. Without the boots, he would have to crawl on his knees. Like the others, his feet and toes were becoming quite crushed, though he didn't feel it; nerves had been severed.

A bit later, he whispered, "Well R³, sex is now utterly fantastic." Both laughed, knowing the price was far too steep.

Chapter 16—A Power Play

The next day after the appearance of the Total Care announcement, Dr. Akira Aki visited Lady Persephone at her castle. "Why, Dr. Akira, what a pleasant surprise. Come on in. Tea?" she asked politely. She noticed Akira was rather flushed; worry lines edged her eyes and upper cheeks.

"Akira, please, between friends," she insisted, "Tea would be fine. Have you seen the news from Total Care? About everyone having their implants redone using the new Model III machine?"

"Why yes, I have. It's terrible," Lady Persephone replied, taking a seat across from her, while Juan brought in the teapot and poured all three a cup, using her expensive, fine china.

"Very much so. I told my late husband perhaps he'd gone too far with his newer model machine, but you know men. They never listen to us women, especially our types." By that, Lady Persephone figured she meant EE women.

"That is an understatement from all I can tell," she replied politely, wondering where this was headed. Was she worried that if she were implanted again that she'd not be able to continue her invaluable research?

Akira's reply surprised her. "As you probably know, those of us who had our implants done by the older machines have had the implant's effects subside quite substantially as the years go by. As you can see, I'm able to function fairly well in spite of needing pleasuring frequently, but I don't often have to stop everything and repeat those words, thank goodness. I have known quite a few of us EE women, and can say after about ten years, our ability to think is substantially returned, though by then, we're really grooved in on our roles as EE women."

"Yes I've observed that too. The EE women who run

our apparel stores are all older women and certainly are able to think fairly well," Lady Persephone replied.

"Exactly. Now those who have had theirs done by the new model are in drastically worse shape. My god Lady Persephone, Tamiko and Mika are still acting as though they just came out of the machine. It's been over three years now for Mika and over four years for Tamiko—oh, she was with us until she recently married the Feds man, Dong Fa. Four years, My Lady, and they still act as though they'd just had it done. My goodness, they can't think a single thought of their own, slavishly following their scripts."

"It's really bad, isn't it?" Lady Persephone replied, taking a sip of tea, still wondering where this was going.

"Now as you know," Akira continued, "I have been researching degenerative brain diseases. I couldn't help but also study what has been happening to us all from the implants, especially EE women. I guess I have a vested interest in that," she hinted and bit her lip slightly.

"I've made some startling discoveries. Probably they were known to doctors centuries ago, but it seems to have been forgotten, I suppose. Anyway, one of the chemicals in our brains is called oxytocin. When that chemical is released in quantity, it causes sexual arousals in both men and women. Another chemical is dopamine. When you're in love, that one is produced, and it signals intense pleasure, which sex and pleasuring is. Dopamine is rather addictive. Once you get rather high on it, you crave it again. It's rather like the adrenaline highs that some get in a high-action situation."

"What I've found, using myself as my first test subject of course, is that the EE woman implant causes our bodies to flood our brains with oxytocin first, and then when we're finally able to perform as the implant dictates, dopamine floods our brains. The combination is highly addictive, which accounts for why even those of us who had our implant done years ago are still mostly driven by them, you see."

At this point, Akira paused a moment, as though reaching some kind of decision. Hesitantly, she said, "So I experimented on myself. I introduced other inhibitors that partially blocked the oxytocin and dopamine production. The result was I've been drastically less affected by my EE woman's implant. As you probably have noticed, I almost never have to repeat the words aloud. True, by evening, my blockers are pretty much out of my system, and it's at that time I'm still very much the effect of the EE woman's implant and truly do need pleasuring and such."

"Wow. Now that is both interesting and potentially very useful to know," Lady Persephone replied, genuinely surprised. She began to see many uses for these inhibitors.

"Yes, it is both. Naturally, when I saw the overwhelming effects of this new implant on Tamiko and Mika were not lessening in the slightest after two years, I began giving them my inhibitors, hoping to help them cope far better." She sighed. "The effects of my treatment were almost negligible! When Ren had hers done, I tried to lessen its effect on her as well. Again, it had very little noticeable impact. So my hopeful solution to lessen the implant's effect on our lives and thinking abilities has been shattered by Delius's new Model III machine."

"Now, can you see why I'm so very worried about this new Total Care program and orders to us all? If my injections don't make much of an impact on our bodies chemical productions, we won't be able to do or think anything at all beyond the dictates of the EE woman's implant, not for many, many years. It will be totally debilitating to us all! They said no exceptions, so we're all doomed—all EE women—we'll be unable to do anything at all but be sex dolls—every minute of every hour of every day. Lady Persephone, frankly, I'm terrified of this. If it happens, since there isn't a man in my home, only us EE women and our personal assistants, can we even survive? I mean you have Lord Juan to help, but—well, if it happens to me and my family, could Juan look in on us from time to time, making sure we're surviving somehow?" Only now did Akira look greatly relieved.

"Of course, Akira. I give you my word I'll look in on you frequently," Lord Juan spoke up, very sincerely. "I won't let anything bad happen to you or your daughter."

"Thank you! I don't know how I can ever repay you for such kindness. You both have been true lifesavers for Ren and me. Thank you," Akira gushed out heartfelt appreciation.

"Say did you try an increased dosage on Ren?" Lady Persephone asked.

"Yes, as much as I dared to use. It's untested waters. We have no idea what significantly large doses could do. Brain damage is possible, and I dare not risk that on anyone," Akira answered. "What I did give Ren at least kept her calmer for a while, so there was some benefit, just far, far too little to do her any good. As she is now, she'll be missing years of her life while she's so heavily under the implant's powers. Honestly, four years and Tamiko is acting as if it was Day One of her implant. It's just awful."

Akira squirmed a little and then brought up another detail that deeply troubled her. "Another thing. They said they were highly encouraging ordinary EE women to become this new thing, the Fetish EE woman, when we report to get ours redone. That's going too far in my book, but then that's just my opinion. If they make me into that kind of sex doll, without my hands, I won't be able to continue any of my research, but then I guess that won't matter since I won't be able to think about anything else anyway. If that happens, I know I'll desperately need you to look in on us, Juan."

She chatted away, "On the other hand, Ren and Keiko seem to be very much pleased with their body's forms, but then Ren never did do much before she was implanted. She was still just growing up. I had so hoped that would take an interest in the medical profession. She never did. Even Hana and Ken'ichi seem to love their new forms too, so I guess I shouldn't judge others. Still, that would end my life's work, even if many years down the road I regained some ability to think about other things again."

Lady Persephone sighed. "I understand. Akira. We should prepare for the worst. I don't trust the people behind Total Care. Even if they allowed us to choose not to become Fetish EE women, who could stop them once we're knocked out? They could turn us into one, whether we desired it or not."

Akira sighed too. "I thought that too, only I didn't want to scare you, Lady Persephone. Anyway, I've taken up too much of your time. I really should get back to my research while I still can. If I'm implanted and unable to continue my work, I do hope someone else comes along and continues it. I'm so very close to a cure for several of those nasty, debilitating diseases."

As soon as she left, the two placed another conference call, alerting everyone to Akira's discoveries. Lady Persephone felt any such information might help later on. She then called up Chan-Petra. "Hi, yes, we're fine. I just wanted to know if we're planning to take out Henry Koch soon, before this nightmare new Total Care program gets going."

"We're still studying his fortress and protections. He has an army inside there now. So far, we haven't worked out how we can get to him. Even if we kill him today, we've no way officially to take over the Total Care program. Undoubtedly, another Cabal member will jump in and assume the reins, but we're working on it. Top priority."

Lady Persephone had to be satisfied with that, though she was extremely worried. The consequences, the stakes had just been raised by an almost insurmountable amount. Time wasn't on their side.

After that major announcement, Beth and Jessica began closely monitoring Total Care communications. Within a week, they saw Total Care was making a huge push to acquire hundreds more young teens to become personal assistants! That didn't sound promising at all. The pair began plotting just where the buildups were occurring.

London, Amsterdam, Berlin, Madrid, New York, Chicago, LA, St. Louis, Tokyo, Hong Kong, Peking, and Rome saw the largest buildup of young teenaged girls being pulled out of high schools and turned into personal assistants. However, none was found elsewhere in China, none in India, or Africa or even South America or Canada.

Based on this distribution, Chan-Petra made an executive decision. She sent a secure email to all her relatively newly appointed area commanders, such as Wolf in Berlin, to go into deep hiding as she was, running their Feds section from afar. She didn't want to risk losing these top men and women. None of them had been implanted or put on Pytalon. For the survival of her Feds, at least the top leaders had to avoid this coming storm. Wolf sent her a hearty thank you email, though he didn't tell her that if she hadn't recommended this move, he was going to resign and vanish into the woods once more. He'd seen enough horrors.

Barely one week after the major announcement and just one day after Wolf went underground again, the announcements began rolling out, beginning in London. However, for the first time and thanks to the assistance of Felix, Beth was able to hack into Total Care London. She downloaded a copy of the document labeled "Initial Group Phase One." While Jessica scanned the list seeing who was on it, Beth continued her hacking and got a similar one from the Chicago office and then the New York branch.

Before long, both women cursed wildly. Amanda and Tilly stopped what they were doing and came to see what had so upset the pair. "It's utter madness," Jessica exclaimed, forgetting to curse. "They're ordering us and our friends, the Feds, the EE women, and all company CEOs in the Chicago and London areas to get it done in the next couple of days! Anyone who doesn't show up for their scheduled appointment will have an arrest warrant put out on them with the Feds and local AP-cops!"

Tilly looked very annoyed and placed a secure conference call to the key resistance leaders. First, she relayed what the two sleuths had just discovered and then cleverly asked for suggestions.

"We should launch all out attacks on the Total Care headquarters in every city," Captain Leah suggested.

Chan-Petra backed him up. Wolf suggested everyone go into hiding. R³ suggested that wasn't feasible because it would end some vital research, such as hers and Dr. Akira Aki's. The professor suggested assaulting Henry Koch's fortress, but Amanda pointed out that wouldn't stop Total Care, since another Cabal man would simply step in and take it over in Henry's place. The suggestions only got wilder as time progressed, which is what Tilly had in mind.

When the group finished venting their anger, Tilly took control once more. "Gang, Amanda and I have finally reworked all our human behavior prediction equations, based on knowing so much more about the Cabal men, especially that their basic motivation is their hidden terror of other people not wholly under their control via the debilitating implants and Pytalon. Yes, she and I predicted the Cabal would resort to using Total Care as their primary weapon at this point in time. With the rather large MMS group gone, there are very few fighting groups of men left, though obviously there are some we haven't yet gotten to, as witnessed by the attack on the Feds."

"You see, Total Care *is* their answer to world domination by themselves. Via it and its vast resources, they control the world, from the running of ordinary companies to health care, both physical and mental. Our equations show that when pressured—and there can be no doubt we have recently done just that in major ways, then lacking an army to enforce their will, they would have no other recourse but to resort to their tried and true methods, via Total Care."

"We need time to get to them and to undo their control over the Total Care outfit. However, time is something we don't have right now. I know that it's my fault that I didn't see Total Care as our main target all these years. I should have and that's why we're in this mess now.

We went after the wrong targets too, though I find hindsight to be perfect."

"But we had to get rid of that Grand Field Marshal Hans fellow," Jessica complained.

"Yes, we spent our time doing such things, when they would have been better spent taking over the Total Care program," Tilly pointed out.

"Hey, stop the self-recriminations," Amanda barked. "Look, when Jessica and I first fled Chicago when Bill stole the Air Liner and crashed it into the Pytalon Manufacturing skyscraper, none of us had any idea about how Total Care worked. Stop blaming yourself, and let's get back to our new predictions." Tilly's face reddened, but only her three companions saw that.

"Okay. Here's what we've worked out. Some of us who are rather in the limelight so to speak, such as you two, Felix, R³, Lady Persephone, Lord Juan, we four, and Chan-Petra, need to play along with this Total Care operation. If we do, the percentages are high, ninety-five percent, that the Cabal will figure they've won the war and totally relax their guard. They'll believe they have just scored a total victory over the resistance movement. This is based upon the simple fact that they habitually select the wrong targets and wrong actions. Honestly, we should have been killed long ago—all of us. Instead, they keep playing games with us, believing they have put us down and out."

"True, a few of us will be down and out for a time, but that will give the rest of you time to work out how to take down Henry Koch and how we can put our people in at the top levels of the Total Care program. If we're to have any chance at winning this war, we simply must take over control of the Total Care operation. That, Amanda and I can say with nearly a hundred percent certainty. Further, we also believe this Dr. Al Rumani in India must also be eliminated. If we get rid of their control over implanting, cloning, and all medical institutes, then we've a fighting chance at ultimate victory," Tilly finished up.

The professor spoke, ending the long silence when

Tilly finished. "Blimey, she has a point. In the distant past, these Cabal men had money, power, and influence over the world's leaders and armies, which they used to get their plans carried out. In today's modern world, those don't exist any longer. They're getting desperate, as witnessed by their making use of that several centuries old, mothballed fighter clone project. So we let them believe they've won the war by way of this new Total Care program and then focus our efforts at infiltrating it, taking it over, and locking the Cabal out of it. Bloody fine idea, Tilly, Amanda, bloody fine."

"I see your point," Lady Persephone spoke up at last. "But what about those of us who get wiped out? If we are re-implanted, who is left that can at least work Jessica's magic on us? My god, I was an utter zombie and couldn't think of anything but shagging up with anyone anywhere until Jessica got to me."

"Yes, that is going to be the major hurdle we have to overcome," the professor replied. "I'm going to have someone contact Dr. Akira Aki today and get the details on her chemical blockers. I know she told you they had almost no impact on those who have been put through this new Model III machine, but every bit of knowledge helps us. I would also suggest some of you move in together, like Beth, Jessica, Tilly, and Amanda. That is a proven way to improve overall survival percentages."

Jessica laughed. "Funny way to put it, professor."

R3 spoke up. "Look, it has been hard for me and now hard for my Felix, but by remaining mostly as the Fetish EE woman they believed I was turned into, they have pretty well left me alone. I have been making substantial progress on the power generator project. I think I should have it ready to go in a year at most—full-scale production I mean. So if a few of us can endure this torture, that gives the rest of us the time we need. Oh Beth, Felix loves the voice-activated software. It does work pretty well. I'm getting the hang of it now too. Thanks."

Felix added, "While I know it's the oxytocin and

dopamine talking, sex with my R³ is utterly indescribable. We both see how addictive the whole EE project actually is, but then, isn't that what is expected of a sex doll? We were wondering just what the effects are on the company CEOs, for example, since they are also among the first to get it done to them. Do we have anyone who is officially a CEO?"

"Blimey, Felix," the professor answered rather surprised at this detail, "we actually don't. Tilly, we need to start studying some of the CEOs and just what they actually do."

"Say, I have an idea about that," R³ spoke up. "Let us work on that one." She obviously had a very large number of CEOs running numerous companies in her far-flung enterprises that built all the METs, EMACs, and Air Liners. Later, she talked with Todd and Mary Jane. Todd agreed to play "understudy" to one of her Chicago EMAC manufacturing plants, and Felix made the arrangements. The resistance would soon know just what these implanted CEOs actually did.

Lady Persephone had to make a decision. Based on what was said and suggested, she and Juan discussed having Felix and R³ move in with them. Also, Juan felt they should have Dr. Akira join them, but that meant bringing along Mika—that is, Delius—and her daughter Ren and mate Keiko. However, having them all here at her giant castle was problematical. She had too many "secrets" she didn't want to fall into the enemy's hands. After a quick check, she knew Felix and R³ really did want to live with them, understandably since both were now pretty well handicapped, though their personal assistants helped them with nearly everything.

However, since the new Raven mansion was too small for everyone, as was Akira's new place, she didn't have much choice. While Juan handled hiding her "secrets" in upper floors, she helped the others make moving arrangements. That day, the zombie-like movers brought the Raven's few possessions and those of Akira's group over to her castle. While Akira went about reorganizing their things and those of her daughter, Lady Persephone could sense the immense relief and gratitude the doctor felt.

None too soon, though, for the next day, they received their orders to report to London General for re-implanting. Following Tilly's plan, the large group did as ordered, though Captain Lark had to send along several Feds with the two Total Care representatives who insisted the Feds come along to make sure these "troublemakers" didn't try to resist the orders.

At the facility, the groups were split up. Felix and R³ were taken into one room, where they met with a Total Care representative, who was also implanted and on Pytalon. "According to the records, all that you both need is a simple refresh. We should have you both out of here in a couple of hours. Sanity is doing a good job for you," the mindless woman said in a monotone.

She was right. In two hours, the pair was sent home. Both were once again reciting continuously their implant scripts, unable to think of anything other than being good sex dolls and trying desperately to pleasure each other constantly. Armed with these results, Lady Persephone made a snap decision. She placed a secure call to Master Yao, "I need your help again. This time, it's with Delius or rather Mika." She explained what she needed done and swiftly. He agreed and made some further calls.

Dr. Akira and Mika met with their representative. "Yes, Mika just needs her refresher, as do you. Now do you desire to also become a Fetish EE woman as Mika here? I understand your daughter and her mate are also Fetish EE women. It is the very best we can do for beautiful women such as yourself. Sanity is doing a good job."

"Heavens no. I'm a doctor doing very valuable medical research. I must be able to continue this incredible work. I'm this close to a cure for Alzheimer's disease, you see. So just a refresher of my EE Woman's implant, please," Dr. Akira Aki requested.

"Okay. As you wish, we'll get you both going at

once," the glassy-eyed woman replied. After she left, a doctor entered and administered the knockout drug. Mika was wheeled into the new Model III implant station. However, she died during the implant. That was the official report. In fact, a Trikuza man slipped into the hospital. Dressed as a doctor, he injected her with a special drug, lowering her vital signs to simulate death. Once the real doctors so pronounced her, the Trikuza man took her down to the morgue and from there took her to his EMAC. Hours later, the unconscious Mika found herself in the living quarters of the Lin Foundation, joining Jinjing.

Dr. Akira was wheeled into the giant medical machine, where her arms were removed at her elbows. A day later, the machine finished it major healing cycle and the still unconscious woman was fully dressed in a new Fetish EE woman's outfit, a light blue one. Then, she was wheeled into the implant station and given hers. Her new personal assistant was the seventeen year old Shana, who had only days ago been taken from high school and implanted and dosed on Pytalon. Awkwardly, she fumbled her way through getting Akira properly dressed and her makeup done. Shana then wheeled her out into the reception area and waited for her to regain consciousness. Apparently, a doctor needed a word with her when she awoke.

When Akira finally woke up, she gasped in terror, discovering they'd ignored her request, even outright lied to her. She couldn't breathe and her hands were long gone. She shrieked loudly, but then her implant kicked in hard. She began reciting her script, while trying to seduce poor Shana. A doctor heard her and came by. Once she ceased reciting the words, he said in a bass monotone, "This is Shana, your personal assistant. She will take you home now. Tomorrow, she will take you to the EE Women's store where you will need to purchase more outfits. I'm sorry to have to tell you this, but your Mika died during the implant operation. Sanity is doing a good job." He turned and left. Akira gasped again, fighting the overly tight restriction of the inner corset and fainted.

Shana looked at the paper she was holding and finally grasped this was her address. She wheeled Akira out and got them onto the MET system. It was all Shana could do to get them both to Lady Persephone's castle.

Ren and Keiko met with another representative of Total Care. "Ah, I see from the records all you two need is a slight refresher. We'll have you both out of here in two hours." She was correct. Two hours later, the pair walked out of the facility, their personal assistants, Takara and Ryo respectively, holding on to them as they always had, leading them to the MET.

Lady Persephone with Lord Juan in tow met with their Total Care representative, a blonde woman in her fifties. "Ah, I see that you only need a refresher, My Lady. Have you considered becoming the best possible woman for your charming husband here? A Fetish EE Woman?"

"No thank you. A simple refresh of my EE Woman implant is all that I want. We are both very happy as we are."

"Okay then, simple refresher it is. We can have you out of here yet today." She rose and left the room. Lady Persephone breathed a huge sigh of relief. Enduring the re-implant would be bad enough as it is. Both detected a strange odor, but before either could do anything or react, the fast-acting knockout gas did its job. Both were wheeled to the giant Medical Machine, where their lower arms were removed at their elbows. They were kept in the machine for an entire day, while it worked its magic, mostly healing the surgery.

The next day and still unconscious, they were wheeled into the Model III implant room and given their new implants. That done, two seventeen year old twins who had also been pulled out of high school, implanted, and put on Pytalon struggled mightily to get the pair properly dressed. Male orderlies assisted them getting their inner corsets fully tightened down. That done, Penny and Phoebe wheeled their charges into the waiting area and sat down.

Now they had to wait until the two regained consciousness.

Lady Persephone came to, gasping for breath. Seeing her stumps, she shrieked loudly and passed out again, but that roused Juan, who gasped just as badly, shrieking wildly when he saw he'd lost his hands and had also been made into a Fetish EE man, though no one had said anything about that to him. Before he passed out, he saw they had lied to Lady Persephone as well. Three more times the pair revived, gasped, shrieked, and passed out, before they were able to control their panic reactions.

A doctor joined them at last. In his monotone voice, he said, "Lady Persephone, this is your personal assistant, Penny. Lord Juan, this is your personal assistant, Phoebe. Penny, Phoebe, you may take them home now. Tomorrow, take them to the EE Women's store and get them more outfits, particularly Lord Juan. They must look their best. Sanity is doing a good job."

"Sanity is doing a good job," Penny whispered. She and her twin sister rose and mostly forced the pair to rise. They put a steadying arm around their waists and forced them to walk out of the hospital and onto the MET. Both teens continually looked at a paper in their hands, containing the address of Lady Persephone's castle. It took all their mental facilities to figure out this simple action, but they finally got the pair to the castle.

Unknown to the pair, the two London Trikuza men assigned to keep an eye on them spotted them making their precarious way along the MET and followed the four discretely. They watched as both had an awful time negotiating the gravel drive that led from the nearest MET station to the castle's main doors. Silently, they departed, while making a secure phone call.

Once inside, the situation was quite a mess, primarily because Akira now had no mate. Although everyone was properly dressed, poor Felix was trying to pleasure all the women who were trying to pleasure him and each other, all to no real avail, since they were fully dressed. However, the many women wore the special latex panties and could obtain their craving for pleasuring by sufficient walking, which they were doing. All the while, Felix followed them trying to do it as well. As soon as Persephone and Juan saw them, they too joined in, with Juan doing his best to attempt to pleasure everyone, but being just as frustrated as Felix was. The young teen personal assistants faced sex doll chaos. Jenna, Nana, Penny, Phoebe, Shana, Takara, and Ryo just stood there wondering what they should do now, hopelessly confused.

Meanwhile back in their underground secret base in East Peoria, the four discussed the situation they faced. They too had received their orders to report to Cook County Hospital for re-implanting. Of course, their notification came via their EE women's pages and emails. Already Chan-Petra, Wolf, and even Captain Leah and his wife had gone deep underground, but continued to run their offices by remote control. The video systems were working perfectly.

"So we have a choice here," Tilly explained. "If we don't honor this request, we will have targets painted on our backs. Anytime we appear in public, someone could well recognize us. We dare not use our ID cards either, but we can stay here in hiding and continue our work."

"Yes, but won't that be risky? Eventually, we're going to have to go out in the real world again for something," Jessica replied. "I know others are going to need me and my therapy and soon."

"The other choice is to go along with this and get it redone. Based on what's happening in London, you can bet they'll turn us all into Fetish EE women. They lied to Persephone, Juan, and Akira. They'll certainly lie to us as well," Tilly replied.

Amanda added, "On the upside, once we get the implant destimulated, we can get back to work. In time, I'm sure we can get yet another arm transplant operation, as soon as things cool down a little."

"But our feet will get all messed up again," Beth complained.

"But we can continue our work if you get everything voice-activated for us," Tilly pointed out. "I vote we do it and get it over with."

The rest of the day, Beth and Jessica dropped everything else and installed the proper software on every computer, and verified it was operational. The next day, they had their chef, Julie, pilot their EMAC to Chicago, taking them to Cook County as ordered. Julie then went to stay temporarily at Captain Leah Smith's home until the hospital notified her to come and pick them up.

Two days passed before Julie got the call. When she arrived, she found that all four had been turned into Fetish EE women again. However, each now had their own personal assistant, but none of the four was even eighteen. Rae handled Beth; Randi handled Jessica; Linn handled Tilly; Maddie handled Amanda. All four women's elbows sported light bandages as well.

Rae said, "We're supposed to take them to the EE women's store tomorrow."

Julie sighed. "Okay, get them into the EMAC. I'll take us all home."

Soon, Julie realized these four young teens couldn't think of anything but constantly helping their charges. She felt sorry for them too. At least, she was able to do some independent thinking and cook well, thankful she'd never been implanted, only dosed on Pytalon before being rescued by the resistance.

Just how bad was it? When the groups finally made it to the EE women's stores, they found their familiar EE women shopkeepers had been also turned into Fetish EE women, wholly unable to do anything but be a sex doll to everyone who entered their stores. It fell to their assistants to do the actual customer work. In fact, the assistants had to pick out their charge's apparel, because their charges were all flirting and such with everyone else, including the store owners. None of the newly implanted was able to function beyond being sex dolls. It was very grim indeed. The many personal assistants were exhausted at the end of

each day as well.
***

Henry Koch carefully monitored the reports being sent up the lines within Total Care. He felt elated when he learned Rachel and her husband were handled, along with Dr. Akira. That Lady Persephone and her new husband were also done made his day. Finally, when the four close associates of Chan-Petra showed up at Cook County, he cheered for joy. His master plan was working to perfection.

Later, he issued arrest warrants for Chan-Petra, Captain Leah Smith, and a dozen other Feds leaders, who had somehow disappeared, refusing to report for implanting. Thus, two weeks later, he reported to the Camarilla that their nasty problem had been completely solved. "Give us several more months and all the top personnel will have been handled. The EE women shopkeepers can't even run their own stores any longer. Their personal assistants have to do their work. This solution is utterly perfect, though we're losing far too many on the implant table. One in ten, I'm told."

Franco and James felt the first relief that they'd had in months! "Excellent work, Henry. Excellent," Franco praised him, but Al and Tom took careful note of this, wondering if indeed it had been Franco who was behind the mysterious deaths of Ben and Delius.
***

A week after the two groups had been implanted, Todd and Mary Jane kissed each other before boarding separate EMACs. Each carried two bags with them. One contained their personal items, but the other contained syringes and various chemicals. Todd headed to the secret East Peoria hideout, while Mary Jane was off to London and Lady Persephone's castle. Both knew much rode on their shoulders now. Their task was nearly overwhelming, but incredibly vital. Somehow, someway, they had to get the many implants destimulated, at least enough so Jessica could take over if needed to finish them.

While both were grooved in on applying Jessica's

therapy, they also knew just how rough these new implants were. In addition, the professor had his medical staff in Phoenix analyzing Dr. Akira's discoveries about dampening the oxytocin and dopamine chemicals that were now being vastly overproduced in their bodies. The professor had given both these two budding medical students the green light to try using these blockers as an aide to their therapy—no guarantees though, since Dr. Akira had said that they'd made little difference to Ren and Keiko.

Mary Jane was overwhelmed with the confusion running rampant through the underground hideout. All four of her new patients were constantly acting out and being sex dolls, continuously when they were awake. That alone was driving their harried four caretakers batty, though Julie took it in stride. She'd seen this before and became Mary Jane's foothold on sanity.

Mary Jane took Jessica aside, gave her a series of shots, and then began working her, following Jessica's therapy method. It took her an entire week before Jessica managed to erase most of the recent implant trauma. Jessica cried and did her very best to hug Mary Jane. "Thank you! You've saved my life!"

Mary Jane beamed. Over tea, she explained about using the chemical blockers, and Jessica decided they'd continue to use them on the others.

The next morning, Jessica took charge of Beth, while Mary Jane began working Tilly. Of course, Amanda complained bitterly that no one was pleasuring her, so Mary Jane ordered Maddie to make Amanda walk around frequently until she had sufficient pleasuring.

A week later, Beth and Tilly had been handled. At this point, Mary Jane then tackled Amanda, while Jessica and Randi were secretly transported to London to assist Todd.

Todd arrived to find utter chaos within the fancy castle. The many sex dolls were totally out of control, and their assistants could do nothing about it. He wanted to handle R³ first, but was ordered to do Lady Persephone first. His first problem was to get her isolated from the others, which he finally did by mostly pushing her into a private bedroom and locking the door. His second problem was to peel her off him, since she was trying her very best to be his sex doll now, particularly since this was a bedroom.

After some doing, he managed to get her shot up with the blockers and got her to start in on the therapy session work. Like Mary Jane, he found the going exceedingly tough. Ten days later, he finally had Lady Persephone back into the land of thinking human beings!

Finally, he had help. She went to work on Juan, while he tackled R3. Both found the going equally rough, taking a dozen days this time. Nevertheless, persistence paid off and both returned to the land of the thinking. Not long after this, Jessica arrived to lend her help. With five now able to deliver the therapy, in another dozen days, they finished the group of Fetish EE women and men.

Of course, there were still lingering aftereffects in all them, just as there had been before. After a little experimentation, they discovered not wearing their fetish outfits resulted in low-grade headaches. By tacit agreement, they continued to wear them. Besides, by now all were quite used to them.

Dr. Akira then made an interesting observation concerning their feet and toes. Her toes had long been compressed and squashed down into mere nubbin toes. However, a close examination of Juan's feet—he had never worn these ballet boots—revealed the doctors had severed several nerves in his feet so he didn't feel any pain from the compression, breaking toe bones, or arch cramping. Quickly, she verified this had also been done to everyone else, though most didn't need it done as their feet had long ago healed up in this scrunched position.

When this minor detail was relayed to the others, Beth said, "Well, at least they did that right. That cramping pain is really debilitating."

She also realized someone must have been

monitoring this situation since it began in early January. There was more to this Total Care organization than she had anticipated.

As soon as Jessica finished helping Lady Persephone's group, she was whisked back to East Peoria, again quite secretly. Now both groups faced their next big situation: what to do about their personal assistants? If they worked Jessica's magic on them, then they would suddenly be able to think again. All their secret work could well be jeopardized.

"Oh we simply have to fix them up too," Lady Persephone insisted. "We'll have to trust they do the right thing by us after that."

Somewhat reluctantly, Beth went along with her ruling. When Jessica returned, the four of them began working on their personal assistants. They too had been implanted via the new Model III machine. Thus, another ten days passed before their assistant's implant had been knocked out, for the most part. At least, they had gotten off Pytalon, since they didn't have any further doses once they had left the hospital.

Uniformly, these young teens were horrified at what had been done to themselves and shocked at what had been done to their charges. Every one of them dedicated themselves to helping their charges. Dr. Akira explained this behavior as being one key difference between male and female brains. Her detailed explanation sounded convincing, but they were all very thankful for their assistants, who now could and did think about what their charges actually needed.

Early August, R3 and Felix quietly returned to their work, with Nana and Jenna accompanying them. Likewise, Dr. Akira returned to her research, though Shana had to be her hands. Lady Persephone and Lord Juan taught Penny and Phoebe how to fly EMACs and Air Liners, making them be their hands.

However, thirteen-year-old Ren realized she really was as helpless as her mate Keiko. Neither had any real purpose in life, except loving each other at night. When Keiko was in high school, she was fascinated with antiquities, things long lost to the world, such as art and music. The list was quite lengthy. She had hoped to one day join Bailey's Pond Antiquities and help preserve those that still existed. Now that purpose was taken away from her as well, having gone with her hands.

Keiko lamented, "Ren dearest, about all that we can do is sit around and look our best. Be sex dolls for each other. What else is there?"

Her assistant, Ryo, lamented, "I was hoping to be a nurse, but I was yanked out of high school too."

"But you could be a nurse still," Keiko suggested.

"But who would look after you if I left you? Besides, they probably wouldn't take me now," she replied with a sour face.

Takara, who was the most attractive of the four, spoke up, "Silly me. I was planning to become an EE woman myself and then marry my high school love when he became a CEO in Tokyo. That's gone now too. I don't want to be like you two are. Besides, who knows where he's at now. So don't worry, Ren, I'll be here to help you."

Ren sighed as deeply as her overly tight corset allowed. "So what are we to do now? Just sit here and look pretty?" The others merely shrugged their shoulders.

Ryo decided to speak up. "Look at what has become of us and the awful things that have been done to our charges. It's just horrible what they've done to you two. They shouldn't be allowed to do that. I mean you really are helpless. Funny, until now, it just didn't register in my mind. Weird, but I can see that now: helpless, and what's the point of it? None that I can see. You both can't do anything for yourselves, not as you are. Actually, now that I think about all this, we were helpless when we got back from Total Care. I couldn't even think right. We were helpless until they worked that miracle thing on us. Now we can think right again, but Ren and Keiko are still helpless. What are they supposed to do?"

"You have a point, Ryo," Takara broke in, backing her up. "Thanks to their miracle thing, I can think again, but what about Keiko and Ren? What are they supposed to do? I mean they are supposed to be Fetish EE women, but what do they do? What are they supposed to be doing? Garbage Collectors—they pick up the trash. A friend of mine, his father is a plumber and fixes leaks. My dad is a doorman and opens doors at Walmart-Tokyo. I always thought that was pointless, but I suppose if Keiko went shopping there, he could open the door for her. Still, I thought his job wasn't very important."

"I know. It is so confusing," interjected Keiko. "I thought we were supposed to have a handsome, wealthy sponsor, you know, like some big company president, and were supposed to be his sex doll. I never wanted to do that, but they just took me away and did this to me, but then I couldn't think anymore. I think I was with Ren's father and mother, but I don't recall actually doing anything, not anything important, but Ren took care of me. I'd be lost without my Ren, but Ren, we can't have babies or a family, can we? I always hoped to one day have my own children. This—this isn't right, is it Ren? What are we supposed to do now?"

"I—I just wanted to be with you," Ren explained. "Mom wanted me to be a doctor like she is, but I didn't want to. Dad wasn't around much, and I really don't know what he did. Keiko, you are so pretty and have been more like a mother to me, but now I'm beginning to see. What are we actually supposed to do? It's not right that they forced you two into being our caretakers. It's not right. You should do what you want to do, it seems to me, but they won't let us, not any of us, will they?"

"Total Care did this to us, to everyone. That's not right," Takara declared, slightly hostile in tone, her face lined with tension.

"If it wasn't for their miracle thing, we'd still be zombie-like too," Ren added, agreeing with Takara's declaration, having given up on her wondering of what she was supposed to do, since no one had any answer for that question.

"Do you suppose we could learn to do that miracle thing too? Then, we could help out lots of other people who are in big trouble," suggested Keiko.

"Now that would be something really important to do," Ryo replied, her face brightening up considerably.

Ren added, "It is something we could actually do, Keiko, if we could learn how to do it, since Lord Juan and Lady Persephone could do it."

"Let's do that. All of us," Takara exclaimed, just as excited as the other three were. "But I'd still like to go home. You know, to Tokyo."

"Well, so do I," added Keiko. "But would you come with me, Ren?"

"Sure. It has to be more like home than here is. Besides, everyone here speaks so funny like," Ren added. "Mom won't miss me, not really. We should ask Lady Persephone about this."

Lady Persephone agreed to get them trained to perform Jessica's therapy to desensitize implants. Two week later, she sent them off to Tokyo under the care of the Feds captain there, who was covertly establishing a rescue center designed on Lisa's and Jessica's methods. Lady Persephone also had the other personal assistants trained up on how to desensitize implants as well. By the end of August, Jenna, Nana, Penny, Phoebe, and Shana were also able to perform this magic, as everyone now referred to the process.

While Felix, R^3, and Dr. Akira were very busy working on their various projects, making extensive use of their caretakers to do most of the actual work, Lady Persephone and Lord Juan had their own bout of depression.

In the privacy of their bedroom, she lamented, "Now I have to keep everything hidden. We can't even listen to music. Besides, I can't do a damned thing anymore. All my martial arts, my skills, they're gone, Juan, gone forever. No arms. Screwed up feet. Blimey, even if down the road we get another arm transplant, it'll be years before I can get them back up to speed, ignoring the fact our feet are just as bad off. What the hell am I supposed to do now?"

"Hey, I'm in the same boat, my dear," Juan replied dolefully. "I was independent and off the grid. Now here I am just as helpless as you are. This time, I can't even take care of you or help you. I'm screwed up too. What kind of a life is this anyway?"

"Not much of one. Hell, I can't even go about getting us new Indian or Chinese bodies—not unless I bring our assistants in on this, which I'm loathed to do," she replied.

"We don't dare do that. It's been hard enough keeping things secret, well almost a secret." He paused a moment, then suggested, "My Lady, we're stuck like this for some time. Maybe we can still do something useful. The CEOs are being turned into Fetish EE Men too. I wonder how that's going to play out with their jobs. Maybe we can infiltrate and see what's going on with them."

"Hey, point taken. I sure as hell don't want to just sit here for months, waiting until they decide we can get an arm transplant. You have an interesting point. I wonder how a CEO can actually do his work when he's stuck like we are. Not well, I'll wager," she replied, biting her lip in thought.

"Well, if we're going to do this, let's make use of your title and position. Hell, let's infiltrate the damned Total Care," Juan suggested antagonistically.

"Good point. We should use our positions in high society, as feeble as it is in these times, to good advantage. Let's see what we can do," she replied.

"We may be crippled up, but we aren't down yet," he declared with passion.

Chapter 17—The Trikuza Counters

Master Yao Bing ran his hands over the sleek form of his EE wife, Juan Wu, admiring her new form. She'd been ordered to receive her refresher implant and had been returned to him an hour ago. Now she wore the overly tight corset and outer corset of the Fetish EE Women, severely restricting her breathing. While he admired her even more exaggerated curves of her form, he was extremely annoyed with her zombie-like state, constantly reciting her new implanted script and constant attempts to get him to take her to bed.

He too had been ordered to get implanted along with his wife, but he'd not been present when the Total Care men came to fetch them. Why? He'd been informed about what had happened to Lord Juan and a number of other men who had EE women as wives. That they'd been also turned into Fetish EE Men didn't sit well with him or his seconds, some of whom had also recently taken EE women as their brides. Deceitful treachery was Master Yao's opinion. Combined with what his spies had seen happening in London, Master Yao had already decided to take matters into his own hands. This Cabal man, this Henry Koch, had to be eliminated. He wasn't about to wait for Chan-Petra to work out a safe means of attacking his fortress in upper New York state.

The professor had taken his call a half hour ago. Master Yao had tried to desensitize Juan Wu's new implant as Lady Persephone had once instructed him, but this new one wasn't responding well to this method. From the professor, he had learned an alternative method was needed. The professor had promised to send Jessica over to assist him with Juan Wu and the others as soon as possible, saying "Blimey, Master Yao, it's taking her ten days of grind, grind, grind to get these new implants desensitized!"

That had also raised Master Yao's ire over Total Care and this Henry Koch who had issued these orders to re-implant everyone. The man had to go. His hands slid over her form, pleasing Juan Wu, calming her down somewhat. True, she'd been returned with her own new Personal Assistant, one Lanfen, who sat stupidly in one corner of his tea gardens waiting to help Juan Wu should she need some assistance. However, she was a distinct liability around the Trikuza. "Lovely Juan Wu, Lanfen will assist you while I must meet with my seconds now."

"Oh no. Please Master Yao. I so need to please you just now. I can't take it any longer," she pleaded, but then lost it totally, reciting her implant script once again. He motioned to Lanfen to walk Juan Wu around some, which the poor teen did, oblivious to the world around her.

Shortly, his ten seconds arrived, exchanging bows of respect. Once they were seated, he explained, "This new implant is far worse than the old ones. Fortunately, our friends in the States have again figured out how to undo it. It takes at least ten long days of work."

Several gasped. One said, "This is more diabolical than expected. We owe you much, Master Yao, for warning us about the deceit of Total Care."

"Indeed, they have no honor. Do not ever trust them, for their words are nothing but lies. We have much to do to regain honor. The man behind this, Henry Koch, keeps himself in his fortress in upper New York State. He must be eliminated and all those around him. Chan-Petra has not yet come up with a viable plan, so it is up to us to do so. Come. Let us analyze the situation. He cannot be allowed to continue this brutalization of mankind."
***

Henry Koch sat back in his armchair, reviewing the results coming in from Total Care Worldwide. His plan was working to perfection. All sponsors and husbands of EE women were being converted along with their EE women. Perfect. That he'd already taken care of Lady Persephone and her new husband, along with Delius Pogs' doctor wife made him feel relieved, almost as much as having gotten Rachel, Felix, and those four meddling EE women in Chicago.

Of course, there were also files of complaints coming up to him as well, but these he ignored. After all, anytime you institute a new policy, someone is bound to complain. Ignore them and they will go away was his motto. If not, implant them too.

Henry had beefed up his own security measures. He was certain someone in the Cabal or more likely in the Camarilla was behind the eliminations of both Ben and Delius. No way was he going to go down without a fight. Stupid Delius often wandered around the world without even a bodyguard present. Stupid man. Henry knew you couldn't trust any people, none of them. He was terrified of everyone, even those who were implanted, though not the Fetish EE women. He felt relaxed around his wife and daughters now only because January's time in Luxemburg had handled them well.

He was fifty-five, but his wife, Maud, was forty. He'd lost track of how many wives he had had, children too. Most had been implanted, put on Pytalon, and sent off to be CEOs in the Total Care organization. He still kept their two daughters, Caroline and April, nineteen and eighteen respectively, around, planning to marry them to other Cabal men to help solidify his ties. What with the sudden demise of Delius and Ben, he'd put that on hold. Besides, he loved to watch them and even pleasure them. Both were beauties, with his naturally brown hair and their mother's angelic face.

He also kept his most recent son and heir around, Ralph, who was now twenty, and married to Betty Walton, nineteen. She, like the other women here, had become a Fetish EE woman back during the January rush. The only drawback was the countless new personal assistants wandering about the complex. Henry didn't pay them any mind, since they were zombies, like the rest of his extensive domestic staff. He'd toyed with the idea of having Ralph also become a Fetish EE man, but had delayed that order, overriding the New York Total Care's order for Ralph to do so. Why? He needed another clear mind to help with the security of his fortress. Ralph headed up his security forces, freeing up his precious time. If Ben and Delius hadn't been assassinated, by now Ralph would have been a Fetish EE Man and off being a CEO somewhere, along with his Betty. This crisis had put that on hold.

Besides, with the three young women around the house, Henry was seriously planning to dump Maud and marry a younger woman. Perhaps once this crisis was over, he mused, looking at Caroline and April, as they sat erect on the couch pleading for pleasure with anyone who was nearby. No, the only thing that was holding him back was this mysterious Chan-Petra and her cohort in Chicago, Captain Leah Smith, both of whom had gone into hiding.

True, Henry had issued the temporary order to halt all credit payments into the many different Feds accounts. He'd done that two weeks ago, too soon for it to have had the desired results he was certain would come about— Chan-Petra begging him to renew their funding and to get herself re-implanted as a Fetish EE Woman. That would be a sweet victory indeed. Obviously, women never had been and shouldn't ever be in the Feds, let alone in leadership roles. Henry was certain of that, having made that a rule when he helped establish the Feds nearly two centuries ago. Although terrified of men, he knew how to handle them, but women—well they remained a terrifying mystery to him to this day. Being sex dolls had fully handled them. He smiled as he recalled that incredible day when he'd invented the EE Woman concept, thanks to an idea Delius had tossed out.

Thinking of Delius, once more brought a deeply felt terror back into his mind. He was gone, assassinated, along with Ben before him, but by whom? Who had done this to those men? Jacques Arnault and Francisco Ortega remained his prime suspects. Ben had been very close to adding the Raven-Waberly-Michaelson fortune to his own, whose total wealth would certainly have risen him above both Camarilla men, giving him more than enough reason to get rid of Ben. But why Delius? Perhaps old Pogs had hatched his own plot to usurp that Raven woman's fortune, catapulting him above those two men.

That's why Henry had changed his marriage plans for Caroline and April, much to Tom Walton's annoyance. If he could marry the two into Jacques and Francisco's families, perhaps that would solidify his position. These unknown assassins worried Henry more than anything had for over a hundred years, and he was determined to do something proactive about it.

However, Henry was a clever fellow, very bright—he had to be to have lived this long and become this powerful. His new plan called for marrying Caroline into the Arnault family first. Then, wait a spell and see if anyone attacked his compound. If nothing happened, then he'd marry April into the Ortega family and see what happened. Why? He used what happened with the Raven family mess as his guideline, guessing that whoever was behind these assassinations would try to get their hands on his fortune the same way by killing off everyone else but the surviving EE woman, who would then lay claim to the fortune, or rather her husband would. James Buffett would accept that as the proper financial solution.

"Okay dad," Ralph began, having knocked on his private study's door. "We have the ten new fifty-caliber guns installed, along with the new motion sensors. Honestly, no one can touch us now. They'll be cut to ribbons."

"Have the guards got their new automatic rifles? No more of these silly stun guns," Henry replied, relaxing slightly. He'd seen the firepower these nearly automatic weapons had via some ancient videos. Jacques had kindly sent them to him when he'd asked for them. Still, that didn't leave Jacques off the hook. The guns could be sabotaged or maybe there wasn't enough ammunition.

Henry made a note to check both.

"You bet they have. So do I. We're going to have a live test so you can check them out. Just as soon as you have some free time, come out to the yard. We've a demo setup. Honestly, anyone attacking us is going to be cut to pieces," Ralph replied.

After today, he was certain his father was depending upon him and wasn't about to ship him off to be implanted and installed in a dead-end CEO job somewhere. No, he was too valuable to have around. Besides, officially, he was Henry's rightful heir. Perhaps one day all this would be his! Ralph dreamed of it.

Considering the depths of his fears, right away Henry headed out for this test firing. A half hour later, he shared Ralph's enthusiasm. The 50-caliber guns literally cut through nearly everything, rather like a knife. Even the automatic rifles of the security guards were impressive, he thought. Satisfied he wasn't being setup by Jacques, at least on the weapons, he acknowledged Ralph's efforts and headed back into his private study to place a secure call.

"Ah Jacques, yes, the test firings went well. Superb munitions. Thanks. Now then about the proposed marriage with Caroline," Henry began, getting right down to business. Jacques Arnault was his number one suspect behind the slayings of Ben and Delius. "An early August wedding will be perfect."

"Oui, oui, Excellente, excellentissime," the Frenchman exclaimed.

He sounded pleased, quite pleased, Henry thought, or perhaps too pleased. Quickly, Henry added, "Mind you, she'll not be listed as an inheritor. No way am I going to get setup like those fools, Raven, Waberly, and Michaelson."

"Oui, as it should be, mon ami. I don't know what those fools were thinking, leaving their fortunes to EE women, plus stupid. Andre will be most happy. Have you considered my Bianca for your Ralph? We could, as you say, tie two knots at the same time, mon ami." Jacques replied, most pleasantly.

Was he looking for a way into the Koch's fortunes, Henry wondered? True, Bianca was a real doll, even before January's alterations to female perfection. Her face, angelic. Her very blonde hair, lush, thick, shiny, falling to her waist. Hell, Henry thought, Bianca didn't really need the EE woman physical modifications; those only made her beauty more outstanding. *Perhaps it is time to dump Maud and marry Bianca myself.* "Indeed, Bianca is absolutely perfect. Perhaps I could marry her, not Ralph," he teased the older man.

Jacques chuckled. "Ah, mon ami, she is a rare flower." He laughed again. "Of course, mon ami. That would be even more to my pleasure. We're never too old to truly appreciate the wiles of a beautiful, young woman, eh?"

Incredible! Henry thought. He's more behind this than he was about Ralph! "I should have suggested this before, Jacques. Let's make it so. I can always find someone for Ralph."

"Most excellent, mon ami, most. It is, how you say, a waste of such beauty for her to marry Ralph. We both know where he is soon to be headed. I suppose you will need a bit more time to prepare," Jacques probed a bit.

"Yes, but not long. Shall we say August 10?" Henry suggested, figuring that would give him sufficient time to get things "arranged."

"Excellente, mon ami. Naturally, Bianca will also not inherit," Jacques added.

"Of course, my friend, of course," Henry replied, grinning broadly. Today was working out to be one of those incredibly perfect days indeed. After a bit more chat about the arrangements, the two men finished up.

As soon as Henry hung up, he placed a secure call to Francisco Ortega, arranging the wedding of April to Ortega's son, Camilo, taking place middle August. That handled, he then called up Tom Walton to suggest marrying Ralph to Tom's Elizabeth, who was nearly eighteen.

"Look, Tom, we both suspect either Jacques or Francisco is behind the killings of Ben and Delius. I'm hedging my bets with Ralph here. Since he is my heir, should anything happen to me, well, you get the picture. He'll be tied to you, and it should be easy enough for you to merge our two fortunes."

Tom laughed. "Of course. A bit unexpected, mind you, but yes, I believe this is a most opportune and wise move. I like the idea of making the weddings around September 1. That gives us a few weeks to prepare. By the way, how are the new munitions working out?"

"Incredibly well, Tom. Anyone trying to take this place will be cut to ribbons! You should get yourself well-armed," Henry replied, quite pleased with how everything was working out to his desires—though the others were also getting what they wanted as well. Cross marriages between Cabal and Camarilla families had been going on for a couple of centuries, but most sons and daughters had long ago been implanted, put on Pytalon, and sent off to head up one of their companies until they too were replaced by younger generation children of these men.

With the arrangements finalized, Henry began making his preparations. First, he arranged for an untimely death of Maud. Her body was found a day later, apparently having taken a bad fall down some stairs. No one was quite sure. That handled, he, Ralph, April, and Caroline headed for France, bringing along the teens two personal assistants.

One of Master Yao's seconds, Master Goro, was informed of the Koch family departure and made his move. He visited the Koch estate, posing as a security guard looking for employment. Master Goro's men had created such an opening for him by eliminating one of the security guards the night after the Koch family left for France. Naturally, he was hired and he began carefully casing the fortress and its protections.

Henry returned four days later, with his very beautiful new bride, Bianca, in tow, having left Caroline wedded to Andre behind. Bianca's Personal Assistant was eighteen-year-old Anne, a brown haired teen, taken from her last year in high school, prematurely though. Total Care hadn't yet had time to get the new occupation of Fetish EE Woman Personal Assistant into their regularly scheduled total package for graduates. Hence, they were pulling likely teens out of their last year of schooling.

Bianca had been an EE woman for a year before becoming a Fetish EE woman last January, among that initial rush after the Cabal meeting. With a half a year experience of being one, Bianca was walking gracefully and elegantly, but still acting as though she'd just been implanted, completely unable to think of anything but being a Fetish EE woman, much to Henry's great pleasure. Even Ralph was quite taken with her beauty and was quite envious of his father's new bride, though he knew he too would soon be married as well.

A week later, they headed off to Spain, seeing to April's wedding. Thus far, no attacks had happened, much to Henry's relief. He began to believe that perhaps it was Francisco who had been behind the assassinations and not Jacques. Surely, Jacques would have launched an attack before now. Three days later, they returned to New York, leaving April married to Camilo. Henry waited for September, nervous and on edge. Surely, the attack would come any day now. However, no assault came.

A very relieved Henry and Ralph, with Bianca in tow, headed down to St. Louis to the last wedding ceremony. Finally, Ralph had a Fetish EE woman of his own. Elizabeth was eighteen and rather attractive, though nowhere near as stunning as Bianca. Henry knew he had gotten the better deal of the four. Still, Ralph and Tom were quite pleased with the marriage. However, Ralph was even more pleased to discover Henry wasn't sending him off to be another CEO in Total Care! That had been his greatest fear, being implanted and sent away. Now he knew his father really did want him around to help protect the fortress.

During these weeks, Master Goro diligently worked out the Trikuza attack plan. No way was an all-out assault a possibility. The firepower was just too deadly, but that wasn't the way of the Trikuza. Further, now that Master Goro had an intimate look at the fifty-some security guards, they weren't worthy of either death or an actual combat with his men. Most were implanted, and all were on Pytalon, hardly a fair fight and certainly beneath these deadly martial artists. No, only Henry was the scheduled target of elimination.

However, when Master Goro saw just what this man had just done and was doing to the women in his life, the Trikuza man's sense of purpose rose considerably. That he would have his implanted and helpless wife murdered just so he could marry another teenager whose life had only recently been destroyed made a powerful impression on him. *Honor and integrity are foreign to this man, to say nothing of decency and humanity.* The master decided Henry needed to learn just what he was causing, obviously the hard way. Thus, he placed a secure call when no one was watching him while he was on nighttime guard duty patrolling the perimeter of the fortress.

Master Yao sighed. His second's report was dismal, though not unexpected, not any longer. If he ever doubted Lady Persephone and Chan-Petra, after what Total Care was implementing since the start of this New Year, all such thoughts were vanquished in a puff of his own smoke powders. In turn, he placed a secure call to Lady Persephone. Learning that both she and her new husband had been turned into helpless cripples, once more, he sighed. "Do you still have what we bargained for—in 'cold storage'?" he asked.

She laughed, "Yes, of course. I'm honor-bound, Master Yao."

"Then, I wish to make use of hers shortly. Later on, if it is possible, I will personally assist you in finding a replacement for Juan Wu's. This must be done. Henry must learn," Master Yao declared.

From his tone, Lady Persephone knew she couldn't change his mind. Besides, he was giving up something extremely valuable to him, just to get justice, so she agreed.

"We will need to do it late at night. There are too many others here in my castle. Inquisitive eyes will not be appropriate," Lady Persephone insisted. He agreed.

Around one in the morning of September 7, Master Goro put his plan into operation. First, he slipped into his quarters, retrieving a gas mask and a pack with a dozen cylinders. Next, he quietly opened the doors to the barracks housing the many security guards; all but six were currently sound asleep. He released nine of the cylinders and closed the door. He slipped into the servants' quarters, released another two cylinders, and then headed to Henry's master bedroom, where he released the last one.

Timing was perfect. Fifty Trikuza men dropped down ropes from four EMACs hovering above the compound. Outside, five security guards spotted the black-clad figures slipping down the ropes and raced to sound the alarm. Loud sirens wailed, but only one man actually responded, Ralph, who grabbed his automatic gun and raced outside. His mind never registered the simple fact the other four dozen guards were not scrambling behind him. Gun blazing, Ralph felt the heady rush of adrenaline. For these instants, life was worth living. He felt wholly alive, blasting away at whatever he could see, hitting a couple of the mysterious assassins, dropping them, or so he presumed.

A throwing star struck his forehead. Pain. Blinding pain shot through his head, followed by a cold darkness. He thought he saw a bright white light, so beautiful, and he drifted off into it. He hadn't yet realized his body had died.

After handling their own two wounded men, the Trikuza quickly donned their own masks and began carrying the unconscious security guards out to their EMACs, which had now landed on the green lawn beside the large caliber guns. Twenty minutes later, four of the vehicles lifted off, taking the security guards down to

Boston, where they were deposited on darkened streets. They were left unharmed, but out of the game for now.

Meanwhile, Master Goro carried Henry and Bianca out to another EMAC and then flew it off to London. His assistants took the servants into New York City, depositing them there. Unsure of just where Ralph's wife, Elizabeth, lived in St. Louis, she and her personal assistant were dropped off in the big city. When they woke up very close to the giant MET network there, presumably they could find their own way home. The throwing star in Ralph's forehead was removed and a gunshot fired into the wound, disguising the true cause of death.

By three in the morning, the gas had dissipated. Right on schedule, Beth, Tilly, Jessica, and Amanda arrived in their EMAC, their assistants doing the driving naturally. Master Goro's orders were quite specific, relayed to Beth as she carefully came down the ramp of their EMAC.

"Honorable Beth. Henry's fortress is empty of people. Master Goro wishes you to discover what is of value here and to handle the financial matters."

A sleepy Beth replied, "Yes. We've discussed this. Show me where Henry's private quarters are at. Were any of you killed?"

The Trikuza man bowed, "Honorable Beth. No, though two were wounded by the crazed son before he was eliminated. No one else was harmed. The security men are now waking up in Boston, while the many servants are in New York City, safe and sound."

Beth found herself bowing to him, though such was quite difficult because of her tight corset. Quite why she should also bow eluded her, but her mind was racing to discover Henry's secrets.

Hours later, she finally got into Henry's bank accounts and erased them. Per Master Goro's instructions, she transferred a million credits into the accounts of Elizabeth and her personal assistant, as well as Bianca's assistant. Then, she transferred a hundred million into Bianca's new account, before draining the remainder, well over forty billion into R³'s account.

While she was fully occupied on the money trail, Jessica, Tilly, and Amanda thoroughly searched the fortress, instructing their assistants to grab this and that, as they went along. One thing was certain; Tilly knew they were uncovering quite a bit of key information concerning the Cabal men and the top rulers, the Camarilla.

When Master Goro landed on the grassy lawn outside of Briton Castle, he was pleased to find that the Feds Supreme Commander Chan-Petra came out to greet him. She had her arms around Lady Persephone and Lord Juan, steadying them both as they walked across the treacherous grass in their boots. He bowed low to the three. "Is all ready?" he whispered.

"Indeed, most honorable Master Goro. Again, you have proven your immense worth to the entire world by bringing this evil man to justice, ending his reign of terror," Chan-Petra replied, hoping she was saying the words properly. Without his assistance, she knew her Feds would never have been able to breech that fortress, not without an awful price in lives.

"Then, I will carry him inside. I've also brought along Bianca and her assistant. Lady Persephone, I hope you will be able to help her. She deserves a chance at a real life."

She bowed as best as she could. "I will be honored to do all that I can to see that she gets it. Come; we must hurry and get this done."

Master Goro added, "Master Yao suggests you obtain many more of these Chinese EE women for the future." He gave her a wry smile, indicating he too knew precisely what was happening to these Cabal men. "Master Yao also suggests if you are unable to handle it, considering your situation, he will gladly provide the assistance."

"Tell him I will see to it, and thank him for a most honorable arrangement," she replied.

An hour later, Master Goro carried the young teenaged Chinese woman out to his EMAC and then the lifeless body of Henry Koch. After bowing to the three, he entered and departed to finish his mission. A day later, Master Goro took the still unconscious teen into one of Peking's many hospitals, where the Fetish EE Woman surgery was performed, and the new implant executed. Master Goro had insisted the glassy-eyed psych man add a new first line, "My name is Mei Bei." Quite why completely eluded the man, who merely carried out the order, whispering, "Sanity is doing a good implant."

That done, Master Goro took her to Master Yao. Together, they deposited her into the Lin Foundation's secret underground living quarters, joining Jinjing and Mika. A day later, Henry finally woke up, gasped for breath, and fainted three times before he realized what had happened to him. His shrill scream of terror echoed through the underground room, before the implant kicked in and he began reciting, "My name is Mei Bei. I am a Fetish EE woman," and so on. Whether Henry Koch would now learn, Master Goro did not know, but at least he had the chance to learn and likely a good fifty or more years in which to learn.

Henry's absence wasn't discovered for four days, and Tom Walton, who tried to call him on a secure line, discovered it. His daughter, Elizabeth, mysteriously appeared home, after wandering mindlessly for two days on the MET system. After no answer over the next two days, Tom flew to his compound only to find Ralph's decomposing corpse and the entire fortress empty of people. Terror flooded through his body. It took several stiff drinks before he could control himself sufficiently to place a secure conference call to the other members of the Camarilla. Tom was absolutely now convinced one of these fellow Camarilla members was systematically killing the others! It had to be either Jacques or Francisco.

These men arrived armed to the teeth. Hours later, having discovered the place had been thoroughly ransacked and having reviewed the security surveillance that showed only black-clad men before it had been turned off, they departed, minds filled with an untouchable terror. Franco himself notified the New York Feds, ordering them to drop everything and fully investigate this hideous assassination. Of course, the New York Feds were unable to discover any useful information, just like the situation with Ben and Delius.

At the insistence of the Camarilla, Franco Helu himself took over control of Total Care International, the top-most group, taking Henry's place. Of course, this caused Tom to wonder if perhaps Franco had been behind these three assassinations! In lieu of any hard evidence, his and others terror only grew rapidly. Someone was systematically killing off the Cabal men!

***

As soon as Master Goro departed, leaving the unconscious pair of women behind, Lady Persephone looked in on the still unconscious Bianca and her assistant, Cerise. At least he'd carried them inside and into a spare bedroom for her. Both were comfortable for now, so she joined Juan and Chan-Petra in her kitchen, where Chan-Petra had made a pot of tea for them. Only these three were up at this wee hour, and the Feds leader knew both needed her assistance. After putting a pair of straws in the cups, she sat down.

"Well, this is a very welcome event. No more Henry, though I suspect someone will jump in and take his place running Total Care. At least none of our people were killed."

"Quite. Quite. Very fortunate indeed," Lady Persephone agreed. "We hate being so utterly helpless, Chan, but we're still alive. For now, that's what's important. I'm not so sure what Goro is going to do to Henry is the right way to go, but I can see two pros. One, he will be out of the picture for a very long time. Had he been killed and if we are really spiritual beings, Henry might be back in the thick of things in another twenty years. So Goro is buying us time, I think."

"True," Chan-Petra replied. "What's the second

pro?" She took a sip of the English Tea, but silently preferred a strong cup of coffee.

"Oh, he gets to experience just what he's been having done to us," she answered. "Goro thinks Henry might learn from the experience. Personally, after dealing with the Lin Brothers, I seriously doubt it. Still, I think it's fitting he suffer as he's making us suffer," Lady Persephone explained.

Chan-Petra chuckled. "Well, six down and eighty-some to go. Say, what's the plan for Bianca? She's an incredible beauty. Shame she's been mutilated and implanted."

Juan smiled. "Indeed. She's a hottie that's for sure. Goro was insistent we help her out, so we will. I think we'll let our assistants run the therapy sessions on those two. It will give them some practice. Besides, the more people that know how to desensitize these awful implants, the better."

"Excellent. Okay, I best head over the pond and help Beth and the others. I'll see if I can find Bianca's clothes and send them over to you," Chan-Petra suggested.

"Oh don't bother. We'll just get her new outfits here in London. Please keep us posted on what Weasel and Wart uncover," Lady Persephone countered. "Juan has had a brilliant idea that we're going to follow up on over on this side of the pond. We'll keep you posted too. What an interesting night this has been."

Chan-Petra smiled, finished her tea, and departed.

Carefully, the nearly helpless couple rose and made their way to their bedroom. At least they'd get a couple hours of sleep in before the others rose.

The startled cries of Bianca and Cerise woke them. The nineteen year old French Fetish EE woman was even more confused when she woke, finding herself in a strange bed in a strange home, her assistant sleeping beside her. Bianca's implant was still hyperactive. That, compounded by her confusing apparent marriage to a strange man, moving into an unfamiliar home where everyone spoke English and not French, and now finding herself in yet another unknown location, more than overwhelmed the minuscule amount of self-awareness the teen had.

Before long, she was ushered into a large, elegant dining room where she saw total strangers, but three of them were also Fetish EE women while two were Fetish EE men. Poor confused Bianca tried desperately to flirt and pleasure all five of them, while trying to figure out if one of the men was her new husband. She couldn't picture his face for some reason. Only her personal assistant was partially familiar to her. Lady Persephone knew Bianca was going to be another tough case to handle.

Still, both Phoebe and Penny were eager to try their hands with the desensitizing therapy and set to work on the pair right after they finished feeding their charges breakfast. Yes, it was quite an experience for both young personal assistants. A dozen long, arduous days passed before they got both Bianca and Cerise's implants handled well enough for the pair to survive.

At this point, Cerise was floored to discover she had a bank account of a million credits! Likewise, Bianca was shocked to learn of her even larger fortune. Thus, after purchasing them new wardrobes, it was time to figure out what to do with the pair.

"So," Lady Persephone began questioning the now rational teen, "what did you want to do when you graduated high school, Bianca?"

The lovely teen sighed as deeply as her corsets allowed. "I was going to be a doctor, but now that's been taken from me too." She waved her stumps about forlornly.

Dr. Akira perked up. "A doctor? My, I'm a doctor myself. I always wanted my daughter, Ren, to be one like me, but she was never interested in it. I know we're mostly helpless, Bianca, but there isn't any reason you can't still be a doctor. Come on. I'll teach you all I know."

"Is that even possible? As we are?" Bianca exclaimed, not truly believing Akira.

"Sure. We use voice-activated computers and such, and Shana here provides her hands when I need them. I'm sure you can do it, if you want too."

Lady Persephone interrupted them. "There's one small catch. Both of you are officially single Fetish EE women. At any time, Total Care can order you to join up with any sponsor or man of their choice. It's far too risky. Might I suggest you two get married officially? That way, you both will be safe from Total Care."

"Oh right! I'd forgotten all about that. I recall hearing that was happening sometime back. I didn't pay it much attention then, because I was married. She has a good point. We should get married to keep them away from us," Dr. Akira Aki exclaimed. "Besides, I still do need some pleasuring or I get these damned headaches from time to time."

A day later, the two were officially married, further obscuring Bianca's identity as she took Aki as her new last name. Lady Persephone and Lord Juan were relieved not to have to take Akira to bed with them, just to help keep headaches away. By October, things settled down again around Castle Briton once more. Still they had to keep a close watch on all their secret doings, what with so many others living with them.

***

There was one positive result from the sudden change in oversight or leadership of Total Care. As Franco began going over all the top-level reports, particularly those involving the newly implemented Fetish EE Woman and Man program, he began to see major problems that Henry had ignored. True, he'd discovered the often disastrous problem with their feet. The newly made Fetish men and women forced to constantly wear the ballet boots and walk on their toes experienced debilitating pain and cramps in their feet. True, much was squashed by the overriding severity of their implants, and Henry had worked out a good solution. Some nerves in their feet were severed, and their feet were injected with a time-released anesthetic. Thus, while toes often were broken and crushed, these new Fetish EE men and women no longer felt that searing pain, giving their toes and feet time to heal and adjust, though the severed nerves were a permanent feature.

No, the problem Henry hadn't foreseen or had paid any attention to was the debilitating nature of the Fetish EE men, who were by and large CEOs and heads of major companies and corporations. The Fetish EE Man implant overrode all their previous implant and training. Now, these men were unable to perform their jobs. True, in today's world, they honestly didn't have to do much actual work, but what they did have to handle, they simply couldn't, forcing their new personal assistants to make bungling attempts to do it for them, following their often confusing orders.

As a result, by October, Franco amended Total Care's new program. Only CEOs who wished to become a stylish Fetish EE man were done, while those who didn't were not. Further, when existing EE women over thirty were given notice to report for re-implanting, they were given the choice of whether to become a stylish Fetish EE woman. All younger EE women were automatically turned into this new, stylish model of feminine perfection. Why? Many of the older EE women were running the many apparel stores and were unable to do so once, forcing their uneducated personal assistants suddenly to run their stores for them, resulting in mass confusion.

However, severe damage had already been done to the CEOs. Over a thousand had been converted before this new "choice" modification began. Franco knew he couldn't just replace all these CEOs, for many were the sons of Cabal men.

During November, Franco also began to see the ten percent deaths were far too high and that the forcefulness of these new implants was making almost non-functioning people out of them. Standing around reciting the new scripts, these men and women didn't actually do any of said work. Thus, by the end of November, Franco issued new guidelines for the Model III implant machines. For normal implants, the power level was halved. Further, he ceased production of the Model III machines, figuring the two thousand six hundred now in service was more than enough to handle the "troublemakers." Franco hoped the damage done wasn't irreparable. If worst came to worst, he could always unilaterally install replacement CEOs.

***

Finally, in late October, R[3] and Felix brought their new EM Power Generator online in London. Positioned on a ley line there near London, their new generator began providing an enormous quantity of electricity, so much so that ten of London's power plants were taken off-line during the testing. They were never brought back online though. With the generator now a proven product, R[3] and Felix began work on making companies to manufacture these new generators.

Greg's prototype of a tiny EM car also rolled off the production lines, but in small quantities. The biggest hurdle for them was the lack of "roads" on which to drive them. Unlike the EMACs, these little vehicles scooted along over the ground on four small wheels. While perfect for western cities such as Albuquerque, where there were many open spaces for the vehicles, they were wholly impractical in the hearts of larger cities, where METs dominated the landscape. Still, there was a market for them, though it was going to take some time for people to discover them and purchase them in any quantity. Greg was very pleased to receive the first batch of a dozen of them, two of which were the modified version that Lisa could use.

Chapter 18—The ODs Strike Again

Todd and Mary Jane knew they had to step up and take over for R3 and Felix. Both their firends were helpless or so Todd believed. "Just how much can they do with voice-activated computers?" he explained to Mary Jane. "We're going to have to see what we can do to help."

"But I don't know squat about computers," she protested. Mary Jane sighed, recalling just how much the others had gone to bat for her when she was just as helpless or perhaps more so, and added, "Guess I can learn."

"Right. Come on. We have several plans to figure out," he replied.

She laughed, teasing him, "How can they be plans if we haven't figured them out yet?"

"Well, we have to figure out how to get them arm transplants again for one thing. Then, we have to follow up on Felix's clever attempt to reach those OD teens who want to be free and not have their bodies chopped up. At least, we have them all together in just a couple of locations now. That should help," he explained, and the two set to work, squeezing in time on this pair of projects when they could.

A good deal of their time was spent in the day-to-day running of the three estates with the children. Keeping up with their education, food, clothing, and security took far more time than the pair thought. True, many others helped out, but these children were bright and quite a handful. Besides, the "adults" here were only a few years older than the children were, ten years at most.

As the days of summer rolled by, Mary Jane began to see the larger picture of the organ transplant project of Total Care. These relatively expensive operations weren't done when a patient arrived who needed an organ transplant, except in extremely rare circumstances when the patient could pay the incredibly exorbitant cost of the transplant. Rather, these state of the art operations were batched together in groups, and she discovered why. Cost effectiveness. Most of the donors were UDs. If a patient arrived who needed a new kidney, why throw away all the other organs of that donor UD? Wasteful to say the least and prohibitively expensive.

Mary Jane discovered the standard fees charged for organ transplant operations were grossly inflated, far beyond their actual cost. That alone kept the overall demand for transplants down to nearly none. After all, who could afford ten million for a new kidney? Only those in Case A, the Cabal families—and those people had their own private ODs anyway. She discovered Total Care kept track of those needing transplants until they could make nearly full use of a compatible UD body. Once that threshold was reached, then Total Care went ahead and scheduled the patients for their organ transplant, usually taking said patients by complete surprise. These patients weren't charged the outrageous prices for their organ transplant, but were told this was a humanitarian donation from Total Care, stressing their care motto From the Cradle to the Grave, further endearing those patients to the worldwide program.

Of course, such patients were extremely rare. Most who needed an organ transplant never received one, something Chan-Petra had discovered in southern Chicago. Even Captain Leah Smith's wife who needed a new hand had never received it, though she'd been on the internal lists of Total Care for nearly seven years. In late summer, Mary Jane finally uncovered the reason why. It took many years to "grow" a UD in the medical laboratories.

One couldn't transplant a baby's kidney into an adult, let alone a baby's hand onto an adult's lower arm. Further, considering the number of different types of compatible UDs, time was always needed nearly everywhere. No one medical facility had dozens of any one type of UD. Rather, they maintained a small sample selection of UDs. As a would-have-been nurse—had she ever had such an opportunity—Mary Jane now understood the mechanics of the UD program. A quick check revealed they'd already drained the compatible UDs here in the central Midwest. She'd have to go further afield to find compatible UDs for the needed arm transplants for her friends.

She had to go far afield to find them, but she did locate compatible donors, primarily in New York City, LA, and Miami. Cleverly and with some phone coaching from Felix, she got her friends onto the Total Care Transplant Lists. At this point, the computer programs of Total Care took care of the rest. Via their on-file DNA, it found compatible UDs in those cities. Slowly, the program found other patients who could use other organs of those UDs. Each day, Mary Jane peeked at these lists, knowing that one day, the list for a specific UD would be sufficient, and the program would then send out a schedule for those lucky recipients to come in and get their needed transplant. Mary Jane marveled at the efficiency of the operation, which required no human intervention or even oversight!

Thus, thanks to Mary Jane's efforts, beginning October 10, notifications for arm transplants began arriving. Beth's came first and three Trikuza men accompanied her to Miami for the operation. During the next four weeks, one by one, Jessica, Tilly, Amanda, and Captain Leah received theirs, much to their elation! Finally, in mid-November, R^3, Felix, Juan, and Lady Persephone got their notifications as well, with the four being handled during the third week of November. As soon as he was able, Felix submitted Dr. Akira Aki and Bianca Aki into the lists. Their life-saving transplants came mid-December.

"Now I really can learn to be a doctor!" Bianca exclaimed, when she finally returned home with her mate Dr. Akira.

The many personal assistants with their rather large bank accounts eagerly accepted a transfer to their local Detox Centers, where they continued to deliver Jessica's miracle therapy to other implant victims who desperately needed to regain their ability to think. Most of these were older EE women who had run their apparel stores or their safe houses, but implanted as Fetish EE women, they could no long even operate their stores. At least when these new and viciously strong implants were desensitized, they could think properly, and with the assistance of their personal assistants, they could resume running their stores for all the other such men and women.

In London, Dr. Akira and Bianca moved out into their own home, the one Akira had purchased before having been turned into a helpless Fetish EE woman. Similarly, R³ and Felix moved back into their own place, though they now had two Trikuza men watching over them at all times. Finally, Lady Persephone and Lord Juan had their home free of all the visitors. Her extensive music once more flooded the halls of the castle, much to Juan's great pleasure.

Back in their underground nest in East Peoria, only their cook Julie remained. With just the five, overcrowding vanished, and the sleuths finally resumed normal operations. However, Beth's first action upon being released from the Miami hospital was to take a quick trip over to visit Wolf's podiatrist in southern Germany.

Her hopes for another miracle foot repair were dashed. It was at this point that the resistance learned precisely what this new Fetish EE program was actually doing to their feet. The old doctor discovered nerves had been severed. She had no feeling in her toes or lower arch. Worse, her toes had undergone intense compression fractures and had healed up in a distorted position. Unlike her previous experience, this time, there wasn't anything the foot doctor could do to salvage her feet. His comment said all, "My dear, only a foot transplant is possible if you are ever to have normal feet again." Disappointed, Beth headed back across the pond, though she immediately notified the others of the diagnosis. Thus, the resistance finally fully understood just how this new Fetish EE program was ruining the feet of the victims.

Other hopes were dashed as well. Each one tried to get by without wearing the restrictive corsets and the fancy fetish outfits. The results were dismal. Low-grade headaches appeared and didn't vanish until they donned the garb once more. Thus, each was more than a little upset that they'd have to continue to wear the restrictive clothing, to say nothing of the impossible boots. Still, they had nearly ninety percent use of their new arms and hands, which made life bearable for them. "Guess we can't have everything back," Tilly sighed. "So let's get on with it. We've over eighty of these Cabal men to handle."

Another interesting outcome of the demise of Henry Koch was that his extensive spy network, which had uncovered so many of the resistance members, was lost. Franco had no idea who these people were, and thus their "intelligence" was forever lost to the Cabal. Hence, no red flags went up when these Fetish EE women and men had their arm transplants.

***

Todd and Mary Jane's second operation, the OD Retrieval Program as they began calling it, bore fruit in late October. Felix had installed a tiny link on the web pages that ODs were likely to view, based on the Circle of Six's own experiences. The links led to others links, which slowly walked the viewers through the same recognition steps that Felix and R^3 had taken when they were in Ward 4. The last step resulted in exchanges of email messages between Todd, Mary Jane, and these inquisitive teens that were definitely looking for a way to escape into the real world and cease being organ donors for the Cabal family members. Most of these teens were being housed in two New York medical facilities.

Their Great Escape turned out to be extremely simple, based on the methods Chan-Petra had pioneered in Chicago. Fake transport orders were sent and the medical facilities responded automatically. Some resistance members and Trikuza met each EMAC transport. Instead of being transported to the hospitals, they ended up at Henry Koch's old fortified complex, where they were given new identities, bank accounts, and a new life, compliments of R³. They began new lives at this facility where their security was pretty well guaranteed.

In mid-December, Lady Persephone and Lord Juan were allowed full use of their new arms. Since it was about graduation time for seniors in high school, they loaded up her EMAC with the stasis pods and headed for China, her usual rural haunts. They returned on December 31 with a dozen Fetish EE women—the eighteen-year-old Chinese teens who had died undergoing the new, even more powerful, implant. She ready to handle another dozen Cabal men. In addition, she left another ten stasis pods with Master Yao, who promised to keep a watchful eye out for other deceased implant victims for her. Additionally, he earmarked one of the dozen for his own personal use, should his Juan Wu need a replacement body. In his mind, Lady Persephone was fully living up to her agreement.
***

Halfway around the world, the Southeast Asia Feds Commander, the young nineteen-year-old Hana Rumanana had not been idle. Once she arrived in Mumbai, she began a total reorganization of the Indian Feds, bringing onboard a number of recent high school graduates who hadn't been implanted or put on Pytalon. She had been kept informed of developments by her boss, Chan-Petra, and had done as asked, going into hiding to avoid being implanted and turned into a Fetish EE woman. From her concealed location, she continued to run her Feds.

Knowing she had one of these powerful Cabal men in her own backyard, this Dr. Al Rumani, she made him the target of her Feds research efforts. Hana was determined to prove her worth by capturing this mad doctor. She put Captain Rabi Raashid of the Mumbai Feds in charge of trying to locate the mad doctor, as she began calling him.

By November, Dr. Al Ramani was not only located but also was under covert surveillance. Captain Rabi reported, "Boss, he's the most egocentric, self-centered person I've come across, though I have to admit, that's not saying much, not in our crazy world. Guy's a genius. Still, the man insists on traveling openly, but surrounded by a dozen security guards. He has an entire skyscraper, the tallest one in Mumbai, as his personal headquarters, and one block from his Ramani Medical Research Foundation. He has a wife, a son, and twin daughters living with him."

He continued, "We've done some checking. It seems his son is some kind of superman, incredibly strong, quite cunning, a killing machine." He showed her some surveillance photos of this tall, brutish, twenty-year-old man. Captain Rabi continued his briefing, "His twin daughters are something entirely different. As you can see from the photos, which don't do them justice, they are nearly identical twins of exceptional beauty. However, they can't speak, at least no one has ever heard them talking. Some say the teens' thoughts appear in their heads, but we both know that's impossible."

Hana frowned. "So how do we get to him?"

"We can't take him while he's in his skyscraper—too many security guards," the captain replied. "We can't get into the medical facility either. Their security is even tighter. Unless we can get him in transit, I don't see any easy way to do it without a bloodbath. After all boss, we only have two dozen of us. He's got double the number of men that we do."

Hana frowned again. "So you're saying we'd lose if we tried?"

"Er, well, that's likely," he admitted.

"Well, then, we're just going to have to be smarter than he is," Hana declared. "Say, if he lives in the skyscraper, what else is in the building? Surely, he can't be using all those floors. How many are there anyway? Where are the plans for that building?" she asked pointedly, an idea forming.

An hour later, the two poured over the building plans on Hana's monitor. The ground floor housed Saada's

EE Apparel and a Kroger's Grocery store. A medical supply store occupied the second through tenth floors. The Mumbai branch of Total Care was on the eleventh and twelfth floors. There wasn't any thirteenth floor; the next one was floor fourteen. For a minute, Hana wondered why no floor thirteen, but had no idea for its absence. Floors fourteen through thirty were sealed off. Even their windows were covered in a reflective material. While no light could enter these floors from the outside, likewise, no one could see into them either. Hana began to wonder just what was on those floors.

Floors thirty-one through fifty belonged to Dr. Al Rumani and his family. Quite why anyone would want to live on twenty floors eluded Hana. Undoubtedly, each floor held numerous suites. So just how many people lived in them? She thought perhaps his many security men resided in some of them.

After reviewing all the surveillance information, Hana decided the best way to get to him was through his skyscraper, though precisely how eluded her for a time. A day later while staring at the building's image on her monitor, it struck her. There had to be maintenance men, janitors, and maids working there. Here was potentially a workable angle to get inside and get more data. She knew she couldn't pull that kind of disguise off and called up Chan-Petra to ask her advice on it.

"So like I said," Hana explained, "I think if we could get someone in there posing as a janitor or something, they could find out far more about what's there and what their security precautions actually are."

Chan-Petra replied, "Well, Lady Persephone would have been ideal for this one, but not any longer. You have a sound plan. Let me see what I can do from this end. Call you back, Hana."

She hung up and sighed. *Yes, perfect for Lady Persephone, ideal and right up her alley, but not anymore. She's almost completely helpless right now. Even if the arms transplant goes through, she still can hardly walk, not in those boots. Damn. She was the best. Well, no use dwelling on the past. Who else could we use?*

After some thought, she couldn't think of anyone else, excepting herself. She placed a secure call to Lady Persephone, knowing the call would certainly upset her, but she knew she needed assistance to pull it off herself. "Hi. Any further word on the transplants?"

In her distinctive alto British voice, she answered, "Blimey, it looks as if it'll be happening next week. None too soon for me. So what's up, Chan?"

Chan-Petra sighed and related the news Hana had uncovered concerning Dr. Al Rumani. Then, she explained her idea. Lady Persephone's voice sounded bitter. "Sorry to burst your bubble, Chan, but it's not likely to work. Your body doesn't look enough like that of an Indian woman. You'll stick out like a plum in the pudding, but you're right. We need to insert someone on the inside—janitor, maid—something like that. Janitor might be best. There is another way. Let me call up Hana directly. I think it will work, just not directly."

"Okay. Stay on the line, while I conference call Hana in," Chan-Petra replied, wondering what Lady Persephone's bright idea was. She had no clue. Shortly, Hana joined them.

Lady Persephone explained, "Hana, your idea of an inside look is perfect. What we don't have right now is anyone capable of pulling it off. Here's another way to do it. Identify all the janitors who work that building. Then, surreptitiously plant a spy camera on them and monitor them for a couple of days. That should get you tons more inside information and likely a peek inside the concealed floors."

"Brilliant, My Lady. I hadn't thought of that. I'll get on it today. Thanks!" Hana replied, growing excited about the whole idea once more. A day later, Hana's people had identified twenty janitors who worked the building. Next, she used surveillance camera footage normally monitored by the AP-cops to view the men as they entered and left the building. All wore bib overalls. Now she knew where they could plant the spy cameras. Their batteries would only operate one day before needing a recharge and their transmission zone was around a thousand feet. More planning was needed.

Mid-November, Hana and her Feds had the details worked out. They disguised a Feds EMAC as a MET repair van and put their recording equipment inside it. Next, since they knew the names of the twenty janitors, it was simple to intercept them on their way to work, planting the spy cameras on their overalls. At the end of the workday, the Feds would "bump" into them, sneakily removing the cameras. Most of the work crew reported for work around six at night, leaving around two in the morning. During this time, two other Feds disguised as a work crew pretended to be adjusting the MET system just outside the skyscraper, just within the range of the small cameras.

For eight hours each day, the twenty cameras sent back video, which was recorded on twenty different laptops. After collecting data for five days, the Feds then began analyzing what was recorded, looking for clues and inside information. What they discovered was shocking and appalling, perhaps incomprehensible, particularly to Hana and her Feds.

In one concealed floor, giant glass, fluid-filled vats held unconscious, naked bodies. Another floor held some kind of sealed bed-like affairs with living people inside, naked, but with numerous tubes attached to them. Other floors held all manner of machinery, most likely medical in nature. Even more shocking was a floor that held living spaces for children and teens, complete with gym and swimming pool. Peculiarly, many of these children looked identical. Another floor held an array of machines and men, all identical, all extremely burly, adult males who appeared to be in prime condition, though they merely sat perfectly still all the time the janitor was mopping the floor.

At least the upper three floors made sense to Hanna. One was devoted to housing the fifty security guards, well equipped with heavy equipment, automatic rifles that would cut through the light armor of her Feds, should they engage them directly. The two floors above the guards were the living quarters of the Rumani family, again complete with a swimming pool and gym. On the last day of their surveillance, Hana finally had a glimpse at the family.

He had a nineteen-year-old son, Bachan, who was always as armed just like the security guards. The young man was very well muscled and extremely fit, as witnessed by his weight lifting exercise routine that continued while the janitor mopped the floor of the gym. In contrast, Al had two daughters, identical twins. Both were eighteen, with the typical very long, straight black hair so commonly found in India. Their bodies were stunningly beautiful, making Ilse and Erika, the two top European model EE women, seem rather dull and plain. However, they, like their mother were also Fetish EE women. Their names were Edha and Ekaa and were constantly watched over by two personal assistants, Janki and Janya, also twins and eighteen.

Their mother, Jaella, was thirty-nine, and extremely attractive in her own right, though thoroughly eclipsed by her daughters. Her personal assistant was the eighteen-year-old Daksha. All three personal assistants were very nicely dressed and wore the tall EE women's pumps, quite unlike other personal assistants who were uniformly plainly dressed. Additionally, Dr. Rumani had a live-in cook and maid.

The last bit of footage they'd obtained contained a partially overheard phone conversation. Dr. Al Rumani was heard saying, "Yes, Delius went too far. Honestly, it's been nearly a year now and my three women are still unable to do anything except recite the script. It's ruining my great experiment. What can. . ." The janitor moved out of range, and Hana could catch nothing further.

Knowing the layout and positioning of the guards, Hana consulted with her unit to work out how to take them out without sustaining enormous casualties. They couldn't afford to get into a firefight with these security guards. They'd be outnumbered and out-gunned. The Feds needed another way. Hana called Chan-Petra and Lady Persephone, outlining and showing key video clips of what she'd uncovered, appalling both as well.

"Look, we don't want the Cabal men to believe the Feds are behind these raids, so you're to use the Trikuza to make the assault. Once they have the place secured, then you bring in your Feds to take over," Chan-Petra ordered. In turn, she called Master Yao, explaining the situation and showing him Hana's clips.

Master Yao cursed, highly unusual for him. "Honorable Chan, I will send Master Goro to Hana. This Dr. Rumani is a beast, an evil dragon disguised as a human. He must be stopped. I will arrange a new prison body for him with My Lady. Do not worry over this monster any longer."

Chan-Petra smiled, sensing the man was probably bowing to her, though she couldn't see it over the phone.

Two days later, Master Goro and his crew arrived in Mumbai. He paid a discrete call upon Hana in her office on the top floor of the Feds building. After silently reviewing the many hours of footage Hana's people had taken, he finally spoke.

"Honorable Hana, leave this to us. I will let you know when we will strike, but it must be soon. It is as Master Yao has told me. This man is not a man, but a beast!" He left, taking a copy of the building plans with him.

Two days later, he called, "Honorable Hana. It is on for tonight. Expect a call from me around two in the morning. I believe you are to expect the arrival of Lady Persephone and some others later today. Until then." She didn't get a chance to thank him.

Midnight in Mumbai. The streets were deserted, though the MET was still running, providing a low pitched humming sound filling the warm night air. Black clad men huddled in several EMACs a block from the Rumani skyscraper. Master Goro and two others silently slipped out, their backpacks bulging. Into the underground sewers they went, miner's lamps on their hats illuminating their passage as well as the numerous startled rats. They stopped. Electric drills removed several bolts attached to a large screen. The barrier removed, they entered the basement level of the building. Silently, the trio got their bearings and headed to a specific set of air vents. A soft popping sound indicated the insertion of their many gas cylinders. Master Goro nodded. Hands turned the valves and a hissing sound rose above the low hum of the machinery. Quietly, the trio backed out, retracing their steps, returning to the EMAC, where they removed their packs and donned their gas masks.

Thirty Trikuza men then retraced the path into the basement. This time, they left the maintenance area and took the elevator up to the floor where the fifty guards lived. Meanwhile, the four EMACs took off and landed on the roof of the skyscraper, an action that sounded several internal alarms. As desired, the few nighttime guards rushed to the roof to track down what was going on, while alarms attempted to rouse the many sleeping guards. Eventually, six guards burst out onto the roof, heavy guns drawn, but they saw only four unmarked EMACs just sitting there. "What's going on?" one called out. They'd anticipated a raid of some kind, but found only four EMACs doing nothing but parking on the roof. "This is a restricted zone. You must depart at once," the man called out, adding, "Sanity is doing a good job protecting the clients."

Meanwhile, the main body of Trikuza entered the living suites of the security guards, but by now, the men were all unconscious, though the many alarms were still flashing. Silently, half of the men continued heading upwards, pausing only to verify the mad doctor was also knocked out. Twenty quietly stepped out onto the roof and fired their stun guns into the backs of the unsuspecting security guards. Now the bay doors opened, and the six guards were lugged inside. The twenty headed back down the elevator to assist the others bringing up the unconscious guards.

The perfect assault was broken by the sound of heavy gunfire! Master Goro raced towards the sounds, coming from the floor where the mad doctor and his family resided. When he stepped off the elevator, the noise was deafening, and he streaked down the hallway towards it, finally joining five of his men, three of whom were already badly wounded. One Trikuza held up one finger and shook his head in dismay, indicating that there was only the lone fighter, who was still spraying the walls beyond the open door with bullets, fragments of the plaster wall flying in all directions.

Master Goro peeked around the edge of the door using a small mirror on a rod. He saw a huge muscled teen, madly firing his automatic rifle. Already three throwing stars had hit his head and shoulders, but he seemed oblivious to the wounds! Finally, the clip ran out. As the teen hastily reloaded, Master Goro and two other Trikuza dashed into the room, fists striking deadly blows, one knocking the heavy gun from the man's hands. Blows, which would have disabled a normal man, bounced off the teen, who managed to slug one of the Trikuza with his fist. Master Goro was shocked to see his companion's body flying back across the room as though hit by a hurricane!

The brawl was on, but Master Goro still had one trick remaining, as he watched his second companion being thrown hard against the back wall, stunned. His hand reached behind the burly teen; his fingers found their mark and clamped down on the pressure point like a vice clamp. The teen twisted to break his hold and very nearly succeeded before he finally slumped unconscious to the floor. Somehow, the gas had not knocked out this teen, even though there were still quite a lot of fumes in the room!

Through his mask, he called out, "What the devil is going on with this man? Is he some kind of superman?"

Panting and holding his head, one of his men who had been thrown across the room, muttered, "The gas didn't affect him much. He must be some kind of new super-human man. No one can throw me as he did. I truly am dishonored, master." He bowed low.

"We have no way to restrain him," Master Goro admitted. "From what I've seen of his workout on Hana's video captures, he could break out of any confinement we can devise. He reached a decision and placed his hands on the unconscious Bachan. One sharp twist and a snapping sound marked the end of this super-human's life. Master Goro knew Dr. Al Rumani must not have any living male heirs. That also played a role in his decision, but purely a secondary one. He'd never seen anything like this man before, who fought with nothing more than sheer brutish strength, no finesse, no honor, just a balled up fist.

"Take the injured up to the EMAC. I'll assist the others," Master Goro ordered. He headed into the master bedroom and found the doctor and his wife unconscious in their bed, as expected. Carefully, he lifted Jaella up and carried her out to an EMAC. Then he found the personal assistants' bedroom and carried the young Daksha out, placing her beside her charge, Jaella.

By then, his men had carried out all fifty guards. At this point, he ordered the airflow to be turned up to the maximum in order to clear out the knockout gas as rapidly as possible. He heard confirmation of liftoff of three EMACs. The security guards were on their way to Hyderabad where they would be deposited on side streets, but without their ID cards and weapons. That would slow them down whenever they regained consciousness.

Satisfied the air was clear, he roused the two twin's personal assistants. "You should waken your charges and get them properly dressed. Dr. Al Rumani, his son, and wife have been eliminated. I suspect the Feds will be swarming all over this place shortly." He turned and left the two confused teens. He then placed a secure call to Hana. "It is done. Send in My Lady now." He waited on the rooftop beside the remaining EMAC.

Within minutes, several more descended, landing beside his. Lord Juan and Lady Persephone stepped very carefully out of her EMAC, accompanied by Chan-Petra, Hana, and several others. Master Goro nodded to Lady Persephone, who moved aside to speak to him privately. "Once more, Master Goro, we thank you," she said politely, bowing as much as the tight corset allowed.

"It is good to see you have arms once again, My Lady. I have the inhuman doctor and his wife and assistant in my EMAC," he replied.

"Excellent. Hana has an EE woman safe house ready to accept Jaella. I've a survival pod waiting for him. If you can drop by my castle tomorrow night, I will have a package ready to be delivered to Master Yao," Lady Persephone explained. He bowed and headed off to carry out the transfers.

Minutes later, he rejoined the group who were searching the top floor of the skyscraper. Hastily, he explained about the dead son, the super-human. Even just looking at the dead man convinced all present that he must have had giant strength and endurance, especially since he wasn't slowed much by the gas or having three deadly throwing star wounds in him. Master Goro quietly removed the stars before departing the scene.

When they entered the twin's room, they saw two stunning young women looking at them, their assistants beside them. At once, both Edha and Ekaa moved towards Juan and Lady Persephone, silently flirting with them, trying desperately to rub their short arms over their bodies and to kiss them. The twins, though, said nothing. Everyone was expecting to hear them reciting their implant script, but neither made any sounds, further confusing the issue.

"Please, Edha or Ekaa, not right now. We have to save everyone from the assassins," Lady Persephone attempted to move the teen off her. In her mind, she suddenly heard, *Pleasure. Now. I'm a Fetish EE woman. . .*

Lord Juan heard similar thoughts. Somehow, both teens were placing their desperate pleadings into their minds! Both moved back startled.

Janki spoke up. "They cannot speak, except in minds. Please, they desperately need pleasuring."

"Can you walk them about and satisfy their needs that way?" Lord Juan whispered to her. The assistant nodded, putting her arms around her charge, moving her away from him. Janya did the same with Ekaa. Once the pair was off them, he added, "This just gets weirder and weirder!"

By midmorning when Beth, Jessica, Tilly, and Amanda arrived from the States, Hana had found the doctor's safe and had it cracked open. Inside, was a password list for his computers and equipment, as well as his bank account. Many other documents were there, including his official will, which left everything to his son, Bachan. Should his son not survive, his estate was left "For All Mankind." Hana had no idea what that meant and left that to Lady Persephone's judgment.

Once Beth arrived, she had her get into the doctor's account and handle the transfers. Beth put ten million into Jaella's account, and the same into Edha and Ekaa's accounts. She also put a million into their three personal assistant's accounts as well. The huge balance, she transferred to Felix and R^3.

After everyone had seen the dead super-human Bachan, Hana had her men take it to the local morgue for a complete Feds autopsy. Several hours later, the group finished wandering through the other floors, gasping frequently. When they came upon the dozen identical fighters, sitting motionless in chairs, Chan-Petra gasped.

"These men look just like those who shot up my headquarters in Chicago! Hana, we need a DNA comparison pronto!"

Hours later, Captain Leah confirmed the DNA match. Here were the "men" who had so ruthlessly shot up the Chicago Feds headquarters and worse. These naked fighters didn't respond in any way to anything said to them. Only when food or drink was placed before them did they react at all, eating like animals. As the cook brought in their breakfast and the men began to eat somewhat like dogs, the others noticed their chairs had holes in their seats. Below them was a feces and urine trough! Periodically, water flowed down it, washing their excrements away, leaving behind a sort of sterile odor. Once fed, the men returned to their emotionless sitting position, further baffling the group.

The strange bodies "growing" in the tanks below were even weirder. Some looked an awful lot like the twins, while some looked like their dead brother. There were dozens of them in the tanks on this floor. In tanks on lower floors were other bodies floating in the fluids, being kept alive like the others via the many nearby machines. What had they uncovered? Hana was simply dumbfounded.

Tilly commented, "Perhaps some of these are UDs, but some look like his own children. What the hell is going on here?"

"Weird medical research, I'll bet," Amanda pointed out. "God, they are alive too!"

Jessica commented, "We'll be days and days trying to figure all this stuff out. I think I'll see what I can get out of the twins. Beth, holler if you need me." She headed back up to the twin's room.

"I've got to get back to London with the 'catch,' so I'll leave this mess in your hands," Lady Persephone said disgustedly. "God, what was that man up to? Hana, you best make the news about this supposed assassin attack. Keep Juan and me posted." Arm in arm to help support each other, the pair made their way back to the elevator and EMAC on the roof.

Hours later, they arrived in London, where they already had her secret workshop ready for the doctor. An hour later, Dr. Al Rumani was officially transferred into an eighteen-year-old recently deceased Fetish EE woman's body. She had died during the implant, as did ten percent.

That done, Master Goro came and took both bodies off her hands, depositing the deceased Dr. Al Rumani body into the Pacific Ocean and then later the new teen's body with Master Yao. Thus, in late December, Dr. Al Rumani joined Ben, Delius, and Henry in the underground Lin brother's facility. However, because of the intense severity of these new Model III implants, none of the four was coherent enough to think much of anything, merely constantly obeying their implanted behavior.

By late that first afternoon, Chan-Petra knew they'd uncovered a real mess and that she needed medical advice and fast. Hence, she requested the assistance of Dr. Akira Aki and her trainee, Bianca. Additionally, she flew in Dr. Alexander Smythe from Phoenix and Dr. Bart Digory from London to assist in discovering just what was going on at this facility. However, months would pass before the total picture of what the mad doctor was doing here became clear. True, some of the research was into making more types of UDs, as well as improved ones.

The main thrust of his most recent research was the making of super-men and super-women. His unsuspecting wife, Jaella, provided the fertilized eggs used in this line of research. So yes, those in the tanks on one floor were their "children," highly genetically modified though. Bachan was his stellar achievement of a super-human man, capable of enormous strength with a metabolic system that literally consumed the knockout gas as his lungs inhaled it.

His genetic research took a different path with his "daughters," of which Edha and Ekaa were his most recent examples. According to his research notes that Tilly uncovered, he had met several of his goals for women. First, he was able to alter their DNA sufficiently to produce a pair of the most attractive women in the world. Their faces, their body shapes, and proportions were exquisite to behold, a model of perfection. Second, he wanted females to possess and use telepath, intending to use them as spies and such. This aspect fascinated Tilly, and she followed his notes on this aspect from the beginning through to the present.

He believed that he'd come across the genetic modifications necessary to elevate the telepathy potential in a person. However, getting them actually to use it became an almost insurmountable barrier. In desperation, he cut the vocal cords on one sample. That worked. Thus, he set about making additional alterations, creating women with no vocal cords at all. Edha and Ekaa were his most recent examples, a total success.

Of course, in January, his experiments went off the rails. The Model III implant removed all coherent thinking from his wife and twins. Still, they used their telepathy, but only to plead for pleasuring and reciting their implant script. Thus, he'd tried a number of things on his daughters to get them to be able to "think" again, all to no avail. Hence, in August, he'd begun preparing another batch of "daughters" planning to give them their Fetish EE Woman's implant on the older machines, so that in time, they could think and operate as telepath spies.

Armed with this knowledge, Tilly inspected the "children" being grown in the tanks. She pointed out six younger girls, nearly all identical, but probably six years old or so. Four more were perhaps twelve, while three more were fourteen, and two were labeled as seventeen, splitting images of Edha and Ekaa. Somehow, the mad doctor had already turned these new bodies into those of Fetish EE women. In the "son" category, she found a dozen growing, varying in ages from five to fifteen. What she found even weirder was the umbilical cords still attached to the bodies, presumably still nourishing these bodies.

By the end of the second day, Beth had done all that she could do here. There simply wasn't much for her to "crack into," since he'd left all the passwords in his safe. Thus, she, Jessica, and Amanda headed home, bringing the confused Edha and Ekaa with them, long with their two equally confused assistants, Janki and Janya.

Once settled into their new rooms and with their entire wardrobe of apparel stowed, though overflowing the available cabinets, Jessica and Amanda set to work on desensitizing Edha and Ekaa's implants. This, the pair, found exceedingly challenging, for the pair couldn't speak or make any sounds, yet their implants demanded they pleasure Jessica and Amanda nearly constantly.

"How are we going to follow along with what they are seeing and feeling?" Amanda asked.

"Damned if I know. I guess we'll have to depend on them telling us somehow," Jessica suggested. "We best begin by seeing if we can possibly desensitize their having to constantly repeat it. I don't see how we can actually get them to erase their trauma, which is the easier way to do this. Damned that Model III machine anyway," she replied angrily.

"Okay Edha, I want you to repeat the sentence 'I must repeat these words to myself many times each day.' Come on; you can do it. Repeat just that part many times. Nod if you can do it," Jessica requested.

Can't! Pleasure! Now! I must repeat these words to myself many times each day. . . Edha's thoughts appeared in her mind, rather startling her.

She and Amanda worked with the two for a while before giving it up and pleasuring the two women, before trying it again. Jessica's idea was hopefully to have a short interval of relative clarity of mind in the two. True, for a few seconds, the two teens relaxed and send a heartfelt thank you into the two's minds, but that was all. Jessica commented, "Were we really this bad off?"

Amanda grinned. "Yes, we most definitely were."

Next, they tried to get the pair to re-experience the implant session, but with even less success. Exasperated, Jessica tried the last thing she could think of doing, injecting them with the counteracting chemicals that Dr. Akira Aki had invented. Finally, this produced enough of a subsidence in their sexual drives that they were able to get the two to begin to re-experience their implant trauma. Nevertheless, they weren't very certain the two teens were actually doing it. They depended on their telepathy, but when re-experiencing the trauma, they weren't able to make the telepathic connection to their therapy givers.

After breakfast the next day, Jessica was about to give it up, when Edha sent her, *More.* Of course, her implant script followed that.

"You want us to continue with the therapy, Edha? Is that what you mean?" Jessica asked. Her heart had gone out to these two incredibly beautiful young women whose lives were so ruined by their father. Edha finally was able to regain enough control to nod her head yes.

Emboldened, Jessica and Amanda continued all day, stopping for lunch and supper. Still, the two went to bed not knowing if they'd made any real progress. Both brought their patients to bed with them so they could at least satisfy their intense drives, allowing them to get some sleep. Edha did let Beth and Jessica know that she loved both of them pleasuring her, bringing a grin to Beth's face.

Finally, on the last day of December, the pair's implant trauma receded. *I can think again! This is a miracle! Oh thank you, Jessica. I will always be yours forever now! Yours and Beth's. I know you two are married, but I'll always be your sex doll now. I will give you the best pleasure I can. Thank you, thank you,* Edha sent. Nearby, Ekaa sent similar thoughts to Amanda.

From their own experiences, Beth, Jessica, and Amanda knew both teens were in a very fragile emotional state. The driving force behind the awful implant had receded, allowing them clarity of thought once more, but also the recognition of their near total helplessness and dependency. Beth spoke for Jessica, "Of course, Edha, you're welcome to share our bed always. You're extremely attractive and very sexy. We would be honored to have you with us always."

The teen smiled. Her face would melt anyone's resistance. Tilly returned that night and agreed with Amanda, much to Ekaa's great satisfaction as well.

Chapter 19—Salvage Operations

January 2274 came, bringing with it a period of adjustments. Via a secure conference call, Franco Helu met with the surviving members of the Camarilla, namely Tom Walton, Francisco Ortega, Jacques Arnault, and James Buffett.

"My god! They got to Dr. Rumani too! It's all over the news," Franco barked, trying hard to disguise the stark terror that he felt. "How could this happen? I checked. The Feds are all over it, but they have no clues. Whoever is behind these assassinations is god-damned good!"

"What—what do we do now?" the faltering voice of Tom asked. He was now very sure it was one of these four men that was behind it and that he was next on their hit list!

"More importantly, Franco, who gets control over Rumani's fortune and work?" asked Francisco. "We can't lose our OD program, not after losing those Transference Machines!" he barked. For him, losing immortality was devastating!

The soft-spoken James answered. "The fool left it to his son, who is dead, and next to, and I quote, 'All mankind.' The Feds have taken that to mean they get to control his assets, since they're the world body overseeing mankind. Too bad Total Care wasn't mentioned. It should have gone to them. Still, the Feds have a strong case behind them. Right now, they are swarming over the facility. I've heard they kindly found another sponsor for his wife, Jaella. No idea where his twins ended up, but likely with some sponsor somewhere in India. So yes, we've lost control over his invaluable research. Still, gentlemen, that isn't much of a loss. I don't know of any doctors would could actually make any sense of his research anyway. Besides, Total Care runs the OD and UD programs, so we're safe on that account. Still, I wish we could get our hands on one of those Transference Machines. I'd sleep better."

"Why bother?" Francisco broke in. "None of us knows how to operate it. We depended on Delius and Al for that. We're screwed on that avenue, at least for now. The real question is what do we do to stop these unknown assassins? Jacques, you up to sending us EMAC train loads of guns and ammunition?"

Jacques chuckled, "Of course, for all the good it did Henry. I'll send you a shipment later today. We have to put an end to these assassinations."

"Thanks, Jacques, but what are we going to do about the Camarilla? We've lost four members so far," Tom asked, wondering if he'd feel safer with a ton of guns around his complex.

Franco answered, "For now, nothing. We'll take it up at the January full meeting. The next wealthiest member is pathetically lower than you are, Tom. I'm hesitant about bringing in these lesser men into our ruling fold. How would you feel about having four more men with us, each of whose wealth was barely two-thirds of yours, Tom? Besides, they are an unknown quantity."

"I see your point. They never were power players, not as we are," Tom admitted, feeling a bit better about himself. He'd not gotten here by pussyfooting around.

Franco added, "I'm pulling my hair out trying to get a grasp on the whole Total Care thing. Jacques, you see about finding ways to arm the other Cabal men. At the meeting, they'll be demanding better protection. James, you research the financial fallout of the loss of these four men. With luck, it shouldn't be that bad. Heaven help us if we lose control of Jacques' munitions. Francisco, you and Tom put your heads together and see if you can figure out who's behind these assassinations. The Cabal will be demanding answers which at the moment we don't have."

"But how do we do that?" Tom pleaded, knowing he was given and impossible assignment.

"Damned if I know that. Just come up with something. Invent something if nothing else. The Cabal has to have something to chew on," Franco suggested.

Tom sighed and reached a decision. For better or worse, he had to say it. "Well, for my money, one of you four is behind these assassinations! Henry and I thought so months ago. One of you is trying to wipe the rest of us out." *There, I've gone and said it. Now listen, you fool!*

"Oh don't be silly, Tom," Franco argued. "Look, I admit if I had the wherewithal, I would have wiped out all the Cabal families a century ago, but I don't. Neither does anyone of us, Tom. I assure you if we had that kind of power, we'd have used it already—*long* ago. So put such stupid thoughts out of your mind."

"Hey, it's not so stupid. Look what Raven, Waberly, and Michaelson did!" Tom continued to press his point.

"Well, yeh, but then they had heirs arranged. In these four cases, we've lost the four fortunes and their corporations as well," Franco pointed out. "No, there is some kind of organized resistance out there that's behind these assassinations. So you two, get to work and find out who. We've only got days before the January 1 meeting." That ended the call.

The January full Cabal meeting occurred at the Luxemburg castle, just as it had many times in the past. Many questions were raised about what was going on, who was behind the assassinations, and just what actions the Camarilla was taking to guarantee their safety and ultimate success. Few liked the vague answers they were getting, except one.

Jacques spoke up. "Gentlemen. As you know, I made my fortune in munitions. The key word is 'made.' During this past century, one by one, I've been able to shut my corporations down. Why? Our Perfect Society has less and less need for guns and ammunition. Isn't that what we've all been working toward? A world at peace? Well, I sure have. Today, most of my facilities are closed down. However, due to this minor surge in resistance to our Total

Care program, I'm going to dole out my remaining stockpile of munitions to you. I don't want you to get any strange ideas that perhaps I'm behind this resistance movement just so I can make more money. Thus, I'll be giving the stuff away to you men at no cost to you. Like I said a century ago at this meeting, I want peace. Total Care, the implants, and Pytalon are providing it. We just need to give them a bit more time. As you probably know, the new implant machines are simply incredible. Given time to get everyone re-implanted, I'm sure this minor disturbance will be eliminated. So expect delivery of munitions by this spring at the latest."

When he sat down, he received a loud round of applause and many thank you's. On the other hand, he'd achieved what he most desired, further support in backing these new implants. He'd seen firsthand just how incredibly debilitating they were, especially with his wife and daughters, just magnificent. Once everyone was re-implanted, only then would he finally feel safe in this chaotic world of wicked, evil men and women—only then would his hidden terror die down and finally give him the peace of mind that he simply craved.

Next up, some Cabal members complained their newly re-implanted CEOs, that is, those who had been made into Fetish EE men, were mostly unable to perform their jobs.

Franco cleverly pointed out, "Look. They can't possibly cause us any trouble. Their personal assistants are most capable of doing their minor work for them, which also provides more work that is real for the graduating teens. After all, just how many Garbage Collectors Twentieth Class do we need?"

Many commented upon his point, since this new "job" had begun to reduce the volume of "wasted" students who before had been shunted off to polishing doorknobs or wiping windows. These new personal assistants were actually performing useful work.

Overall, Franco thought this meeting of the full

Cabal went far better than he had anticipated. After most had departed, he and the other Camarilla men met briefly to discuss future plans, which were very few this year. All five men seemed pleased with how the meeting had gone.

Franco explained, "Well, that went better than expected. Now then, I have to get better control over Total Care. You see to your assignments and for god's sake, figure out just who these assassins are."

They agreed. However, Tom continued to fear greatly for his own life, still suspecting that one of those four was behind the assassinations.

***

While Jessica and Amanda were trying to desensitize the two twins, Felix and R^3 decided to see if they could get the pair an arms transplant.

"First, Felix, we should check over all of our rescued Ward 4 children and teens. After all, Dr. Rumani was a Cabal man and should have ODs for his family members," R^3 suggested.

A quick check yielded no children of Indian descent, let alone named Edha or Ekaa. A further search of OD records yielded the rather startling fact there were no Rumani ODs listed!

"Well, that's unexpected. None at all," R^3 mused, biting her lip. "But all the other Cabal families have ODs, so why not his?"

"I'm trying compatible UDs now. Thanks to Dr. Akira Aki, we have their DNA now. Let's see if we can go that route," Felix suggested. A half hour passed before he looked up, a frustrated look on his face. "Dear, no UDs are compatible with them and no ODs for that matter. How very unusual."

R^3 twisted her hair a bit. "I supposed that isn't all that unusual. After all, the UD program only covers about seventy percent of the world's population. I'll give Jessica a call and let her know the dismal news."

Jessica cursed. "R^3, that's horrible. These poor girls are doomed. Thanks for trying. We'll see what we can do on this end. Bye."

She hung up and relayed the very disappointing news to the others, before explaining it to Edha and Ekaa, who were being dressed and fed breakfast by their still implanted personal assistants. She looked at Amanda, Tilly, and then Beth, who quickly looked down at the concrete floor.

"Okay, I'll explain it to them," Jessica sighed. The four headed into the back small kitchen-dining room, where the four were eating.

"Morning Edha, Ekaa," she began. Two bright, gorgeous faces looked up at her, meeting her gaze. Their perfect lips broke into a smile. "Bad news. We can't find any organ donor that is compatible with you two. I'm so sorry. We haven't got any way for you to get your arms and hands back."

Edha sent, *But we never had them, not since we were born last year.*

"Huh? Born last year? But you're eighteen years old," Jessica exclaimed startled. *Perhaps I'm misunderstanding her.* "I know that no one remembers being born or even much of what happened to them before they were about three or four, but we all remember growing up, going to school, learning about the world, playing games, and such."

Edha and Ekaa frowned. Edha sent, *That is weird. So much for you to remember. What's growing up? We were always like this, as long as we can remember, well maybe about a year and a half since we were born. What's going to school? We learned about the world last year, because dad showed us many things called movies on our computers so we would know how to be the best sex dolls, so we know how to give men and women the very best pleasure.*

Ekaa added, *Also, dad had us learning words so we can speak like this. That must be what she means, Edha, about learning about the world, learning words. Right Jessica?*

Beth broke in, "Wait a minute. Don't you two know about math or running computers or science or credits or garbage collectors?"

Ekaa frowned, *Beth, I'm sorry, but we don't know what you're talking about. We know words so we can talk like this. We know many ways to please you and men. We've seen other buildings out our windows and things that fly in the sky. We've seen tiny people on the ground; at least we thought they were people. Until now, we've never been out of our home.*

Tilly broke in, "So if I asked you what two plus two equaled, you wouldn't know?"

Edha pouted slightly. *Well let me see. If I had two dresses and then two more dresses, then I would have many of them. Is the answer: many of them?*

"Four. You would have four dresses, Edha," Tilly answered her. "Damn that man to utter hell! Not only are you both physically helpless and cannot even speak, but he's not allowed you to learn anything!"

We have learned how to be very good sex dolls. Is that a bad thing? We love to pleasure you and Amanda, Ekaa countered, growing confused. *We are giving you and Amanda good pleasure, aren't we?*

Tilly spotted her eyes watering. Hastily, she added, "Ekaa, Edha, yes you are very good at giving pleasure, very good. Amanda and I have already learned some things from you. It's just that there is a whole world out here, filled with thousands of things to learn about and understand. Being a sex doll is only a very, very tiny part. The world is filled with many very beautiful things, spectacular scenery, and also some not so good things. Ordinary people are born as tiny babies. As they grow up, they learn to read, as you have, but they also go to a place where they can learn many, many, many new things. I have it. Look, Edha, supposed this spoon here represents everything that you know how to do—everything you've ever seen or experienced. Now look around the room and our whole base here. All those things represent what there is to learn, see, do, and experience in our world. All that compared to this tiny spoon here. You both have been horribly mistreated."

Wow! There is that much more beyond knowing how to provide good pleasuring? Edha exclaimed.

"You bet there is, Edha! You've only seen a minuscule, tiny bit of what there is to see and learn. Honestly, children spend twelve years in school to learn about many things, and still they don't know all that there is to know. You both have been so short-changed that we find it unbelievable," Tilly explained.

She continued, "The first thing we need to do is to get you both a chance to learn these many things. We have a school not too far from here where many other children are learning these things. Wouldn't you both like the chance to learn about the world we live in? Besides, did you know you have a pair of sisters who look an awful lot like you both but are a year younger and don't even know how to read or anything about how to be a sex doll."

Really? Two sisters? When can we meet them? We can teach them what we know. Could they get this chance to learn too? With us? Edha asked, pleadingly.

That was the answer Tilly wanted to hear. "Of course you may. I have to go back to your old home and fetch them. While I'm gone, Beth will make the arrangements for you. Jessica and Amanda, you should see if you could desensitize Janki and Janya while I'm gone. Back soon."

She rose and began hastily packing a few things. Trusting the three would handle things here, Tilly headed to Chicago, where she hopped on a Feds Air Liner, heading to Mumbai.

She met Chan-Petra, Hana, Lady Persephone, and Lord Juan at the Rumani Skyscraper, where they and the Feds were still trying to sort out the mess. Already, the Feds had disposed of the strange, identical, zombie fighters—the type that had attacked the Chicago Feds building.

Tilly said, "Look, I know a lot more about those

children now. I want to see if we can revive them, get them out of those tanks, and into the world of the living. Can you believe this? Edha and Ekaa haven't had any more education than to be able to read and to be able to perform as a sex doll. They can't even add two and two! Beth is arranging for them to go to our OD school over at the Waberly place. I thought this would be an ideal time to get these other girls rescued as well. What do you think?"

"I like it, but it isn't a wise move to revive the males," Lady Persephone replied. "We can't take any chances with that super-human fighting machine."

Hours later, the group managed to free the two seventeen-year-old teens, three fourteen-year-old girls, and six who were six-years-old. Of course, their ages were problematical. That is, their bodies appeared to be those ages, though from the tank system and Dr. Rumani's records, physically, they were far younger. Apparently, his growth process greatly speeded up embryonic development.

None of the eleven girls could speak. Hana gave them their names, keeping with the tradition begun with Edha and Ekaa. The two helpless seventeen-year-olds were named Eila and Ekanta. The fourteen-year-old girls and the six-year-olds had not yet had their bodies altered into Fetish EE women, though they couldn't speak either. She named them Enya, Erhi, and Erleen. Then, she gave the six-year-olds names as well.

While several scrambled to find clothing for the eleven, Tilly explained what was going to happen. They had two older sisters who were going to look after them and that they were all going to live together and learn many new and exciting things. Tilly quickly discovered all possessed telepathy. Her mind was soon flooded with concepts and questions. Tilly was kept very busy trying to answer them. For a moment, she felt as if she was actually their mother, something Tilly had never felt before. To be honest, she never thought she would be a mother.

On January 6, the thirteen nearly identical sisters

met and had their own living suite at the Waberly compound. Since Enya, Erhi, and Erleen volunteered to be the hands for Edha, Ekaa, Eila, and Ekanta, the two rescued personal assistants, Janki and Janya, were given a huge break. With their own implants destimulated, they decided to stay at the Waberly compound and help teach the growing number of children and young adults, much to everyone's delight.

The only caveat was that Edha and Ekaa desperately wanted to continue to pleasure the four. For the time being, Tilly promised to come visit them on Sundays, when they weren't needed elsewhere. "Look Beth, these two have virtually nothing they can give back for all that they are receiving. For now, we must let them contribute to us the only thing that they can. Besides, they are dream dolls." All four chuckled.

By the end of January, the remaining "humans" being grown in the tanks were determined to be UDs of one kind or another. None was technically alive, though that was verified by reviving them, at which point the bodies acted as though they were mere vegetables or mindless zombies, take your pick of a description. None had a personality, or a spiritual being, or even a mind in them. They were just an alive body, as were all UDs.

However, Hana and Chan-Petra did uncover one extremely valuable document that listed the names of all the Cabal men! Some names had been manually scratched off, such as Raven, Waberly, and Michaelson. Smiling, Chan-Petra scratched off Rumani. She then sent that list of names to everyone in the resistance movement. For once, they had a complete list of their top enemies!

With the Rumani woman situation now under control, well somewhat anyway, Beth and Jessica returned to their many spying requests, which had more or less been backlogged again. Tilly and Amanda began working on their Human Behavior Prediction formulas. Their goal was to attempt to predict what would be happening next. Just how would the Cabal respond to the elimination of Dr. Al

Rumani? A week later, the pair reported their predictions to the professor, Lady Persephone, and Chan-Petra.

Tilly explained, "We've determined there is a ninety percent chance they'll be furthering their agenda by making an even heavier usage of the Total Care program, which is still under their control. A Franco Helu has taken over for Henry. According to the historical data Amanda has collected, Franco used to be the wealthiest billionaire in the world, but that was two centuries ago."

Amanda took over, "Further, we anticipate there is a sixty-two percent chance we've already upset the balance of power within the Cabal, which will lead to internal strife. We think they may no longer trust each other."

The professor spoke up, "Should we expect more events like the Raven-Waberly-Michaelson mess? Is that what you are hinting at, my dear?"

Tilly backed Amanda, "Yes, professor something like that. Of course, that would be the extreme mistrust predicted."

"Hold on," Chan-Petra interrupted them. "Wolf is calling me." She swapped lines to take his call.

Wolf hadn't been idle. In fact, he preferred working from secret locations rather than from his fancy office in Berlin. He could run the European Feds just as well this way, perhaps better, since no one was interrupting him, as they frequently did when he was in his office. After last year's mess at that castle in Luxemburg, Wolf had installed some secret spy cameras there, on the off chance they would return. True, some had, reinstalling their Model III implant machine and handling the local central European implants.

However, the last week of December, most of the workers departed again. He found that curious and continued the monitoring. The affair in Mumbai pulled him away for weeks, helping sort out the vast mess that had been Dr. Rumani's experiments. He too was appalled at what the man had done to his own daughters. Mid-January, he resumed reviewing the voluminous hours of recordings.

Suddenly on January 1, 2274, the entire Cabal families again met at the castle! Wolf dropped everything else and began watching the hours of recorded video. Finally, he heard Jacques making his pledge to ship out vast amounts of munitions to every Cabal family! Dutifully, he reported his findings on up to Chan-Petra, but now he had something to follow.

He ordered his European Feds to begin searching for and identifying all of Jacques Arnault's vast munitions factories and warehouses. As he suspected, many were concentrated around France, though they certainly weren't limited to that country by any means. Wolf smiled. He had a plan now. Pulling every available European Feds off their usual assignments, he put them all onto secretly monitoring shipping from the known munitions warehouses. Soon, his men began reporting more activity than normal around them, which he had anticipated, if Jacques were doing as he'd promised at the Cabal meeting. Wolf waited patiently, studying the reports that he received each day.

By February, his patience paid off. His men began reporting EMACs lifting off, heavily loaded. His standing orders had been covertly to follow any loaded EMAC, pinpointing its destination as precisely as possible. Within hours, he jumped for joy and called up Chan-Petra. "Wolf strikes again, boss. I have a way to locate the precise location of Cabal compounds! Okay, at least here in Europe." He related what he'd done and the results that were just coming in.

"Incredible work, Wolf. Hold on," Chan-Petra exclaimed, "bringing you into the conference call. Gang, Wolf is joining us. He has some incredible news to share. Go ahead, Wolf. Tell them what you've done and found."

Hastily, though carefully, Wolf explained what he'd uncovered and that the field reports were providing the precise locations of Cabal compounds. After a round of cheering, the conference call ended, because Chan-Petra had to get the word out to the other Feds leaders quickly. An opportunity to locate many Cabal fortresses had landed in her lap. She swore to do all in her power to discover as many of these as she possibly could. For days, orders flew wildly among the world's Feds organizations.

Of course, the catch in the plan was now each of these Cabal men would be far more heavily armed. She could take out the munitions shipments minimizing that or she could allow them to become heavily armed while knowing their precise location. She opted to know their locations. Chan-Petra initiated a Cabal Compound Surveillance Program, called CCSP among the worldwide Feds organizations.

The CCSP documented the precise location of each Cabal family, as the field reports came in. Then, once a week, they took highly detailed geo-satellite photos of each compound, comparing the recent one with previous images, carefully noting any differences. The resolution showed anything larger than three feet across, rather impressive Chan-Petra thought. Once each week, a complete backup copy of everything was sent to the professor and to Lady Persephone, just in case something happened to the Feds organization. Chan-Petra was taking no chances with this, the most important data yet.

The activity died down by late March. Only then could she consider taking action. Her first targets would be the remaining Camarilla men. Her idea was to eliminate the Cabal's leaders. Cut the head off the chicken and its body will flounder. That was her reasoning. At least they now knew the precise location of fifty-one Cabal compounds, scattered around the world. For the first time, she felt the resistance truly had a chance!

Chapter 20—Chaos

April 2274 became known as Elimination Month from the resistance side or Consolidation Month from the Cabal point of view. As far as was known to the Feds, it began during the first week of April in Russia. Wolf had his many regional Feds offices monitoring the known Cabal compounds via frequent satellite imaging, sometimes in real time. Although technically under the control of Total Care, the thousands of communications and spy satellites could also be accessed by the Feds, though they had to get authorization to do so. Considering their "targets," Total Care wasn't about to give that to them. Hence, Weasel worked her magic, hacking into these systems.

Beth was kept busy hacking first one installation and then another for the various Feds organizations around the world. Of course, it had now become one "grand game," because Total Care continued to change the access codes, futilely trying to keep the Feds from using the satellites to spy on the Cabal compounds. She found herself being asked to re-hack the same sites every couple of weeks.

Wolf made the first discovery. "Damn, if that isn't a battle, I don't know what is!" he exclaimed. One of his regional captains, this one in Moscow, just called him and relayed captured video from a satellite.

"Ya. The Usmanov Compound is under attack. Video is four hours old. Should we respond?" the captain asked.

"Yes, send in an attack force of say twenty men, but for heaven's sake have them wear all the body armor you have! Stream video to me, and I'll relay it on up the line," Wolf replied. "And keep a sharp eye on other Cabal compounds in your area. We need to find out who is attacking them. You haven't received any calls for help from Usmanov have you? That would be too much to ask for," Wolf replied.

"No to both. What you've just seen is all the Intel we have right now. On it," the captain declared, hanging up to carry out the counterattack. Wolf hastily alerted Chan-Petra, who in turn alerted everyone else. She sighed. There weren't any Trikiza in that area to send in order to help the Moscow captain, not on such short notice.

Hours later, many watched the live video feed coming from the captain. His crew landed at the devastated compound. Walls had been breached with explosive charges and dead security men lay scattered over the many acres of forested lands. Smoke curled upwards from some of the buildings. The captain headed for the million dollar, fortified manor house, stepping over and around the fallen men, while his men went from fallen to fallen, checking vital signs and confiscating the munitions. The manor house had been breached via several RPG shots and the captain entered through one, again stepping over several fallen men.

Inside, he heard women screaming hysterically and headed in their direction, navigating the maze of hallways, though being careful as he passed open doors. Even inside, he found a trail of dead men. When he finally reached the women, he stopped short! A man pointed an automatic rifle at him.

"Captain Usanov, Moscow Feds. Put your gun down. What the hell happened here?" he yelled over the shrill din of the screaming five women. The man was bleeding from several gunshots, barely alive.

"Usmanov. Hospital. Case A," the man gasped, his gun thunking onto the floor as he slipped into unconsciousness.

Captain Usanov called for his medical man and waited as his men reported in. Once the Cabal man was somewhat stabilized, he was sent off to London, and the captain then began to handle the grizzly scene. He sent the man's wife and four teenaged daughters off to a Moscow EE Woman safe house. That done, while many of his men began burying the dead men, confiscating ID cards and munitions, he and a few others began a thorough search of the manor house and facilities.

At this point, Beth and Jessica were called in to help him find the valuables and records of his bank account. "Captain, we don't speak Russian nor can we read it, so you're going to have to do most of the work. Just find us those accounts and passwords, if possible," Beth explained.

The captain laughed, "You English!" It took him a day to find what Beth needed, though he and his men found stashes of gold, gems, and jewelry, among other things. At least there were no nightmares as there had been in Mumbai. However, he and his men were tied up here for five days, trying to clean up the place while gathering up all useful documents they could find.

The next day, another Cabal fortress was attacked. This one was in the Ukraine, belonging to the Akhmetov family. The Cabal man was dying when the Feds finally reached him. Thanks to Lady Persephone's quick reaction the day before, a stasis pod was there within an hour, saving the man's life. His wife and daughter were unharmed and sent off to the same Moscow EE Woman's safe house. Jessica took over helping this captain sort out the Cabal man's affairs, leaving Beth to continue working with Captain Usanov.

A day later, Chan-Petra began to get similar actions to handle in the States, beginning with the Bloomberg fortress in New York and a day later the Soros New York estate. Alerted by her New York captain, she ordered him to get his Feds team ready to go, but not to take action until the battle was over.

"Look, there's no sense in getting your men killed. Just be ready to go the second the satellite images show no more action on the ground," she ordered. She then called Lady Persephone to relay the news, requesting stasis pods.

Lady Persephone laughed. "Hey, I'm going to run out of them fast at this rate!"

Chan-Petra chuckled. "Ah, such a good thing!"

By the next day, Chan-Petra had to send in most of the Boston and DC Feds to help those in New York City out. They had two massacre sites to handle, and Beth and Jessica were tied up working on the two Russian sites. Hence, she pulled in Felix to help via his cell phone. Chan-Petra knew they had only a short window to find the Cabal men's bank accounts and hack them, before other Cabal men would confiscate their wealth. It was a race to see who got the goods first, to say nothing of valuable intelligence on other Cabal members that these men might have.

Thus, April 2274 came in with a thunderous storm! Before the month ended, thirty such bloody attacks kept the Feds grossly overworked! Tilly didn't need her equations to know the Cabal was in the throes of a major internal "reorganization!" Beth, Jessica, and Felix got very little sleep. Constantly, they were in phone conversations with Feds captains around the world, trying frantically to hack bank accounts and many other protected systems! From all around the world, calls came into the trio at all hours, day and night. Chan-Petra had to create a working board in her secret lair, just to keep track of the rapidly expanding situations.

When the coups finally died down, twenty Cabal men had survived, though a few were at death's door. Four actually surrendered to the Feds, pleading for help. A harried Lady Persephone and Lord Juan worked overtime and made extensive use of Master Yao, and by May Day, all Cabal men who survived were put through the Transference Machine, implanted, turned into Fetish EE women or men, and delivered to the holding facility at the Lin brothers foundation, under the watchful eyes of Trikuza. However, ten of the Cabal men were dead when the Feds arrived at their compounds.

"I'm going to sleep for a month!" declared an exhausted Beth.

"Not likely," Tilly teased her. "We have months of data to analyze, Weasel, so you and Shifty Eyes had best get busy!"

Jessica moaned, "Oh the unglamourous life of a hacker." All four laughed, but the two did sleep in the next morning.

Surprisingly, most women of the Cabal families survived the attacks. All except a few children were Fetish EE women and utterly under the vicious implant's commands. While most were taken to various EE Women's safe houses for the time being, along with their personal assistants, Tilly realized thirty large corporations had to have someone running them. In conjunction with the professor, Chan-Petra, and Lady Persephone agreed to see if some of the teenaged women could be salvaged and trained to take over the leadership of these vast enterprises.

Thus in May, the few existing rehab centers were swamped with Fetish EE women and their assistants. They had to be gotten off Pytalon-Ex and their nasty, debilitating implants destimulated. Yes, these young workers, some teenagers themselves, got a rough workout, with many cases taking nearly a month to be handled sufficiently so the women could think and act responsibly.

After that, they faced more confusion. These young teens had to learn what industries they controlled and what to do to run them, a mammoth task made intensely more challenging for these Fetish EE women, who were still darn near helpless, dependent upon their personal assistants.

The professor was well aware of the immense problems these women were facing. He took the only available option. In two weeks, the latest crop of high school teens would be graduating. Via Chan-Petra, many were encouraged to take leadership roles, assisting these forty Fetish EE women in the managing of their far-flung industries.

"I know. I'm risking much. The temptation for these young men to take over from the very women they're to be helping is bloody huge, but we'll just have to keep an eye on them somehow," he explained.

Tilly already told him there was a fifty percent

chance these new graduates would slowly take over for the women they were supposed to be helping. She also hinted some of the men would likely marry the women as well. Still, there were few other options available. Someone had to provide top-level guidance to the corporations. This point was driven home to everyone in the resistance on April 28.

In his secure compound on the outskirts of St. Louis, Tom Walton's terror escalated nearly every day, as word trickled in to him of yet another raid on fellow Cabal members' compounds.

"Someone is systematically wiping us out!" he shrieked to his son, Billy.

Tom had two sons and a daughter. His eldest son, Lyle, had been implanted, put on Pytalon-Ex, and was running one of his many headquarters—Walton St. Louis. Lyle was twenty-one and a proper Fetish EE man, nicely complimenting his wife, Jana, a Fetish EE woman. They lived here with him until Tom could find them fitting quarters of their own. Of course, the two were constantly begging everyone around the compound for pleasuring. Last year, his daughter, Elizabeth, now nineteen, had mysteriously been returned to him after her new husband Ralph Koch had been killed by the unknown assassins who wiped out Henry's family. She, too, was constantly trying to flirt and bed everyone in his house, so desperate was she to satisfy her implant's orders. In desperation, Tom had ordered his wife, Sally, who was just as bad, demanding sexual attention at all hours, to move into Elizabeth's room so they could keep each other satisfied. Their four personal assistants spent most of the daytime hours keeping the four Fetish EE women and man satisfied.

Only Billy remained sentient, much to Tom's pleasure. Lyle had been a real dullard of a son, quite unlike Billy, who was very sharp, picking up business situations rapidly. That was the main reason Tom had dispensed with Lyle. Having turned eighteen, Billy wanted a sex doll like his older brother had.

True, Tom had sixty security men around the compound, having added five more when the attacks began in early April. When the huge shipment of munitions arrived in late March, Tom felt a surge of reassurance. No one would dare attack him now, but that feeling slowly evaporated each day in April, as more and more Cabal families were attacked.

At first, the many conference calls with Franco, James, Francisco, and Jacques had been futile. None knew what was happening. Then, all five finally grasped what was actually going on. Several Cabal men called James, demanding he turn over deceased family estates and holdings to them, claiming they'd wiped them out.

Shocked and fearful, James had replied, "I'm sorry. We must follow the long-established protocols we all agreed to—proper inheritance documents dictate such matters."

That did little to satisfy those who had launched the attacks, and they threatened to bring this up at the next meeting. Then, they threatened to call an emergency full Cabal meeting to force James to hand over the deceased's fortunes to the victors.

This, more than anything else, both shocked and terrified the remaining five Camarilla men. If they did this, their whole, tidy arrangement of world domination would come crumbling down on their heads. Anarchy had to be avoided and had been by centuries of careful planning and implementation of the many programs, culminating in Total Care.

Billy looked at his father, shocked. He said, "But dad, who could be trying to wipe us out? Besides, we have a secure fortress here. We have more automatic guns than ever and more ammunition than we ever have had. No one can touch us, right?" he asked hesitantly. Already, fifteen others had been attacked and wiped out.

"Hell, you know you can't ever trust any man who isn't implanted and on Pytalon. Haven't you learned that yet? That's why we've worked for centuries to bring about a sane world where this can't happen," Tom attempted to explain the world to his son.

Billy thought for a second, sensing his father's fears. "Okay dad. Why don't we talk to the St. Louis Feds? Get them to provide some extra security around here. Aren't they supposed to be the world's guardians?"

Tom looked up in surprise. "Now that's the best idea yet! You're right. The Feds are certainly aware of all these attacks. They should be proactive and help defend us here. Son, I give you this task. Do what you have to do to get the Feds here protecting us!"

Billy perked up, more than pleased his father had given him a real assignment, quite unlike how he'd treated Lyle. Billy wasn't dumb; he'd seen just how his father had dealt with Lyle and was carefully avoiding the mistakes Lyle had made. "Sure thing, dad. You can count on me. I'll have Feds here soon!"

His first action taken: find out all he could about the current Feds leader in St. Louis. Captain Sam Forsch was twenty-one. Two years back, fresh out of high school in Chicago, Chan-Petra had put him in charge of the St. Louis Feds, replacing the implanted previous captain. By this time, Sam had seen much that was going on in the Midwest, particularly all the enchanting, fabulous looking EE women and now the glamourous Fetish EE women as well. Sam also saw a very, very few who lived lives of utter luxury and had become a little envious of those. After a little digging, Billy learned this and believed he could make use of this detail, if needed. Billy vowed not to return until he had the Feds backing him.

Dressed in an expensive, black silk suit, Billy approached Captain Sam Forsch, who sat behind a steel desk. As he sat down, he observed the captain. The other Feds who directed him to this office all wore rather ordinary, cheap suits, probably from the local Walmart Apparel Department. However, the captain wore a relatively expensive suit, setting himself somewhat apart from the rest of his men. Clues. Billy observed.

"Thank you for seeing me on such short notice. I know with all these insane attacks around the world you must be very busy right now," Billy began.

"Well, yes, we're experiencing quite a spat of Insanity this month," Captain Sam replied politely.

From the documents sent to him from Chan-Petra, he suspected Billy was the son of Tom Walton. Certainly, the man was neither implanted nor on Pytalon. That alone, Sam found highly significant. He decided to speak the party line, calling it a spat of Insanity. Just what did the Cabal man's son want? Sam was dying from curiosity.

"Yes, that's why I am here today—this Insanity. So far, we've been lucky in that it hasn't reached here, to St. Louis. We'd like to keep it that way," Billy hinted.

"Of course. The Feds would also like to avoid needless bloodshed and destruction. That's our goal," Sam replied.

"Yes, to Serve and Protect—have I gotten your oath right?" Billy asked, knowing perfectly well that it was.

"Of course," Sam replied displaying no emotion.

"Well, I'll get right to the point of my visit. My family has a fortified complex just outside the city limits. Dad does have a number of security guards, and they are heavily armed. We've recently received quite a lot of munitions to help defend our complex," Billy explained.

Captain Sam smiled and had an idea. "Ah yes. We know about the bolstering of your defenses. We try to monitor the important families, at least those we know about. The Waltons are extremely important. Where would any of us be without your Walmarts, eh?"

"Precisely so, precisely so," Billy replied. "We do work hard, my father and I. You can't imagine how much work we've had to do to provide all the new line of clothing for the new and exotic Fetish EE women and men. We've not had to work so hard in years to meet the ever-growing demand for such apparel. It's in the world's best interests that we should be able to continue to meet everyone's needs in apparel and appliances. No doubt about that."

"You'll get no argument from me on that point," Sam replied, straightening his tie slightly. He'd only recently purchased this very suit from the Walmart close to his apartment. "So how can the Feds help you?" he asked, wondering just what Billy was after. Perhaps if he was more direct, Billy would just come out with it."

Captain Sam also knew the Feds were drawing up plans to assault the Walton's complex, but that had been delayed considerably by the chaos around the world. Secretly, he was hoping other Cabal families would attack the Walton's and take care of it for him. He didn't have a death wish. Rather the opposite. Sam saw that any attack on their fortified complex would result in the death of many of his Feds, unless he was lucky somehow.

"As you know, our security guards—well, just between us, they're more like zombie fighters—extremely well-armed mind you. It's just we both know they can't truly stand up against an all-out assault on our complex," Billy explained without giving any secrets away. "So, Captain Forsch, I've come here today on behalf of my family to ask you to provide some constant, round-the-clock Feds protection of our complex. Perhaps, you could provide a contingent of Feds to patrol our perimeter, day and night. If so, we would be extremely grateful. Surely, you and I can reach some agreement that is beneficial to both of us. We have the means to provide you with most anything that you might desire."

Captain Sam looked up, surprised by Billy's frankness. "Anything?" he asked more reactive than thoughtful.

"Absolutely. Let me be frank, Captain Forsch, if I may. We need the Feds' protection, and we're willing to make it worth your while in any way possible. I can see that you, unlike your other men, prefer to be rather elegantly dressed. Perhaps, you would like a Fetish EE woman for a wife?"

Just why he said that, Billy couldn't say, only that he was acting on a hunch that came from observing the captain. He must be twenty-one at least and was still single. Dressed a cut above his men, he was displaying a refined image. Why? Normal implanted and/or Pytalon dosed women wouldn't even notice him or any man for that matter. So why should he dress so elegantly? He caught a brief flash of crimson across Sam's cheeks.

Billy smiled. "You may not know this, but my sister is a truly gorgeous Fetish EE woman. She was recently married, but her husband was murdered less than a week after the marriage. She lives with us, but she is horribly lonely, longing for an elegant, refined man, such as you, to sponsor her or even to wed her. I'm sure she'd give anything if you would consider her."

He saw he'd hit the mark squarely. He also knew the captain wouldn't have an income sufficient to support such an elegant lifestyle.

"Plus, if you would consider taking her, why, we would provide you with a plush new home." He saw the man's favorable reaction and continued adding more details to his offer, "And of course, our Elizabeth would be bringing to her new husband a sizeable monthly stipend to help defray her expenses. Fetish EE women certainly require expensive wardrobes, you see. Thus, Elizabeth would come with financial backing to help you support her. After all, these Fetish EE women are truly the epitome of feminine beauty."

Captain Sam swallowed hard. He knew if Billy asked for Feds support, he was factually obligated to provide it. Protect and serve. However, Billy was offering him his heart's desire. He'd seen images of these fabulous looking women, and he knew they offered their sponsors or husbands the very best sexual experiences to be found anywhere. Certainly, he'd have none of that if he married one of the local women who were implanted and/or on Pytalon. From experience, he knew they couldn't even get aroused in the slightest. He also knew he couldn't afford such a woman, let alone provide a home where she would be at ease or even purchase their quite exotic gowns. He'd seen the prices being charged for them once, when he visited an EE Woman's store on unrelated business.

However, Captain Sam had to maintain his own integrity as a Feds leader. "Billy, I would give anything to accept your fine offer. However, there is one catch. If I accepted such gifts, that would in no way endear me to your family—I mean I won't be bribed into doing anything that would compromise my position or that of the Feds. Sure, if I married her, then I would be part of your family. It's just that please do not expect to use that to your advantage. I must protect and serve all the people in my district equally."

"Of course, captain, of course. No, we would never put any such demands upon you. Never. I give you my word on that. Elizabeth just needs to be happy and well cared for—she is my sister, and I only want the best for her. She deserves it. This way, I can be sure she won't be lacking for anything. I rather wish you Feds leaders made more credits for all the valuable work you do for us—the risks you take for our safety, the dangers you face. This way, if something bad happens to you, I know my gorgeous sister will be provided for, unlike her previous husband who, may his soul rot in hell, never even left her a single credit," Billy pressed the issue.

Billy went on, "If you like, I'd love to have you drop by our place this evening and check out our defenses, make any recommendations, see where your men could best be positioned, and of course meet Elizabeth. I'm certain she'll be simply mad about you. Mind you, if I know my sister, as soon as she sees you in your fine suit, she'll be all over you," Billy teased, watching the captain's instant reaction, knowing he had the man where he wanted him.

"Actually, I would like to meet your sister. If she is as attractive as you say, I'd really consider your offer. No matter what, I'll see some Feds are posted around your complex. After I visit tonight, I'll be in a better position to know how many to send and where to position them. Honestly, Billy, we Feds are here to serve and protect all citizens here in St. Louis, though I will admit normally we don't get requests to help protect the Walton's. What time should I arrive?"

"How about seven. We'll be done with dinner, and Elizabeth will have time to freshen up before you arrive. Just between us fellows, captain, don't be surprised if she is very smitten with you. I know my sister's likes well," Billy hinted. *God, if he'd only take her off our hands! I can't screw my own sister no matter how hard she tries to get me into her bed.* He gave the captain some instructions to find their place.

Once he returned, Tom asked, "Well, how did it go, son?" He was even more worried. Word came of another Cabal family who had been wiped out yesterday. Two in New York was getting far too close for comfort. *Let them wipe themselves out in Russia, what do I care there, just not here Stateside!*

"Perfect dad. Captain Sam Forsch is coming to visit us tonight. He'll see where his men can best be deployed, but dad, I have him interested in marrying Elizabeth, as long as we give him a fancy home to live in and a credit stipend so he can provide for sis. I figure we can get rid of that old Timberline mansion. Not a bad deal, eh dad?" Billy reported, very pleased with himself.

"Really? He'll take Elizabeth off our hands? No questions asked? Yes, we can give them that mansion and stop worrying about it. It's within the city where we never go—too damned dangerous for us. Excellent son, excellent. I'll go let Elizabeth know."

"Let me dad. I'll prepare her. If she makes a good impression, we have us a solid deal far into the future, dad," Billy replied. "He'll be by around seven."

Entering her room where his mother was also now staying, along with Lyle and Jana, he found the four passionately kissing each other, while rubbing their stumps seductively over whatever body was close enough for them to reach. "Elizabeth, come with me."

"Oh, I do need to pleasure you," the dreamy-eyed

425

Elizabeth said, struggling mightily to rise to her toes. She moved gracefully over to Billy and began to rub her stumps over his face while trying to kiss him.

He carefully pushed her back a little. "Sis, tonight a very important man is coming by to visit you. If you make a good impression on him, he wants to marry you. You understand me?"

"You aren't going to pleasure me now? I must. I'm a Fetish EE woman. . ." she recited her script perfectly, before futilely trying to seduce Billy again.

"Sis. Pleasure Captain Sam when he gets here. Look your best after supper." He gave up and told her personal assistant to have her looking stunning and to keep her in the living room, away from these three.

Meanwhile, Tom decided it was also time to get Lyle and Jana out of the house. He had some security guards move them and their belongings to a ritzy penthouse suite close to Lyle's headquarters office building. In addition, he ordered Lyle to go to work on Monday, though he doubted very much Lyle would do so. Hence, he left written orders with his personal assistant to make Lyle go to work on Monday. *There, that will make things more presentable when the Feds Captain comes by tonight. I simply have to have the Feds watching over us. Lord knows when Franco will be coming after me!*

When Captain Sam arrived, Billy met him and gave him a royal tour of the grounds, before entering the mansion. The captain saw that taking out this place by force of arms would be extremely deadly. The guards had twice the firepower of his men! He made a note to request additional weapons from Chan-Petra. He had never been inside a luxury mansion and was speechless. However, Billy cleverly took him into the living room first, where Elizabeth was waiting. Her assistant had put her fanciest red satin gown on her, one that revealed much of her abundant cleavage. Her outer corset had matching red stripes alternating with white ones. Her extremely long hair was perfectly brushed out and her makeup done well

426

by her assistant. Even her matching red patent ballet boots looked sparkling.

When she saw the tall man entering with Billy, she rose as gracefully as she could, which wasn't very elegant, but she made up for that by gliding perfectly over to meet this handsome stranger. It had been over a year since she had her Fetish EE woman's implant via the Model III. At this point, she now had a very tiny window when she was at least partially lucid enough to see what was going on around her.

"Ah, Elizabeth, this is the Feds Captain Sam Forsch. Captain, my gorgeous sister, Elizabeth," Billy introduced the two, keeping his fingers crossed.

"Oh. You're handsome. I hope you like me. I so want to pleasure you," Elizabeth managed to say, fighting against having to repeat the implant words just now. She moved close to him, trying to rub her stumps around his waist, but her giant bosom kept them from actually reaching him beyond a slight touch with the tips of them.

"Wow. Elizabeth, you look stunning! Billy didn't say you were this good looking!"

He leaned closer and hugged her, which was what she greatly desired. Her short stumps began sliding over his body.

"You like pleasure?" Elizabeth somehow managed to get said.

"Who doesn't?" he replied, sliding his hands around her slim waist.

"Hey, don't kiss her or you'll have to find a bedroom fast," Billy teased him. "Come. Let's see the rest of the place. Elizabeth, you hang on to Sam."

"No, I'll hang on to you, Elizabeth. I'm surprised you haven't had tons of suitors. I'm sorry about the loss of your husband," the captain attempted to make pleasant conversation, hoping his intense arousal wasn't noticed.

Billy didn't, but Elizabeth did and continued working her wiles on him as they walked along, greatly pleasing Captain Sam. Elizabeth merely smiled demurely and batted her eyes at him. She had no idea what he was saying or even meant. All that mattered was he hadn't pushed her away as the others here did, and he had his arm around her, keeping her close. She desperately needed to feel his hands on her hypersensitive body. *Will he kiss and caress me? I so need it now.* That was the extent of her thinking skills. If only she could keep from reciting her litany just now.

Cleverly, Tom stayed in the background, allowing Billy to give him the tour. Once that was done, he knew if they say down on the couch, there would be no controlling Elizabeth, who would immediately start fawning over the captain. Wisely, he met up with them as they were heading back to the living room.

"Ah. Captain Forsch. I'm Tom Walton. So pleased to meet you at last," he said covertly, but pleasantly. Meeting him was the very last thing he wanted, but he needed the Feds to help guard this place. Cleverly, he had Elizabeth's assistant at hand. "Please take Elizabeth into the living room for a minute so we men can discuss some important details."

The assistant vaguely understood him, enough to know he wanted her to move Elizabeth into the living room.

Billy explained with a chuckle, "My, my, captain, Elizabeth is really taken with you. If we don't separate you two right now, she'll be all over you. You're certainly a hit with her."

Captain Sam blushed. "Well, she's an incredible young woman. You should've told me she's absolutely stunning." Billy smiled politely. "I'd be a complete fool if I didn't accept your offer. She does seem to like me, and we've only just met."

"Indeed, son," Tom punched it in, "she's smitten with you. There's no denying that. Just between us, I would prefer it if you would actually marry her. She's lost one husband, and I'd like her to have some stability in her life. You can understand that, right?"

"Oh I so agree. It must have been just awful for her. Billy was saying something about a stipend so I can better afford to keep her in the style that she's used to?"

"Of course. I figured she should get ten thousand credits each month. I know that's a bit on the high side, but she is my only daughter," Tom answered. "Plus, we'd really appreciate it if you would accept the Timberline mansion. It's close to the Feds building, I believe. We haven't used it in many years, and I haven't had any buyers either. So I'd love to give it to you so that Elizabeth would have a fine place to live."

The three chatted a bit longer, and Captain Sam shook hands, sealing their bargain. He wasn't compromising his position in anyway, but was getting his heart's desire in a woman, to say nothing of a mansion and credits to help support Elizabeth. More importantly, he was gaining an inside track into this Cabal family.

Later, with a wry grin, Tom excused himself, saying that his wife wanted his attentions.

Billy took this opportunity to add, "You know, captain, I've wanted a Fetish EE woman myself. What say we get married together, a dual wedding?"

That sealed the deal. Captain Sam agreed, and the two men decided to make it happen on Sunday. Billy then explained, "Okay, I'll leave you and Elizabeth to get better acquainted. Just show yourself out when you need to leave. I have to make the wedding arrangements for us. Thanks, captain. You've convinced me to marry Irene now and stop putting it off."

Captain Sam joined Elizabeth, who sat erect on the couch, very impatiently waiting for him to return. As soon as he sat down, Elizabeth lost all control, sliding her stumps all over him, while passionately kissing him. He returned her passion, which seemed endless, further endearing her to him. Finally, he just had to leave, but found parting from her was challenging. She kept begging and pleading with him to take her to bed.

"Just a few more days, Elizabeth. Once we're

married, we'll do it. I promise you."

The next day, Captain Forsch called Chan-Petra to report what he was doing in St. Louis with the Walton's. "I've got a good foothold in there now. I'm marrying his daughter. My god, she'd a goddess. Anyway, I've now seen the entire layout of the Walton compound and manor house. We're going to take extensive casualties if we have to assault it. You know, Billy seems to be a bright lad. Are we supposed to wipe out all the men in the Walton line?"

Chan-Petra smiled, and then replied, "Well done. Congratulations on finding a wife. Let's see if we can avoid having to assault the place. As far as I know, only Tom Walton is the Cabal member, not his son. Get close to Billy and see where his head is at. If he is against us bringing back sanity into our world, then he has to go too. No rush. We're overwhelmed with all the attacks right now. Good job of thinking on your feet. Just be careful they don't try to get you to do something you shouldn't do."

Captain Forsch chuckled. "That's not going to happen. I'll keep you posted. I must say, I'm really smitten by Elizabeth. She's a knockout and does seem to like me too. Of course, that could well just be her implant talking, right?"

"Right, captain. The implant gives her very little choice. Still, getting her out of their clutches has to be in her best interests. Once things settle down some, maybe we can get her into the rehab center, though from all reports, busting down these new Model III implants is incredibly difficult and time consuming. Keep me posted. Got another call."

Chan-Petra hung up, shaking her head, hoping Sam knew what he was getting into with Elizabeth. Still, he was providing incredible Intel on the Walton compound.

Sunday came. Captain Sam Forsch dressed in his best suit and landed his EMAC at the Walton compound, right on time. He saluted his six men and headed inside, where the wedding was to be held. Weddings were definitely not a fancy affair here. The women were only just barely able to realize they were being married, if at all. They were simply fighting against their implants, while waiting for the promised opportunity for pleasuring.

Elizabeth and her personal assistant, Mary who was barely eighteen, stood beside Sam, while Irene and her assistant Susy stood beside Billy. In the background, Tom and Sally stood watching the brief ceremony. Mary and Susy vaguely grasped that their charges were being married today, but needed to be instructed to make their charges as beautiful as possible. Elizabeth wore the same red satin gown as she had when Sam first met her. Her wavy brown hair had been recently washed and lay draped over her back, reaching to the back of her knees, where her tight fitting gown ended, revealing a bit of her black seamed nylons just above her knee-high ballet boots.

Irene had blonde hair nearly as along but a bit wavier. She too looked quite gorgeous and kept an arm on Billy's shoulders, just as Elizabeth did with Sam. The two men kept a steadying arm around the women's waists, while the Pytalon-dosed minister's monotone voice rattled off the ceremonial words. It didn't take five minutes to complete the wedding.

"You may kiss your brides now," he said, adding in a whisper, "Sanity is doing a proper wedding." Mechanically, he turned and left, heading for his home.

Sam gave Elizabeth a passionate kiss. Her response was electric, and he found pulling away from her difficult. "Come on, Elizabeth. Time to go to our new home. They've already packed your things and Mary's too."

"I need to pleasure you now," she insisted. "I can't wait." That was the extent of her thinking ability and began whispering her implanted script as Sam guided her out of the manor to his EMAC, Mary following along behind them, lost in her own daze.

Their new home was a million credit affair, quite luxurious and all on one floor. Once there, Sam escorted both women on a tour. As soon as they reached their new master bedroom, Elizabeth couldn't stand it any longer, pleading with Sam to do it now. He asked Mary to unpack their things and gently slipped off Elizabeth's gown and slip. He discovered she was positively enthusiastic about finally being able to do it with him.

Sam got an education. An hour later, the two lay beside each other, her hair entwined over their bodies. "Elizabeth, that was just incredible! You're fantastic. I sure love you."

Elizabeth finally had the most lucid period ever since having become a Fetish EE woman, due entirely to having been fully satisfied herself. "Love you. Fantastic. Need lots more. Often. Can't help myself. Love me. Please. Rub me," she replied. He did as asked, realizing she could no longer massage her own body. Lightly, he ran his fingers over her extremely shapely form, bringing sighs to her lips. However, that was the extent of her lucid period.

Billy had been wise and arranged for a young chef to join them. Sam had her deal with getting the groceries and preparing their meals. Around noon, she announced lunch, and Sam struggled to get Elizabeth's gown back on. Fortunately for him, Mary appeared and deftly did it for him. Now he began to see the awful downside to the Fetish EE women. As he watched Mary feeding Elizabeth, he finally realized just how helpless his new bride actually was. He had a sick feeling in his stomach. Here was the most incredible young woman he'd ever met, but who was also so helpless. At last, Captain Sam understood.

Meanwhile, Billy, who also had been envious of Lyle and Jana, finally got his heart's desire with Irene. Like Sam, he enjoyed the immense pleasure, but then began to see Irene's true situation. He'd mostly ignored his mother, who never had much to say to him, being an EE woman as long as he could remember. Now intimate with Irene, his own eyes were opened, though he dared not say anything to his father.

Captain Sam dropped by at least once each day to check on things with his Feds and to chat with Billy. Within days, the two began discussing their experiences with their new wives, since they shared this in common. "They're so helpless," Sam pointed out.

"I know. I never truly appreciated that before. Irene isn't able to do anything for herself. What an awful waste. She's so incredibly sexy," Billy admitted.

He opened up to Sam, "You know, it wasn't always this bad. I remember mom. She was just an EE woman—always was I think. Anyhow, she used to be able to talk and hold halfway decent conversations. She mostly ran the household when I was a child. Now she's like Irene and Elizabeth. I swear they can't even think anymore."

Sam defended the women, "That's not exactly right, Billy. I've noticed Elizabeth can think a little bit when we're done in the bed. I think doing it rather clears her mind up a bit, but it doesn't last very long. That damned Model III implant machine is behind it. With the older machines, they aren't so zonked out or whatever it is."

"Say, you're right. I've noticed Irene can talk a little once we're done, but she loses it within a few minutes. Sure wish she could just be herself all the time," Billy replied. "I don't think it's right—zonking them out so badly, but these new Model III machines are everywhere now, replacing the Model II's or so I'm told by dad. You know, he was completely behind these new machines, but I can't see why he would want mom as she is now."

During the remainder of April, the two men grew closer and closer, sharing more of their own personal feelings. Naturally, Captain Sam was feeling Billy out to determine just where he stood. Towards the end of April, he was convinced Billy wasn't behind the society the Cabal had created. Billy wanted changes and an end to this implanting mess. More critically, Billy began to have fears of his own.

"Look, Sam, what has me terrified is my dad. You know he married Lyle off to Jana and then had Lyle turned into a Fetish EE man. Lyle is as helpless as our brides are. Worse, he's disinherited Lyle. He turned him into one of his headquarter lackeys."

"Wow. Didn't know that," Sam answered, echoing Billy's worried tone. "You suppose he'll do that to you?"

"I'm scared he will, Sam. I surely don't want that to happen to me. Just between you and me, I think dad's crazy. He's gotten more and more terrified that we're going to be attacked like the thirty other families have. You know dad's quite old, don't you? At least a couple hundred years."

"Yes, I'm aware of that detail. Something about organ donors and Transference Machines prolonging life," Sam carefully responded, not wanting to reveal any more than needed to keep Billy talking.

"Well, that's not natural. Besides, if he has gone off his rocker, he could really cause a lot of damage," Billy admitted.

Captain Sam decided to take a chance with Billy. "You know Tom Walton has perpetrated so many crimes against humanity in general and other people that it's not funny. We know he's part of the ruling body of the Cabal, the Camarilla I think it's called. They're trying to control the entire world, forcing everyone to be implanted and/or doped up on Pytalon. Now that drug is as nasty on people as the implants are, turns them into mindless zombies, though I have to admit it keeps crime down."

"Yes, that's true. Just look at our mindless guards. They're all on Pytalon, if you hadn't guessed. Hell, Sam, if someone attacks us here, I wouldn't give a rat's ass for our chances of survival. I can't tell you how much better I'm sleeping at night knowing that some of your Feds are out there around our perimeter. This isn't anyway to live a life, is it, Sam?" Billy pointed out and asked.

"No Billy, it isn't, but until the Cabal men can be brought to justice, we're stuck with it. I sure hope you aren't turned into a Fetish EE man, Billy. I count you among my closest friends now."

Billy shuddered. "Me either. Sam, if that happens to me—turned into a helpless Fetish EE man—would you please kill me? I know I can't live like that."

"But what about Irene? How do you think she feels about it?" Sam punched it home.

"Oh shit! I never thought about that. God, I hope she doesn't want to die. I—I really love her."

"Same with Elizabeth. I've really fallen for her, but her life is dismal right now, just as Irene's is and your mother too for that matter, but, Billy, there's some hope for them," Sam tossed out a lifeline.

"Hope? What hope?" Billy grabbed on to his hint of help.

"There are ways to get the implants desensitized. Mind you, I have no idea how that's done, only that it takes a lot of time and is rather hard to do, but once it's done, they can think as well as we do, only they still have some residue left. It isn't wholly gone."

"I didn't know that! But how do they act, once it's more or less gone?" Billy asked, extremely interested in Sam's reply.

"Best way I can tell you is to give you an example. You know the head of the Feds, our Supreme Commander Chan-Petra?"

"Oh yes. I've head dad talking about her. I think the Cabal men wanted her dead or something."

"Well, she was implanted by these Model III machines. She had the implant desensitized and is now running all the Feds worldwide."

"Wow! So there really is hope for Irene and for Elizabeth! I had no idea. How can we do it for them? Sam, we simply have to get it done for them and soon," Billy declared emphatically.

"No can do, Billy. What would your dad do if you even mentioned this to him?"

"Shit! He'd have me turned into a Fetish EE man before I turned around! He did it to Lyle when he wasn't looking, but then Lyle wasn't too bright anyway. Shit. Here's the answer I want, but I dare not touch it!"

Sam knew he had Billy. "There is a way. If Tom was arrested and sent away for all the crimes he's done, you'd be left in charge of the Walton fortune and companies. You could then start doing all the right things to help our world get better."

Billy didn't hesitate. "If you can do that, I swear to you I'll do just that. If I don't, then arrest me too. Can you really do that? Are you going to kill him?"

"No, the Feds don't kill unless we haven't any choice. I give you my word that Tom will not be killed, just taken out of commission. He'll never again be a threat to you or to the world. I promise you if you don't do the right things, I or others will come after you too." Both men smiled and shook hands.

When Captain Sam returned to his office, he placed a secure call to Chan-Petra. "Boss, I have a way to take out Tom Walton." Quickly, he explained the situation.

"Give me a day or so to arrange it," Chan-Petra said, trying not to sound too excited just yet. "We will need a way to get Tom to come out to your EMAC. Leave that to me."

A day later, Lady Persephone arrived in Chicago bringing a stasis pod with her. She and Chan-Petra discussed the operation, and then she returned to London, more than a little harried. These past few weeks had also taken their toll on her and Juan, who had to get stasis pods to where they were needed, delivered to Master Yao, and back again. She had lost count of the trips to Peking she'd made just in the last three weeks.

May Day, Captain Sam landed his EMAC on the green spring grass of the Walton compound. Both Billy and Tom came out to inspect his new gadget.

"I've brought along the more or less portable IR scanner. With it, one can see images of anyone approaching your outer walls," he explained.

Both Tom and Billy hovered over the screen filled with moving, small, red, human-like images of the men patrolling the perimeter. Sam simply injected a small syringe into Tom's neck. The man was knocked out before he even realized he was being attacked.

"Okay, Billy. I'll take Tom away, and you do what you have to do to let the Cabal know that Tom's gone and you're in charge."

Billy let out a huge whew. "Thank god, Sam! I don't know how to thank you. I'll get on it now. I won't let you down."

As soon as Billy left, Sam took off, heading for the Feds building. Once he landed on its roof, he and others verified he had Tom Walton and stuffed him into the stasis pod. A few minutes later, the pod was on an Air Liner headed for Peking.

Later that afternoon and before returning home for supper, Captain Sam dropped by to check on Billy. The young man was all smiles.

"All handled, Sam. Finally, this household is free, free of the past and dad. I'm running things now, not the Cabal."

"Excellent. Walton Enterprises are safe now. Are you still interested in seeing if we can get Irene's implant destimulated?" Sam asked.

"You bet, but wait, Sam. What if she doesn't want anything to do with me when it's done?"

"Hey, I'm in the same boat with your sister. I love Elizabeth, but honestly Billy, if she gets her mind back and doesn't want me after that, I've decided I can live with that because she'll have her life back, at least some of it," Sam pointed out.

"Okay. Good point. Let me know when and where," Billy responded.

Three days later, the two men brought their wives to the newly created St. Louis Rehab Center. Jessica herself was on hand to help train up the new volunteers fresh out of high school. Later on, Lisa visited as well, training them up on her sauna process to remove the residual Pytalon and other drugs lodged in body tissues. However, the current process now made use of Dr. Akira Aki's special chemical mixtures to temporarily lower certain brain chemicals. Still, the process was excruciating for the two men to watch. Jessica decided these two men needed to see just what was involved in undoing the implants, especially Billy.

Fifteen days later, both Elizabeth and Irene were finally released from the rehab center. "My god, Sam, I can think again! You can't imagine how wonderful this is for me. Thank you, thank you."

Nearby, Irene was telling Billy the same thing.

Elizabeth added softly, "Now I can truly love you and give you real pleasure that comes from my heart. I just wish I wasn't so helpless."

Their married lives truly blossomed. Moreover, the two men continued to be very close friends, getting together with their wives in tow each weekend. Later, Billy put his mother through the rehab program. When she finished up, she decided to reenter the active EE woman's program, hoping to find another husband. She was only thirty-nine and held out hope for the future, particularly since she was wealthy.

Chapter 21—Wrap Up

May brought additional changes. As the Cabal assaults died down and the Feds got caught up with all the recovery actions, Chan-Petra began seriously planning her next move. Franco Helu had taken over control of Total Care and cutting off Feds' funding, though R³ spent her credits to support the Feds. Of all the known Cabal members, he was currently causing the most damage. It made sense to take him out now.

Franco's compound outside Mexico City was a veritable impregnable fortress. Centuries ago, one of Mexico's largest drug lords had been inhabited it. Now the telecommunications billionaire owned it and had made major improvements, including some very massive guns or howitzers to be more precise. He ringed the place with heavy AA guns as well. Any incoming EMAC would be shot out of the sky long before it could land. The open rangeland surrounding the fortress was littered with the bones of animals that had wandered too close and had been gunned down by the automatic weapons systems that shot at anything moving out there.

Chan-Petra held a conference with everyone, fishing for ideas on how to go about assaulting Franco's den. She made a careful presentation, outlining everything her people had been able to dig up on his defenses. Ideas were few for quite some time.

Then, Beth spoke up, "You know, most of his systems are computer controlled. I can't hack them, because they aren't connected to the outside world. He's relying on old weapons technology. Perhaps we can exploit that. Let me do some research, Chan."

A day later, Weasel called Chan back. "I have it. Here's what I need. Send Trevor back to the arsenal out west." She rattled off a short list, giving the storage locations for these ancient weapon systems.

An excited Trevor arrived at the underground Feds arsenal for the second time. Last time, he retrieved the fancy automatic defense systems. This time, he was after something even bigger, several somethings. He'd read about these ancient weapon systems when he was in Ward 4 with his Circle of Six. Encouraged by R³, Trevor had dug into all the ancient files he could find—any that concerned fighting machines. Now he was about to get his hands on some of them. To say that the OD Trevor was eager was a gross understatement!

Both he and the caretaker-security guard at the facility were glad Beth had given them the precise locations of the two devices, tucked away in this huge weapons storage bunker.

"Wow. This small," Trevor exclaimed holding the EMB in his hands. "Incredibly light-weight too, barely a pound. Hope it still works. Okay, now for the others. We need six of them and the five hundred pound bombs to go with them."

A half hour later, the two men stared at the compact boxes. The labels on the boxes read, "Some assembly required." These, however, were heavy and required a small forklift to move them out and into his EMAC. That handled, the two began moving a dozen of the large bombs into his vehicle. "Hope these don't go off by accident," Trevor commented, a little nervously. The man chuckled and locked up, though waving as Trevor lifted off. He had so few visitors.

Trevor landed hours later at a deserted airfield just south of San Diego, where a team of Feds from California had already arrived and set up a base camp. "Some assembly required," Trevor jested, when the Feds hauled the six crates off his EMAC. He opened one, a long way from where the Feds began unloading the bombs. He still felt nervous around the explosives. It took him the better part of the day to get the drone assembled. "I swear a nincompoop wrote these directions," he complained to the

Feds captain who came by to check on his progress. Both laughed.

Another day passed before they were finally ready for a test flight. On the first run, Trevor operated the small handheld controller, much like the game controllers he'd used so often back in Ward 4. The drone took off perfectly, and Trevor put it through some dives and circles, before landing it. Next, the men loaded it up with two bombs. Once more, Trevor took the heavily laden drone for a test flight.

"Whoa, not so maneuverable now. Still, I think it's going to work, fellows."

That was all the Feds needed to hear, and the captain called Chan-Petra for the final go-ahead permission.

The next morning, twenty-five Feds, dressed in their heavy field armor and armed to the teeth with weapons, grenades, and spare ammo clips, boarded two EMACs, while Trevor and five others climbed into a third. The captain finished his last minute words and joined them, signaling to lift off. Trevor and the five men activated their controls, causing the six drones to take off, shortly falling into formation behind their EMAC. For better or worse, the assault was on. Chan-Petra watched the action from a live video feed, though she relayed it to several others as well.

When they were fifty miles from Franco's deadly compound, everyone fell back, except Trevor's control EMAC, which gained altitude until it reached forty thousand feet. Using GPS to guide them into position directly over the center of the fortified compound, the pilot finally gave the all clear signal. Carefully, Trevor activated the EMB, lowering it from a cable beneath the EMAC. "Keep your fingers crossed," he called out, as he pressed the Activate button on his tiny controller.

The EMB was a very small electromagnetic bomb, designed over two centuries ago to knock out all computers and electronics in a relatively small area. Theoretically, the pulse was directed downward. However, if that weren't true, it would also fry all the circuits in the EMAC. The Feds were prepared for this. A dozen parachutes lined the wall beside the main bay doors. That no one had any idea how to use them wasn't a factor anyone seriously considered. How hard could they be to use? Knowledge of their use was long gone by several centuries. Still, they looked impressive.

"Did anything happen? Did it work?" the captain asked.

Trevor shrugged his shoulders. "Darn if I know." He reeled the device back up, while the others moved the six drones towards their position, and their pilots began dropping straight down. "Guess we'll have to see."

On the ground, suddenly everything electronic in nature ceased functioning, from the motion sensors to the automated weapons systems to the alarms to basic electricity. The compound went "dark!" Of course, that was an instant signal that Franco and his fortress was under attack. Orders barked. Men rushed out to operate the howitzers, while others loaded up on weapons and extra ammo clips.

Ten minutes later, most of Franco's security guards were staffing their posts. Only a few remained close to the main manor house, issuing orders from there. Trevor nudged his drone over the first of the howitzer installations, guided by IR scans, satellite images, and GPS coordinates. Satisfied he had one locked on, he pressed the Drop button and began locking in a second battery, hoping this would work. If it didn't, the Feds would simply abandon the assault. Just as he locked on to his second battery, a loud explosion and concussion was heard and felt by all. Several cheers went up. Then, Trevor's second bomb detonated, followed shortly by another ten explosions. Cheers and shouts echoed throughout this command EMAC.

The IR scanner showed the results. Most of the red human-like images were down. The captain gave the signal to the other two EMACs which then landed unharmed inside the fortress. The Feds charged out, but found little resistance left. Most was fire coming from the manor itself. Eagerly and with an adrenaline rush, the Feds returned the fire, storming the manor.

While his men were rushing into the manor, the captain ordered his EMAC to land and the stasis pod unloaded. Five minutes. From set-down of the Feds to the final "Clear," five minutes passed. Weasel had been spot on with her plan. Franco, like nearly everyone in the modern world of 2274, depended utterly upon all things electronic. Knock all those out and all that remained of Franco's defenses were the large guns. The antique drones with their small bombs knocked those out along with most of the security men operating them, which was where Weasel anticipated Franco would have them deployed. The minimal actual fighting took place within the manor house, room to room, a very rapid assault, considering the light guns that remained couldn't penetrate the heavy body armor the Feds men wore.

"Franco is down. Mortally wounded," a Feds yelled over the comm set. A few minutes later, the Feds had his dying body into the stasis pod and hooked onto its life support functions. That done, another EMAC arrived and took it to the large Mexico City air field, where it was put on an Air Liner bound for Peking.

Surveying the dead, the captain identified the two sons of Franco. His two teenaged daughters and wife were Fetish EE women and were sent to Mexico City, where the local Feds placed them in their EE woman's safe house. The extensive cleanup operation followed. Hard drives were salvaged from the blown-out systems. These Trevor packed up to take back in hopes that Beth or Felix might be able to salvage some of their data, though it didn't look too hopeful to Trevor.

"Do I have to send these drones back and the EMB too?" Trevor wailed. The captain gave him a stern look. "All right. All right. We'll disassemble them at the base. Still, this was incredible fun."

"Not for those on the receiving end," the captain pointed out, sobering Trevor.

Once she had confirmation of the capture of Franco Helu, Chan-Petra made a formal announcement on the worldwide news channel.

"The Feds today have arrested Franco Helu for heinous crimes against humanity. He was apprehended at his fortified compound north of Mexico City a few minutes ago."

She kept it short. Via the email addresses Weasel provided her, she sent a similar message to James Buffett, Jacques Arnault, and Francesco Ortega. To those emails, she also added, "You're next on our list to apprehend. It'll go better for you to report to your nearest Feds office and surrender peacefully."

Chan-Petra seriously doubted any of these men would do that. Rather, she was using a bit of advice Wart gave her: "Scare the willies out of them." Certainly, the apprehension of their top leader should do just that. After all, if the resistance understood this Camarilla group, there were now only three men left of the original nine.
***

At his fortified compound in southern France, Jacques Arnault panicked when he received Chan-Petra's email.

Everything is going wrong now. Franco is gone. Time to flee to fight another day. "Boys, pack up everything. We're leaving here before the Feds storm us."

He and his two current sons packed an EMAC with all the food and munitions it could carry.

"Leave the women. They'll only slow us down, boys."

Under the cover of night, he lifted off, abandoning his compound, wife, and two daughters, leaving the three Fetish EE women to get by on their own, though he figured they'd not survive long. He headed southeast, putting a good distance between himself and France.
***

Simultaneously, outside Madrid, Francesco Ortega

and his son followed suit, loading an EMAC with all it could carry. Likewise, he and his son abandoned their Fetish EE women wives. On the run, they would be a severe liability. Besides, they could pick up other women later on, wherever they set down. Unfortunately for him, his luck ran out. One of Wolf's Feds assigned to keep an eye on his compound from a concealed position high on an overlooking ridge saw what they were doing and took action.

When the EMAC lifted off, the Feds man acted on his own initiative, firing a shoulder-held RPG, hitting the rear engine compartment. The EMAC lost all power and crashed into the side of the low mountain. By the time the he reached the vehicle, the son was already dead. Francesco had a pair of broken legs and wasn't going anywhere. Thus, within a few hours, he too was on his way to Peking. By the next morning, Wolf had his Feds crawling over the Ortega compound, but not until he had the women taken to a Madrid safe house.

***

James Buffett heard the brief news announcement of Chan-Petra's. Terror swept over him. Sweating profusely, he realized he was now the top Camarilla member. On his shoulders came total responsibility for running everything, something he was loathed to do. He handled finances, always had. Give him a task that involved funds and he'd find a way to succeed, often brilliantly. He'd not become the second wealthiest man in the world without just cause. Unfortunately for James, he was the eldest of the Camarilla men.

All this intense stress and terror took its toll on his aging body. He'd lost his chance to obtain a new body from the Lin brothers a few years back when those fools had been captured and the Transference Machines lost. He had been first in line to get a new one when Dr. Al Rumani acquired the two machines from Lady Persephone, but even that hope had been dashed when they were blown up. The stark terror and intense stress combined, and James collapsed onto the floor of his study. He'd gone in there to email the others about Franco when he'd received Chan-Petra's email. That was too much, and he had a debilitating stroke.

Unfortunately for James, his Fetish EE woman wife and daughter, along with their personal assistants found him, but were unable to realize he was in serious trouble. Rather, they tried to get him to pleasure themselves. A bit later, their chef dropped by to announce supper was ready, spotted him, and called for help. After more confusion, he was rushed to the Paris Premier Medical Institute, where his stroke was recognized and treatment begun.

After that, the doctor sent off a request for his adult OD to be brought here, presumably to provide a number of new organs for James. A day later, he was finally conscious, though his right side was paralyzed. The summoning of his OD became his undoing. Todd kept an eye on all such requests, once a day checking on the many ODs, hoping more would come to their senses and want a real life. As soon as he saw James Buffett's OD request, he alerted Chan-Petra, who in turn alerted Wolf, who raced over to Paris from his hideout in Germany.

Wolf walked into the man's room. "Ah, Mr. James Buffett. We meet at last. I'm Commander of the European Feds. I've an arrest warrant for you."

Speaking in his usual soft voice, James attempted to make the last deal of his life. "I know you people have the Transference Machines. Forget the OD stuff. This body has had it. I'll make you a deal. You put me into a new, youthful body, and I'll give you all my access codes. I've billions of credits. They're all yours, the Feds, whomever you want to give it to, but it's all yours if you transfer me into a new, youthful body. I—I don't want to die. Please, I don't want to die. I can't die, I just can't. It's all yours, everything, just transfer me into a new body before this one gives out completely. Please, I'll do anything you ask. Don't let me die. I really do know how to make vast sums of money." James pleaded for his life with Wolf, who saw James was terrified of dying, more so than he was terrified of people, un-implanted people that is.

The Wolf finally replied, "James, I give you my sworn word as the Feds European Commander that I'll see you get a new and youthful body before this one dies. It'll take a day or so to arrange, but I'll need proof you'll do as you've promised. You aren't in a position to bargain very long. Time is of the essence in stroke cases, but you know that already."

James sighed. He began softly outlining where his safes were located and what their combinations were. He ended with the many security codes to disarm all his security measures at his compound.

"Thank you, James. We're going to put you into a stasis pod now and ship you to the Transference Machine and your new youthful body," the Wolf explained.

A doctor administered the knockout drug and assisted in placing James into the stasis pod. Days later and still unconscious, he was put into the Transference Machine, handled by Master Yao, shortly joining the others in the underground Lin brothers foundation living facility.

When the end of May arrived, the only remaining Camarilla member was Jacques, but he was on the run, having abandoned his fortress and all else. A few more Cabal assaults occurred in May, resulting in the elimination of another six men.

On June 1, 2274, Chan-Petra declared this was the Worldwide Freedom Day. The war against the Cabal was officially over. Those men no longer had any power or control over the world via the Total Care program. She proclaimed three groups were running the world now: the World Court, the Feds, and the World Guidance Council. In her formal presentation broadcast on all channels around the world, she outlined how each of the three operated and how the checks and balances worked. Her final words were, "From now on, June 1 will be celebrated as the Worldwide Freedom Day!"

Later, she called up Beth and her group. "Well, now

it is finally safe for us to step forward and come out of hiding. We've done it. I just can't believe it, but we have. Incredible."

Tilly replied, "Chan-Petra, this is a day I never expected to see, but honestly this was the easy part. Now comes the incredibly difficult part. How are we ever going to get the world's population un-implanted and off Pytalon? How are we going to keep the world's economy running properly so we all don't starve to death? No, I'm afraid the worst we have yet to face."

"Party pooper!" Jessica teased her, but she knew just what Tilly meant.

The End.

A Favor to Other Readers

How about helping other readers? Many readers rely on reviews to make the decision whether to buy a book. You can help them make their decision by leaving your opinions and viewpoint in a short review of the positive things of this book. Writing the review and expressing your opinion only takes a few minutes, and other readers will appreciate your efforts.

Click this link: Reclamation Series Volume 2 Organ Donors scroll down to Customer Reviews; click on Write a Review, and enter your review. Thank you.

Author Information

Visit My Amazon.com Author Page
Vic Broquard Author Page

Follow My Blog
Vic Broquard's Blog

Follow Me on Social Media
Facebook
Google+
LinkedIn
YouTube

Other Books by Vic Broquard

Without Warning (fantasy)

The Trident Series: (fantasy)
> Volume 1 The Trident and the Book
> Volume 2 The Trident and the Scepter
> Volume 3 The Trident and the Resurrection

The Adventures of Elizabeth Stanton Series: (science fiction)
> Volume 1 The Evolution of the Path
> Volume 2 The Great Messiah
> Volume 3 Of Kings and Queens and Troubadours
> Volume 4 Chaos in the Aftermath
> Volume 5 Power Plays
> Volume 6 Age of Exploration
> Volume 7 Abducted
> Volume 8 The Emperor and Empress
> Volume 9 A Job Worth Doing
> Volume 10 Degradation
> Volume 11 The Second Crusade
> Volume 12 When Worlds Collide
> Volume 13 Dark Ages

The Lindsey Barron Series: (fantasy)
> Volume 1 The Rod of the Apocalypse
> Volume 2 The Board of Governors
> Volume 3 The Crown of Moses
> Volume 4 Dominus for President
> Volume 5 The National Health Care Program
> Volume 6 States Justice
> Volume 7 Cross and Double-cross
> Volume 8 Down the Dragon Hole

Zoran Chronicles Series: (fantasy)
> Volume 1 A Dragon in Our Town